BAYOU HEAT
COLLECTION ONE

BAYOU HEAT

COLLECTION ONE

Laura Wright and Alexandra Ivy

ISBN: 0989990753
ISBN 13: 9780989990752

RAPHAEL

By
ALEXANDRA IVY

LEGEND OF THE PANTERA

To most people the Pantera, a mystical race of puma shifters who live in the depths of the Louisiana swamps, have become little more than a legend.

It was rumored that in the ancient past twin sisters, born of magic, had created a sacred land and claimed it as their own. From that land came creatures who were neither human or animal, but a mixture of the two.

They became faster and stronger than normal humans. Their senses were hyper-acute. And when surrounded by the magic of the Wildlands they were capable of shifting into pumas.

It was also whispered that they possessed other gifts. Telepathy, witchcraft, immortality and the ability to produce a musk that could enthrall mere mortals.

Mothers warned young girls never to roam alone near the swamps, convinced that they would be snatched by the Pantera, while young men were trained to avoid hunting anywhere near the protected Wildlands.

Not that the warnings were always successful.

What girl didn't dream of being seduced by a gorgeous, mysterious stranger? And what young man didn't want to try his skill against the most lethal predators?

As the years passed, however, the sightings of the Pantera became so rare that the rumors faded to myths.

Most believed the species had become extinct.
Sadly, they weren't entirely mistaken…

CHAPTER ONE

S LUT. Whore.
Worthless piece of white trash.

The words were still ringing in Ashe Pascal's ears as the door to the trailer slammed behind her.

She grimaced as she gathered her clothes that littered the front porch and headed for her piece-of-shit clunker that was parked near the curb.

For once the drunken insults flung by her mother managed to hit a nerve.

Not that she was a whore. It wasn't like she'd gotten paid for spreading her legs, was it?

Hell no, she'd spread them for free.

Or at least she assumed she had.

How else could she be pregnant? Immaculate conceptions might happen in the good book, but in the bayous of southern Louisiana women got knocked-up the good old-fashioned way.

A damned shame she couldn't remember what happened.

If she had to pay the piper she should at least have enjoyed the dance.

With a shake of her head, she yanked open the door of her car and tossed her clothes on the cracked leather seat before climbing behind the driver's wheel.

Shoving her key into the ignition, she breathed out a sigh of relief as the engine rattled to weary life. The way her pissy luck was running she'd expected the battery to be dead. Again.

She supposed there was an irony in the fact that she'd promised herself that she would start looking for a new car just as soon as she'd paid off her mother's latest bar tab. She'd even driven to the bar to tell the owner that she was done being her mother's personal banker.

And that's when the trouble had started.

Barely aware that she'd shoved her car in gear, Ashe absently drove through the small town that hovered on the edge of the bayou, pulling to a halt across the street from the only bar in town.

The two story wooden building with a tin roof had at one time been painted a cheery yellow, but over the years it'd faded to a miserable mustard, with heavy green shutters that could offer protection during hurricane season. The entire structure was built on heavy stilts to keep the main floor off the ground. A necessary precaution in this area. The danger of flooding was a hundred percent, which no doubt explained why less than a few hundred people lived in the town.

She gave a humorless laugh at the neon sign that blinked in the thickening gloom.

'The Cougar's Den'

It sounded like a hang-out for the local football team, or maybe a taxidermist's shop.

Instead it was filled with a motley crew who she assumed came in from the oil fields, the shrimp boats and the dark shadows of the swamps. And of course, locals like her mother who were so desperate for a drink they were willing to ignore the thick air of aggression that filled the entire building.

The rest of the town avoided the place like the plague.

Including the pack of stray dogs that terrorized the rest of the town.

The Cougar's Den was a cesspit of danger.

Her grim thoughts were abruptly interrupted as the humid spring breeze swept through her open window, tugging at her long, black curls and caressing her skin that remained a pale ivory no matter how much sun she got. Her eyes, as dark as a midnight sky, narrowed.

There was something in the breeze.

Something beyond the hint of azaleas, and newly bloomed roses from Old Lady La Vaux's garden, and even the more distant smell of rotting vegetation that wafted from the swamps.

What the hell was that scent?

Not cologne, but...musk.

Yes. That's what it was. A rich, intoxicating male musk.

Without warning, a flash of memory seared through her brain.

She was in the cramped barroom, trying to ignore the flat, unfriendly glares from the large group of men who were gathered around the pool tables at the back of the darkly paneled room.

One in particular had separated himself from the pack, staring at her as if she were a creature from another planet.

He was big. Six foot two at least. And powerful, with sleek, chiseled muscles beneath his tight white tee and black jeans.

In the dim light he looked like some exotic god.

His shoulder-length hair was thick and shimmered like molten gold in the dim light. His features were lean, stunningly beautiful. And his eyes...

Words couldn't capture their beauty.

They were the same gold as his hair, but flecked with hints of jade and in the darkness they glowed with an inner light.

Abruptly her memory took a leap forward.

She was no longer in the public room, but lying on a bed in a room upstairs.

It was dark and that aromatic male musk saturated the air.

A low, male voice whispered in her ear.

"*You're so wet, ma chère. Do you want me to lick your cream?*"

She groaned, her legs parting as she felt soft kisses blaze a trail down her quivering belly.

"*Raphael, please.*"

"*Tell me what you want.*" *A command.* "*Say the words.*"

"*You.*" *She clutched the soft quilt beneath her, her body on fire with need. It'd never been this way. Not this raw, frantic hunger that clawed through her with an addictive force.* "*I want you.*"

There was a low chuckle and she gasped at the feel of his hot breath against the sensitive skin of her inner thigh.

"Where do you want me?" he teased. "Here?" The stroke of a rough tongue through her wet slit.

Sucking a sharp breath, Ashe shattered the strange vision.

Was the memory real? Or just her mind trying to sugarcoat the hideous truth?

With a low cry, she shoved the car back into gear and stomped her foot down on the accelerator.

There were no answers here.

What she needed was a hot meal and somewhere to sleep for the night.

Tomorrow she would worry about how she was going to take care of a baby when she could barely take care of herself.

———

Standing in the shadows beneath the bar, Raphael strained against the large man who kept him from charging after the sorry excuse for a car currently speeding away.

"Release me," he growled, his eyes glowing with a luminous gold in the darkness.

"Goddammit, Raphael." Bayon shared Rafael's golden good looks although his hair was a shade paler and his eyes held more green. He was also built on bulkier lines. "Leash your damned animal and listen to me."

Raphael battled through the primal instincts that had nothing to do with humanity and everything to do with raw, animal desire.

Holy hell.

Of all the Pantera, he was the one who'd had the best control over his primitive nature.

It was the reason he'd been chosen by the elders to become one of the most trusted diplomats for his people, traveling away from the Wildlands to meet in secret with various world leaders. At least that was his public persona. In truth, his primary duty was heading up his peoples' vast network of spies who infiltrated the various governments and scientific communities.

He could travel for weeks away from the reservation without being debilitated by his need to shift. And more importantly, he'd developed the ability to mimic the humans so he could function in their world.

He was still a feral feline at heart, but a feline with manners.

Now, however, he was at the mercy of savage need that thundered through his body with the force of a tsunami.

"I'm not going to tell you again," he growled. "Let me go."

Bayon leaned in until they were nose to nose. The bastard was one of the few who had the *cojones* to get in Raphael's grill.

"This has to be a trick," the younger warrior snapped. "We've tried for the past fifty years to discover human women who can carry our seed—"

"You don't have to remind me of our history."

And he didn't. Raphael knew better than anyone the struggles of the Pantera.

It'd started slow.

Fewer and fewer females going into heat. And those who did were unable to carry their babes to full-term.

At first the elders believed that it was the fault of the human contact with the Pantera. They shut off their borders and became increasingly isolated from the world.

When that didn't work, they began to fear it was a genetic anomaly. The Pantera had, after all, interbred for centuries.

So discreetly selecting the finest specimens of human females who agreed to become surrogates at an enormous price for their secrecy, they'd brought the women to their high-tech medical facilities. They were the rare few who realized the Pantera were more than mere myths.

The human females, however, had been unable to breed with the Pantera. Not even with the most potent fertility drugs.

So his people had no choice but to seek answers outside the Wildlands.

5

Keeping a low profile, a handful of Pantera scientists had covertly gained employment at various research facilities, seeking information from the humans' work on DNA.

At the same time, the 'Suits,' or Political Faction of the Pantera, had sent spies to infiltrate the various governments.

They needed to know if there was some physical change that was affecting the magic of their land.

Toxic waste. Global warming. Bio-chemical warfare.

It could be accidental or deliberate sabotage, but if the humans were involved then Raphael intended to uncover the truth.

He had just been returning from his latest trip abroad when he'd stopped at The Cougar's Den, needing to blow off some steam before traveling to the Wildlands and making his latest report.

The elders weren't going to be pleased with his lack of progress.

Hell, he wasn't pleased.

The last thing he expected was to be blindsided by a human female. Or to find himself returning to the decrepit bar week after week in the hopes of spotting her again.

And now...shit.

Giving Raphael a shake, Bayon glared at him, his anger causing the temperature to spike.

"Then you realize it's impossible for that female to be pregnant with your child."

Raphael met his friend glare for glare. "Impossible or not, I know what I smelled."

"Think about it." Bayon's eyes glowed with golden power. "A strange woman just happens to stroll into a bar where the Pantera gather. She magically stirs your mating urges despite being human, and now she deliberately parks her car close enough that you were bound to pick up her scent before driving away like a madwoman." He gave Raphael another shake. "Does she have to have T R A P tattooed on her ass for you to get it?"

Raphael made a sound of frustration. His friend wasn't saying anything that Raphael hadn't already told himself.

Hell, he'd be shocked if it wasn't some sort of trick.

But until he discovered exactly what was happening, he wasn't going to let the female out of his sight.

Or out of his bed, a treacherous voice whispered in the back of his mind.

"There's one way to find out."

With a strength that caught Bayon off-guard, Raphael shoved them away and headed toward the road.

"Wait," Bayon called. "What are you going to do?"

"To find my woman and discover exactly what she has tattooed on her ass," he snarled.

"Christ, Raphael."

Focused on the rapidly fading scent, Raphael jogged away from the bar, his dark jeans and black tee allowing him to disappear among the shadows.

He expected the female to head to her house. The more respectable citizens of the small town tended to be tucked safely behind closed doors as soon as the sun went down. They might not logically believe in voodoo or ghosts or even the Pantera, but they were smart enough to know that strange creatures crawled out of the swamps at night.

No reason to become easy prey.

But instead of heading toward the wooden houses that ran in tidy rows facing the red brick schoolhouse and attached community center that doubled as a church, she turned in the opposite direction toward the town square that was framed by a handful of small shops.

At last she parked her car next to the three-story hotel that was squashed between the beauty shop and post office. Raphael stood beneath the draping branches of the weeping willow in the center of the square, watching the slender female enter through the glass door.

Did she work at the hotel?

Or was she there to meet someone?

Some man?

A low snarl rumbled through his chest, his cat twisting beneath his skin with a primeval fury.

The woman was his.

Branded by his passion and bound to him by the babe she carried in her womb.

Mine. Mine. Mine.

The words whispered through his soul as he strolled across the street to enter the cramped lobby of the hotel.

His nose wrinkled at the stench that clung to the ugly green and yellow diamond-patterned carpet and the mold that had multiplied into a thriving community behind the warped wood paneling. There was a wilted fake plant shoved in a corner and a reception desk at the back of the room. Currently a bleached-blonde woman was leaning on the desk as she flipped through a glossy magazine.

Lifting her head at his entrance, she gave a low whistle, her chubby face flushing with pleasure as her blue gaze made a slow, thorough survey of his body.

"Can I help you?" she murmured, tugging at her loose top to better display her massive rack.

Clearly the middle-aged woman thought her breasts worthy of putting on public display.

A delusional belief, but Raphael wasn't a trained diplomat just because he could travel away from the Wildlands.

With his most charming smile he strolled forward, halting near the desk so he could covertly take note of an office to the left where two small dogs were yapping at his arrival and, to the right, a back door that led to the alleyway.

"I was passing and I thought I saw a friend come in here."

The female gave her blouse another tug. "Lucky friend."

"Maybe you would recognize her. She's tall, dark-haired… beautiful."

"Oh, you mean Ashe Pascal."

Ashe. He silently tested the name. A Native American name.

Did she carry their blood?

"Yes."

The woman eyed him with a growing curiosity. "She just went to her room. Do you want me to give her a call?"

"That's not necessary." He shared another dazzling smile. "Is she a guest here?"

"For tonight." The bleach-blonde curls bounced as the female shook her head in a gesture of disgust. "That mother of hers kicked her out. The damned bitch should be flogged for the way she treats her daughter."

Raphael's brows lowered. "Ashe never speaks of her family."

The woman shrugged. "What's to say? Her worthless father walked out when she was just a babe and her mother's a drunk. Ashe spends every penny trying to keep a roof over her head and the bills paid. Not that Dixie Pascal appreciates what Ashe does for her. Most nights she's down at that nasty Cougar's Den swilling cheap vodka." She grimaced. "Just as a warning, if you're new in town, you'll wanna give that bar a miss. It's not a place for decent folk."

A pure shaft of fury pierced his heart.

The Pantera were a close-knit society who protected their young with a ferocious intensity.

But Ashe had been treated like trash. Tossed onto the streets by her mother.

She'd been left vulnerable, her child…*his* child…put at risk in this shabby hotel that was barely a step above sleeping in the gutter.

The knowledge was unacceptable.

Sensing the hotel manager's growing curiosity, Raphael leashed his anger.

He would deal with Ashe's worthless parents after he had her safely hidden in his lair.

For now he had to make certain that his savage obsession with the beautiful female wasn't blinding him to an obvious trap.

"I'll keep that in mind," he murmured.

The older woman tilted her head. "Are you wanting to see Ashe?"

With every fiber of his being.

He forced himself to shake his head.

"Perhaps later. Unfortunately, I have a meeting, but I can't remember the exact address." He held the manager's pale gaze allowing a tendril of his musk to fill the air. It wasn't enough to captivate the woman, but it would loosen her tongue. "I don't suppose you've seen any strangers hanging around here?"

"Here?" She frowned, considering the question. "I've had the usual crew from the oil rigs and the Jenkins family came in from Baton Rouge for a reunion."

"There hasn't been anyone around town asking questions?" he pressed.

"The only strangers in town are down at The Cougar's Den." The woman heaved an exasperated frown as the dogs caught the whiff of his musk and went into a whining frenzy. "What the hell is wrong with them dogs? *Excusez-moi.*"

Raphael waited until the woman had stomped into the office to pacify her terrified animals before silently sliding out the back door.

He stepped into the shadows, disappearing from prying eyes as he allowed his senses to absorb his surroundings.

He caught the sound of mice tunneling through the trash cans. The buzz of the street lights at the end of the alley. The breeze that carried a threat of rain.

And, overwhelming everything, the sweet perfume that had haunted his dreams for the past six weeks.

Sucking in a deep breath, Raphael focused on the window where he could sense Ashe.

He would wait to slip into her room once she was asleep.

And then…

Then he would have the truth.

Chapter Two

ASHE hadn't expected to sleep.

Even when she'd stripped off her clothes and crawled beneath the sheets buck-naked, she'd assumed she was too worried to actually relax enough to rest.

But the emotional upheaval of the day, combined with the hormonal changes that were already affecting her body, soon had her tumbling into a welcomed darkness.

Not that her rest was peaceful.

She'd barely fallen asleep when her dreams were filled with the memories of a hard, hot body pressing her into the mattress.

She moaned, her head twisting on the pillow as seeking lips trailed a line of kisses down the column of her neck. Her hands ran a restless path over the wide back, savoring the feel of rippling muscles beneath the silken skin.

Raphael.

Her legs parted as he settled between them, the steel-hard length of his erection pressing against her inner thigh. Her entire body was on fire, shaking with the need to feel him deep inside her.

It'd never been like this.

Never before had she experienced this savage…hunger.

She felt the head of his cock penetrate her, but while her hands moved to clasp his hard ass, he refused to deepen the thrust. Instead his lips blazed a path of devastation along the line of her collarbone, kissing and sucking the sensitive skin.

Her hips lifted in a silent plea, her breath wrenched from her lungs as his mouth traveled over the soft globe of her breast and latched onto her nipple.

She whimpered.

Oh…god.

It was good. So good.

His teeth closed over the aching tip, biting hard enough to send a jolt of sizzling excitement through her.

Please.

What do you want?

You.

Only me. Do you understand? You're mine.

Yes.

Say it.

Only you.

She heard a rumble of satisfaction deep in his chest, the intoxicating musk filling her senses. Oh, hell. How had she ever thought sex an overrated pastime?

This was mind-blowingly fantastic.

The inane thought was shattered as he pressed his hips forward, entering her with a slow, ruthless slide that stretched her with a delicious friction.

He was huge.

A gasp of pleasure was ripped from her lips as his hands gripped her hips, tilting her so he could sink even deeper, invading her with the promise of paradise.

Raphael.

I'm here.

Jerked out of her dream, Ashe lifted a hand to her ear, feeling the lingering warmth. As if lips had just brushed the delicate shell.

Shit.

Slowly sitting up, she tugged the sheet over her breasts as she impatiently brushed her tangled hair out of her face.

"Hello?" Her eyes searched the darkness, sensing a presence even though she couldn't see the intruder. A chill inched down her spine. "I know there's someone here."

"You smell so sweet." The male voice was low, whiskey-smooth. And terrifyingly familiar. "Like night-blooming jasmine."

She didn't scream. Instinctively she knew that he would pounce before she could be heard.

Her hand fumbled for her cell phone.

Where the hell was it? She'd left it on the nightstand, hadn't she?

"I have a gun," she tried to bluff.

She heard a soft footfall, but the intruder remained in the shadows while she was bathed in the moonlight that slanted through the window.

The *open* window.

No need to ask how he managed to get in.

"That's what first caught my attention," he continued, ignoring her threat. "That scent…" She heard him suck in a deep breath. "It intoxicates me."

"I'll shoot," she tried again, even knowing it was futile. "I swear I will."

"And then I caught sight of you." His words seemed to brush over her skin, creating tiny sparks of awareness. "The exquisite lines of your profile. The sexy tumble of ebony curls. The ivory satin of your skin. The elegant lines of your body." There was a low rumble. Did it come from the man? "You were a purebred, all pride and nervous energy."

Her mouth went dry and she forgot her search for her missing phone. Instead her fingers went toward the lamp.

"Who are you?"

"No, don't turn on the light."

She shivered at the command in his voice. "Then answer the question."

"Raphael."

So, she hadn't imagined knowing his name.

Christ. Did that mean the rest was true as well?

The thought should terrify her. Or at least infuriate her.

It sure the hell shouldn't cause a treacherous heat to bloom between her legs.

"Just Raphael?" she rasped.

"Just Raphael."

"Why are you in my room?"

There was a beat of silence, as if he was startled by the question.

"You know why."

A sudden premonition stole her breath. "No."

"You carry my child."

"Shit."

The panic that should have hit the minute she woke with a strange man in her hotel room belatedly thundered through Ashe. Without conscious thought she was shoving aside the sheet and preparing to leap off the bed.

She didn't know where she intended to go.

She was naked, broke and currently homeless.

But anywhere had to be better than locked in a room with a lunatic.

There was no warning.

One minute she was struggling to untangle her feet from the covers and the next she was flat on her back, a heavy body pressing her into the mattress.

Oh…hell.

This was it.

Her dream.

Except in her dreams he was naked. Now his denims scraped against her upper thighs and a soft tee brushed the aching tips of her breasts.

Unbelievably the sensations were almost as erotic as the feel of his bare skin.

Or maybe not so unbelievably.

Even with a layer of clothing between them she could feel the searing heat of his body seeping into her, stirring her blood. And that musk…

How was a woman supposed to think clearly?

Her lips parted—whether to scream or moan she would never know—as his head swooped down and her mouth was taken in a savage kiss.

She gasped, shocked by the jolts of sheer pleasure that ravaged her body.

It was like being struck by lightning.

Dazzling. Electric. Stunning her with an instant need that made her pussy clench with anticipation.

She squirmed beneath him, pressing the aching tips of her breasts against the heat of his chest. Oh god. It felt so good.

With a groan, Raphael ripped his mouth from hers to bury his face in the curve of her throat.

"That smell," he muttered, his nose lingered against her thundering pulse as his hands pinned her arms over her head.

His heavy legs held the bottom half of her body motionless, but even with her mind clouded by lust she realized that he was taking great care not to press any weight against her stomach.

The knowledge sent an odd flare of tenderness through her. A sensation that was far more disturbing than the desire pulsing through her blood.

Instinctively, she tried to put some distance between them.

"No." A warning growl rumbled deep in his chest as he lifted his head. "Don't move."

Her hair rose at the prickles of heat that filled the air. "Are you going to hurt me?"

"No. But your struggles…" His golden eyes suddenly seemed to shimmer with a luminosity in the darkness. "Excite my animal."

Those eyes.

Those magnificent golden eyes that had glowed with hunger as he'd ridden her with a rough urgency.

"Oh god, it was you," she breathed.

"Yes."

A surge of anger merged with her lust, forming a combustible combination.

"You're right, you are an animal," she snapped. "What kind of man drugs and rapes a helpless woman?"

He hissed in genuine outrage. "There were no drugs and there sure as hell was no rape." He lowered his head until they were nose to nose, his breath a warm caress against her face. "You begged, *ma chère*."

"A lie," she muttered.

He brushed his lips over her cheek until he could whisper directly in her ear, his tone pitched high as he mimicked her words.

"Please don't stop," he breathed. "Please, please. I need your cock deep inside me."

Her lips parted, but the protest died as she could hear the words in her own voice echoing through a dark room.

She *had* begged.

She'd even grabbed the steel-hard length of his cock to try and steer him to her sweet spot.

"It was the drugs," she muttered.

He nipped her earlobe. "No drugs."

A violent shudder racked her body, her legs spreading as he settled between them, the ridge of his erection pressing against her inner thigh.

"There had to be," she insisted. "I don't have sex with strangers. And even if I did I wouldn't forget—"

Her words faltered as he did something with his hips that aligned his cock directly against her throbbing clit.

"Mind-shattering climaxes that left us both gasping for air?"

Her breath was wrenched from her lungs even as she dug her nails into the hands that gripped her wrists above her head.

"Stop it," she moaned, wanting nothing more than to wrap her legs around his waist and rub herself to climax. This wasn't her. She didn't become hot and bothered just because some guy wanted to have sex with her. Even if he was a gorgeous stud who was built like a freaking Greek god. "You did something to me."

"No, we did something to each other." He caught her bottom lip between his teeth, giving it a sensual tug before nibbling at the corner of her mouth. "Something that shouldn't be possible."

"I don't know what you're talking about."

"And that's the problem."

Hell, there were a whole lot of problems.

And this man making her go up in flames was the cause of all of them.

"Could you please get off me?" she demanded, lifting her hips as if she could actually buck him off.

His hands tightened on her wrists, his breath hissing between his clenched teeth.

"Stay. Still."

Her heart halted as something seemed to shift behind his glowing eyes. An…awareness that was watching her with a feral hunger.

"Christ."

He sucked in a deep breath, a muscle clenching in his jaw. "Listen, *ma chère*, we need to talk. But if you keep moving, I'm going to forget everything except my instinct to fuck you."

Moisture gathered between her legs, a raw craving clawing through her.

"Don't…don't say things like that."

"Does it excite you?"

Yes. God, yes.

She wanted to be fucked.

Here. Now.

She swallowed a moan.

"It disgusts me," she forced herself to lie. "*You* disgust me."

His low chuckle brushed over her heated face. "Is that why you're wet?" he teased. "Why you've got your nails dug into my hands as if you're terrified I might leave before I satisfy that ache inside you?"

She shuddered. He was right.

It would be unbearable to be left to suffer the overwhelming lust that was spiking ever higher.

"God."

"Shh." He brushed a gentle kiss over her lips. "Right now I just want to talk."

She refused to be comforted. "Before or after you drug me?"

17

"Dammit." The austere beauty of his face tightened with annoyance. Then, with an obvious effort, he struggled to keep his temper. "Have you heard of the Pantera?"

She blinked.

Of all the questions she'd been expecting, that had to be at the bottom of the list.

"The beast-men who roam the swamps?" she asked in confusion.

His lips twisted. "I suppose that's one way of describing them. What do you know?"

She shrugged. Like every child who grew up near the swamps she'd heard the stories of the strange beasts who were part man, part animal, who roamed the darkness.

Her own grandmother had sworn the mysterious race had openly interacted with the townsfolk when she'd been young, but the old woman had often been confused. Hell, she'd all but implied that Ashe's father had been some sort of magical shaman instead of a lazy jackass who'd bolted the minute he discovered her mother was pregnant.

"I know they're about as real as Rougarou and Bigfoot," she said.

"They're real." There was a deliberate pause. "*I'm* real."

Her mouth went dry, a sharp-edged fear slicing through her heart. "You're saying you're a beast-man?"

The beautiful face was set in a grim expression. "I'm Pantera."

She tried to laugh, only to have it come out as a shaky moan. "Yeah, right."

"Look at me, Ashe." The eyes glowed brighter, as if there were a fire burning deep inside them with flecks of jade. They were…magnificent. Stunning. But they sure as hell weren't human. "You know I speak the truth. You've sensed I was different from the moment we met."

Of course she'd sensed he was different.

No mere man could move with such graceful speed, or hold a woman captive with one hand.

And then there was that enticing musk that clouded her mind and made it impossible to think.

"I didn't know you were a freaking animal," she rasped.

He flinched, his nose flaring with irritation. "Careful, *ma chère*, the child you carry is Pantera."

Abruptly she squeezed her eyes shut. It was too much.

Too. Damned. Much.

"God, please let this be a nightmare."

"Do you intend to act like you're five and hope you can close your eyes and wish away the monster?" he chastised. "Or are you going to look at me and discuss this like an adult?"

Her eyes snapped open.

Did he think a child of a raging drunk had ever been allowed to pretend she could wish away monsters?

"I was an adult at five," she said, coldly.

Something that might have been regret softened his aquiline features.

"Then you understand that we have to face the consequences of our actions."

"Easy for you to say. I don't even remember our...actions." She narrowed her gaze. "You did something to me to make me forget, didn't you? Is it a power you have?"

He shrugged. "One of many."

So she hadn't blacked out that night.

She didn't know if his confession made her feel better or not.

Actually, she didn't know what she felt.

She licked her lips, shivering as his glowing gaze lowered to study her mouth with an unsettling intensity.

"Are you—"

"What?"

"Part beast?"

CHAPTER THREE

RAPHAEL lifted a brow.

Christ. Did she actually think he had furry parts when he was in this form?

Then he bleakly reminded himself that while every kiss, every soft moan as he plunged deep inside her, was branded on his mind, she had only flashes of memory.

The thought stirred a startling compulsion to repeat the performance.

To fuck her so long and so thoroughly she would never, ever be able to forget his touch.

To mark her so no other man would ever dare lay a finger on her.

Mine.

He swallowed a low snarl. Dammit. He'd been chosen as a diplomat because he was one of the Pantera capable of controlling his emotions.

How did this female manage to destroy that restraint?

"Yes, I'm part beast," he said dryly. "And before you try to peek, I don't have animal parts when I'm in human form."

With a remarkable courage, considering all she'd been through over the past few hours, she met his gaze, determined to learn the truth.

"I assume that means you have more than one form?"

"When I'm on my native soil I can shift."

"Shift?" She blinked. "Like a werewolf?"

He made a sound of disgust. "No, I'm a puma, not a mangy dog."

She slowly absorbed his words, her face pale. "How?"

Raphael hesitated, battling against his instinctive urge to ignore her question.

Over the past fifty years the already elusive Pantera had become increasingly isolated, sensing they were in danger but unable to pin-point the precise threat.

Only those individuals necessary for survival of their race actually left the Wildlands and they remained incognito except to a rare few, trusted humans. Well, and the politicians who had the power to screw with their homeland.

But even as he struggled against his training, he knew deep in his gut that this woman was innocent.

He would have been able to sense if she were lying to him.

She truly had no idea what Pantera were or that the child she carried was supposed to be an impossible dream.

"You'll have to discuss the subject with our philosophers if you want an exhaustive explanation," he at last answered. "But the short story is that the Wildlands possess a magic that created my distant ancestors."

She frowned. "Turning them into pumas?"

"Giving them the ability to shift into animal form. It's still hotly debated whether they could have chosen any animal and settled on pumas since they were the most lethal predator capable of surviving in the bayous, or if it was the only form the magic allowed."

Her face paled another shade, emphasizing her fragile beauty. "What else can you do?"

Feeling a jab of regret, Raphael loosened his grip on her wrists, skimming his hands down her bare arms.

This had to be difficult for her.

Unfortunately, he didn't know how to make it any easier.

"Like humans, we each have our own talents."

She shivered with growing excitement, but her expression remained hard with suspicion.

"That's…evasive."

His concentration was shattered by the feel of her satin skin beneath his fingertips, the cat inside him stirring with restless hunger.

It didn't understand this need to talk.

It wanted to pounce. Devour. To mate with this female who was warm and wet beneath him.

"We're a secretive race."

"No shit," she breathed. "Why?"

"We have our reasons."

Her eyes darkened as his hands traced her shoulders before heading down the line of her collarbone, her own concentration obviously beginning to fracture.

"Just tell me, is one of your talents seducing humans?" she hissed through clenched teeth.

"We produce a pheromone that can be an aphrodisiac," he said, not surprised when her eyes widened and she wildly grasped for the excuse to explain her violent arousal whenever he touched her.

"I knew it," she rasped.

He shook his head. "Ashe, that's not what happened between us."

"You just said—"

"I said it's possible to produce a pheromone, but believe me I had no need to do anything," he said, his voice thickening as his dick began to throb with an insistent craving. "You walked into the bar and the air combusted between us."

He could hear her heart miss a beat as her nipples hardened into tiny nubs of temptation.

"So you're saying I caught sight of you and instantly climbed into the nearest bed?"

She tried for scorn, but there was no missing the dilation of her pupils and the scent of her arousal.

He sucked in a deep breath, savoring her sweet scent. "I don't have an explanation beyond the fact that we saw one another, the mating heat hit, and not a force on this earth could have kept me from claiming you."

"Mating heat?"

"When a female Pantera is fertile she—"

"Don't." She pressed a hand over his mouth, a complex tangle of emotions rippling over her delicate features. "I'm not Pantera."

"No," he swiftly agreed. "And even if you were, I should have been able to control myself. I might have the soul of an animal, but I'm still human."

She studied his somber expression, searching for the truth. "Did you truly make me forget?"

Raphael forced himself to meet her gaze. He wasn't proud that he'd used his power to scrub her mind.

But the bald truth was that he'd been as shocked as she was by the intensity of his desire for her. And while he'd had sex with any number of human females, he'd never lost control like he had that night.

He couldn't be entirely certain that he hadn't given away the fact he wasn't a normal lover.

Now he knew that his little stunt was only going to complicate their already fucked-up relationship.

"I have the ability to cloud your memories," he reluctantly admitted.

She stiffened beneath him. "You can manipulate my mind?"

"No," he growled. "I can only…urge you not to remember. It's a small trick that has allowed my people to keep our presence hidden from most of the world."

He could feel her stiffen beneath him. "That's what you call it? A small trick?" she snapped, her eyes flashing with midnight fire. "I thought I was going crazy when I went to the doctor and he told me I was pregnant. Then I started getting flashes of memories. It terrified me. I didn't know if they were real or if they were fragments of a growing insanity."

"I'm sorry," he said.

And he was. The thought of causing this woman one second of pain was abhorrent. But as he slowly began to accept that the child she carried was no trick, that she was actually pregnant with his babe, he couldn't regret that he'd given into his primitive urges.

To have this woman as his mate, and a child to call his own…

It filled him with a fierce happiness he never expected.

Her lips flattened. "That's all you have to say? I'm sorry?"

His gaze lingered on her mouth, his cock twitching as his cat reached the end of its patience.

"It shouldn't have been possible."

"The memories?"

"The memories or the pregnancy."

"You used protection?"

"No." His gaze returned to meet the challenge in her eyes, once again struck by her courage. Most humans, male or female, would be cowering in fear. But not his beautiful Ashe. His cat preened with pride. "I'm incapable of catching or carrying human diseases so you were in no danger. And there's never been a human female impregnated by a Pantera."

"Never?"

"Not one in recent memory."

Her eyes widened. "Then maybe this baby isn't yours."

"Ashe—"

"You said yourself you screwed with my memories. Maybe I left you and had sex with some other man…" She gave a small scream as his teeth sank into her neck. Not hard enough to break the skin, but with enough force to claim his ownership. "Shit, Raphael," she gasped, her nails digging into his shoulders as she squirmed beneath him.

Not in pain.

But pure excitement.

"No other man has touched you," he snarled, his nose pressed against her skin as he breathed deep of her scent, seeking to calm his animal.

She shivered, her head pressing into the pillow to arch her neck in unconscious invitation.

"How can you be so certain?"

"Because you're mine." He soothed his bite mark with tender kisses before heading downward. "You even taste like you're mine," he murmured, trailing his tongue down to the tip of her nipple.

Ashe moaned, her fingers shoving into his hair. "What does that mean?" she demanded.

"You taste of sunshine," he whispered, his tongue continuing to tease the hard nub, "and rich, fertile earth, and magic. You taste of home."

Her eyes squeezed shut, a flush staining her cheeks. "What are you doing to me?"

"Nothing you don't want, *ma chère*," he promised, his lips tracing a gentle path of kisses to her stomach. "Mine," he murmured, his superior senses already able to detect the tiny babe in her womb.

Whispering a soft hello, he shoved himself off the bed, ridding himself of his clothes with a minimum of fuss, relishing the sensation of her avid gaze taking in the hard muscles of his naked body and the tattoo on his upper chest. He paused, taking a heartbeat to simply appreciate the sight of Ashe stretched across the mattress, her slender body painted in silver moonlight and her dark hair spilled across the sheet.

Like an exquisite sacrifice to the gods.

Then, placing a knee on the edge of the bed, he bent down to kiss the sensitive arch of her foot before nibbling each tiny toe.

She gave a choked groan as he slowly explored up her calf, relishing the intoxicating smell of her arousal perfuming the air.

With a low groan she restlessly stirred on the sheets, and Raphael grasped her hips, holding her still.

He intended to feast on her, making her scream with pleasure before he was done.

Giving her a punishing nip, he worked his way upward, spreading her legs as his cat gave a low snarl of anticipation.

"Raphael." Her fingers clenched in his hair as his tongue discovered her moist heat.

He slid his hands beneath her hips, finding the perfect angle before returning to his single-minded task.

Lapping at her cream, Raphael savored her sweetness, dipping his tongue into her tight little passage.

Holy hell. Her taste was intoxicating. Better than the finest wine.

He stroked back to the top of her clit, finding her tiny bundle of pleasure to suck between his lips.

Her hips bucked upward, her hands tugging at his hair as her moans became shortened pants.

He could taste her nearing climax on his tongue, making his cock twitch in protest.

As tempting as it might be to stroke her to completion, he needed more.

He wanted to look her in the eye as he thrust deep inside her, completing the most intimate connection possible between lovers.

With a last, lingering lap of his tongue, Raphael surged upward, claiming her mouth in a kiss of stark hunger. He would never have his fill of her.

Never.

Her legs wrapped instinctively around his waist in a silent offering and Raphael gave a rough groan. He was quivering with the need to slam his cock into her, pounding them both to a swift, satisfying climax, but he was acutely conscious that she was far more fragile than a Pantera female.

He had to be careful.

Peering deep into her dazed eyes, he pressed the head of his cock at her entrance, halting to appreciate the sensation of her moist flesh wrapped around his crown.

Oh, hell. He could come just like this, it felt so good.

Beneath him, Ashe whimpered, her nails digging into his upper arms as she struggled to tug him closer.

"Why are you stopping?" she pleaded. "I need you."

"Easy, *ma chère*," he murmured. "I don't want to hurt you."

"You won't...oh god..."

She lifted her hips, taking another inch of his throbbing erection inside her. They both groaned, the air spiced with the musky scent of his cat who was dangerously close to the surface.

This was a Pantera at his most primitive, stripped of the layer of civilization that gave him the appearance of being human.

He slid his hands beneath her shoulder blades, lowering his head to claim her lips even as he thrust forward and claimed her with his steel-hard erection.

With him buried to the hilt, they clutched at one another, the pleasure rolling over them in searing waves.

"You have enthralled me," he breathed as he slowly pulled out of her to surge back with a roll of his hips. She gave a startled gasp that was choked off as the swelling excitement held them in sexual thrall. "I am yours."

Scattering kisses over her damp face, he drove himself into her heat, keeping the pace relentless, but gentle. Man, he wanted this to last all night, but already he could feel the building pressure of his orgasm. Burying his face in the curve of her neck, his fingers flexed against her back, his nails unconsciously digging into her tender flesh.

He was lost.

Lost in the overwhelming sensation of her pussy clenched tight and hot around his surging cock.

Continuing his relentless pace, he waited for her to tense beneath him, the sound of her thundering heartbeat echoing inside him with a pagan rhythm.

Still it wasn't until she gave a soft cry of release that he unleashed his cat, unknowingly using his claws to slice through her skin, marking her on a most primal level.

With one last thrust he buried himself until his balls were flush against her ass and allowed his climax to smash into him with mind-numbing force.

God. Damn.

Was the world still spinning? It felt as if it must have come to a shuddering, cataclysmic halt.

Raising his head, he studied Ashe's sated expression, a smile of smug satisfaction curving his lips.

The scent of lust and his personal musk was thick in the air, along with…

Blood?

With a stunned sense of disbelief, he turned to the side, rolling her over so he could inspect the scratches that marred the satin skin of her upper back.

Marks made by claws, not human nails.

They weren't deep, but he knew beyond a shadow of a doubt that they would leave four silver lines on each shoulder that would forever claim her as his mate.

No. It wasn't possible.

A Pantera couldn't shift unless they were in the Wildlands.

Their eyes glowed in the dark, or when their emotions were aroused, and they produced a musk that was directly connected to their cats. But they couldn't actually change body parts.

So what the hell had just happened?

CHAPTER FOUR

RAPHAEL didn't try to prevent Ashe from lying back on the mattress, a frown chasing away her earlier glow of post-coital bliss as she regarded him with a wary suspicion.

"What was that about?"

"This is madness," he muttered.

"I agree." Her chin tilted to a defensive angle, yanking the sheet over her body still flushed from her recent climax. "Sex with a stranger who says he's not even human is most certainly madness. Even worse, I'm now stuck with an unwanted pregnancy."

His stunned reaction to yet another impossibility becoming possible was shattered by her stark words.

While he'd been reeling at the sight of his mating marks, she'd been left feeling raw and exposed by their explosive passion. He should have been cuddling her close and assuring her that she was precisely where she belonged.

In his arms.

Now she was scrambling to resurrect her protective walls.

Christ, could he fuck up the situation any worse?

He leaned on his elbow, meeting her guarded gaze with an expression of open concern.

"You don't want the baby?"

Her defiance faltered, something heartrendingly vulnerable visible in the depths of her dark eyes.

"I…haven't had time to think about it."

His hand moved to cautiously touch her lower stomach, struggling against the sudden, brutal fear that she might actually do something to end the pregnancy.

"Ashe, I'm not exaggerating when I say this is a miracle," he said softly, not minding the edge of pleading in his voice. His child might very well prove to be the savior of the Pantera. "My people—"

His words came to abrupt halt as he tensed, turning his head toward the door.

"What is it?" she demanded.

"I'm not sure."

With a fluid movement he was off the bed and pulling on his jeans and T-shirt before moving silently across the room.

He pressed his ear to the door, his heightened senses picking up the unmistakable scent of two human males walking up the steps and the metallic tang of the guns they carried.

It wasn't the stench of their weapons, however, that made his cat snarl in warning.

There was something…off in their smell.

Not drugs or disease.

But a sour smell that was just wrong.

Without hesitation he spun on his heel and headed back across the room. He didn't know who the hell these men were, but he wasn't hanging around to find out.

Not when his mate and child needed his protection.

Reaching the bed, Raphael leaned down to wrap the sheet around a startled Ashe, scooping her off the mattress and cradling her against his chest as he headed toward the open window.

"What the hell are you doing?" she rasped, futilely battling against the sheet tangled around her limbs.

"We're leaving."

"But I'm—"

He covered her mouth with his hand, bending down to whisper directly in her ear.

"Shh. We need to get out of here. Now."

She tensed in his arms. "You're scaring me."

"I'm not going to let anything happen to you." The words were a vow that came from his very soul. "Hold on."

Her eyes widened as he held her out the window, and she belatedly realized his intent.

"No," she choked as he gave a shove with his feet and they were falling through the air.

He landed softly, keeping her tightly pressed against his chest as he allowed his senses to search the darkness.

Only when he was certain that there were no strangers lurking in the alley did he jog toward a nearby side street, heading south of town at a speed that could never be mistaken for human.

Right now he didn't care if he exposed his superior skills or not. He needed to get Ashe somewhere safe.

Still struggling to get her arms free so she could no doubt punch him in the face, Ashe at last gave a hiss of frustration.

"Dammit, let me down."

"Not until we're safe."

"Safe from what?"

He met her narrowed black eyes, knowing nothing he said was going to make her happy.

"I'm not sure."

"You're dragging me naked through town in the middle of the night and you're not sure why?"

"That about sums it up."

"Sums it up?" She kicked her feet in fury. "Take me back to the hotel."

"Not a chance in hell."

"I'll scream. I—" She bit off her words as he reached the outskirts of town, jogging along the edge of the swamp before heading straight for The Cougar's Den. "Why did you bring me here?"

He ignored her question, heading up the back stairs and slamming his fist against the steel door.

There was a tense wait as security checked him out on the monitors, then the door was finally shoved open to reveal a furious Bayon.

"What the hell are you doing?" the younger Pantera snarled, glaring at the female in Raphael's arms.

Raphael stepped past his friend, entering the storage room of the bar.

"Make sure we weren't followed," he commanded.

For a moment Bayon bristled, as if he might demand an explanation. Then, muttering something about crazy cats in heat, he slipped out the door and melted into the shadows.

Tightening his hold on a still furious Ashe, Raphael crossed the storage room to kick the edge of the wooden shelves, watching the wall swing inward to reveal the secret chambers hidden behind the bar.

He halted in the communal room, where the Pantera visiting the area could gather in private.

It wasn't fancy. Nothing more than two overstuffed sofas and a handful of padded chairs sturdy enough to endure the roughhousing that came with a race of people who were cats at heart.

It was, however, the only place they could talk in privacy.

The attached room was dedicated to high-tech security that kept watch on the fringes of the swamp, monitoring everything and everyone who entered the bayous, while the upper story was set aside for private bedrooms.

There was no way in hell he was going to take Ashe to another room that included a bed.

Not until he was convinced there was no threat.

Gingerly setting Ashe on her feet, Raphael stepped back, but not before she managed to take a swing, clipping him on the chin.

"How dare you kidnap me?" she snapped, covering her seething fear behind rage.

Rafael rubbed his chin. More to give her the satisfaction of believing she'd hurt him than in any true pain.

"I'm going to protect you and my child whether you want me to or not."

She tugged the sheet until it was wrapped tightly over her breasts, her hair spilling over her bare ivory shoulders like a river of ebony.

"Protect me from what?"

"That's my question," Bayon interrupted, stepping into the room and folding his arms over his chest.

Instinctively, Raphael moved to stand protectively at Ashe's side.

"Ashe, this is Bayon," he said, his warning gaze never leaving Bayon's grim expression.

"He's a—"

She didn't need to finish the question for Raphael to know what she was asking.

"Pantera. Yes."

Bayon scowled. "Shit, you told her?"

Feeling Ashe shiver, Raphael wrapped an arm around her shoulder and tugged her close.

"She carries my child."

Bayon hissed in shock as Ashe's back was exposed, revealing the rapidly healing scratches.

"And your mark." Bayon gave a disbelieving shake of his head. "Dammit, Raphael. What the hell is going on?"

"The question is open for debate."

"Yeah, and until we can find out the truth, you shouldn't have brought her here. She can't be trusted."

"I can't be trusted? Is that a joke?" Ashe broke into the argument, her eyes flashing fire. "I didn't emit some sort of lust odor to get an unsuspecting woman pregnant and then mess with her mind before kidnapping her."

Bayon's brows snapped together. "Why did you come here that first night?"

Ashe stiffened. "It's none of your business."

Bayon took a step forward. "Who sent you?"

"No one sent me."

"Then why were you here?"

"I was paying my mother's bar tab. She's the town drunk," Ashe snapped, seeming to realize that the stubborn Pantera wasn't going to let it go. "Satisfied?"

"Not even close."

Bayon reached out a hand and a red mist clouded Raphael's mind. He didn't truly believe his friend meant to harm Ashe, but it didn't matter.

Between one beat of his heart and the next, he had Bayon pinned to the wall, his forearm pressed against the man's throat.

"Don't. Touch. Her," he warned, the air prickling with the threat of violence. "She's innocent."

Bayon stilled, accepting that he'd pressed Raphael too far.

"You can't be certain."

"Yes. I can."

"How?"

Raphael held his friend's gaze, allowing him to see the truth in his eyes.

"Because she's mine."

Bayon scowled, but a hint of uncertainty flashed through leaf green eyes.

"That's impossible."

"We can argue about it later." Raphael forced himself to lower his arm and step back. "For now I need your skills."

Bayon cast a swift glance toward the tense Ashe before returning his attention to Raphael and offering a slow nod.

"For what?"

"I caught the scent of two men entering the hotel."

Bayon blinked. "Is that the start of a bad joke?"

"They were armed."

"Everyone in this godforsaken town carries a gun."

Raphael shook his head. "Not enough to start World War III."

"They could have been poachers," Bayon pointed out with a shrug.

"They smelled…"

"What?"

"Wrong."

Bayon held Raphael's gaze as they both recalled the warning from Parish, the leader of the Hunter Faction, that there'd been reports of Pantera running across humans with scents that repelled their inner cats.

Parish had been certain they were attempting to spy on the Wildlands.

Now Bayon gave a sharp nod. "I'll check them out."

Waiting for his friend to shut the door behind his retreating form, Raphael moved to stand directly in front of Ashe.

He didn't for a second believe her momentary silence and stoic expression were a sign of resignation. Unfortunately he had to make a call to the Wildlands to warn them to put extra guards on the borders.

"I need you to stay here," he said, trying to console his raw nerves with the knowledge that there was no way she could escape even if she wanted to.

The locks were specifically designed to only respond to the touch of a Pantera. They wouldn't budge for a human.

She frowned, clutching the sheet with a white-knuckled grip. "Where are you going?"

"To call…a friend."

"And you expect me to wait here?" She glared at him with a seething fury. "Do you think a few bouts of hot sex have given me Stockholm syndrome?"

Lowering his head, he claimed her lips in a kiss of sheer frustration.

All he wanted to do was sweep her into his arms and carry her to his homeland where they could celebrate the new life they'd created.

Instead he was plagued with a growing fear that an unseen danger was lurking just out of sight.

"Just stay here and behave yourself."

Chapter Five

ASHE was still reeling as Raphael left through a narrow door on the far side of the room.

Of course, she'd been reeling since the doctor had called with the shocking news of her pregnancy.

That was one of the reason's she'd gone to the hotel instead of trying to convince her mother to let her return home.

She'd needed a few hours to consider her options in private.

But instead of a few hours of peace, she'd been accosted by the man who'd impregnated her, discovered he was a creature she'd long believed to be a myth, seduced all over again and kidnapped.

She grimaced as she lifted her fingers to lips that still tingled from his touch.

Okay. Maybe it wasn't entirely fair to claim he'd seduced her.

She'd all but begged him to ease the desire that had been on a slow simmer for the past six weeks.

And if she were honest, she'd admit that her treacherous body was ready and eager to repeat the performance.

Which was precisely why she needed to get the hell away from the disturbing man.

No…not man.

Pantera.

Beast.

Absently she reached over her shoulder to touch the scratches that had seemed to shock Bayon. They didn't hurt. In fact, they tingled with a pleasure that was as disturbing as the implication that Raphael had deliberately marked her.

Yeah. She was in dire need of some space to clear her head.

Crossing to where they'd first entered the room, she placed a cautious hand on the silver doorknob.

She didn't know what she'd expected.

Ringing alarms. A trap door opening to drop her into a pit of alligators. An electric shock.

Something to prevent her from leaving the private rooms.

But stepping into the back storage area, there was nothing to break the silence beyond the thundering beat of her heart.

Still, she remained on edge as she tiptoed to the outer door. It was quite possible a silent alarm had been activated. Or that there would be guards outside that she hadn't noticed when she'd first arrived with Raphael.

And, of course, there was the mysterious danger that Raphael insisted was stalking him.

Until she was far enough away from the bizarre creatures she would have to take extra care.

Surprised yet again when the door opened easily, Ashe crouched low as she darted down the steep staircase, and headed directly toward the cars that lined the narrow street.

She shivered, feeling a strange chill of premonition. As if unseen eyes were following her every movement.

Damn. She needed to get back to the hotel.

She was going to get dressed, get her car keys and head out of this town as fast as possible.

After that…

Well, she'd worry about that once she was far, far away.

Pausing to tuck the sheet tighter around her body, Ashe sucked in a deep breath and gathered her shaken courage.

She'd endured a childhood of neglect interspersed with episodes of terrifying violence from a mother who'd never loved her. She'd been humiliated and bullied throughout school. She'd been forced to work as a secretary for a bastard who couldn't keep his hands to himself, just to keep a roof over her head.

She had truly discovered the meaning behind 'what didn't kill you only makes you stronger'."

Now she stiffened her spine and gave one last glare toward the shabby bar that glowed in the neon lights.

"Behave myself?" she muttered. "Not in this lifetime."

Kicking the folds of the sheet away from her bare feet, she turned to gaze at the untamed edge of the swamp across the street. She had no genuine desire to wade through the muck, not to mention risking the endless dangers that haunted the bayous. But she couldn't walk down the streets in a sheet without attracting unwanted attention, not even in this podunk town.

She would have to skirt the swamps until she was closer to the hotel.

The decision made, she dashed across the road, grimacing as the gravel dug into the soles of her feet. God almighty. Would this night ever end?

The thought had barely formed when a strange buzzing flew past her ear. She waved an impatient hand, assuming it was one of the humongous bugs that filled the night air.

Some grew to the size of small birds.

It wasn't until there was an audible thwack in a cypress tree just behind her that she turned her head to stare at the arrow stuck in the trunk.

She stumbled to a baffled halt.

It wasn't that unusual for the locals to hunt with bow and arrow.

Some preferred following in the traditions of their forefathers. Some preferred the challenge of hunting old-school. And some just didn't have the money to buy a gun.

But who would be out hunting this time of night?

And why would they be so close to town?

Stupidly, it wasn't until the second arrow clipped the top of her shoulder as it whizzed past that she accepted that she was the prey, not some hapless rabbit.

Shit. Shit. Shit.

She hadn't thought Raphael's buddies would actually try to kill her.

Unless it wasn't his friends, but his supposed enemies?

But why would they shoot at her?

Not that the *who, what* or *where* mattered at the moment.

With a muffled cry she darted toward the nearest clump of bushes, kneeling down to peer through the thick branches.

It was too dark to see more than vague outlines of shapes. She thought she could see something running along the roof of the closed lumberyard, and…was that someone creeping between those trucks?

Oh god.

For a crazed second, panic threatened to overwhelm her.

She had no phone, no clothes, no weapons that could help protect her.

Worse, she didn't know if a scream would bring help or more danger.

Then her hand unconsciously slid to her stomach, a protective burst of determination stiffening her spine.

Dammit, she wasn't going to wait here like a sitting duck.

She had a child to protect, which meant she had to get away.

Wrapping the bottom of the sheet around her arm so it was above her knees, she scooted backward. If she could reach the actual bayou she had a chance of shaking the bastards.

She ignored the sound of approaching footsteps, and the strange smell that made her nose curl in disgust. Her only hope of survival was slipping away before her stalker could pinpoint her precise location.

Concentrating on backing away as silently as possible, Ashe froze when a low, enraged snarl reverberated through the air.

It was the sort of full-throated roar that caused a terrified hush to spread through the area.

A feral predator on the hunt.

Barely daring to breathe, Ashe listened as she heard a muttered curse from just beyond the bush and the sound of rustling, followed by the unmistakable click of a gun. Either the person wasn't the same psycho Robin Hood who'd been flinging arrows in her direction, or he'd decided that approaching danger was worth pulling out the big guns.

Literally.

But, even as she prepared herself for the deafening blast of the gunshot, there was another snarl and a blood-chilling scream that she knew beyond a shadow of a doubt would haunt her dreams for nights to come.

Barely realizing she was moving, Ashe straightened to peer over the top of the bush. It wasn't so much a desire to see what was happening. Hell, no. She had a hideous suspicion it was going to be awful. But she needed to make sure the stalker was too busy fighting off the rabid animal to notice her escape.

She needn't have worried.

The man who'd been standing by the bush wasn't going to be firing arrows at her or anyone else.

Paralyzed, Ashe's gaze roamed over the man who was now sprawled on the ground, his throat ripped out and his face mangled. His dead eyes stared sightlessly at the star-studded sky, his arms flung wide with a gun in one hand and his empty bow in the other.

She gagged, a hand pressed to her mouth as her stomach threatened to revolt against the grisly sight.

She'd never seen a dead man before.

Especially not one who had been mauled by a wild animal.

Then her shattered disbelief was distracted as a sleek form detached from the shadows, gliding toward her with an uncanny silence.

"No," she breathed, taking in the sight of the large cat in stunned amazement.

The color of rich caramel, the fur was thick and glossy in the moonlight. The broad head had small rounded ears and large golden eyes that studied her with an unnerving intensity. His body was chiseled muscle with long legs and a tail that was tipped with black.

Any other time she would have found the animal a beautiful sight.

Lethal certainly, and due proper respect, but…beautiful.

This wasn't any other time, however, and facing the deadly predator with his most recent kill mangled on the ground between them only ratcheted up her fear.

She held out her hand. Like that was going to help.

"Stay back."

"Ashe?" She jerked at the sound of her name being called, turning to watch Bayon appear from behind the large cat. The male came to a sharp halt as the animal whirled to hiss at him in warning. "Holy shit." His gaze focused on Ashe as she took a step toward him, giving a fierce shake of his head. "No, don't move. He won't hurt you."

"How do you know?" she demanded, her voice as shaky as her nerves. "Is this your pet?"

"Pet?" A humorless smile twisted his lips. "No."

"Then how do you know he's not going to hurt me?"

"He's trying to protect you."

Her heart slammed against her chest as a disturbing suspicion began to form in the back of her mind.

"A wild animal is trying to protect me?" she tried to scoff. "Yeah right."

Bayon held her wary gaze. "He may be wild, but he's not entirely an animal."

"Don't." She turned her attention toward the cat who had moved to stand directly between her and Bayon. It was one thing to be told of humans who could transform into pumas and another to see it in the flesh. Literally. "You can't seriously expect me to believe that...that creature is Raphael?"

The green eyes blazed with sheer male aggravation. "It doesn't matter what you believe."

"But—"

"Who was that man?" he interrupted her protest.

She grimaced, reluctantly turning her gaze to the bloody corpse. "I don't have a clue. I assumed he was a friend of yours."

"No." Without warning, Bayon leaned forward to spit on the dead man. "Tell me what happened."

Yikes. So not a friend.

"I…decided to return to the hotel."

He narrowed his gaze. "And Raphael just let you go?"

She tilted her chin. Arrogant ass.

"I didn't have to ask for his permission." She met him glare for glare. "Or yours."

He went rigid, seemingly startled by her words. "You opened the doors?"

"Of course I did. I'm not helpless."

He studied her with a disturbing intensity. "The locks are specifically designed to respond only to Pantera. They should never have opened for you."

She frowned, recalling her own amazement that her escape had been so easy.

Was it possible…

No.

God. She was so tired she couldn't even think straight.

"Then they must have been left unlocked," she said, her tone warning she was a breath away from snapping.

He hesitated, as if he wanted to press her, but meeting her panicked glare, he at last gave an impatient wave of his hand.

"What happened next?"

"I was trying to get back to the hotel without everyone realizing I was waltzing through town in just a sheet when this…" She waved a hand toward the corpse. "Whack job started shooting arrows at me." She shook her head. "I mean, who uses a bow and arrow when you have a gun?"

"Someone who wants to kill without attracting unwanted attention."

Her breath tangled in her throat. Oh. Yeah. Good point.

She shivered, vividly aware of how close she'd come to death.

"I was trying to sneak away when I heard a roar and—" Her words trailed away as she glanced toward the puma staring at her with glowing golden eyes.

"Raphael?" Bayon helpfully supplied, his own gaze trained on the big cat.

"He attacked."

Bayon shook his head. "Astonishing."

"Astonishing?" She made a choked sound. "A man is dead."

He lifted his head to stab her with a fierce glare. "A man trying to kill you. Would you rather Raphael had allowed him to finish his task?"

No. The answer came without hesitation, her hand once again pressing against her belly. To protect her child she would have done anything.

Including killing the man herself.

She shuddered, unthinkingly stepping toward Bayon. She might not trust him, but she desperately needed a hot bath, a warm bed and a return to sanity.

Instantly the puma turned, opening his mouth to display his impressively sharp teeth.

"No," Bayon snapped. "Stay there."

She scowled in frustration. "If it's Raphael then why is he keeping me trapped here?"

"He's keeping me away from you."

"I thought you were friends?"

"We are, but his beast is convinced you're his mate and he won't willingly allow another male near you."

Mate.

She pressed her fingers to her throbbing temple. "God…this can't be happening."

"You have no idea," Bayon muttered.

"What's that supposed to mean?"

"A Pantera can only shift when we're in the Wildlands."

Ashe stared at him in confusion. She was still trying wrap her brain around the whole 'shifting' thing.

"This town is part of the Wildlands?"

"No."

"Then I don't understand."

"Neither do I." There was a dangerous edge in his voice. "But I intend to find out."

Keeping his gaze trained on the cat, Bayon began to whisper in an unfamiliar language, the haunting words resonating deep inside her, like a bell being struck.

Ashe bit her lip, ignoring the terrified voice in the back of her head that urged her to flee while Bayon was distracted.

Where would she go?

Certainly nowhere that she wouldn't be constantly looking over her shoulder for fear there might be an arrow trained at her back.

Besides, she couldn't avoid the truth any longer.

Raphael was a mythical Pantera and no amount of denial was going to change the fact.

Or the chance that the child she carried was going to be one as well.

She had to find out as much as possible about these mysterious people if she was going to keep her child safe.

Inching away from the body lying lifeless on the ground, she watched with a growing fascination as Bayon lowered himself to his knees and continued to whisper as he looked directly into the eyes of the beast.

Ashe felt a breathtaking surge of electricity dance over her skin, then her eyes widened as she watched a silver mist form around the puma, nearly disguising the sight of the limbs twisting and elongating, the fur seeming to melt as if by magic.

Fascinated, she took several steps closer, unable to tear her gaze away.

It was odd. She would have assumed watching an animal shift into a man would be revolting.

Instead it was…poignantly moving.

How many people could say they witnessed magic with their own eyes?

The mist dissipated, leaving behind an unconscious, and extremely naked, Raphael.

"Oh." She furtively licked her lips. "Where are his clothes?"

"This wasn't a natural shift. When I force a Pantera to change from human to cat, or cat to human, my magic strips him down to his most basic form. Clothing, jewelry, sometimes even tattoos are lost in the transition."

Still caught in a sense of wonder, Ashe watched in silence as Bayon grabbed his friend around the waist and with an unbelievable display of strength heaved his limp body over his shoulder.

Rising to his feet, he spared Ashe an impatient glance. "Let's go."

She flipped him off behind his back, but she obediently followed him back to The Cougar's Den.

Her decision had been made.

She would stay with Raphael until she could be absolutely certain her child was safe.

After that…

She shook her head, hitching up the sheet as she climbed the stairs leading to the back of the bar.

Right now it was enough to take it day by day.

Hell, it was enough to take it minute by minute.

Bayon led them back through the storage area and into the hidden room she'd been in before, but he never paused as he continued through a door at the back that led to a narrow staircase.

She grimaced, feeling an odd sense of déjà vu as they headed to the top floor. A feeling that only intensified as he entered one of the rooms that lined the long hall.

Absently walking toward the double bed in the center of the wood-planked floor, she barely paid attention to Bayon as he slid the still unconscious Raphael off his shoulder and onto the mattress.

This was the room she'd been in over a month ago.

She was certain of it.

There was a foggy memory of the hand-carved headboard that matched the wooden rocking chair in the corner. And the paintings of graceful plantation homes that were framed and hung on the walls. And of course, the patchwork quilt that covered the bed…

Sorting through her vague recollections, Ashe sensed Bayon step toward her, but it wasn't until she felt something cold snap around her wrist that she realized her danger.

With a gasp, she glanced down to discover that she'd been handcuffed to the sturdy headboard

The jackass.

"What the hell?" she growled, glaring into his impassive face. "I'm not going run again."

"No, you're not."

With those words he headed toward the door.

"Wait." She tugged at the metal bracelet holding her captive, achieving nothing more than a painful welt on her wrist. "Let me out of this thing."

He didn't even bother to acknowledge her plea as he stepped out of the room and closed the door.

"Bastard."

Cursing the day from hell that refused to end, Ashe awkwardly climbed onto the bed. She was too weary to work up a proper fury.

Not that she was the forgive-and-forget type.

Next time she crossed paths with Bayon she was going to kick him in the nuts.

Managing to keep the sheet wrapped around her, she moved until the handcuff wasn't biting into her skin and turned her attention to the man sprawled in the middle of the mattress.

Did they always pass out after shifting back to human?

It didn't seem very efficient.

Or had he been hurt?

Leaning to the side, she inspected the bronzed perfection spread over the quilt.

Her mouth went dry as she tried to concentrate on searching him for injuries. She'd never seen a man so magnificently… proportioned.

A broad, chiseled chest. Powerful shoulders. Washboard abs. Long, muscular legs. And a huge…

Yeah. Magnificently proportioned.

Her gaze moved back to his chest, lingering on the stylized tattoo that resembled a puma crouched to pounce.

She had a hazy memory of exploring that tattoo with her tongue the first night they'd shared this bed.

Did it have a special meaning?

Raphael made a low sound, his head turning in her direction. Without thought, she reached out to brush the silken golden hair from his face, her fingers tracing the prominent line of his cheekbones before moving to the lush curve of his lips.

She'd tried to fight against the sense of connection that she'd felt from the moment she'd opened her eyes to find him in her hotel room.

Now she simply savored the comfort of having him near.

No one had ever tried to protect her.

Certainly not her mother or deadbeat father.

It made her feel…cherished.

Shuffling through her unfamiliar emotions, Ashe wasn't prepared when Raphael's eyes snapped open, something that might have been panic flaring in the golden depths before he was surging up to grab her face between his hands.

"Ashe."

She barely had a chance to brace herself before he was covering her lips in a kiss of stark need.

"Raphael," she muttered, when he at last lifted his head so she could breathe.

"I thought I'd lost you." He spread desperate kisses over her face before he bent down to place his mouth against her lower stomach. "I thought I'd lost you both."

The heat of his lips seared through the thin sheet, and without thought she combed her fingers through the satin gold of his hair.

There was no mistaking the stark fear that continued to haunt him.

"We're fine," she soothed, stroking him in a comforting motion.

"Ashe." His hands brushed down her shoulders, his lips nibbling a tender path upward. "I couldn't bear to lose you."

"Raphael, I—" Whatever she was about to say was lost in a haze of pleasure as his lips reached the edge of the sheet.

"What?" he whispered.

"I don't remember."

He chuckled as his hands drifted down her arms, pausing when he reached the handcuff.

With a sound of surprise he lifted his head to meet her darkening gaze.

"What's this?"

She made a sound of disgust. "Your pain-in-the-ass friend was afraid I might try to escape again."

"But the locks…" His gaze narrowed as he belatedly remembered she'd escaped before. "How the hell did you get out of here?"

She rolled her eyes. Like she knew?

"I just walked out." She shook her arm, making the handcuff rattle. "Get this off me."

A slow, wicked smile curved his lips. "I think we should leave it in place for now."

A treacherous heat flared through her body. "Don't tell me you're kinky?"

"Desperate," he corrected, his smile fading as his eyes smoldered with a naked hunger. "I need to be inside you, *ma chère*," he said with blunt honesty. "My cat needs to know I haven't lost you. Say yes."

Ashe shuddered at the simple plea. She found it oddly erotic to know just how much he wanted her. It gave her a sense of power that she rarely experienced.

"Yes."

He hissed, as if he was caught off guard by her ready capitulation, and then with a slow motion he was pulling open the ends of the sheet.

She forgot how to breathe as the night air hit her skin, her heart pounding as his fingers gently cupped the small firmness of her breasts.

"Beautiful," he muttered, stroking his thumbs over the hard points of her nipples.

Ashe knew she wasn't beautiful.

Her own mother had lamented the thick dark hair and prominent nose that Ashe had inherited from her father. And then there was her body that was too skinny, and her skin too pale.

But beneath his predatory gaze she felt beautiful.

Snarling deep in his throat, Raphael turned her until his lips could stroke down the sensitive scratch marks that were nearly healed on her back. His touch sent jolts of shocking arousal through her, but she made no effort to pull away.

In this moment she needed him as much as he needed her.

Turning back to face him, she boldly ran her free hand over his chest, astonished by the satin smoothness of his skin. He was completely furless. A perfect bronze velvet draped over steel.

Enjoying her exploration, Ashe barely noticed when Raphael gently arranged her against the pile of pillows, careful to keep her shackled arm above her head. Not until he bent over her to capture a nipple between his teeth.

She moaned as his tongue teased the sensitized tip, tormenting her until she was moving restlessly beneath him. Good lord. She'd never gotten so hot so quickly.

It was as if his touch had a direct connection to her libido.

"Oh, yes," she moaned, arching upward as his lips traced the curve between the mounds of her breasts before moving to the other aching nipple.

Her fingers impatiently threaded through his hair. The satin strands brushed her skin, only heightening her pleasure.

"Do you like that, *ma chère?*" he breathed, his hands skimming over her hips and down her thighs. His touch was searing hot, matching the molten heat flowing through her veins.

Tugging at her nipple with the edge of his teeth, Raphael eased his hand between her legs and sought the moist heat.

She grasped the strong column of his neck, hanging on for dear life as he stroked his fingers over her clit, finding the sweet spot of her pleasure.

She was falling into a whirlpool of sensation that bordered on pain, it was so intense.

"Raphael."

Easily sensing the raw edge of need in her voice, Raphael lifted his head to nuzzle his lips just below her jaw.

"I have you…*ma chère,*" he softly soothed. "I will always have you."

She shivered as her hips instinctively lifted to press more firmly to his caressing finger.

"I know."

He lifted onto his elbow and peered deep into her wide eyes. "Are you ready for me?"

For a long moment she merely gazed into his beautiful face. With his golden hair tumbled over his shoulders and the muted light playing over his stark features he looked barely civilized.

Feral.

Her lips parted, her breath coming in short pants.

"Yes."

His mouth covered hers as he rolled to settle between her parted legs and impale her with one smooth thrust. He swallowed her cry of pleasure as her hips left the mattress and her nails scored down his back.

Yes. God, yes.

She grasped the headboard as he plunged in and out of her, always careful to keep his weight off her stomach.

It was swift and raw and exactly what she needed.

She was being consumed by Raphael and she couldn't make herself care. For this one priceless moment she wanted to be overwhelmed. She wanted to belong to this man on the most basic level.

Thrusting his tongue between her willing lips, Raphael fucked her with an increasing intensity. Ashe clutched at him as the pressure built to a looming crescendo.

She was perilously close.

"Raphael."

"I know, *ma chère*," he muttered against her mouth, his body pressing deeper.

Her breath came in jagged gasps as the pleasure tightened and spiraled toward a shimmering point. His strokes quickened, sinking him deep in her. At the same time, he angled his head to bite the vulnerable curve of her neck.

The pleasure/pain hit a critical point and her entire body tightened. For a breathless moment she hovered on the edge, then with explosive force the bliss shattered through her and she was soaring through paradise.

They lay in dazed astonishment for a long moment, Raphael groaning as he emptied his seed. Ashe held him tight, savoring the rare moment of absolute peace.

At last Raphael gently pulled out, cradling her face as he spread delicate kisses over her flushed cheeks.

Boneless, Ashe watched in silence as he reached into a side table to grab the key to the handcuffs. Removing the steel bracelet, he gently kissed the red mark that circled her wrist before covering both of them with the quilt.

"That was…" She released a shaky breath. "Amazing."

He pressed a lingering kiss to her lips before pulling back to regard her with a searching gaze.

"Why did you leave the bar after I told you to stay?"

"Why?" She met his accusing gaze with a frown, her sense of contentment swiftly fading. She might be slowly accepting that her life was now tied with this male, but that didn't mean she was ever going to follow orders. "Because I don't appreciate being held captive."

"I was trying to protect you," he growled.

The rasp of male possession made her frown deepen. Okay, this was something that needed to be nipped in the bud.

Raphael had the sort of alpha personality that would ride roughshod over her if she didn't take a stand.

"A protection that wouldn't have been necessary if you hadn't gotten me caught in the middle of your gang war."

He stiffened, his brow furrowing in confusion. "Gang war?"

"That man obviously thought I was with you and wanted to make a point."

"We are Pantera, not a gang," he said. "And we certainly aren't at war."

"Then why was that lunatic shooting arrows at me?"

He held her gaze. "I don't know, but it's you they're after."

A chill inched down her spine. "That's ridiculous. I've lived here all my life without having people trying to kill me."

His hand moved to lie gently against her lower stomach. "You weren't carrying this."

She studied his grim expression, the chill spreading through her body.

"My baby?"

"*Our* baby."

"But…" She licked her dry lips. "No one knows I'm pregnant."

He arched a brow. "No one?"

She shrugged. "My mother, but she wouldn't tell anyone."

"Not even if she was drinking?"

She flinched as his words hit a nerve. Her mother was notoriously chatty when she was sitting on a barstool. There wasn't a person in town who hadn't heard when Ashe had her first period or when she'd been stood up on prom night.

Thankfully, people had long ago started ignoring the increasingly incoherent woman.

"Who listens to a drunk?" she muttered.

"You might be surprised." The edge in his voice suggested he'd spent more than a few nights cross-examining an unsuspecting, inebriated fool. "Anyone else?"

She chewed her bottom lip, knowing the question was important. "My doctor."

"Local?"

"Yes."

"When did you see him?"

"Two days ago." Her lips twisted in a rueful smile. It seemed a lifetime since she'd walked into the small clinic believing she was suffering from a bout of the stomach flu. "He called earlier today with the results."

"Time enough to share the information."

She frowned. "With who?"

He caught her chin in his fingers, forcing her to meet his determined gaze.

"Until we can find out, I need to get you to the Wildlands."

"The Wildlands?" She shook her head in disbelief. Until a few hours ago the name had been nothing more than a place in legend and myth. Now he wanted her to leave her home and travel there? "I can't."

"Ashe, it's the only place you and our baby will be safe."

"But—"

Her protest was drowned out by a sudden thump on the door.

CHAPTER SIX

SENSING Bayon standing in the hall, Raphael muttered a curse as he leapt off the bed and headed toward the dresser.

Yanking open a drawer, he removed a pair of gray sweats, pulling on the bottoms before tossing the matching top to Ashe.

It was three sizes too large for her, but it did fall to her knees, providing a small amount of modesty.

It would have to do until he could send someone back to the hotel to pick up her suitcase.

Pulling open the door, Raphael stepped aside to allow his fellow Pantera to enter the room, his cat keeping a watchful eye on the male to make certain Bayon didn't stray too close to his mate.

No doubt sensing Raphael's unease, Bayon remained close to the door, his pale green gaze never straying from Raphael.

"Glad to see you back, *mon ami.*"

Raphael grimaced. He was still reeling from the combination of shifting despite being away from the Wildlands and the shock of being yanked out of his animal form.

"I assume you were the one to trance me?"

Bayon nodded with regret. "Sorry I had to put you out. You were too hyped for me to convince you to return to human and I needed to get you away from the kill."

Raphael waved aside the apology. Although it was rare to use the words of power that would force a Pantera back to his human form, he knew his cat would never have allowed his friend near.

"You did what you had to do."

Bayon folded his arms over his chest, his expression grim. "The obvious question, is…why did I have to do it?"

"Damned if I know." Raphael's memories were hazed by the surge of adrenaline that had gripped him from the minute he'd realized Ashe had left the safety of the bar. "I was tracking Ashe when I caught sight of the stranger." His voice thickened with fury. "When I realized he was trying to skewer her with an arrow, my cat took over."

"Did the stranger do anything to you?"

Raphael arched a brow. "Do?"

"Shoot you with a poison arrow?" Bayon asked. "Cast a spell? Use a secret military weapon to force you to change?"

He snorted at the moronic questions. "It didn't have anything to do with the stranger. I changed when I came close enough to feel Ashe's aura."

Both men glanced toward the silent woman standing in the center of the room. Instantly she held up her hands in a gesture of innocence.

"Hey, don't look at me. I didn't do anything."

"Could it be the child?" Bayon suggested.

Raphael frowned, considering the precise second he'd shifted.

As he'd sprinted across the dark street there had been terror that he was going to be too late. And a blinding fury that anyone would try to hurt his mate. But his last memory was the sweet smell of lush land and female magic.

Ashe's scent.

"I'm not a medic or a philosopher," he at last said with a shrug. "All I know is that my cat decided this female was mine at first sight and it wasn't going to let anyone or anything hurt her."

"Maybe the elders have some idea," Bayon muttered. "We need to get her home."

"My thought exactly."

"Wait," Ashe protested. "This town is my home, not the middle of the swamp."

Glaring toward Bayon, who parted his lips to demand Ashe's compliance in his usual blunt style, Raphael moved to stand directly in front of her, his finger brushing over her too-pale cheek.

"Is it truly your home, *ma chère*, or somewhere that you live?"

"I—"

"The truth."

Their gazes locked, her dark eyes revealing the lonely, wounded child who'd been unwanted her entire life.

Until she'd walked across his path.

Now she would never, ever be lonely or unwanted again.

Cupping her cheek in his hand, he prepared to convince her just how desperately he needed her, when Bayon made a sound of impatience.

"I hate to interrupt, but this touching scene will have to wait."

Raphael glared at his friend. "Are you deliberately trying to piss me off?"

"It's in my job description."

"No shit."

Reaching into his back pocket, Bayon held out a scrap of material. "Here."

"What's this?"

"Open it."

Raphael's sensitive nose curled at the stench of rotting flesh and something else. That same 'wrongness' he'd smelled on the humans entering the hotel earlier. With reluctance, he flipped aside the folded material to reveal the patch of skin cut into a perfect six by six square.

He hissed in shock.

Not at the fact that he was holding a slab of flesh. He was a predator who'd just ripped out the throat of a man.

But at the sight of a brand that portrayed the outline of a raven with wings spread in front of a full moon.

"Where did you get this?"

"I returned to dispose of the body," Bayon answered. "This was branded on his lower back."

Beside him Ashe gave a gasp of horror. "Oh my god, is that his skin?"

Raphael flinched, wishing he could protect her from the darker side of his nature. Christ, it was bad enough she'd had to witness him tearing apart a man just a few feet away from her without having to endure the gruesome prize he held in his hands.

Unfortunately, this brand changed everything.

"The Mark of the Shakpi," he breathed. "This is—"

"Impossible?" Bayon took the word out of his mouth. "Yeah, there's a lot of that going around."

Ashe cleared her throat, struggling to hang on to her severely tested courage.

"What is the Mark of Shakpi?"

"It's an ancient legend that speaks of the origin of our people," Bayon answered, his flat tone intended to bring an end to the conversation.

Of course Raphael's stubborn mate wasn't going to be intimidated. "And?"

Raphael took charge of the story. "The legend claims that the bayous gave birth to twins," he said, sharing the oral history that every Pantera learned while still in the nursery. "Opela was able to call upon the magic of the land, eventually creating the Pantera. Her sister, Shakpi, grew jealous of Opela's love for her children and tried to create her own children to rule the Pantera. The children twisted the magic, using it for evil, and Opela had no choice but to have her sister imprisoned."

Ashe frowned. "Imprisoned in the swamps?"

He shrugged. "No one knows where she was sent."

She gave a slow shake of her head. "There are a lot of stories about the bayous."

"Only one that our people believe."

"So you really think some mythical woman has escaped from her secret prison and is now going around branding her personal Robin Hoods?"

Did he?

Raphael glanced back down at the branded skin, a primitive fear lodging deep in his gut.

A part of him wanted to laugh it off as an old wives tale. As Ashe pointed out, there were a dozen stories that came out of the bayous.

But he didn't laugh.

He wasn't human. He was Pantera. A creature of magic.

And the fact that this brand was discovered when their people were unable to breed…well, it had to mean something.

"It's one explanation," he murmured.

She pressed a hand to her temple, as if her head was throbbing. "I really have fallen down the rabbit hole."

Raphael gave a short, humorless laugh. He felt exactly the same way.

Six weeks ago he'd been a respected diplomat for his people, in absolute control of his life.

Now he was mated to a human, expecting a child, and growing increasingly convinced his people were being hunted by an evil, ancient goddess.

Yeah, that was one hell of a rabbit hole.

Giving a shake of his head, he thrust aside his rising panic and turned his attention to Bayon.

"The most important thing is to keep Ashe and our babe safe," he announced.

"Agreed," his friend swiftly agreed. Then they both froze as that now-familiar scent drifted through the open window. "Raphael."

"I smell them," he rasped.

Bayon pulled a gun from the holster at his lower back, his eyes glowing with power.

"Get her out of here while I distract them."

Raphael didn't bother to argue. Not only would it be pointless to try and keep Bayon out of a fight, but his duty was to protect Ashe and the child she carried.

Moving forward he laid a hand on his friend's shoulder. "I'll meet you back at the Wildlands. Take care."

"And you." Bayon flashed a smile of anticipation before he was running across the room and leaping out of the window with reckless valor.

Raphael returned to his mate's side, staring down at her frighteningly pale face.

She'd been through hell and back in the past six weeks. More than anyone should have to endure. Let alone a pregnant woman.

His heart clenched with regret. God dammit, he had to get her somewhere safe.

"Ashe, will you trust me?" he asked.

"Yes."

Something connected inside him at her swift, unhesitating agreement. A sense of completion, as if two separate pieces had just clicked together to form a perfect whole.

He paused just long enough to savor the unexpected sensation before leaning down to scoop Ashe off her feet.

"Don't make a sound," he whispered next to her ear.

Barely giving her time to wrap her arms around his neck, Raphael moved toward the door, glancing down the hall as he used his senses to search for enemies.

Below them he could hear the scramble of Pantera to meet the unexpected threat outside. Which meant the attackers would be occupied. At least for a few minutes.

Holding Ashe tight against his chest, Raphael darted down the hall and shoved open the door that led to a maintenance closet. He locked the door behind him, then, tilting Ashe's slight weight so he could hold her with one hand, he gave a leap upward, knocking aside the trap door that led to the roof.

He landed lightly on the flat surface, his finger touching Ashe's lips as they parted to utter a small shriek.

In the street below he heard the sound of gunfire and a scream of pain followed by the unmistakable scent of blood that made his cat snarl with the need to be in the middle of the fight.

Raphael battled back the instinct to shift.

The only way to get Ashe to safety was to remain in his human form.

Staying low, he headed to the far side of the roof, halting at the edge to once again whisper in Ashe's ear.

"I need you to hold on tight," he commanded.

She gave a shaky nod, her dark eyes wide with fear. He paused long enough to brush a kiss over her lips, then with a strength only a Pantera could possess, he jumped off the roof and landed on a nearby branch.

Keeping a terrified Ashe cradled in one arm, and the other wrapped around the branch above him, Raphael crouched in the tree, listening intently to the battle that still raged in the street.

There had been no cry of alarm to reveal he'd been spotted.

So far, so good.

Cautiously, he weaved his way through the branches and easily vaulted to the neighboring tree. Ashe gasped, burying her face in his neck as he balanced on a narrow branch, waiting to make sure they remained unnoticed before repeating his stealthy performance until they reached the edge of the swamp.

Once there, he had no choice but to leap to the spongy ground.

His people were skilled at traveling through the trees undetected, but he wasn't going to risk dropping his precious cargo.

Not now. Not ever.

Heading deeper into the swamps, Raphael kept his attention trained on the ever-changing landscape. In the bayous the very ground melted beneath his feet. There were no roads, no permanent pathways. Even the lily-clogged canals could be there one day and gone the next.

A perfect place for monsters to hide.

Thankfully he was the most dangerous monster around.

Or he had been until tonight.

He had only a faint buzzing sound of warning before he felt a pinprick of pain in the back of his neck.

What the fuck?

Carefully lowering Ashe to the thick underbrush, he reached up a hand to pluck the annoying barb out of his flesh.

A dart?

He studied the small weapon with a frown, wondering who the hell thought a full-grown Pantera could be hurt by a mere toy.

Then, a strange chill spread through his body, making him shiver, and worse, numbing his connection to his cat.

"Shit," he breathed, realizing that the poison coursing through his body had made it impossible for him to shift.

"Raphael?" Ashe touched his arm, her expression troubled. "What is it?"

He dropped the dart, gripping her shoulders as he held her worried gaze with a fierce determination.

"Listen to me, *ma chère*, I need you to run as fast and far as you can."

"No." She shook her head. "I'm not leaving you."

"I can't shift. My cat…" He gave a low snarl of frustration. "Dammit. Run. I'll find you." He swooped down to steal a kiss of raw promise. "I'll always find you."

She reached up to cup his face with shaking fingers. "What about you?"

"I can take care of myself," he softly assured her. "But I need you to take care of our child. Do you understand?"

She bit her lip, giving a grudging nod. "Yes."

"Trust me." He gave her a firm push toward the tangle of swamp milkweed that would easily hide her tracks. "Go."

Waiting until she'd disappeared into the thick foliage, Raphael slowly turned, concentrating on the human male he could sense hiding behind the narrow trunk of a tupelo tree.

"Come out of the shadows and face me like a man, you spineless coward," he taunted, oddly unnerved by the pharmaceutical barrier that separated him from his cat.

Although he couldn't shift while away from his homelands—well, until Ashe had crashed into his life—he was always in touch with his inner animal.

To be cut off from that connection was like missing a limb.

Someone was going to pay.

In blood.

That someone stepped from behind the tree, revealing an average-sized man dressed in camo fatigues, with his hair buzzed in a military cut.

Not that Raphael believed for a second the stranger was a part of the armed services.

He'd secretly traveled the globe to meet with world leaders. He easily recognized the crisp movements and precise bearing that marked a trained soldier.

This yokel was a bully who'd been given a gun and the illusion of power.

"I don't fear an animal," the man mocked, his square face and beady eyes revealing a confidence that came from his mistaken belief that the gun he clutched in his fingers gave him the upper hand.

"Good." Raphael moved forward, a taunting smile curving his lips. "Then let's do this thing."

G.I. Joe Wannabe frowned, glancing over Raphael's shoulder. "Where's the female?"

Raphael prowled steadily forward. The idiot didn't even realize his danger.

"Why?"

"She has to die."

Raphael halted, a ball of dread lodged in the pit of his stomach.

It was one thing to suspect the strangers were after Ashe, and another to have it confirmed.

He battled back the red haze that demanded blood and tearing flesh and crunching bones.

Before he ripped the bastard apart he needed information.

"Because she carries my child?"

"Because she carries the magic."

"Magic?" He frowned, baffled by the unexpected words. "What magic?"

The man narrowed his gaze, belatedly realizing he'd given away more than he intended.

"I'll find her." He lifted the gun. "But first I intend to rid the world of an abomination."

He squeezed the trigger at the same instant that Raphael leaped forward.

It shouldn't have been a contest.

Raphael was bigger, stronger, and infinitely better trained.

But whatever drug was coursing through his body had done more than put his cat to sleep. His movements were awkward, lethargic.

He slammed into the bastard even as the bullet sliced through his upper shoulder. Pain seared through him, but wrapping his arms around the man, Raphael drove him into the ground, landing on top of him.

He knocked aside the gun, wrapping his fingers around the man's thick throat.

"Who sent you to kill Ashe?"

The man laughed, the fetid stench of 'wrongness' intensifying.

"This is bigger than you," he choked out, his eyes simmering with the madness of a true fanatic. "This is bigger than all of us."

Raphael tightened his grip, battling back the growing weakness that threatened his survival.

"Tell me who sent you, dammit," he roared.

Without warning the man jerked his upper body off the ground, smashing his forehead into Raphael's with enough force to make him see stars.

Giving a shake of his head, Raphael suddenly found himself being rolled onto his back, the man holding him down as he reached for the gun that lay a few feet away.

Oh…hell.

Raphael wanted answers, but the combination of the unknown poison and the blood loss from his wound was taking its toll.

If he didn't kill the man quickly, he was the one who was going to end up in a soggy grave.

Clearing his double vision, Raphael bared his teeth. He was going to rip off the man's head and feed it to the gators.

The satisfying thought had barely formed in his mind when he caught a familiar scent and his heart forgot how to beat.

Goddammit. That stubborn female was going to get locked in his house and never let out again.

He gathered his waning strength, desperately grasping his attacker's arms to keep him from reaching the gun. At the same time, Ashe stepped into view, her arms held over her head as she swung a heavy stick toward the back of the man's head.

There was sickening crunch as the skull busted at the impact, and the man's eyes glazed.

Raphael didn't hesitate. Grabbing the man's face, he jerked his head to the side with enough force to snap his neck. Instantly the stranger went limp and Raphael tossed his dead body aside.

Rising to his feet, he stepped over the corpse so he could glare down at his mate in frustration.

"I thought I told you to run?"

She rolled her eyes, tossing the stick aside so she could wrap an arm around his waist. Only then did he realize that he was swaying like a drunkard.

"You know how well I take orders," she reminded him with a wry smile.

He brushed his lips over the top of her head, allowing her to keep him balanced as they continued their interrupted journey through the bayou.

Once he reached the Wildlands he would send someone back to check the body for a brand.

For now he had to get Ashe to the safety of his people.

"That's something we're going to have to work on," he assured her.

She tilted back her head to meet his weary smile.

"Together."

"Together," he breathed, wondering if a word had ever sounded so sweet.

Leaning against each other, they managed to stumble their way through the swamp, combining their strength as only a truly mated pair could.

They reached the Wildlands just as the sun crested the horizon, and Raphael wasn't remotely surprised when a cat padded forward to greet them.

Dark as the shadows, the lethal feline regarded them with a predatory gaze.

Then, with a low roar the creature surrounded itself in a silvery mist, shifting to reveal a tall, grim-faced warrior.

"So it's true, Raphael. You return with a mate and a child," the leader of the Hunters drawled with a taunting smile. "I don't know whether to congratulate you or have you thrown into the psych ward."

"And a happy fucking hello to you, Parish."

With a shared chuckle, they stepped into the Wildlands, the magic wrapping around them as overhead a raven screeched in fury.

PARISH

BY
LAURA WRIGHT

CHAPTER ONE

THE baby emerged writhing and covered in amniotic fluid. Cradling the child, unable to curb the proud and relieved smile breaking on her sweaty face, Dr. Julia Cabot reached across the bed and placed him on his weary mother's belly and chest. Annette, one of the three nurses assisting, quickly covered him with a blanket, then suctioned his nose and mouth with a bulb syringe. In seconds, a hearty wail erupted from the infant, the welcome sound pinging off the walls and calling forth a duet of sighs from the baby's father and aunt.

Twenty-one hours of hard labor. This woman's a freaking rock star. Julia glanced at the clock. "9:51 pm."

"Got it," Annette said, scribbling on the chart. "Do you want me to get his scores now, Doc?"

"Right on his mom's chest will be fine." Julia returned to her work, another nurse assisting as she delivered the placenta. "So, Mrs. Dubroux, do you have a name for your beautiful boy?"

"Garth," the woman said, pulling her gaze from her little love and looking up at her husband. "Garth Allan Dubroux, just like his daddy."

The man beamed.

"Nines across the board, Doc," Annette announced, making the note in her chart.

"Well, well, you've got a strong one there," Julia said, pulling off her gloves and letting the nurse take over with the cleaning. She walked around to the side of the bed and eyed the precious new family member. "Welcome to the world, Garth."

As the baby rooted around on her chest, Mrs. Dubroux smiled up at Julia, tears brightening her eyes. "Thank you. Thank you so much."

"You're a godsend, Doctor Cabot," Mr. Dubroux added, his arm tightening around his wife's shoulders. "Marilyn would've been in the surgery room if it wasn't for you."

"It was my pleasure," Julia said, trying to hold back the wave of emotion and sadness at such a lovely ending to her career at New Orleans General. "One of the nurses will help you with breastfeeding if you need it, and Doctor Salander will be coming in to check on the both of you very soon." She gave them one last smile. "Congratulations, and good luck."

"Nice work, Doc," Annette said as they left the room. "Never seen anyone turn a baby like that. You have a gift."

Julia headed for the nurses' station. She needed to fill out some paperwork before she was done for the night. Before she was done, period. She didn't want to be rude, but talking about her work right now…well, it was too painful. She was going to miss this place, the staff, the patients.

Sidling up next to her, Annette clucked her tongue as she watched Julia scribble on Marilyn Dubroux's chart. "Damn shame. Best baby doctor this hospital's ever seen."

The words pinged inside Julia's heart. She was good at her job because she believed in it so much, truly cared about each and every new family that came to the hospital. She wanted their first moments as a unit to be special because after they left, when they got home, sometimes things changed.

"You want to stay at my place tonight, Sugar?"

Julia turned to face the nurse. With her beehive of graying brown hair and warm, chocolate eyes, Annette Monty was hard to resist. She had that kind of older woman, motherly charm that was so irresistible to one who'd lost her own mother at a young age. But encouraging a connection that was just days away from being severed wasn't wise.

"Thanks, Annette," Julia said, giving the woman a soft smile. "But I have a hotel room."

"He paying for it?"

The sour note in Annette's voice made Julia flinch. "No."

"Bastard."

Julia's lips pressed together and she returned to her charts.

"The worst kind of asshole," Annette continued.

Yes. And what a fool she'd been to believe herself in love with him.

"Wish he wasn't my boss." The nurse sniffed with irritation. "If I didn't need this job, I might just walk right into that new office of his and—"

That brought Julia's chin up once again. She eyed the woman seriously. "Don't even think about it. You have three teenagers at home, and Dell is still recovering from knee surgery."

Impassioned brown eyes softened. "You're a good, kind gal, Julia Cabot. That man should be strung up from the nearest light pole for hurting you like he did—not getting a gawd damn promotion."

Head of pediatric surgery. It was amazing how some people were rewarded for bad behavior. Dr. Gary Share: mega-talented physician, desperately disappointing man.

Annette wasn't about to let the subject go. Keeping her voice just above a whisper, she hissed, "Brings you all the way out here from California, promises you a home and a family, and," her voice dropped to a whisper, "takes that *salope* into your bed."

A still shot flashed in Julia's mind, the same one she'd been seeing every day and night for a week. Lunch hour, coming home to bring Gary, who'd been up all night in surgery, a hot meal. She'd heard it, heard them, the minute she'd walked into the house, and yet she couldn't stop herself. She'd walked up those stairs, heart pounding, food clutched in her shaking hands, and into the bedroom she shared with Gary.

It's a surreal experience to see the person you care about and trust most in the world lying on their back, legs spread, with one of the new nurses from emergency on top of them. But it's something else entirely when they don't even stop, when they don't pull out or even have the decency to look horrified when they utter breathlessly, "*What are you doing here, Julia? You're supposed to be at the hospital.*"

"You going to stay here in New Orleans or go back home to Hollywood country?"

Annette's question tore Julia from her unrelenting vision, and she cleared her throat. "I haven't decided where I'm going."

Or when.

It was a little pathetic to admit. She'd given her notice a week ago, been living in a hotel and she couldn't seem to plan her next move. Where should she go? Where did she belong? Her mother was dead, her father had never been in the picture, and she had no siblings, and the few friends she'd managed to make in medical school were scattered around the country. It had been the main reason she'd accepted Gary's offer to move to New Orleans. She'd been smitten with him, surely, and the idea of a new city, a job that was waiting for her. But the one thing she'd wanted above all else was a chance to create a life, a community—a family.

Lucky little Garth.

She smiled to herself as she handed all her files to the nurse behind the desk.

"Come stay with me, Sugar," Annette said, touching Julia's shoulder. "One night. We can play Yahtzee, watch something with a lot of hot men running around without their shirts on, and take down that box of wine I have in my pantry."

Julia laughed softly, shook her head. "Did anyone ever tell you that you are the sweetest, kindest and pushiest woman…" Her words died as her gaze caught sight of something down the hall. Her heart leapt into her throat.

"That they have, Sugar," Annette continued with a soft rumble of laughter. "So what do you say? I'm off in an hour."

Air wasn't getting into Julia's lungs. She tried to breathe normally, but her insides refused to cooperate. Her hands formed fists and her lips went dry. Walking down the hall toward her, all five foot eleven, perfectly cropped blond hair, pressed pants and a coldly charming smile, was the slimeball himself.

Dr. Gary.

God, what was wrong with her? Why was she reacting like this? Insecure and embarrassed? He'd screwed her over! He'd kicked her out of the house he'd made sure to keep in his name, 'suggested' she find a new place to work, then moved his afternoon delight in before she'd even found herself a hotel.

"Turn around, Sugar, and face me. Don't let that towheaded rat bastard see your face."

Annette might have been one of the bossiest, most loveable irritants around, but at that moment, Julia had never been more grateful to have her near.

———

Inside the empty hospital room, Parish crouched near the open doorway, nostrils flaring as he took in the scent of his prey. A delectable combination of vanilla and female sweat. A low growl vibrated in his throat.

"What are you doing, Parish?" Michel hissed behind him. "You sound feral."

Feral? *Yes.* Hungry. *Always.*

She smelled especially appetizing.

As he watched the human female interact with her co-worker, his body stirred, and even though Pantera couldn't shift outside the magical boundaries of the Wildlands, his cat scratched at the base of his skull. The puma was intrigued by her, too.

Granted, he despised humans, didn't trust them with anything but destruction, but he'd never scented anything like her—never *seen* something like her in his life. Skin the color of cream, hair, long and straight and sun-lightened yellow, eyes as pale blue as the bayou sky he awoke beneath every morning, and a smile that was equally sweet as it was sad. She wasn't very tall. With the small heel on her sexy black shoes, maybe she'd reach his shoulder, but he liked that. His hands could easily wrap around her small waist as he gathered her in his arms, crushed her body to his and took off back to the Wildlands.

Another growl escaped his throat, and his breathing changed. Beside him, Michel cursed. The Suit was one of the many spies the Pantera had living and working outside the Wildlands, and was Parish's New Orleans contact. The Political Faction of the Pantera was always on the alert, needing to know about any human-based threat to their species, or a physical one that could affect the magic of their land.

Tonight's mission, however, was something vastly more important. The miracle the Pantera had spent over five decades praying for could finally be upon them, and the female with the addictive scent, sunlit hair and black kitten heels was the key to its success.

"Parish," Michel said with more force than he'd shown all night. "Do I need to pull you back here?"

Parish grinned broadly. *As if that were possible.* "That's my doctor."

"Yes, but you can't just barrel down the hospital hallway and take what you want."

Watch me. His eyes narrowed into predatory slits and he moved forward, but Michel put a hand on his shoulder to stay him.

Parish shrugged him off, then growled, his canines vibrating with their need to drop.

"Goddamit, Hunter." The Pantera spy cut in front of him. The male wasn't as tall as Parish, but he was broad shouldered in his suit and tie, and his green eyes flashed with the thick heat of the bayou. "It doesn't work this way. If we want to keep our alliance with human law enforcement, and the identities of our spies hidden, protocol and rules cannot be broken."

"Rules don't apply to Hunters," Parish snarled.

Michel's frown deepened. "Inside the Wildlands, that may be true. But this is the human world."

Parish didn't care where they were. "Raphael wants a female doctor for his pregnant human. She will help deliver the first Pantera child in decades." His gaze cut once again to the blond woman who was bending over to retrieve her co-worker's pen from the floor. Parish growled softly at her, his assignment. He suspected she would look very appealing on her hands and knees before him.

"I think this is a mistake," Michel remarked dryly. "Perhaps some-one from the Nurturer Faction should be sent—"

Parish's gaze ripped back to the male before him. "Too late. I will have her."

Michel cursed. "This is not a store, and she is not for purchase."

"I'm not buying, Michel, I'm taking."

Even as he said it, the possessive purr in Parish's tone surprised him. He'd never felt such an immediate and intense need for a female. No doubt she'd be afraid of him when he approached. Most females were. Perpetually on the hunt, he didn't have the softness, the easy manners of some other Pantera males. But he would try to be gentle with her.

The male shook his head and sighed. "I don't understand Raphael's choice in sending you."

"Do you not?" It was in fact a job for both himself and his sec-ond-in-command, Bayon. But the other male had been called away on some emergency when they'd arrived in New Orleans. Knowing Bayon, the emergency probably had large breasts, a ripe ass and the morning free. "I am leader of the Hunters, and Raphael's mate carries our future within her womb." One dark eyebrow lifted sardonically. "Never send a Suit or a Nurturer to do a Hunter's job."

Michel reddened and his lip curled.

"You've done your part. Go back to work." Parish pushed past the male, his nostrils already filling with her scent once again.

"Do not hurt her."

Parish didn't even glance back, but his lips did twist into a humor-less smile as the woman left the nurses' station and headed for the bank of elevators. "She will be well taken care of."

CHAPTER TWO

THE French Quarter, the nerve center of downtown New Orleans, was overflowing with people, and yet the moment Julia hit Gravier Street, she knew she was being followed. Living in Los Angeles, always working late, taking the bus everywhere or walking home, her instincts had been tested, proven and finely honed. Just seconds after leaving the hospital, she'd felt something, sensed someone keeping pace with her, but she hadn't stopped or turned around. That was an amateur's move. One that could easily get the looker hurt or killed.

Don't ever let the bogeyman know you know he's there.

Her mother's words, back when she'd still been able to communicate, had fallen on teenage know-it-all ears. But one night after a late class, Julia had found herself on the terrifying and ill-prepared end of a mugger's switchblade. The lesson had cost her a computer, medical school books, ID, credit cards, cash and a week's worth of sleep. From that day forward, her mother's warning remained steadfast in her head.

Don't ever let the bogeyman know you know he's there until you're ready to either lead him directly into the path of a cop, you have a clear and realistic way to ditch him, or you can bring him with you into a crowd of people and make a huge goddamn stink.

The hair on the back of Julia's neck prickled and she quickened her pace, heading directly into the eye of the NOLA bar crawl.

Just a few blocks to the hotel.

As the sound of cool jazz, and the scents of body odor, grilling crawfish and stale beer came at her on the warm air, her eyes searched the massive crowd for a cop, but came up empty.

What did he want? she wondered, the concentrated sounds of revelry enveloping her, driving up her adrenaline, making her senses incredibly keen. Didn't he know she had nothing?

Shit. Less than nothing?

Didn't he know she'd already been robbed this week? Of a life, a future, a promise?

The noise grew in strength, and the crowd thickened. Instead of fear, anger started to stir within her. Anger that had been festering in her chest, waiting, squeezing, aching to find release. Maybe this was it. The time.

The *bogeyman*.

It was in that moment she felt a hand brush her waist. Her pulse jerked in her blood and instinct fed her already jacked-up rage. Coming to a sudden halt, she whirled around and faced the bastard who had just dared to touch her.

Eyes the color of melted gold met her.

Julia froze where she stood, her anger leaking from her gut like a punctured balloon. All she could do was stare at the creature before her. He was stunning, incredible, unlike anything she had ever seen before. Around her, the crowd noise dissipated to a dull hum, but she barely noticed. Her gaze was slowly traveling the length of him, taking in his predatory stance and powerful muscle and tanned skin. He wore plain clothes; jeans and a black T-shirt with scuffed combat boots. But he was the furthest thing from plain she'd ever seen. Far over six feet tall with broad shoulders and long, ink-black hair that was tied back at his neck. A few stray pieces had escaped and were licking at the ridges of his sharply drawn features. His face was shockingly handsome, tan and smooth, except for the two healed scars near his right ear and mouth. Her nails scraped against her palms as she thought about running her index finger over the small white lines.

A low growl sounded, but Julia didn't register where the noise was coming from. Her head was far too fuzzy, and her skin felt uncomfortably warm. It was only when a heavily muscled arm snaked around her waist and pulled her close that she snapped out of the haze enveloping her.

"I like the way you look at me," he said, his voice a dark, sensual rumble. "For once, I am the prey."

His words and the feel of his breath against her face turned her legs to rubber. What the hell was going on here? What was wrong with her that she was reacting like this? She brought her hands to his chest and pushed like hell, but he didn't budge.

"You don't have to be afraid of me," he said, his eyes cutting away for a moment to check their surroundings. "I would never hurt you."

The man's dark, erotic scent rushed into Julia's nostrils and she whimpered. Where were her guts? Why wasn't she screaming in terror? That coveted ability she thought she possessed, the one where she kept her shit together in the face of danger, lay completely out of her reach as his golden eyes, now flecked with blue and gray, returned to hers and all but urged her to relinquish her very soul to him.

Her mind raced, her feet were rooted to the ground, the drunk New Orleans crowd just continued to party around them, and instead of wanting to knee him in the balls and run, she actually wanted to move closer, nuzzle her face against the steely wall of his chest.

His lips curved into a sexy smile, those small white scars calling out to her as he spoke. "I understand Raphael's need for his human woman now."

Raphael.

Human woman?

The words snaked through Julia's brain, tugging at her rational thought, waking her fear center. *Oh shit.* Her pulse jumped in her throat and she swallowed. For the first time since she'd laid eyes on this man, she found her voice.

"Let me go," she whispered.

The gold in his incredible eyes receded for a moment and black irises emerged.

Adrenaline pumping, she eased back from him. "Let me go," she said again, far more firmly this time. Her heartbeat was so loud now she heard it in her ears. "I'll scream. I'll scream so goddamn loud the cops will be on you in a second."

The man's face fell. He looked completely taken aback by her words, maybe even offended. But he didn't let her go. "There's no reason to be afraid, Doctor Cabot."

Julia's insides went cold with terror. *He knows who I am. How does he know who I am?*

She started to struggle, panic causing her skin to prickle. "Why are you following me? What do you want?"

"I was sent to find you."

Sent? "By who?" she demanded, trying to get her arm free, her knee, anything she could use.

"You need to calm down," he urged softly, his arm tightening around her waist as, once again, he looked around, up at a few buildings, then into the crowd. "Your heart beats too fast."

Who would send someone after her? She didn't know anyone outside the hospital. She didn't have family. She didn't—

She stopped struggling and stared up at him, her mouth dry. "Is this Gary's doing?" she said hoarsely as a group of drunk college girls stumbled past them. *Oh god. That bastard.* He'd told her he would hire a lawyer if she didn't go away quietly—if she tried to stake a claim to the house or any of its contents. "Are you a private detective or something? Is he actually having me followed? Because that would be both incredibly shitty of him and unnecessary since I want nothing from him."

"Gary?" The man's nostrils flared. "Is this your male?"

"My male?" she repeated with an almost hysterical laugh. "Gary *was* my boyfriend until I found him in our bed, balls-deep in one of my nurses. Or didn't he tell you that part?"

Dark brows lifted over those extraordinary eyes.

"You can tell that jackass that there's no reason to follow me. I don't want anything from him." Her voice broke. *Goddamit.* She hated tears. They were worthless and made a person look weak. "Except my cat. I want my cat."

That damn cat. She missed him like crazy.

A large hand moved slowly up her back and held her posses- sively between the shoulder blades. "You don't wish to return to this Gary?" the man said with a slight snarl. "This male who betrayed you?"

"I'd rather eat my own hand." She gritted her teeth. "And you can tell him as soon as I'm out of the hotel and living somewhere perma- nent, I'll send someone to get Fangs."

"Who is Fangs?" he asked.

"My cat."

She saw a flicker of a grin on his dark, rugged face. "The female likes cats."

Before Julia could say another word, the man pressed her closer to his chest and took off into the crowd. He moved so quickly that all she saw before she passed out was a blur of city lights, and all she felt were his arms around her and air rushing over her skin.

"What the hell where you thinking?" Raphael admonished.

Pacing near the bed in the medical ward, Parish glanced up and flashed his canines at yet another Diplomat. "I did what I was sent to do."

"You were supposed to talk to her—"

"I did talk to her," Parish cut in. He continued to pace. It both- ered him to look at the woman, unconscious and pale behind the white sheet. He hadn't meant for this to happen. He hadn't known she would pass out from the burst of speed he'd used to get them out of the crowd and on their way to the Wildlands. "She has quit her job and has no family. She's broken things off with a bastard male who fucked another female right in front of her." He growled softly, his cat itching to spring free and hunt down this human called Gary. "Just like a human to go sniffing around when he has something beautiful and perfect in his bed."

"Dammit, Parish." Raphael's green eyes flashed with irritation. "Gathering personal information was not the assignment. You were supposed to talk with her about Ashe and the child. You were supposed to explain our situation and our offer. Invite her to come here. Instead you snatched her off the street, rendering her unconscious in the process."

"I am a Hunter. I do not ask. When you ask, you give your prey the opportunity to say no."

Even as he said the words, Parish's gaze cut to the woman on the bed. As much as he wanted to think of her as prey, as human—as nothing at all to him—there was something inside of him that had already connected to her. She was the most beautiful female he'd ever seen. Her smooth, pale skin called to him, as did her full pink mouth. She had to wake. She must. He needed to hear her voice again, see her eyes flash in anger and heat as he held her against him.

He turned from the bed with a frustrated snarl.

"This is your fault," Raphael called to Bayon. The massive blond Hunter leaned against the doorframe, refusing to commit to entering either the medical room or the conversation. "Running off while one of our wildest takes on a human alone."

Parish quick-flashed the Suit his puma, then drew it back inside before continuing to pace. He needed air, needed his clothes off and his fur on just for a few hours. But he couldn't leave the woman.

Julia.

Just her name made his body stir.

"Parish was with Michel," Bayon said. "The meet, greet and offer with the doctor was all set up. It should've gone smoothly."

Raphael hissed. "Where the hell were you?"

"I had something to take care of."

"That's not an answer, Bayon."

"It is the only answer I'm willing to give."

"Some*thing* to take care of – more like some*one*, right?"

Bayon's eyes narrowed. "Cage your cat before I have to."

"You were off hunting tail instead of backing up your leader!" Raphael roared.

"Enough!" Parish growled, coming to stand between the warring shifters. He would not have Julia upset, awakening to a verbal brawl in a strange room. He turned on Raphael, prowling closer to the dark blond male. "You sent the leader of the Hunters to bring back the best female baby doctor in New Orleans." He cocked his head. "And I did."

Nostrils flared, Raphael seemed to be searching for patience. "She's unconscious, Parish."

The words twisted in Parish's gut. He'd never thought about his reckless, instinctive ways before. Never felt so unsure of himself until now. "It's only for a short time. She is well. Pulse, breathing, vital signs. Our doctors have said so."

"If this gets out, if any of the Diplomats learn of this—"

"Handle it. Suit business is for you to figure out."

"You're right about that," Raphael ground out. "Go. You're done here." He knocked his chin toward Bayon and the door. "I'll make sure this doesn't become a problem."

Panic flared within Parish and his gaze cut to the bed. "But the female…"

Cold authority bled from the Suit's tone. "I'll assign someone to take care of the doctor."

"No!" The sudden rush of anger and possessiveness toward the woman surprised Parish. And Raphael too by the look on his face.

"She's going to need a guard," he said. "Like you, there are many Pantera who do not welcome humans. They're tolerant of Ashe because she carries my child, and the hope for our species. But they may not feel we need a human doctor. They might see it as an insult. When she wakes up, after I have spoken to her, explained things, and if she agrees to remain, one of the Nurturer guards will take her—"

A snarl ripped from Parish's throat.

"—Will take her to and from her quarters and make sure no harm comes to her."

Parish moved closer to the bed, blocking Julia from Raphael's view, his stance aggressive, protective.

"Ease up, Parish." Bayon stepped inside the room, moved toward his leader. "What is it? Are you losing control of your hatred for humans? We can't risk her…"

Parish ground his molars. They didn't get it. Shit, he barely understood his irrational anger and desperate need himself. But the one thing he did know was that he couldn't leave Julia.

He glanced down at the woman. Her color was coming back and beneath her pale lids, he saw movement. His chest expanded with hope. She would awaken soon, and the first face he wanted her to see was his own.

"I found her," he said softly. "I took her. She is mine."

Bayon cursed behind him.

"Yours?" Raphael said.

Parish's hand inched forward, toward her until his fingers met her elbow. As irrational and impossible as it was, he wanted to claim her, announce to both Raphael and Bayon that something had happened on the street in New Orleans when he'd pulled this woman into his arms and gazed down into her lovely face. A connection, a need, a pull he'd never imagined he'd ever feel for a female, much less a human woman. And the idea of being separated from her made not only him but his cat ache.

But he pushed back the urge. He knew such a declaration would sound insane. He would do better to claim her as a Hunter, a protector.

"To guard," he amended, his gaze moving over her face. "The doctor is mine to guard. She will live with me, have my full protection as she cares for Ashe."

Bayon started to laugh, then abruptly stopped when Parish turned and glared at him.

"You're serious? Live with you in the caves? A human female?" The blond male tossed a look at Raphael. "Presuming she actually agrees, she won't last a minute in that dank, uncivilized rock. She'll be running from us."

She won't get far.

"I will agree to you guarding her, Parish," Raphael said slowly. "But it will be somewhere with hot water and clean sheets."

There was nothing Parish wanted more in that moment then to scoop her up in his arms and take her home to his caves, but he knew Raphael's mind, knew how far to push the male when it came to protocol. And perhaps the beautiful doctor deserved a little pampering after what he'd put her through. He nodded at Raphael. "Fine. I'll bring her to Natty's."

"She may very well be afraid of you. She's not going to soften around the feline who shut down her mind and abducted her."

Parish's lip curled, but the ire was more for himself than for the Suit. "I won't be harsh with her. I won't scare her."

The male looked unconvinced. "Can you truly promise that? Your dislike of humans is legendary. And understandably so."

"She is different."

She is mine.

"She is special." Raphael came to stand beside him at the bed, his puma's face flashing momentarily from its normally controlled cage. "I cannot have this go wrong."

Parish knew exactly how important this was, for the both of them. "I give you my word. I will keep her safe and well."

Golden green eyes searched his. "All right. If the woman agrees, she is yours to protect."

The cat inside of Parish purred.

Chapter Three

JULIA returned to consciousness slowly, her mind still wrapped in a delectable dream. One she wasn't all that keen on releasing.

She was on her bed in the hotel. It was night and the windows were open, letting in the glow of moonlight and the balmy New Orleans breeze. Beneath her lay a man with bronze skin and hungry, gold cat eyes. His long black hair kissed his broad shoulders and chest, both of which were beaded with sweat. As she rode him, he growled at her, his hands gripping her hips.

Beside the bed, watching, his expression strangled and confused, was Gary. Blond, buttoned-up, cheater, liar and all around heel, Gary. He kept whispering the words, "You're supposed to be at the hospital, Julia," over and over, but Julia barely spared him a glance. She was close, so close. The one beneath her, the one inside her, the one who growled and snarled at her as he made her come again, was the only thing that mattered.

"You belong to me!"

Julia collapsed onto his chest, his possessive roar echoing in her ears as his hot seed filled her sex.

"Julia?" A voice, female and insistent, was trying to reach her, break in to her wonderful dream.

"Julia?" the voice said again. "Her breathing's worrying me, Raphael. And she looks flushed."

Julia felt something cold on her face and gasped. Body on fire, limbs shaking, her eyes flickered open. It took her several seconds to focus, but when she did fear gripped her. The dream was gone, and the woman who sat beside her, on what Julia could only guess was a hospital bed, was a complete stranger.

"I'm Ashe." Long black hair framed a beautiful, concerned face. "Please don't be scared."

"What's going on?" Julia demanded, trying to sit up, but failing immediately. "Did I pass out?"

The woman glanced behind her and Julia followed her line of vision. A man stood several feet away. He was tall and imposing and reminded her of someone. Why couldn't she remember?

"The effects will wear off," Ashe said, her gaze returning to Julia's. "It just takes a little while."

The effects? The effects of what?

Her heart started to pound.

"Do you remember anything?" Ashe asked gently. "Where you were before you…Who you were with?"

Julia's hands gripped the sheet that covered her. Did she remember? God, she hated this. Her mind felt blank. Fuzzy as hell, but blank. "I was at the hospital," she said, struggling to see past the white noise in her brain. "I delivered a baby. Garth. It was a really difficult delivery, but everything turned out well." She squinted. "It was my last day, and I was going back to my hotel. I was walking down Gravier when I thought someone was…"

She jerked her head up, her gaze crashing into Ashe's. "Oh my god. The guy…"

The woman inched forward on the bed, her eyes heavy with concern. "Please. I need you to stay calm."

Shit. Her heart was now slamming painfully against her ribs. Calm was the last thing she felt. "Did you see that guy? The one who followed me? Did he bring me here? He has black, long hair and golden eyes…" Her head began to pound and she winced. "That sounds impossible, I know. Was I drugged?"

"No." The woman cursed, and once again glanced over her shoulder. "Listen, I'll tell you. Everything. But I need you to promise me you won't freak out until after I'm done."

How could she promise that? How could she promise anything to a stranger? Someone who might know the man who took her, who brought her here. But desperation to know the truth, get any kind of information, had her agreeing. "Okay."

"Have you ever heard of the Pantera?"

Julia frowned, struggling with the fog weighing down her mind. "No."

"They're a group of…people who live deep in the bayou," Ashe explained, her expression uneasy. "They're rumored to have magical powers and an ability to shape-shift."

Julia's head continued to pound, competing for the highest decibel level with her heart. Maybe she was still lost in a dream. Maybe she was in her hotel room. "I don't know," she managed, her mouth irritatingly dry. "I may have heard some crazy legend about cat people or something. But what does that have to do with me? With that guy who followed me? Who grabbed me and—" Her chest tightened as she recalled the feel of his body against her own. "This isn't my hospital, is it?"

"*Ma chère*," called the man at the door, his gaze on Ashe. "Maybe I should talk with her…explain what has happened…"

"No," Ashe insisted, her worried gaze locked with Julia's. "She's here because of me. She needs to know the truth before anything else." The woman gave Julia a small smile. "The Pantera, the cat people you've heard about, are not a legend. They live in the bayou, in a secret, sacred place called the Wildlands. They are shape shifters."

Had she hit her head? Had the gorgeous man dropped her? Was he even real? Or was she imagining him? "I don't believe you. I don't believe any of this." She tried to sit up again, and this time, her brain didn't balk, didn't feel like it wanted to explode. God, she needed to get out of here, back to what she knew to be real.

"You're in the medical facility in the Wildlands," Ashe continued quickly. "You were brought here. For me. To help me."

Julia inched backward into the pillows. "I'm in the psyc ward, right? I had a breakdown over this shit with Gary?" She cursed again. "Seriously, I can't believe I'm this weak."

"You're not weak," Ashe said, reaching out and taking her hand. "And don't say that guy's name again. It's not worthy of crossing your lips."

"You know Gary?" Julia asked, stunned. *What the hell was this? What had she got mixed up in?*

"Parish told us about him. What he did to you." Her eyes narrowed. "Sounds like a real jerk."

Julia shook her head. "Who the hell is Parish?"

A low growl sounded, echoed throughout the room. Julia hunched in terror, ready to throw herself off the bed. Find escape. But the voice at the door froze her.

"I told you to stay out until we spoke with her." It was the man who'd called Ashe "*ma chère*".

"You spoke with her," came another male voice from outside the door. "I heard it. I refuse to walk the halls another goddamn second."

Julia's heart dropped into her stomach. She knew that voice, had just dreamt of that voice and the man who owned it. The man who had followed her from the hospital, who'd held her close and gazed down at her like he'd wanted to consume her very breath. Or was that part of her dream, too? She eased her hand from Ashe's and closed her eyes, trying to sort reality from fiction.

But that voice resumed its assault on her senses.

"How are you feeling, Julia?"

Julia couldn't help herself. She lifted her lids and her gaze shot to the man walking toward her. *Holy shit.* He was real. Flesh and blood, and if it were possible, even more gorgeous than she remembered. When he'd pulled her close on Gravier Street his hair had been back off his face, but now it hung loose and wild and sexy around his beautiful, scarred face. Like before, he wore jeans, but instead of a T-shirt, he had on a black tank that revealed heavily muscled shoulders and arms.

Her mouth dropped open as she stared at him.

"I'm confused," she managed. What had happened? How had she ended up here? And where exactly was she?

His dark eyes, eyes that had once been golden, grew concerned as he approached the bed. "I'm sorry for the way I brought you here. I'm not used to asking or discussing."

That she believed. Her gaze ran up his body. He was so tall, such a fierce presence beside her bed. "What did you do to me?"

He winced, looking guilty, and his gaze cut away for a moment. "The speed at which I move was too disorienting for your mind. And my musk, the one I used to try and calm you, is more potent than most Pantera's. I should've known." His eyes slid back to connect with hers once again. "I apologize."

"Musk?" Julia felt suddenly exhausted. It was like they were all speaking another language. "What's this musk? A drug?"

"No," he said, worry etching his expression. "It's magic we can release—"

"Magic." There was that word again.

"—a scent to calm or soothe or arouse.…It's nothing permanent."

She had to be freaking dreaming.

"You will be able to get up soon, walk—"

"Walk out of here?" Julia said, her pulse jumping against her neck. "I can leave?"

His eyes shuttered. "I would not like that."

"Okay. Go." Ashe pointed at Parish, then glanced over her shoulder at the other male. "Leave. Both of you."

Parish growled, and the sound penetrated Julia's skin and vibrated through her. She practically moaned. "God, what was that?"

"It's Parish being rude and insensitive," Ashe said, her tone nearly lethal now. She glared at the man. "You're scaring her, confusing her. *I* will explain things, woman to woman."

"You heard my female," said the other man, who continued to remain near the door. "Let's go, Parish."

Parish's gaze moved down Julia's body, then back to her face. His nostrils flared. "Fine," he muttered. "But I'll be back."

He turned and stormed out. The other man gave Ashe a quick, tight smile before turning and walking…

Julia gasped, her blood suddenly fire hot in her veins. *Impossible.* She blinked, then stared hard at the empty doorway. The man was now gone, but she swore…*No.* She shook her head. It was the drugs or the head injury or the story Ashe had just told her. She did *not* just see the back end of a large cat where the man had been.

Or a long golden tail.

She let her head fall back against the pillows and closed her eyes, tried to calm her breathing. After a moment, when she felt in control, she opened them and focused on the nearly empty room. It seemed darker now, colder. Julia frowned at her odd reaction. She should be able to breathe easier with him gone, shouldn't she?

Still seated beside the bed, Ashe gave her an understanding, tight-lipped smile. "I know it's overwhelming. They tend to be pretty protective. And possessive. Parish seems to think he's responsible for you after how he handled things. But don't worry, Raphael will take care of that."

"Raphael?" Unbearable confusion tested the last of Julia's patience. She fixed her gaze on Ashe and repeated her question. "Who is Raphael?"

"My mate." She smiled, her eyes softening. "First, let me say that I know exactly how you're feeling. It's confusing and impossible sounding." She laughed. "I'm pretty sure my face had that exact same expression when I found out."

"Found out what?" Julia ground out. "That you were being drugged? That you were living in a dream state?

Ashe shook her head, her eyes bright. "That magic truly does exist. That the man I fell in love with is a puma shifter." She bit her bottom lip. "And that the baby I'm carrying is half human, half Pantera."

"What?" Julia said on a gasp, her gaze slipping down to the woman's flat belly.

"I'm only six weeks along." Ashe grabbed Julia's hand again, her eyes imploring. "I'm scared. I have no idea what to expect. No clue as to how long I'll be pregnant, what the gestational period of a puma/human hybrid will be." She swallowed. "I want this baby to be okay.

And having a human doctor…" She shook her head. "I can't believe Parish just took you without telling you anything."

Parish. Just hearing his name made her skin tighten. This was madness. A puma/human hybrid. Christ. This woman didn't need an OB, she needed a shrink. *And I need to get the hell out of here before I'm sucked in further.*

"I know. I know where your head's at." Ashe leaned toward her. "And I don't blame you. I'm just asking for some time."

"Time for what?"

Ashe licked her lips. "To prove it to you. To show you. Them."

Pale gold fur, a set of feline hips and a long, thick tail moved slowly through Julia's mind. She gritted her teeth against the vision. She couldn't believe Ashe, she refused to. But if she wanted to get out of here, maybe she needed to play their game for a little while.

Julia held the woman's gaze and sighed. "If all this is true, and I'm not saying it is, wouldn't it be better to have a doctor who's a…" Shit, she could barely get the word out because it was so ludicrous. "Shifter?"

"There are plenty of those here. But they've only dealt with puma births. Plus, they haven't delivered a child in over fifty years."

Puma. Births. And yet, her damn doctor's curiosity had her asking, "Why not?"

"The female Pantera either couldn't get pregnant or were unable to carry the babies to full-term. It's a horrific situation. They even tried to impregnate humans, willing test subjects, but nothing happened."

"Until you," Julia said softly, eyeing her sharply.

Ashe nodded.

This poor woman needed help. Serious, professional help. Julia was going to do her best to find a way out of here. Maybe she could convince Ashe to go with her.

"Listen, Ashe," she said in a gentle voice. "I know some really incredible doctors back in the city—"

Squeezing her hand tightly, Ashe implored her, "Please don't say no. Don't say anything. Not yet." Ashe released her hand after one final squeeze and quickly got to her feet. "I'll leave you alone. Let you try and sort this out. It took me a while…Hell, I think I'm still reeling from the truth. But know this: you'll have whatever you need and want here. A home, salary, protection, freedom." She smiled down at Julia with the most stable, yet concerned expression. "If you decide to leave, though, no one's going to hold you here against your will—not even Parish."

Was it true? She could go if she wanted? Julia lifted a brow. "I don't know about that. Parish seems pretty intent on me staying." *And god, I think I like that part of this dream.*

Ashe shrugged. "He's a Hunter. He's wild, untamed, used to taking what he wants. And he doesn't have the best manners. But he's also honorable."

Honorable. She hadn't met an honorable man in a long time.

Ashe was almost at the door when she glanced back. "Like you, I don't have much back home. Nothing I want to run to, anyway. My family is Raphael and...well," she touched her belly again. "Little No-Name here." She smiled. "It would be great to have a friend as well as a doctor."

Julia stared at the woman, watched her leave the room, and as soon as the door closed she pivoted to sit on the edge of the bed. Her head felt light, but okay. She had to find a way out, a way home. To the hotel and the jobless, family-less life. She couldn't stay here. Right? With the crazy lady and shape-shifting Pantera? With the gorgeous, golden-eyed male who looked at her with unmasked desire and hope?

It was reality vs. fantasy. And as a doctor, a scientist, she was nothing if she couldn't choose fact over fiction.

A shaft of light spilled into the room then, snaking across her legs and coating the metal door beyond. Completely taken by its brilliant, pale glow, Julia pushed to her feet and followed its origin. The long picture window was closed, but when she arrived at the glass and looked out over the unfamiliar setting, she gasped in amazement.

———

Parish opened the door and entered with the silent predatory grace he was known for as leader of the Hunters. His gaze went first to the bed, then shifted to the window where she stood looking out over the courtyard. He wondered how long she'd been standing there; poised at the glass, her arms spread, her hands curled around the edges of the sill. His gaze moved deliberately, covetously down her body. The sun was bathing her in its warm light, allowing him to see through her white T-shirt to the curves beneath. Deadly, brain-altering curves. His mouth filled with saliva and his cat scratched to get out, run at her and pounce.

He had to convince her to stay, but more importantly he had to convince her that he was the best male to protect her. Just the idea of Raphael assigning another male to guard her, another puma sniffing around her, looking at her with a desire only he should feel, made him insane with jealousy.

He wasn't willing to admit his claim on her out loud, but he would make damn sure the Wildlands' males felt it, sensed it, scented it, every time they got close to her.

He growled softly, and she instantly turned around. He waited for fear to ignite in her eyes, but all that appeared in her expression was relief. His heart softened, pressed against his chest as if it wanted to get to her. She didn't fear him. Unlike so many other females, she didn't fear him.

"I can't believe this place," she said, turning back to the window. "It's incredible. I thought I might be dreaming, but now I'm convinced of it."

He came to stand beside her. "You shouldn't be out of bed." His words were meant to be gentle, caring, but they came out slightly gruff as his mind conjured images of taking her back to bed himself. Maybe curling beside her and purring against her neck.

"What is it called again? This place?"

"The Wildlands."

"I've never seen anything so beautiful."

Leaning against the window, Parish stared at her. No, neither had he. Far too beautiful for the likes of a scarred Hunter with a bad attitude. And yet, he couldn't look away from her, couldn't stand the thought of her leaving the bayou. How was this possible? Taken with a human? He hated humans. They had no conscience, no honor. They destroyed the good and the innocent.

They'd destroyed *her.*

His gut tightened with pain as it did every time he thought of Keira. How could he even think of caring for a human? Giving his protection to one?

"It's so green." Julia glanced over at him, the smile curving her mouth echoed in her eyes. "But shades of green I've never seen before. I mean, I've been to the bayou. Several times, in fact, but I've never seen anything like this. It's paradise."

He had always thought humans were attracted to electronics, tall buildings, glass and metal. Not the wild, untamed landscape he'd been born to, protected and loved fiercely. But the fact that Julia saw it as he did pleased him.

"Do people know about it?" she asked. "Do they come here?"

"It's masked," he told her. "To keep out intruders."

"Like me." Her eyes flashed with sudden and unexpected humor.

He shook his head slowly. "*Unwanted* humans."

"And you are," her eyes cut to the landscape, then back at him, "what exactly?"

His brows drew together. "Ashe told you. We are Pantera."

"Cat shifters," she said.

"Puma," he corrected.

She laughed softly and shook her head, returned her gaze to the Wildlands.

"You don't believe it." He stared at her. It hadn't occurred to him she would need convincing. Not after what happened on the street in New Orleans. She couldn't have missed the rush of magic. "You must believe."

She glanced back at him. "Why? Why should this unwanted human—"

"You're different," he interrupted in a tone far too fierce for his liking. "Ashe may want you here, but I need you, Julia Cabot."

The humor in her gaze instantly retreated.

Parish turned and rubbed his forehead against the cool glass. "I don't know how to explain it. These feelings I have for you. I'm not good with words. Or making others feel at ease."

"You're doing all right," she said.

Parish turned and looked at her. She wore a confused expression and her eyes looked incredibly blue and vulnerable. The sun blazed in through the window, turning her blond hair almost white. She looked like an angel. What was he to do about this, about her? He reached out and lifted a piece of her pale hair from her cheek, rolled it gently between his fingers. "Soft."

Her eyes never left his, but her lips parted to draw in a shaky breath. Whether she accepted it or not, she was as affected by him as he was by her.

"Will you stay here, Julia?" he whispered, moving closer, his hand opening to cup her cheek. "In this paradise? This dream you're not sure is real? Help Ashe? Allow me to protect you? I would consider it a great honor."

"Parish…" she whispered.

He groaned. "Say my name like that again, Doc, and my mouth'll be on yours before you can take another breath."

Someone coughed. Someone by the door. Then a familiar female voice remarked, "You're up. And Parish is back."

Damn woman. Parish growled blackly as Julia turned away from him. Raphael's woman was really starting to get on his nerves.

In the doorway, Ashe stood beside another female, small and grinning broadly as she looked from Julia to Parish with giddy interest. Parish believed the female to be Nurturer Faction, but in that moment he couldn't care less. He wanted her gone. Ashe, too. He wanted that moment of mutual need between Julia and him back. *Now.*

"Seems like the musk has worn off." Ashe looked only at Julia. "I thought if you felt up to it, we might take you to lunch. There's something I want to show you."

Parish narrowed his eyes at the woman. Forget the males sniffing around his human. What he truly needed to worry about was Ashe. Only one resident of the Wildlands was going to protect Dr. Julia Cabot, and it was going to be him.

Chapter Four

THE Pantera ate lunch as a community. A spirited, tightly woven community who gathered around the fifty or so intricately carved wooden tables that ran along the bayou. Dressed with pale green cloth, each table was piled high with boiled shrimp, crawfish pie, étoufée, potatoes, corn, bread pudding, buttermilk cake and iced sweet tea. For Julia, who normally grabbed a salad or a cup of soup in the hospital cafeteria whenever she had a second free during the day, this sprawling, home-style picnic of a lunch was as overwhelming as it was delicious.

She glanced across the table at Ashe and grinned. "This is the best meal I've ever had."

Ashe laughed. "I know, right?" She offered Julia another helping of creamy grits, then spooned some onto her own plate. "At first I thought it was the pregnancy, but then I realized the food's just different here. Super fresh, homemade, and you know," she winked, "maybe there's a little magic in there."

Julia didn't say anything. She'd been reminding herself how imperative it was for her to find the Wildlands' exit and get back home to New Orleans, that this wasn't real, and there was no such thing as puma shifters. But it wasn't so easy. The land surrounding the charming village was vast and completely rural. Where was she going to go? She didn't know this area. How dangerous would it be to just go walking off into the bayou?

And then there was the undeniable curiosity she couldn't seem to shed. About Parish and the Wildlands. She hated to admit it, and had used her concern for Ashe as an excuse, but she was interested in this place, how it came to be, how it remained off the tourist trade's radar.

"Oh, there's magic in everything here." Ines, the small woman with the dark hair and sable cat eyes who'd come to Julia's room with Ashe, sat at the head of the table. "It's in the air and the earth and the water. Makes the food irresistible." With a grin, she added, "The males, too."

Julia's mind instantly filled with images of Parish and she tried to combat them with a hefty spoonful of grits.

Ashe snorted. "I believe mine was irresistible way before I came to the Wildlands."

"Well, you're special," Ines said, reaching for the ladle in a nearby bowl. "Have some of this, Ashe. Creole alligator. Cook's specialty. He was fresh caught this morning and very tender." Not waiting for an answer, the woman dropped a helping on Ashe's plate. "You'll love it. As will your cub."

Julia looked up from her plate. "Cub?"

"Her child," Ines said, passing an entire buttermilk pie to the table behind them. "It will be half puma. When it shifts for the first time from human form to cat, it'll no longer be considered a baby."

With wide eyes, Ashe glanced over at Julia. "You see why I need a little human help here?"

The woman's face was so momentarily panic-stricken, Julia couldn't help but laugh. She didn't believe what Ines was saying, couldn't, and wanted to scold the woman and find out why they were all feeding Ashe's psychosis. But as she sat there near the slowly moving bayou water, with the fish jumping over the floating vegetation and the sun filtering through the trees above, granting them a gentle, tolerable warmth, she couldn't bring herself to break the incredible mood of this village's picnic.

Maybe she was a coward.

Or maybe the magic of the Wildlands was starting to affect her, too.

"If you decide to stay, Dr. Julia," Ines said, a forkful of buttermilk pie on its way to her mouth. "I would love to assist you. I'm a Nurturer, and trained to work with young, but so far I haven't been able to use my skills."

In that moment Julia turned away from the table and glanced around. She ignored the gentle, sweet breeze on her skin, the laughter, and the incredible scenery, to take in the people – the Pantera – at the tables nearest to them. She hadn't noticed it before, even on the walk over here, but there were no children anywhere. She'd heard what Ashe had said back in the medical facility, but she hadn't given it any thought. She hadn't believed it. The world around the bayou carried no infantile sounds, no cries or coos, no immature squabbles or echoes of pint-sized laughter coming from up and down the shoreline. Her heart clenched. It wasn't possible. Maybe they were at school. This couldn't truly be a community without young.

Her eyes cut to the woman who was leaning back in her chair, her hands spread protectively over her still-flat belly. "How many weeks did you say you were?"

"Six."

"How are you feeling?" she asked, unable to stop herself from slipping into doctor mode.

"With the pregnancy?" Ashe asked. "Good. Strong." She grinned. "Happy."

"No pain? Spotting?"

She shook her head. "I'm a little tired, and hungry. Always hungry."

"Hungry's good. Can I have your hand?" Julia reached out and instantly curled her fingers around the woman's wrist. For one minute, she felt Ashe's steady pulse. "Have you had your blood pressure taken? Any tests?"

"Nothing yet. I haven't been here that long." Ashe cocked her head to the side, her eyes playfully narrowed on Julia. "You're sounding like a doctor, Doctor."

"Hard habit to break."

"Then don't break it," Ashe said, her eyes soft. "Stay."

"I don't think I can," Julia told her. "It's complicated, I'm not sure…"

Ashe's eyes darkened. "It's Parish, isn't it? He's coming on too strongly."

Strongly, sensually, irresistibly.

"He can't help it," Ines said, leaning forward. "Hunters can be very intense, but Parish most of all. He lives in the caves, you know, rarely changes out of his puma state, and I don't think I've ever seen him smile."

"Really?" Julia said, deciding she hadn't heard the part about him rarely changing out of his puma state.

"He's smiling now, Ines," Ashe remarked with a note of concern in her voice.

"What? Where?"

"Over at the Hunters' table." She pointed behind Julia. "I didn't want to make you self-conscious, but he hasn't been able to take his eyes off you since we got here."

Julia glanced over her shoulder, heart jumping into her throat as her gaze searched for the man with the long black hair and eyes that held such intensity, such heat. She'd wondered where he was, if he was having lunch with the rest of them, the Pantera. She spotted him about twenty yards away at a table that sat among a stand of river birch, its four legs submerged in an inch or two of water. Clustered around the table were ten or so of the most wild-looking, barely clothed, heavily muscled men and women she'd ever seen. And at the head, standing on a branch a foot above them all was Parish. He was barefoot and tanned, and wearing only a pair of faded jeans, which rested just below his hipbones. His hair was wild and the scar near his mouth winked in the sunlight. Julia's gaze moved covetously over every inch of him. His narrow waist and ripped stomach that widened to a broad chest, powerful shoulders and lean, muscular arms. He looked ready to spring. And the muscles in Julia's belly turned to liquid fire as she watched him watch her.

"The Hunters moved their table to the water about ten years ago," Ines was saying. "They like to see if they can catch prey from the bank.

I swear they never tire. A wild bunch, but incredible at what they do. Most of the Factions take midday meal together, but Hunters always do."

"He's very taken with you, Julia," Ashe said, not sounding all that pleased. "Say the word and I'll tell Raphael to speak with him, get him to back off."

"No, don't do that." She said the words very quickly, a fact that wasn't lost on Ashe.

"You find him attractive. I can see that, but be careful."

"Yes," Ines agreed. "He is not the soft, gentle human male you're no doubt used to."

Good. I think I'm tired of human males.

She mentally kicked herself for the thought. As the warm, sultry breeze moved over her skin and the trees listed back and forth overhead, her gaze held Parish's. She couldn't look away. She didn't believe in magic, but goddammit, she wanted to believe in him, in whatever this was that burned between them.

"Don't worry, Ashe," Ines continued. "With his history, he won't think of her in a serious way."

The woman's words cut the invisible string that had locked her gaze to Parish's, and she whirled around to face Ines. "What do you mean?"

Ines shrugged one shoulder. "Just that he'll never mate with a human. Not after what happened to his sister."

Julia looked first at Ashe, who shook her head, then back at Ines, who was now loading up her plate with a massive helping of bread pudding. "What happened to his sister?"

"His twin actually, and the leader of the Hunters for nearly a decade. Keira was a complete warrior female. She was brilliant and tough and stunningly beautiful, and she was the only family Parish had. But she wasn't happy here. She wanted to see the world. She wanted to work outside the Wildlands."

"What happened?" Though even as she asked, she felt the answer in her gut.

Ines looked down at her plate and said in a small voice, "She was killed. By the human male she fell in love with."

"How terrible," Ashe remarked.

"Since then, Parish has preferred his puma state, keeping to himself." Ines's eyes lifted, found hers again. "I'm surprised he's showing an interest in you. It'll make our females jealous. Though some fear him, there are many who hope to catch his eye."

Julia glanced over her shoulder again, found Parish standing on the bank near his table. His attention was now on his Hunters, and as he spoke to them, one shuddered almost violently, then stretched his neck abnormally far forward. Julia's heart jumped into her throat. *What was happening to him?* A strange silver mist appeared, from the bayou or out of nowhere, Julia couldn't tell. But it moved over the man, and as it did his clothing seemed to melt into his skin. It was almost tattoo-like until—

"Oh my god," Julia uttered, her gaze pinned on the man. No. He wasn't a man. Not anymore.

This had to be a dream. Or drugs. Maybe she wasn't even awake. She'd hit her head.

She gasped, gripped the table, as another man shuddered. Same stretch, same mist, same shift into golden brown…

"They're going back to work," Ines remarked as though the sight before them was nothing out of the ordinary. "The hunt's tomorrow and they have to secure the borders."

"Oh, Julia," Ashe exclaimed excitedly, "you have to stay now. I've never seen the hunt, but I hear it's amazing. We could go together."

Julia was only barely listening. Her gaze cut to Parish. Two large, golden eyed pumas were bracketing him. Pumas who had once been… human? How was this possible?

"Parish leads the hunt," Ines said with a grin in her voice. "He's incredible to watch. His cat is one of the fastest and fiercest predators I've ever seen."

The very moment Ines stopped talking, Parish looked over at Julia. Her heart thudded in her chest, her ears, her blood. Her lips parted as if she was going to speak, but instead her breath came out in a rush. Before her eyes, Parish shuddered, and in a wave of silver mist, he shifted into a large, powerfully built, slate gray cat. Julia might've said something or whimpered, she wasn't sure. Her heart was pounding so hard she was afraid it would rupture inside her chest. Her entire focus was trained on the incredible magic she'd just witnessed. The magic she could no longer deny. She'd thought the first puma she'd seen shift was beautiful, but he was nothing—absolutely nothing—to Parish. His broad head and luscious coat were formidable, but it was his eyes, gold flecked with blue and gray, rimmed with the darkest, deepest black, that took her breath away.

"Seeing is believing," Ashe said behind her.

Julia stared at the male, the cat.

Parish.

She didn't turn back to face the women as she uttered breathlessly, "It's real. He's real."

He's magic.

The puma opened his mouth and attempted to draw her scent deeper into his lungs. Now that she had proof of what he was, he wanted to see if, as she stared at him, her chemical reaction to him changed. Was she disgusted by his feline form or curious?

The slight hint of arousal that met the roof of his mouth made him growl.

He wanted to spring across the green, over tables and capture her between his teeth, toss her onto his back and return her to her room at Medical. He didn't like some of the looks the other Pantera males were giving her. They would need to be shown just to whom this new doctor belonged.

But before he could move a paw in her direction, two massive gold cats came bounding up to the table.

North border is secure, Mercier said, his deep voice booming inside Parish's head.

It was how they communicated in their puma form, but only when they were on duty. Rules regarding privacy had been established long ago. A Hunter never spoke or listened in to the thoughts of other Hunters unless they were working.

Parish turned to the other for her report. *Rosalie?*

Her silence instantly drew his concern. *What is it?*

Could be nothing, she said, nodding at a few of the other Hunters who stood nearby. *Could be big game or a few nosy locals, but I picked up traces of human male scent near the east border.*

Parish's gut tightened. *How many?*

Three.

Shit. And right before the hunt. He cut his gaze to Mercier. *Let's go. You, me, Rosalie and Hiss. I want to see what we're dealing with.* He turned to the other five Hunters who had already shifted and were calmly and attentively waiting for their orders. *Split up. Run the west and southern borders. I want every inch scented.*

Parish took off along the water's edge, glancing at Julia as he passed. She was watching him with wide eyes and a stunned expression. He'd wanted to stay with her, get her reaction to his cat firsthand and find out when she could be moved to Natty's house. But it looked as though he'd have to wait until later. In the meantime, she would be protected at Medical, and he would make sure she, and every Pantera in the Wildlands, remained safe from those who might wish them harm.

CHAPTER FIVE

THE three-story Greek Revival house sat on an impressive expanse of lawn, with a small stream a few yards from the front door, and several raised Creole cottages in the distance. On her way there, walking through the Wildlands' village, with Raphael at her side and men and women shifting in and out of their puma states as they went about their day, Julia had pretty much stopped questioning her surroundings, the magic, the shifting creatures, and how such a remote spot so deep within the bayou could be the most incredible oasis she'd ever laid eyes on.

Maybe tomorrow she'd wake up to a different reality, but for now, for tonight, she was living among the Pantera.

"I thought this would suit your needs rather nicely." Miss Nathalie, the proprietor of the boarding house, stood in the doorway of the top floor bedroom, her hands on her hips as she looked around. "But I have two others downstairs that're unoccupied I could show you."

Julia smiled at the tall, pin-thin woman who appeared to be in her early sixties. "It's perfect." And it was. Spacious, yet cozy, the room sported white and pale blue wallpaper and linens, elegant handmade furniture, and a clawfoot bathtub in a small alcove that overlooked a massive oak tree. It was like something out of a magazine. "You have a beautiful home," she told her.

The woman grinned, leaning against the doorframe. "Oldest one in the Wildlands. My great, great grandparents built it...or maybe they conjured it with magic." When she laughed, her pale green eyes sparkled with gold. "Never can be sure."

"I'd believe the magic part." Julia's eyes came to rest on the bed. Queen-sized with dark wood that rose to an intricately carved canopy.

"My children did, too," Miss Nathalie remarked a bit wistfully. "They loved it here, but they're gone now. Livin' on their own. Both of 'em Suits. Diplomatic Faction, like Raphael. Not sure how that happened when their papa and I are Nurturer. But the Shaman always knows."

Julia's attention shifted back to the woman. "The Shaman?"

"Ah, yes. She's been here longer than anybody, even the elders." As her grin widened, the woman looked about twenty years old. "She's magic, she is. Predicted the placement of every Pantera cub born."

How incredible, Julia thought, and yet completely in keeping with the mystery of this secret bayou village. "So you don't decide which Faction you're going to be in, or your child's going to be in?"

"No, Gal. The magic decides. You're born to it. It's already inside you. Been a long time since we've seen the Shaman make a prediction." Her eyes suddenly brightened. "But if you stick around you might see for yourself."

She was speaking of Raphael and Ashe's child. The one Julia had been asked to help bring into the world. The more she learned about the history and complications of the Pantera race, the more interested she became, and the more pressure she felt. She wanted to help them, help Ashe, but frankly, she wasn't sure she had the skills. This child, and Ashe's pregnancy, they would be something she'd never experienced before.

"Glad you're here, Gal," Miss Nathalie said as she moved into the room and headed for the window. "Nice to have a female around."

"You don't get many female boarders?"

"Most who come here are males." She turned, pressed her back to the large pane of glass. "Mates who've been sent away by their females."

Julia laughed. "Really? Why?"

"Got mated too quick, without understanding the way a female works."

Julia felt her cheeks warm. "I see."

Miss Nathalie laughed at her expression. "No, no. Not that way, Gal. Every Pantera male is gifted when it comes to sex. Their animal takes over, knows innately how to please their partner. But with the animal comes a lack of personal skills. Some of our males, even the Nurturers, don't know how to listen, comfort, be a friend to their mates. That's where I come in. And this place. They stay, and I talk to 'em, school 'em until they're ready to go home."

"In other words," came an irritated male snarl near the bedroom door. "She has them neutered and declawed."

Julia's heart lurched into her throat and she turned to see Parish standing in the doorway. She always forgot how tall and broad he was. He looked gorgeous, freshly showered, in jeans and a black T-shirt, his expression wicked. And those eyes, they still glowed with the gold heat of his puma.

Julia couldn't tell herself it wasn't true anymore. She'd seen it with her own eyes. And damn, if it hadn't been the most glorious sight ever.

"Your time'll come, Parish Montreuil," Miss Nathalie said with a soft chuckle. "If you ever meet the right gal, that is."

Parish didn't answer her. He was too busy looking at Julia. His gaze raked down her body, a combination of desire, concern and anger shadowing his expression. "Raphael will feel my fangs for this."

"What are you going on about, Hunter?" Miss Nathalie asked, her teasing, motherly tone dissolving as she sensed his ire.

"Looking after Dr. Cabot here. Guarding her." His eyes cut to Miss Nathalie. "She was moved from Medical without my knowledge or my consent."

"Raphael brought me here," Julia said, not understanding his fierceness. "He didn't say anything about me having a guard."

Parish's gaze ripped back to her and he growled softly. "Well, you do. And it's me."

Julia's heart leapt in her chest and she felt slightly breathless. The way this man looked at her, with the animal behind his eyes, was as worrisome as it was erotic.

"Oh my." Her expression brimming with humor, Miss Nathalie turned to Julia, her eyebrows raised. "What do you say to this, Miss Julia? Shall I kick this self-important feline out of my house, or do you want to accept his care?"

"She has no choice," Parish said quickly, moving into the room, toward her.

No choice? *Oh, he wasn't going to take it there, was he?* He might be the sexiest, most gorgeous man she'd ever known, but no one was going to run Julia Cabot's life but her. Not anymore. Not even in this amazing place where magic actually existed. She glared at him as he approached, and spoke slowly and clearly. "I will always have a choice, Parish Montreuil. Got it?"

Dark brows lifted over blazing gold eyes.

Miss Nathalie chuckled. "I like this human gal."

Parish looked stunned, as though he wasn't used to being scolded or contradicted. He moved past her, his gaze going from the tub to the bed. "You need someone to protect you, Dr. Cabot. A human living among the Pantera, it's asking for trouble."

"Maybe I like trouble," Julia found herself saying. *Maybe I'm even asking for it.*

Parish turned to face her. At first his expression was tight, and Julia thought he was gearing up for another verbal argument. But after moment, his face broke into a broad smile, then he started to laugh. "I think I might like this human gal too, Natty."

"Peas in a pot, I never thought I'd see this day," Miss Nathalie uttered, shaking her head. "Cave-dwelling, arsenic-spewing Parish Montreuil, laughing his fool head off."

"I'll be staying for supper, Natty," Parish said, though his eyes remained fixed on Julia. "So make sure it's a good one."

"It's Miss Nathalie to you, and you'll eat whatever I put in front of you. And you'll like it."

He growled playfully low in his throat, and Julia felt the sound all the way to her toes.

"Growl like that at me again, Feline, and I'll have you peeling potatoes with your canines."

"Can't." Parish reached out suddenly, and took Julia's hand. "I'm taking Miss Julia for a walk." He purposefully gentled his tone. "If she accepts my care, that is."

His hand felt strong and callused in hers, and she had the strangest desire to tighten her grip on him. The warmth of him seeped through the skin of her palm and into her blood. She had to force herself to breathe as she looked up at him. "She accepts. For now."

Miss Nathalie snorted. "Well, be back before the sun goes down." She was on her way out the door when she added, "Supper's at six-thirty sharp."

The minute she was gone, Parish rounded on Julia, pulled her close until they were just a foot apart. His dark eyes flashed with gold as he gazed down at her. "Don't do that to me again, Doc."

Breathing still felt awkward. "What?"

"Leave. Without telling me first."

Heat was pouring off his body. "I didn't. Raphael came—"

"I know," he said quickly. "But I'm asking you, wait for me next time."

The strength and intensity of his gaze was affecting her brain, how it processed. "You were worried?"

His nostrils flared and he growled at her softly. "Out of my mind. Until Ashe told me where you were."

"I'm sorry."

"No." He squeezed her hand. "You have nothing to be sorry about. I know I'm overbearing and blunt and a scarred-up wreck of a male, but I have to protect you." He looked like he wanted to say more, but held himself back.

"Because of the baby," Julia prompted, her breathing still uneven and shallow as she stared up at him.

"It should be because of the baby."

"But it's not."

He shook his head, his gaze fierce with wanting.

Julia's skin prickled and her mouth felt suddenly dry. No one had ever looked at her like this. No one had ever said such words as their eyes filled with deep, vulnerable need. And yet, even with her newfound belief in magic and honorable, sexy, shape-shifting males, the fear of failure, of getting hurt, of what had happened with Gary—with all the Garys in her past—clung tightly to her heart.

"You've got to understand something," she began, "I'm just getting out of a relationship. I don't want to—"

"That wasn't a relationship, Julia." His thumb rubbed her palm gently, but his expression was resolute. "That was a lie told by an arrogant, self-centered piece of shit who had no idea what he had. What he was blessed with." As his gaze roamed her face, his eyes turned completely gold. "If I was lucky enough to be claimed by you, I'd never give you cause to wonder."

Tears formed in Julia's throat. His words, his gaze…the blatant sincerity behind both…this man had the power to change her, her heart and her soul, if she would ever allow it.

"Come, Miss Julia," Parish said, turning and leading her toward the door. "You think what you saw today at midday meal and out your window was beautiful, you haven't seen anything yet."

———

She felt like heaven on his back.

The weight of her, the way her thighs gripped the sides of his body. And her hands, fisting the fur at his nape as he ran the familiar course, weaving in and out of trees with the warm bayou air against his face.

Damn, he could get used to this.

Several feet from the bluff, his puma came to a halt. For one exceptional moment, he looked out over his sacred space and purred as Julia leaned down, wrapped her arms around his neck and squeezed. He'd never brought anyone here. It was the secret hideout he and Keira had spent hours playing in as cubs, then the home Parish had created after she'd left. No…after she'd been murdered. A mile from anything Pantera, anything that wanted to talk, lecture or demand, the caves had been his solace. While the scent of the bayou, the sharpness of the rocks, and even the intensity of the heat had become his family. He'd never needed more than that to feel whole, never craved more.

Until now.

Until her.

Parish allowed Julia a moment to slide off his back, then quickly shifted and walked to the very edge of the bluff. As was his daily custom, he took a visual inventory of each curve of rugged hillside and the caves above, the heavy vegetation that hung from the rocks and dipped gently into the warm water of the bayou pool below. He sensed nothing unusual or threatening, and his muscles relaxed.

"Incredible," Julia said behind him, her tone awestruck.

Glancing over his shoulder, Parish eyed her with just a hint of playful arrogance. "Me or the landscape?"

She smiled. "You within the landscape."

"Thank you for that." He smiled back and reached for her hand. When she instantly curled her fingers around his, his cat purred. Her touch did what nothing else could: comforted him, made him feel something remarkably close to happiness.

Keeping her protectively at his side, Parish led her down the incline to the grassy bank near the pool. The scent of bayou coated the insides of his nostrils, and he breathed it deeper into his lungs.

"I'm not sure of the reason," he said. "But the water here is incredibly warm."

"And clear."

"And remarkably free of critters."

She laughed. "Do you bathe in it?"

He turned. "I do."

Her eyes flashed with sensual interest. "I thought cats weren't supposed to like the water."

"I'm not your typical cat."

"Really?"

He nodded.

"Prove it."

His eyebrows lifted. "You want me to go in the water? Bathe in your presence?"

She pretended to think for a moment, then she smiled. "Yes, I believe I do."

He chuckled. "Fine, but you're going with me."

"What?" A choked giggle erupted from her as he slid one arm around her back and another under her knees. "No. Wait."

He lifted her up and started walking into the water. "Don't struggle, Doc. I might drop you."

"Okay, okay," she said, laughing, kicking her feet. "You called my bluff."

"Never dare a Pantera." He waded farther in.

"Come on, bring me back."

"You want me wet and I want you—"

"Parish!" she cried out in shock.

He stopped, the water swirling around his waist, his entire body tense as he gazed down at her. "What did you call me?"

"Parish," she said, this time with a wave of heat attached to each syllable. She bit her bottom lip, suppressing a giggle.

He lowered his head and lapped at that bottom lip with his tongue. "Oh, Doc," he uttered. "I warned you what would happen the next time you said my name like that."

Her eyes flashed. "Yes, you did."

His mouth closed over hers, hard and hungry, and he groaned with the instant and incredible feel of her soft, wet lips. She could drive him insane with just her scent, her warm breath. He suckled her bottom lip, then nipped it, and when she whispered his name again and pressed herself closer, he thrust his tongue inside her hot mouth and claimed her.

Christ, how did he tell her?

How did he form the words, then release them?

How did he make her understand when he himself barely did? She didn't live in his world or understand how things were when a Pantera male claimed a female.

How could he explain to her that there was no going back? That she belonged to him now.

His hands gripped her thighs and waist as he caressed her tongue with his own, then plunged it deep inside her mouth, over and over until they were both panting. *There. See how much I want you, Julia Cabot. Understand that you are mine.*

Water splashed as she suddenly struggled in his arms, trying to turn, reposition herself. When she faced him, her legs wrapping around his waist and squeezing, Parish growled and caged her ass in his palms as he took her mouth again. *Fuck.* She was wet. And not just from the splash of the warm bayou water around them. He could feel her damp pussy through the fabric of her jeans. It ground against him, calling to his rigid cock, begging to be filled, fed. And he wanted to oblige. He wanted take her, rip her clothes from her body and sink himself balls-deep into her tight, tender flesh.

Just the thought of it made him mad with lust. He'd never wanted anything or anyone like he wanted her. The intensity of his desire almost frightened him.

He ripped his mouth from hers and nuzzled her neck, ran his sharp canines gently across her pounding pulse.

"Parish?" she uttered on a moan.

He lapped at her pulse, wondered what her blood would taste like. "Hmmmm?"

She gasped, pressed her breasts against his chest. "You said this pool was free of critters."

"Mmmmmm...Yes..."

"Then...what's that behind you?"

His mind came awake like a shock of electricity. He drew back from her neck and whirled around, coming face to face with a small alligator. The thing was only about two feet long, but it was packing a set of impressively sharp teeth. Protective of his woman, his puma rose to the surface and growled, flashing the small creature his own set of sharp and deadly hardware. The alligator instantly turned around and swam the other way.

"Damn reptile," Parish grumbled, still gripping Julia's sweet ass as he carried her to shore. His body screamed with need, his cock hard as stone and pulsing. But he wasn't risking another encounter with sharp teeth.

Other than his own.

If she was willing.

His puma purred at the thought. For a second, he wondered about taking her to the caves above, where he lived and slept. But it didn't seem right, didn't feel like the proper place to take the female he intended on claiming as his mate. Not for their first time together, anyway. He had enough cold, hard stone to deal with as it was.

At the bank, he gently eased her to her feet and tried to get his mind to focus on something else, something that would make his cock calm the hell down. But one look her way, one brief trip down her body, had the thing creaming at the tip.

Wet clothes clinging to delectable hips, round succulent breasts and erect nipples.

Fuck.

He grabbed her hand and started up the incline to the bluff. "Sun's going down. We should get back." His tone was nearly a growl. "Natty'll have my hide if I bring you home late for supper."

"Can't have that." The thread of unfulfilled desire in her tone was unmistakable.

Parish cursed inwardly. "Nope."

"You're probably hungry."

You have no idea, Doc.

"Parish?" she said as they reached the top of the hill.

"Yeah."

"Was that magic?"

His head came around, and his eyes met her hers. "What?"

She looked disheveled in the sexiest of ways: pink cheeked, and eyes wide and heavy with lust. "Not the alligator or your shift, but what happened in the pool, between us. Was that magic?"

Parish felt his heart squeeze inside his chest. "No, Doc." He drew her closer. "That was so much more." *That was just the beginning.*

Before he took her right there on the bluff, he shifted back into his puma, then waited for her to climb onto his back and fist his fur. He couldn't wait much longer to have her. When the moon rose and stole the bayou heat, she'd lie beneath him, and she wouldn't just be speaking his name. She'd be screaming it.

His puma roared into the coming eve and he took off into the trees.

CHAPTER SIX

DINNER had been fantastic. Or at least Julia assumed it had. Her plate was clean, she just couldn't remember actually tasting any of it. Ever since she'd returned to the boarding house, all her tongue seemed to want to register was Parish. And if that wasn't bad enough, all her mind wanted to bring forth were images of their incredible time at the bayou pool.

She let out a long breath. She could still feel his arms around her, so tight, so possessive, his mouth working hers with soft kisses, hungry bites and snarls of arousal. She'd known what he'd wanted from her. Not because it was pressed against her belly, inciting the blazing heat inside her sex to liquefy, but because it was exactly the same thing she'd wanted from him.

The deepest, most intensely erotic fuck of her life.

Her body contracted at the thought, and she gripped the table. What would it be like to be touched by him? Her back to the mattress, Parish looming above her, the muscles in his arms and chest and stomach pulled tight under sweat-laced, tanned skin?

"Dr. Cabot?" came a soft male growl.

Julia glanced up from her empty plate and caught Parish staring at her across the dinner table with a mask of sensual ferocity, his black hair loose to his shoulders. He was so sexy. Every inch of his face, from his eyes to the scar near his lips, tempted her, made her mouth water.

His nostrils flared. He glanced left, saw Nathalie chatting it up with one of the other boarders down the table, then returned his gaze to Julia as he leaned forward.

"You have to stop thinking about us or I won't be able to stop myself from throwing you over my shoulder and hauling your sexy ass upstairs to bed."

Julia's mouth dropped open. "How did you know—?"

"Your scent."

My scent? She tilted her head in the direction of Miss Nathalie. "Does she know?"

"Probably."

Oh my god. "I'm so embarrassed."

"Don't be. She knows how I feel about you." He grinned, molten gold flashing in his eyes. "And now she knows that as you're thinking about my tongue in your mouth," his voice dropped, his chin too, "I'm thinking about my tongue somewhere else."

Julia's eyes widened, yet everything below her neck went hot and tight. "Stop that," she whispered.

"Impossible. Your scent makes me insane." His canines lengthened.

"You're not the only one," remarked the male down at the far end of the table beside Nathalie.

Julia turned apple red and cursed, while Parish flashed the male his puma. "Don't even think about it, Mace. In fact, keep your eyes on your plate."

The male grunted. "I'm mated, Hunter."

"Then you remember exactly what's running through my blood right now," Parish said with a deep growl.

Nathalie stared at Parish, but spoke to Julia. "Perhaps you should retire, Miss Julia. Might I suggest a bath?" She sighed. "With soap."

At first, Julia was so consumed with the aggressive banter of the two males at the table she didn't catch the woman's meaning right away. But when she did, she closed her eyes and winced with humiliation. She was turned on thinking about Parish, every damn feline in the room could smell it, and she was being told to get upstairs and wash it off. What the hell ever happened to privacy? She pushed back her chair and scrambled to her feet. Her eyes were drawn to Parish. "Are you staying tonight or…"

"He'll be sleeping on the porch," Miss Nathalie said quickly.

Parish hissed at her. "I will sleep wherever I want, Female."

"Outside?" Julia said. "But—"

"Not to worry, Miss Julia," Nathalie continued. "He's used to it."

"Isn't it time to clean up?" Parish growled softly, his eyes narrowed on the older female.

Miss Nathalie ignored him. "After all, he still sleeps in those caves a mile out, don't you, Parish?"

"Dammit, Natty!" He pushed back his chair and stood.

"What?" she grumbled. "Isn't a secret, now is it?"

Julia turned to him, confused. "You live there? Where we were today?"

He didn't answer. His nostrils were flared with irritation as he continued to glare at Miss Nathalie.

Julia stared at him. Why wouldn't he have told her that? And why was he refusing to look at her? Was he hiding something? Or was it that he just didn't think her important enough to share information about his personal life?

A spark of apprehension moved through her. She hated this feeling, that something was being kept from her. That the man she'd just been fantasizing about, had just kissed like she'd needed it, needed *him*, to breathe, wasn't being honest with her. It gave her a killer sense of déjà vu.

She turned from him and offered Miss Nathalie a small smile. "Good night. Thank you for dinner."

She needed a moment to herself. Needed to really think about what she was doing here, and how long—

As she walked out of the room, she heard Parish growl behind her. "Julia."

"Let her be, Parish," Nathalie scolded.

"Like hell I will."

"You're acting like a jackass."

"No," said Mace. "He's acting like a mated Pantera male."

118

Julia only made it to her bedroom door before Parish was upon her.

———

"I didn't tell you about the caves for a good reason." He followed her inside the blue and white bedroom suite.

"They're all good reasons," she said, heading for the windows.

"I know what you're doing, Doc." He kicked the door closed behind him. "Don't compare me to that lying bastard who cheated on you."

"I'm not."

"Turn around."

She heaved a great sigh and turned to face him. Her cheeks were flushed, her eyes a shocking blue against the pale hair that hung about her face.

"I'm not comparing you to Gary," she said. "There is no comparison. He was a mistake, and you…you're a hope, a dream…magic…" Shadows moved over her eyes. "It just scares me, Parish."

Fear was the last thing he ever wanted her to feel with him. "What scares you?"

"I've never wanted to be with anyone more than I want to be with you." Her voice caught as she spoke, and her eyes brimmed with tears. "I actually ache for you. I think about you every second." She shook her head. "My body responds to your voice like it's your touch. That's not normal."

He hated how upset she was, how fearful she sounded because to him her words were his magic, his potential first step back into life, and a future he never thought he'd see. He crossed the room and pulled her into his arms. "Look at me." One hand raked up her spine to her neck. "That's our normal, Doc. My mind is filled with you, too. Your tears make my fucking heart ache. I don't know what to do with this desperate need I feel for you, except…*this.*" He dropped his head and kissed her, groaning at the raw hunger and blatant need between them. When he pulled back, he found beautiful, stormy blue eyes gazing up at him. "Julia…"

"I love when you say my name," she whispered.

His gut tightened. "I didn't tell you about the caves because I was ashamed."

Her brow furrowed. "What?"

"I know you're aware of what happened to Keira." The damned tortured sound in his voice never went away. "Ashe told me. But what you don't know is that she was my everything, my only family, my best goddamn friend, and when she left, when she was killed I...*fuck*...I went to the one place where I felt closest to her."

"The caves," Julia whispered.

He nodded. "I never left. Never wanted to." He reached up and cupped her chin and cheek in his palm. "Until you."

"Oh, Parish..."

He smiled. "I love it when you say my name too, Doc." He captured her mouth again, kissing her frantically. "I want you." He nipped her lip. "Christ, the scent of your heat. It calls to me, begs me to taste." With one hand around her waist, he easily lifted her. "Let me earn my way into your bed."

"You already have," she said breathlessly.

He tossed her onto the bed, then drew back. "Not even close." He stripped bare, and grinned as her gaze moved hungrily over him. "You know what I am."

Her eyes lifted, connected to his. She nodded.

He growled softly at her. "Then open your legs for me, Julia. This cat must have his cream."

Chapter Seven

JULIA had never been undressed so quickly, so frantically, and with such desperate hunger in her life.

And she loved it.

Her back to the mattress, her legs bent and spread, Julia trembled with heat and desire as she stared up at Parish. Without clothes, he wasn't just sexy—he was stunning. Drool-worthy. His powerful body flexed with every movement, each muscle defined. But it was the long, thick muscle standing hard and proud against the six-pack of abdominal perfection that made her mouth water. What would he feel like in her mouth, taste like against her tongue? She almost reached for him when he knelt, placed his hands under her buttocks and yanked her to the edge of the mattress.

His breath fanned her stomach and hipbones. "I've thought about this ever since we met. How you looked, scented..." He lowered his head and lapped at her. Just once. Julia gasped and arched her back. "How you tasted."

How was it possible that just one swipe of his tongue made every muscle in her body jump? He was magic. There was no other explanation for it. She lifted her head to see what he was doing, and the blood rushed to her sex. Nostrils flared, dark eyes glittering with exotic desire, his gaze was locked between her thighs.

A soft growl came from his throat. "You're so beautiful, Doc. Every inch of you is soaking wet. Your pussy's like a ripe peach, juice running down your leg." Once again, he dropped his head, but this time he ran his tongue up her inner thigh.

Julia nearly came right then. His tongue. It wasn't smooth like a human's. It was slightly rough, like a…

She stared at him.

"Cat," he said with a grin, lapping at just the edges of her sex. "So sweet. Christ, I think I'll drown in you."

The heat building inside her burst into flames. Her ass clenched, her breasts tightened into sensitive buds and she felt her pussy cream right before him.

Parish saw it too and his canines dropped. "My cock's crying for you too, Doc. But first I'm going to fuck you with my tongue." Without another word, he curled his fingers around her knees and spread her wider. He purred, his eyes glowing. "Oh, yes…there it is. Your clit is ripe, Doc. So damn pretty. So pink."

Julia's legs shook, her sex pulsed and ached to be filled, touched, eaten. God, she was going to go out of her mind just from the way he talked. "Please, Parish…" she moaned, letting her head fall back on the mattress.

"Spread yourself for me," he commanded, his breath fanning her wet sex. "Wide. I want my entire mouth on you, my tongue thrusting inside you as my lips suck that plump little clit."

With trembling fingers, Julia moved her hands down her belly, over her hips and into her hair. She gasped at how wet she was, how sensitive.

"Hurry, Doc," he growled with need, his fingers digging gently into her thighs. "I want to taste you before you come, and you're so ready."

His shoulders pushed between her legs, and the minute she spread herself wide, he latched onto her clit, suckling gently as his tongue flicked feather-light. In seconds, she came. Spasming on the mattress, her hips slamming upward, pumping as she moaned. *Dammit. It's too soon. Too fast.*

Just as she was about to lift her head, Parish chuckled against her sex, his hot breath making her writhe. "Now, we can begin." Without another word, he thrust his tongue up into her, and fucked her in slow, rhythmic strokes.

Her hands fisting the bedspread, Julia tried to focus but it was impossible. She was so tense, so heated, her body refusing to come down from the orgasm. It wanted more. It craved more.

He drew back then, eased his tongue out of her and replaced it with two thick fingers. "I feel you around me," he growled, thrusting into her so deeply she felt it at her belly. "You're so wet, suckling my finger."

"Oh, god," she moaned as he started licking her again, using his entire tongue in greedy circles.

Julia didn't know what to do with this feeling. She'd never experienced such mind-numbing pleasure. She wanted him so badly, yet didn't want him to stop licking her or thrusting his fingers inside her.

She released her pussy lips and plowed her fingers through his soft, thick, hair. She scratched at his scalp as he ate her. Instantly, he started to purr, the sound making his lips and tongue vibrate against her. Her eyes slammed open and she gasped in a breath. She was going to come. Again.

"Parish, please," she begged, rocking her hips against his face, her juices pouring out of her, down her thighs. "I want you inside me."

But he wouldn't stop. Hungry and determined, he drank her down, his purr coiling around her aching clit.

The climax that tore through her was raw and shocking. For a moment, she was blind and deaf, all her senses pooling below her waist. She cried out, pumping wildly, barely feeling him draw back and loom over her. She could hardly breathe, and her eyes were as wet as her sex. Nothing could feel better. Nothing.

And then she felt something nudge against her sensitive mound. Instinct blossomed inside of her and she reached out and grasped him. Hot, rock-hard cock filled her hand, and she moaned a hungry, "*Yes*." Up and down, she stroked him until he started to breathe differently, moan, curse, and pump himself off in her palm.

"Inside," he growled. "I need you. I need to be up inside you where it's hot and tight and still shaking from your climax."

She released him, and he entered her with one quick, deep, gasp-inducing thrust. Julia gripped his shoulders, her nails digging into his skin. He felt so right there, so perfect.

"Wrap your legs around me, Doc. I want to ride you."

She groaned, closing her thighs, her heels squeezing his tight ass. For one moment, his eyes met hers and he grinned. Then he started to fuck her, deep and slow, all the way to her womb. Oh, the pleasure. The heat.

"You've claimed my heart, Julia Cabot," he whispered against her mouth as his thrusts quickened. "It's useless to anyone else, but full of life and love and desire for you. I want no one but you."

Oh, god yes. She wanted him, too. But…"I'm scared."

"Of what? Being loved? Taken care of? Respected and desired? Of never having to worry about my devotion, my commitment?" His kissed her, then settled in the curve of her neck. "Pantera mate for life, Julia."

She gasped as he bit her gently.

"Tell me I can claim you."

She moaned.

"Tell me you want not only my cock inside of you, but my mark on your body."

"I want you," she cried out, climax so close she could taste it. "All of you."

He growled harshly, "Mine…all mine," as he scored the skin between her waist and navel with his claws and pounded her deep into the mattress.

Julia came with a jolt and a scream, and as she did, Parish roared out her name, pumping his hot seed into her soaked and sensitive pussy. Freefalling, Julia slapped her arms around him, holding on tight as he continued to come inside of her.

Long minutes passed before he rolled to his side, but when he did, he didn't break their connection. His powerful arms curled her snugly against his chest, where she rested and tried to catch her breath. Tears threatened as she gripped him possessively, almost fearfully. Had he truly marked her? Was that the delicious sting she felt on her abdomen? And if so, what did it mean?

Oh, god…

Parish kissed her hair and whispered, his voice raw with emotion. "Tell me you're going to stay. Here. In the Wildlands with me. I need to hear it."

Her heart squeezed. "I want to."

"But something holds you back. What is it?"

She rubbed her face against his hard pectoral. "I don't know. I have nothing back there, nothing but my cat. But how do I trust my wants and desires when they've always led me into failed misery?"

He tipped her face up to meet his, brushed the hair from her cheek so lovingly she nearly burst into tears. "Perhaps this time you should trust your gut and your instincts. I watched you that day in the hospital. You used them delivering the child, didn't you?"

Her breath caught in her throat. He'd been watching her? "Yes."

He smiled. "You have Pantera in you, I think. When I looked at you for the first time I felt need and desire unlike anything I'd ever felt. But you were human, and I was lost in anger and grief. It was my gut and my instinct that told me we belonged together."

Stunned, Julia just stared at him. She'd never heard such a thing. No man had ever talked to her like this, told her to trust herself and her instincts. What more was she looking for? A sign? Christ, she had magic.

Exhaustion overtook her thoughts and she cuddled in close to Parish as he kissed her hair and stroked her back until she fell asleep.

CHAPTER EIGHT

JULIA woke to a strange, yet familiar sound.

The emerging light of dawn filtered into the room, casting shadows on the walls and floor. Beneath the covers she was warm, but instinctively she knew that Parish was gone. The hunt. He would need to prepare before dawn.

Meeeoooowww.

Julia's head jerked around to where Parish had lain on his side, holding her, still connected to her as he soothed her to sleep. He was gone, but something else was curled atop his pillow. Julia screeched with joy, and threw off her blanket. How had he managed it? And when?

Rousing from his own sleep, gazing at her with narrowed yellow eyes, was Fangs.

"How the hell did you get here?" she asked the cat, reaching out and scooping him up, cuddling him to her chest.

He immediately balked at the closeness, clawing and mewling until she let him down. When his paws hit the sheets, he took off toward the headboard, leapt onto the edge and remained there, perfectly balanced on all four feet.

That's when Julia noticed the note, taped to the wood.

He didn't come quietly. At least until he realized who I was bringing him to.

Fangs is here, Doc.
Now you must stay.
Forever.
I will look for you at the hunt.
Parish

Julia stared at the note for long seconds, then glanced down at her belly, her naked flesh, scored with four silvery claw marks. She ran her fingers over the smooth, healed tattoo. He'd truly marked her as his, and given her his heart in both action and deed. The night before she'd thought about and rejected the idea of a sign. Parish didn't have to prove anything to her. She knew that now. And yet…he'd gone to New Orleans sometime in the night while she slept. Broke into Gary's house, and retrieved the only thing she valued outside the Wildlands.

No, this wasn't a sign.

It was love and caring and listening and hoping. It was everything she'd ever wanted, ever wished for.

She gave Fangs a quick rub under his chin, jumped out of bed and headed for the shower.

———

"I've never seen you wound so tight," Bayon remarked, his puma shifting in and out of his leaf-green gaze as he readied for the hunt.

"I'm fine," Parish uttered, his eyes cutting from one entry point to the other.

Where was she?

Raphael had promised to bring Julia early. Didn't the Suit understand how desperately Parish needed to see his woman, scent her? Christ, he wanted her to see him hunt, recognize that he was a worthy male—that he could provide for her, always protect her.

"Rosalie asked if you were going to the swim afterwards." Bayon eyed him curiously. "She's invited the two new apprentices. One of the females is a redhead, both in and out of shift." He grinned broadly. "What do you say? I'd be happy to share."

Washing the blood from their skin in the bayou was always done after a hunt, but playing with females held absolutely no interest for him. He started to pace back and forth over the cold ground. "I'm going to my Julia."

"*Your* Julia?" Bayon repeated. "Since when does she belong to you?"

"I've marked her. She's mine, my family now."

Bayon didn't say anything at first. Parish's second-in-command was undeniably one of the top Hunters in the Faction, but to him females were for play and pleasure, and commitment was to be avoided. Which made his thoughtful, almost gentle gaze pretty damned significant.

"It's good to see," Bayon said finally, as the dawn broke around them and Hunters stalked about in the open field near the shore of the bayou. "You know Keira and I never saw eye to eye—"

"You hated her, and she hated you," Parish said with a quick grin.

A grin Bayon picked up and held. "Yeah, well. She was a hardass, unforgiving, forgot she was a female most of the time, and probably the best goddamn Hunter I've ever witnessed. No offense."

"None taken."

"But when she…" Bayon stared at the ground, shook his head. "I thought you died that day too, brother."

"Yeah," Parish uttered, his own gaze running the landscape. "Well, maybe I did." *Until her. Julia.*

He needed her. He needed her *here*. Had she gotten his note? His gift?

Christ, he could still taste her. All he could think about was being inside her.

Her body.

Her heart.

Then he caught sight of Ashe and Raphael, walking through the trees. His heart pounded in his chest. Right beside them was Julia. Beautiful, desirable, fearful Julia. For a moment it was as if time stood still. He stared at her over the expanse of vegetation, willing her to look at him, and when she did, when her eyes met and held his, he released the breath inside his lungs.

When Ashe and Raphael stopped to speak with a group of Suits, Julia continued forward. Her face split into a wide grin as she jumped up on a rock and raised something above her head. It took Parish a moment to understand what it was. White and thin. Paper.

His note.

The one he'd taped to her headboard just a few hours ago. And there was something written over his words in big, bold red marker. His heart started to pump loudly, heavily in his chest. Was she refusing him? Was she returning to the outside world with her cat, and the heart he'd claimed last night? He narrowed his eyes to read:

CAN WE BUILD OUR HOUSE NEAR THE BAYOU POOL?

Parish would never be able to explain the overwhelming relief and intensity of feeling that surged through him in that moment, but his puma did. Even in his male form, the cat could not be reigned in. It broke from Parish's throat, roaring loudly and clearly and happily into the early morning air as its master ran at her. *Mine*, it screamed. *Mine*, Parish agreed as he jumped upon the rock beside her and pulled her into his arms.

"Welcome home, Doc."

"Thank you." She nipped at his lower lip and grinned. "For everything. Fangs, the magic, for being you. I feel so…"

"Loved?"

Her eyes filled with tears, and she wrapped her arms around his neck and squeezed. "Yes."

Parish growled and nuzzled her neck and felt as if his heart would explode from wanting. He had love and family, and he would never allow anything or anyone to take it from him again.

"Where's my gorgeous puma?" she asked, drawing back, her blue eyes bright.

He growled again, soft and sensual. "I got your puma right here, Doc." He stepped back, grinned, and in a plume of silver mist, he shifted. He roared into the cool, dawn air, then turned on the rock and called out to everyone present, "I've caught the prey of a lifetime, Pantera, but she has come to see a hunt, and we will give it to her!"

Silver mist coated the air around them as they floated down the bayou with the rest of the Pantera spectators. Along with Ashe and Raphael, Julia and two other Pantera, one female and one male, sat within the low-bottomed boat, following the pack of puma Hunters as they raced down river. The strange, six-foot long skiff had no motor, but it was definitely moving through the water as if it did.

Animal or magic? Julia wasn't sure she wanted to know.

"It's the best way to watch the hunt," Raphael remarked, pointing to the gold and black cats breaking through the trees, stopping momentarily, nostrils flaring, mouths open, trying to catch a scent before taking off once again.

Parish's roar after he'd read her note still echoed through Julia's mind and body. She'd hoped he'd have that kind of reaction, and she couldn't wait to curl up against him later and show him just how happy he made her, and how deeply touched she felt about Fangs.

A loud, feral squeal tore through the mist then, and ripped Julia from her thoughts. What was it? she wondered. The prey they sought? Or an injury to one of the Hunters, perhaps?

She felt equal pangs of curiosity and horror, but along with everyone else on the boat, she lifted her chin and narrowed her eyes on the bank. At first she saw nothing but green, stands of trees and moving fur. She heard growling, followed by another squeal, then a cut off feral scream.

She turned to Raphael, so did Ashe.

"That was quick. Parish is fired up." Raphael grinned at his woman. "My cub will have bacon tonight."

Ashe turned slightly pale. "Oh, jeez. Not a visual that's working for me right now, my love."

"Sorry, *ma chère*. I promise, no more details—"

"Look!" cried the female beside Julia. "They're coming."

"Maybe you want to keep your eyes closed, my love," Raphael said gently as the boat slowed, then stopped.

Turning from Ashe, Julia scrambled to her knees. Her gaze shot to the bank. She combed the water's edge until—*There.* She watched as the group emerged from behind a stand of cypress. Julia's heart jumped into her throat and she grinned. Out in front strode Parish's slate gray puma. Broad and fearsome, he searched each boat with his golden gaze. When he spotted her, his cat grinned with pride, blood covering its muzzle and teeth.

Julia beamed, waved at him. She'd never felt so proud, so possessive. That was her puma. The Hunter, the protector.

But her giddiness came to an abrupt halt when the boat jerked violently and she was tossed backwards onto the metal floor. Pain slammed into her elbow, and she saw the male Pantera passenger fall into the water, followed by something else. Her vision blurred and she felt slightly nauseous. All she could think was that they'd hit something, a rock or a tree. The wind was knocked from her lungs, and as she tried to capture breath, she heard Parish's roar ringing in her ears, then Raphael's cry.

Cry? Why was he crying?

She tried to push herself into a sitting position. Her elbow stung and stars swam before her eyes, but at least air was coming in and going out. She heard Raphael again. Then a female Pantera. They were screaming, roaring. But who were they screaming—

Ashe.

Oh, god…they were screaming for Ashe.

The boat rocked and jerked, and Julia heard a loud splash to her right, then water hit her face. She gasped as sound rushed her from all sides. Everyone was screaming, calling out for Ashe.

"The bastard took her over the side with him!" someone yelled.

"Who was it?" said another. "What Faction?"

"I think he's Nurturer."

Julia blinked several times, trying like hell to get her bearings. *What the hell was happening?* Her vision cleared just as Raphael roared from somewhere in the water, "He's swimming toward the other bank! We're close to the border! Go! Fuck! Go after him. I have Ashe."

Fully alert now, her heart slamming against her ribs, Julia scooted over to the edge of the boat. The water and the bank were complete chaos. Pantera were everywhere. She scanned the water for Raphael and Ashe. When she spotted them, her heart stopped. Raphael was swimming madly toward shore, Ashe tucked against him on her back. Julia could see the woman's face clearly in the burgeoning light of day. She looked cold and pale and quiet.

Without thinking, Julia dove into the water and swam hell-bent for shore. Once there, she scrambled to her feet and ran, neither noticing her aching lungs or how dripping wet and cold she was. She needed to get to Ashe, to her patient.

Pantera crowded around Raphael and his mate, but Julia pushed her way through. She slid to her knees beside Ashe, put her face near the woman's mouth and assessed her breathing.

"She's bleeding."

Julia glanced up.

It was Raphael. He stared at Julia, horror-struck, terrified beyond measure. "The baby."

Chapter Nine

PARISH had lost the piece of shit right as he'd crossed the border of the Wildlands.

Poof. Gone.

The instant his traitorous feet had touched down on human soil.

Parish had no idea how such a thing could be possible, or how a traitor had lived among them without detection. Because that was exactly what the bastard was. Ashe was Raphael's mate, which made her and her child Pantera. And when you attack within your clan you're a goddamn, good-for-nothing-but-gator-bait traitor.

But Parish and his Hunters were going to find him. In fact, every Hunter he had was patrolling the border at this very moment. Except Bayon. The male was tight with Raphael, and had insisted on staying by his side at Medical. If anyone could keep Raphael from knocking down the door to Ashe's room, it was Bayon. Julia had made both Bayon and Parish promise to keep Raphael out until she knew what was going on. But it was becoming a nearly impossible task. Understandably, the Suit was losing it. He looked feral, terrified as shit, pacing and cursing and swearing that once he knew Ashe was all right he was going to find and disembowel the one who'd dared to hurt his woman and child.

It had been one hour since they'd arrived, since Julia and several other Pantera doctors had whisked Ashe away. Parish was so proud of his female. He'd never seen hands that worked so quickly, eyes that saw everything, a mind so clear and strong.

"Julia will have news soon," he told Raphael, who looked as though he wasn't even aware of Parish's presence.

"She's a good doctor," Bayon added, his gaze on Raphael even though he was speaking to Parish. "We're lucky in that, as are you, Parish. She's going to make you a fine mate."

It was news to Raphael, but he didn't acknowledge it. He was pacing, hissing, cursing at nothing but his thoughts.

"You must go to the Elders," Bayon continued. "I'd like to see their face when they hear another Pantera has taken a human as his mate." His eyes once again cut to Raphael. He was trying to pull the male back into reality. "Where will you live?"

Parish eyed the other Hunter, nodded. "Not in my cave. Can't have a female and child there."

"Child?" Raphael stopped in his tracks. "She's not pregnant?"

Bayon released a breath, cursed.

"Not yet," Parish told him. "But if you can make cubs with your human, so can I. For now, we'll take a house close to town, and to Medical."

The door behind Parish opened then, and Julia, along with three Pantera doctors, emerged. Her thoughtful blue eyes flickered momentarily to Parish, then quickly focused on Raphael.

"First, let me say, the baby's perfect. All vital signs are normal; heartbeat, fluid within the—"

"Ashe?" Raphael demanded, his expression terrified as he rushed toward her. "Is she all right? Tell me!"

"Easy," Parish said, holding the male's shoulder.

"She's okay," Julia said quickly. "Stable, and her vital signs are good."

Raphael seemed dumbstruck, his breathing shallow. Parish had never seen a male react this way, and yet he knew that if it were Julia inside that room, he'd be acting the same way. Maybe worse.

"Do you know what happened?" Bayon asked her.

"As far as I can tell, she was injected with something."

Raphael growled, his canines dropping. Parish and Bayon drew nearer to him as calm, cool Dr. Julia Cabot explained, "I believe whoever did this was aiming for her uterus—"

"The child?" Parish uttered, slightly stunned. The attack was not on Ashe. It was on the baby.

Raphael hissed. "I will bleed that bastard out so slowly and painfully he will beg me for death."

Julia swallowed, her face tight. "Ashe must've deflected somehow, and under the water. She's already an amazing mother. The needle didn't puncture anything vital."

"I need to see her," Raphael said, advancing on her. "I need to see my Ashe."

Julia blocked the door, her eyes down.

"What is your woman doing, Parish?" Raphael said with a terrifying growl.

One Parish matched with his own. "Stop and listen, Raphael."

"I know this is hard," Julia said, taking a deep breath, then letting it out. "As I said, she's physically well, healing properly, and all her vitals are stabilized." She glanced at the Pantera doctor to her right.

The male Nurturer stepped forward. "I have only seen this once in our lifetime, brother. But whatever your woman was injected with… well, it has made her…" He paused.

"What!" Raphael roared.

"Unstable," the male finished. "Dark magic now runs through Ashe's bloodstream." He locked eyes with Raphael. "Something is trying to possess her."

BAYON

BY
ALEXANDRA IVY

THE LEGEND OF OPELA
AND SHAKPI

Deep beneath the bayou, Shakpi stirred in the darkness of her prison. For centuries she'd been trapped beneath the choking layers of magic. Her sister, Opela's, last gift to her beloved Pantera.

Ancient fury surged through her, sending out shockwaves that shook the land above her. It was all the fault of those damned cats.

In the beginning, it was just her and Opela. Twin sisters born of magic, meant to rule the world. They had done everything together, never needing anyone else.

Then Opela became obsessed with her desire for children. She'd claimed that there was no point of existence if she couldn't possess creatures to love. Without thought for anyone but herself, Opela created a new race, the Pantera, to call her children.

Shakpi had done everything in her power to stop her sister. They'd had each other. Why did they need anyone else? But Opela had refused to listen to her pleas, instead lavishing her love and devotion on her Pantera.

Consumed with envy, Shakpi had plotted to kill the freaks of nature. Mortal creatures weren't meant to be blessed with Opela's magic. Or given the ability to shift into puma form. They were an abomination that had to be destroyed.

She'd been confident that her sister would understand her desire to return to the life they'd had before. A time when they'd both been happy. Together.

Born to destroy, Shakpi was unable to create her own children to act as instruments of her revenge. Instead she infected humans with her malevolent toxin, giving them the power to spread it among the bayou, destroying the magic that gave the Pantera their power.

How could she possibly have suspected her sister would make the ultimate sacrifice? That Opela would use her life-force to entrap Shakpi in this tomb to save her children?

But the bitch had underestimated Shakpi.

After centuries of being locked in stasis, her tentacles were at last reaching beyond her prison, touching the weak, the desperate, and the greedy.

Her infection was spreading and this time nothing would stop her from destroying her enemies…

Chapter One

The Wildlands deep in the bayous of Louisiana would never be considered a place of peace.

The magical land of the Pantera was filled with puma shape shifters who had all the aggression of their animal nature plus the usual volatile emotions of their human nature. It was a combination that encouraged plenty of passion and conflict. Which meant that more than a little blood had been shed over the centuries.

But never before had there been enemies capable of slipping past the Wildlands' borders to directly attack the Pantera.

The shockwaves were still rippling through the gathered Pantera as Bayon raced to the edge of their territory. He couldn't help Raphael, who remained with his pregnant mate, Ashe. He had no talent for healing or for combating the mystic evil that was trying to destroy the babe she carried.

Bayon was a Hunter. A tall, golden haired man with eyes that fluctuated from leaf green to deep gold when he was aroused, and the solid muscles of a warrior. His talent was tracking down the bastards who dared to come into his homeland, and destroying them.

Well, first he intended to torture them. Slowly. Painfully. He needed to know who they were and if they were actually disciples of Shakpi, the Pantera's ancient enemy.

First, however, he had to complete his current mission for Raphael.

He slowed his blinding speed as he neared the private house that was practically hidden among the weeping willows.

Most Pantera preferred to live in the main community with their various factions. There were the Diplomats who dealt with all things political, including their network of spies, as well as the Geeks who performed their magic with computers. There were the Nurturers who had built one of the world's finest medical facilities as they searched for the reason the Pantera had lost the ability to procreate. There were the elders who were the ultimate rulers of the magical race of puma shifters, and their spiritual leaders.

And then there were the Hunters.

The warriors who protected their people with a ruthless efficiency.

There were, however, a few Pantera who sought isolation.

Parish, the leader of the Hunters, had lived in the caves at the far side of the Wildlands after his sister had been killed by humans. Everyone had understood his need to mourn in private.

Bayon didn't know what had driven Jean-Baptiste, one of their finest Healers, to shut himself off from his family and live so far from everyone else, and he had no intention of asking. Pantera might live as a tight-knit community, but that only meant they had to have firm boundaries when it came to privacy. Shoving your nose in someone's business was a good way to get it snapped off.

Vaulting onto the wraparound porch of Jean-Baptiste's cabin, Bayon slammed his fist against the heavy wooden door, frowning when no one answered.

Dammit. He knew Jean-Baptiste was inside.

So why the hell was he ignoring him?

"Jean-Baptiste," he growled, his voice edged with impatience. He didn't have time for this shit. "I know you're in there. Open the fucking door."

A string of ugly curses reverberated through the cabin before the door was yanked open to reveal a six foot plus, male Pantera with dark brown hair that hit below his jawline, and eyes a peculiar shade of amber. He was dressed like Bayon in faded jeans and shit-kickers with a white T-shirt pulled over his leanly muscled torso. But unlike Bayon, he was wearing a heavy leather jacket that covered the numerous tats that Bayon had only glimpsed from a distance. Oh, and he had the sort of piercings that made him look like he should be in a motorcycle gang, not walking the halls of a hospital.

"What the hell?" Jean-Baptiste snarled.

"You're needed."

The amber eyes narrowed. "Why?"

Bayon's hands clenched, the raw fury still pulsing through him. "Raphael's mate was attacked."

It was obvious the news hadn't yet reached the Healer. "Where?"

"Here. In the Wildlands."

Jean-Baptiste jerked in shock at Bayon's blunt explanation, the air prickling with his angry disbelief.

"Impossible."

Jean-Baptiste was right. It should have been impossible.

Which only pissed off Bayon more.

"Yeah well, tell her that," he said.

There was a long silence as Jean-Baptiste struggled to wrap his brain around the unprecedented event.

"When did it happen?"

"During the hunt."

Stepping onto the porch, Jean-Baptiste paced the wooden planks with a grim expression, his thoughts obviously dark.

"Who would dare to enter the Wildlands?"

Bayon peeled back his lips, revealing his elongated canines. "That's what I intend to find out. But first, Raphael wants you at the infirmary."

Jean-Baptiste came to a sharp halt, his jaw clenched. "In case it escaped your notice, *mon ami*, I'm not on duty."

"Too bad," Bayon said, in no mood to tiptoe around his friend's feelings. Whatever shit was going on with this male was going to have to be put on the back-fucking-burner. Nothing was more important than saving Ashe and her baby. "You're needed."

The amber eyes glowed with the power of his cat. "No."

Bayon stepped forward, one of the few not afraid to get into this male's grill. "Look, I don't know what bug crawled up your ass—"

"There are other healers who are better suited to treat a human," Jean-Baptiste snapped.

Bayon refused to back down. "Raphael doesn't want your healing abilities."

His companion stilled. "Then what?"

"They sense something is trying to possess Ashe. Or the baby," he revealed. "They need you to travel to New Orleans to find a gris-gris to hold off the evil until we can determine the source of the attack."

"Shit." With a grimace, the Healer shoved a hand through his hair, knowing this wasn't a duty he could decline. Their very future might depend on saving the babe. "Tell him I'll—"

"You tell him. I'm a Hunter, not a damned messenger," Bayon growled, already heading toward the edge of the porch and leaping over the thicket of yellow cow lily.

By the time he touched the ground he'd already shifted into his cat form, the surge of magic jolting through him with heart-pounding pleasure.

His roar echoed through the thick, humid air. *Mère de dieu.* There was nothing as intoxicating as releasing his animal to hunt. His lips stretched over his massive teeth, as his cat reminded him there was one thing more intoxicating.

Hot, balls-deep sex that made a woman scream with pleasure.

No. Not just a woman.

The *right* woman.

Something denied to him for far too long.

With an impatient shake of his head, he dismissed the painful thought. Now wasn't the time.

Running lightly over the marshy ground, he used his acute senses to search for any trace of the intruders, finding nothing until he reached the narrow river where Ashe had been attacked. He growled low in his throat as he caught the sour scent of the intruders and followed the stench to the edge of their territory.

The intruders had either been the luckiest bastards in the world to have entered the Wildlands and stumbled across the very person they wanted to kill—or they had a way to track her.

Magic? Or a more mundane human technology?

He made a mental note to have Ashe searched for a tracking device small enough to have been hidden beneath her skin. Raphael said she'd been to a doctor just before the strangers tried to attack her the first time.

The medic could easily have tagged her without her knowing.

Sensing Parish's approach, Bayon reluctantly returned to his human form, straightening to watch the glossy slate gray cat prowl forward. With a shimmer of magic, Parish shifted to human form revealing a man over six feet tall with broad shoulders and long, inky black hair. His face was angular, speaking of a predatory nature emphasized by the two healed scars near his right ear and mouth.

"They crossed here," Parish snarled, looking more feral than usual. Together they studied the opening between the cypress trees where the attackers had entered the Wildlands. "Goddammit. I should have done a more thorough search. We have sensed a growing danger for years."

Bayon shook his head. The leader of the Hunters was as hard on himself as he was on his warriors.

Harder.

Parish had never quite forgiven himself for his sister's death.

Maybe now that he'd finally mated he could find some peace.

"Yes, sensed, but we had no tangible proof until recently," Bayon pointed out. "There's nothing we could have done, Parish."

"I cannot change the past, but I can the future." Parish jerked his head toward two large pumas who slid silently through the tangled foliage. "The guards will be doubled until further notice."

Bayon squatted down, absorbing the sour scent of the intruders. It made the hair stand up on his nape.

"How did they get through the magic?" Bayon demanded.

"That is what you will discover."

It was, indeed. Bayon had no intention of returning until he had some answers. "I'll need my weapons."

Parish nodded. "Do you want to take backup with you? I can send Talon."

Bayon narrowed his eyes. "Are you trying to piss me off?"

"We cannot judge the level of danger," Parish reminded him, his features carved from granite. "If this is truly the work of the ancient evil we fear, we cannot afford for anyone to take chances."

Bayon shuddered.

All Pantera grew up with the legend of the twin sisters who created the Wildlands. Opela was the ultimate mother of the Pantera, while her sister, Shakpi, had grown jealous of Opela's love for her children and tried to destroy the Pantera by using human disciples who'd been twisted by her evil. Eventually, Opela had no choice but to imprison her sister.

Was it possible that Shakpi was actually still alive? That she was trying to break out of her mystical prison? Perhaps even touching the world with her evil?

His thoughts shied from the possibility. He had to focus on finding the bastards responsible for hurting Ashe and her baby.

He'd leave the potential threat of a malevolent goddess seeking revenge in the hands of the elders.

"I won't take any chances," he muttered, raising his hands as Parish eyeballed him with a stern expression. "I swear."

"Fine. Keep in contact."

"Aye, aye, Captain." Bayon turned to head back to the rooms he shared with his fellow Hunters, but before he could take off, Parish was standing in front of him.

"Bayon."

"What?"

"I know you enjoy testing the limits of my patience by doing your own thing," the Pantera warned. "If I do not hear from you I will come hunting your ass."

"I'll call." Bayon rolled his eyes. "Cross my heart and hope to die."

Keira didn't know how long she'd been locked in the cage hidden in the suffocating attic.

In the beginning of her captivity, she'd used a rock to scratch the passing days on the floor. She'd needed some way to maintain her sanity.

But the days became weeks, and then months, and then endless years, making it impossible to keep track of the time that was slipping away from her.

She knew this wasn't her first prison. She had a vague memory of waking up surrounded by gray cement blocks that had held her beneath the ground. After that had been a cramped space that she'd assumed was a storage shed, followed by a root cellar that had smelled of damp earth and rotting potatoes.

There were others, but her memories were so muddled she couldn't sort through them.

They were like her. Broken. Fractured. Some of them shattered beyond repair.

Most days she knew her name. Keira. Keira Montreuil. She repeated it over and over, desperate to cling to her previous life.

And she knew she was a Pantera, despite the fact that she couldn't reach her cat no matter how desperately she tried.

But beyond that, her world was a blur punctuated only by occasional visits by her captors to bring her food.

And speaking of the devil…

She smelled him before he ever climbed the steps to the attic.

The rank, sour stench that assaulted her senses and made her gag in disgust.

With an effort she forced herself to her feet. She felt constantly lethargic, no matter how much she ate or rested, convincing her that she was somehow being weakened. Her guess would be the metal collar she wore around her neck. Her captors used it to send an electrical jolt through her when they wanted to punish her. But she suspected there was something in the composition of the collar that kept her debilitated.

How else could they keep her trapped?

A cage, no matter how well-built, would never hold her prisoner. Not if she was at her full strength.

And it wasn't as if the attic could contain her.

The window that overlooked a small backyard was narrow, but she could easily squirm through it. And if nothing else, she could climb onto the stack of dusty boxes in the corner to bust through the rotting timbers of the roof.

But she wasn't at her full strength.

That had been stolen from her, just as the comfort of her cat had been stolen.

And it didn't matter if it was the result of the metal collar or poison or some magical curse. The end result was that she felt so exposed and embarrassingly vulnerable she wanted to curl in a corner and hide.

Instead, she was standing in the center of the cell when a human male crossed the warped floorboards and shoved a tray of mush that passed as food through a small slot in the door. Keira grimly moved to catch the tray before it fell. The shit tasted bad enough without having to eat it off the floor.

The man smirked, his brown hair greasy and his narrow face in need of a shave. He wore jeans and a flannel shirt that always looked like it needed to be washed. There was a cunning intelligence, however, in the mud-brown eyes and a sadistic hunger in his gaze as it slid slowly down her slender body.

Thanks to the old-fashioned cheval mirror in one corner of the attic she knew precisely what he was seeing. Sleek black hair that was pulled into a braid hung halfway down her back. Eyes that looked a dull yellow. Delicately carved features. Skin that was pale from a lack of sunlight. And a sleek, too-thin body that was covered by a pair of spandex exercise pants and matching sports bra.

"How's my pretty kitty today?" the man taunted. She didn't know his name. Why would she? He was just one of a long line of tormentors she'd endured. But she'd privately named him the 'Ferret'. "Are you ready to purr for daddy?"

Setting the tray on the narrow cot that was the only furniture in the cell beyond the small TV, she turned back to the man with a mocking smile. She didn't know why she found it so important to remain defiant in front of her guards. She was trapped like a rat.

Helpless. Abandoned. And closer to the edge of insanity with every passing day.

What was the point?

But some stubborn, rebellious part of her refused to accept defeat. She would spit in the face of fate until the madness consumed her.

"Come and get it, fucker," she taunted.

He deliberately licked his lips. "Someday."

It was a constant threat, but so far the guards hadn't sexually attacked her.

Not yet.

Keira didn't know why they hadn't. They'd humiliated, shamed, and taunted her in every other way. But if sexual assault was coming, she desperately hoped her luck held until she was too insane to know what was happening.

"Yeah, and someday I'll rip your heart out and eat it with special sauce on a sesame seed bun," she retorted.

"Naughty kitty." The bastard touched the band strapped around his wrist, sending a jolt of electricity through the collar around Keira's neck. She hissed, her heart missing a painful beat. "But don't worry. You won't be in your cage for much longer."

Keira frowned. "Why?"

"The word has started to filter down the ranks. Our time is finally here."

"Your time? You sound like a cheesy super villain."

The Ferret stepped forward, his eyes glittering with a fevered lust. "You won't be nearly so funny when we don't need you anymore. I'm going to fuck you to death."

She kept her smile in place even as a sick dread clenched her gut. There was a smug cockiness in his voice that warned her it wasn't yet another empty bluff.

He was truly confident he was soon going to get his hands on her.

Shit. Shit. Shit.

"With that miniscule dick?" She tilted her chin, refusing to let him see her fear. "If I'm going to be screwed, at least send a man to do it."

"You bitch."

He pressed his finger onto the switch that sent the electrical pulses out of the collar. But this time he continued to hold it down, sending jolt after jolt through her body. Keira's teeth ground together as she fell to her knees. Holy shit. She'd gone too far. The bastard was going to kill her.

Her head was bowed and her mind going dark when the sound of a male voice floated from the doorway at the bottom of the stairs.

"Roger."

Roger? Her lips twisted despite the agony searing through her rigid muscles. His name was Roger?

Ferret fit him better.

Abruptly the pain stopped as the Ferret muttered a curse. "What?"

"Meeting."

"Another one?" the Ferret shouted. "What the hell is this one about?"

"I didn't call it," his companion groused. "We leave in ten minutes."

The Ferret moved to stand near the bars of Keira's cell, his stench only adding to her misery.

"Maybe it's good news. Maybe we're going public and I can finally have you flat on your back where you belong."

With a laugh, he turned and left the attic, allowing Keira to take a deep, cleansing breath as she struggled to clear the fog from her mind.

"Be careful what you wish for, asshole," she muttered, pressing her fingers to her temples that throbbed from the massive amount of electricity that had scorched through her.

Remaining on her knees she waited for the nausea to pass, surviving the time by picturing the various ways she could kill the Ferret if he was stupid enough to unlock her cell.

Snapping his neck would be the most efficient, but it was far too clean a death for the loathsome creature. She wanted something slow. Something that would cause maximum pain.

An hour passed. Then two. Darkness slowly filled the attic as she wearily curled into a tiny ball on the floor. Later she would try to choke down the sludge they called food. For now, she was alone with no need to act brave.

"Keira. My name is Keira," she murmured. "I'm strong. I'm brave. And those bastards aren't going to break me."

Softly chanting the words over and over, Keira nearly missed the faint sound of footsteps that crept up the stairs. She frowned, a strange fear clenching her heart. Those steps were too light, too graceful for a mere human.

What was coming?

She remained curled on the floor, lost in the shadows as she glanced warily through the gathering gloom.

A large, male form appeared, but with obvious caution, he circled the entire room, searching for hidden enemies before at last turning his attention to the cage in the center of the floor.

Only then did he suck in a horrified breath as he caught sight of her cowering form.

"What the hell?"

The man stepped forward and Keira's heart missed a beat as she took in his golden male beauty. He disturbed her. Not like the ferret-man. Or his various human partners. This was…different. Somehow more personal.

"Is this a trick?" he breathed.

She scowled. "I don't understand what you're asking."

"You're dead."

His stark words sliced through the muddle in her mind. She blinked, struggling to process them. Dead. Bizarrely, the thought didn't frighten her.

Actually, it explained so much.

"So this is hell?" She gave a short, near hysterical laugh. "I hope I earned a spot here by partying my ass off. *Laissez les bons temps rouler.*"

There was a short, nerve-scraping silence before a soft word floated on the air.

"Keira?"

A startled hiss was wrenched from her throat. Her name. It was the one thing that she'd been able to cling to from her past. It had kept her grounded when her captors did everything in their power to crush her will. Or when her mind threatened to become lost in the dark depths of despair.

And through it all she'd kept it protected.

No one knew that secret, precious name.

No one but her.

"Don't," she breathed, her voice humiliatingly weak. "That's mine. Only mine."

"Holy shit." The man took another step forward. "Is it really you?"

Keira scrambled backward, her defiance forgotten as she caught the warm, male scent. Pantera. He was like her.

"Who are you?" she rasped.

With a graceful leap, he was standing directly in front of the cell door, his beautiful leaf green eyes serrated with gold, glowing with a stunned joy.

"Oh my god."

"No." She held up a hand, her heart racing. She didn't know what was bothering her. On some level she knew she should be fiercely relieved. This man was one of her people. But there was a part of her that was terrified by his scent. "Stay back."

He frowned, watching her with a searching gaze. "Keira, it's me. Bayon."

Bayon. She silently tested the name. It was...familiar. *He* was familiar.

But the confusion in her mind was too tangled to pull out the memory.

"Stay back," she repeated, her voice harsh. She didn't understand what was happening, and that was as terrifying as any torture.

"Is it a trap?" He tilted his head to the side, sniffing the air. "Keira, honey, will I trigger an alarm?"

She shook her head, her mouth dry. "You have to go."

He studied her pale, frightened expression, then without warning he grabbed the bars and ripped the door off the cell.

Keira vaulted onto the cot, her palm pressed to her thundering heart as he ruthlessly moved toward her. He reached out a hand, but rather than grabbing her as she half expected, he ran his fingers over the collar around her neck.

With a hiss he yanked his hand from the metal.

"Shit. There's something toxic in the metal." He gave a shake of his head. "I have to find a key. I'll be back."

She watched in silence as he ran lightly back down the stairs, leaving her alone.

Mutely she studied the mangled door of her cell, a voice in the back of her head urging her to make a run for it. She could slip out one of the windows, drop from the roof and take off down the road before the…before Bayon ever realized she was gone.

Her limbs, however, refused to move. They felt as if they'd been locked into place by a compulsion she couldn't understand.

Instead she remained crouched on the cot, her breath a loud rasp as she heard the sounds of Bayon moving through the house. There was a tense wait before he was jogging back up the stairs and returning to the cell.

She hissed as the warm musk of him filled her senses, reminding her of…what?

Something her mind wasn't ready to accept.

She trembled, shaking her head as he slowly crossed the cell and perched on the edge of the cot.

"Just hold still, Keira," he urged softly, his gaze never leaving her face as he reached to unlock the collar and remove it. With a grimace he tossed it aside.

Then, his fingers returned to her throat to lightly soothe the flesh that had been rubbed raw by the metal. Instantly she was pulling away, her heart slamming against her ribs at the odd sensations that streaked through her at his soft caress.

"No." She surged off the cot and pressed against the bars of the cell, hating herself for acting like a fucking mouse, but unable to halt her violent reactions. "Don't touch me."

"Okay." Rising to his feet, he held up his hands in a gesture of peace. "We have to get out of here."

"Out?" She licked her dry lips. "Where are you taking me?"

"Back to the Wildlands."

The rising panic flooded through her, closing her throat until she struggled to draw air into her lungs. "No. I can't."

Bayon frowned, his fingers twitching as if he was battling the urge to physically force her from the cell.

"Keira, we can't stay here," he at last managed to murmur in soothing tones. "Will you come with me? Please."

Keira glanced toward the door. She wanted out. Desperately. And some part of her understood that this man wouldn't hurt her.

Still, it took every ounce of her willpower to give a jerky shake of her head. "All right. Just...don't touch."

"Okay." He backed out of the cell, watching her with a carefully controlled expression. "Whatever you need, honey, just tell me."

"I need space."

"You got it," he promised without hesitation. "Follow me."

She did. But it was at a cautious distance as they crept silently down the stairs and then out a small kitchen with cracked linoleum floors and a pile of filthy dishes on the counters.

Once in the backyard he paused, searching the darkness for any hint of a trap. Behind him Keira trembled, her dulled senses tingling to painful life.

Christ, was this real?

The brush of a warm breeze on her cheek. The grass beneath her feet. The distant sound of a child laughing.

Over the years she'd too often dreamed she was free, only to wake and discover she was still trapped in her cage.

She couldn't bear to discover this was just another hallucination.

At last convinced they were alone, Bayon led her toward a gate that had been left unlatched and into a narrow alley that smelled of rotting trash and human feces.

She slapped a hand over her sensitive nose, grimly concentrating on placing one foot in front of the other. Nope. This was no dream. Her imagination wasn't capable of producing such a foul odor.

Relief surged through her even as her weakness increased with every step. Grimly she refused to slow her pace. She didn't care if she had to crawl. Nothing would make her return to that prison.

They reached the end of the alley when the Pantera male halted, motioning her to stay behind him as he peered into the window of a derelict garage.

"What are you doing?" she demanded, nervously glancing over her shoulder.

Dammit. Why was he hesitating? Her guards wouldn't be gone forever.

"We can travel faster in a car," he muttered.

"No." She shook her head, a painful flash of memory searing through her confusion. She was hogtied with a hood over her head as rough hands stuffed her into the trunk of a car. There were male voices that sliced through her with the pain of a dagger. "I can't," she muttered.

Bayon glanced over his shoulder, his expression concerned. "Why?"

"It's a cage," she muttered.

A stark, brutal regret darkened his eyes before he gave a sharp nod. "Then we run."

Running.

The wind in her hair. The earth pounding beneath her feet.

The stench of the humans fading from her senses.

"Yes," she breathed. "God, yes."

CHAPTER TWO

Bayon fought for control.

He was acutely aware of the woman sprinting mere inches behind him even as they moved through the thickening shadows of Melton, the small town several miles north of the bayou where he'd tracked the bastards who'd attacked Ashe. Keira needed him calm. His mind focused on escaping into the nearby swamp before the humans returned to discover she was missing.

Not acting like a raving lunatic who wanted to grasp her by the shoulders and demand to know what the hell had happened to her.

Holy shit.

The memory of the day she'd disappeared was seared into his brain.

Twenty-five years ago, she'd left the Wildlands to visit her human lover and then…nothing.

Her brother, Parish, had sensed she was in distress, but he hadn't been able to reach her before she'd vanished off the face of the earth.

Eventually they'd had to accept she was dead, and Bayon had secretly gone into a mourning that had matched Parish's. Only his was worse, because while Parish had received the sympathy of the entire Pantera community, Bayon had been forced to keep his own grief shoved deep inside, pretending as if his life hadn't come to a shattering end on that day.

Now…now, he didn't know what the hell to think.

Keira was alive.

But she wasn't the same bad-ass female who'd been the leader of the Hunters.

Once she'd stood tall and proud, her body lean but powerful. Her dark hair had been threaded with hints of fire and her skin kissed with a deep honey tone. And her eyes had been a magnificent gold with starbursts of emeralds in the center.

Now her hair was limp, her skin pale, and her eyes so dull he barely recognized her. Even worse, her mind was obviously broken to the point she couldn't even remember him.

But she was alive.

His cat snarled deep inside him, struggling to reach out to the woman who'd once touched him at his most primitive level.

His emotions were a dangerous brew of elation, shock, guilt, and overall a murderous rage at whoever was responsible for keeping this exquisite woman locked in a cage like a fucking animal.

Keeping himself from exploding was taking everything he had as they traveled silently through wetlands surrounding Melton, the dusk turning to night as they left behind civilization and eventually arrived at the edge of the Wildlands

Which explained why he hadn't immediately noticed, when he passed over the magical border, that she'd halted on the other side.

Belatedly realizing she was no longer behind him, Bayon whirled around to discover her crouching at the edge of their territory, that look of terror marring the beauty of her face.

His heart twisted as he cautiously made his way back to her shivering form. He could sense her bone-deep weariness, but this was more than just collapsing in exhaustion.

She was being tormented by some inner demon.

"Keira?" He kept his voice soft. "What is it, honey?"

She shook her head. "I don't remember."

He reached out to stroke a hand over her dark head, only to yank it back. She'd asked him not to touch her.

It was a request he intended to honor.

"Remember what?" he prompted.

"Anything." She frowned, her fingers twisting together as she stared at the lands that she'd once known with the intimacy of a lover. Her duty as the leader of the Hunters meant she'd patrolled every inch of the Wildlands. Night after night. "No, that's not right. I have memories, but they're like puzzle pieces I can't put together." There was a long pause, her heavy breathing emphasizing the effort it was taking not to bolt in terror. "How long?"

Bayon frowned. "What?"

"How long was I gone?"

He grimaced. This wasn't a conversation he wanted to have. Not until she was stronger.

"Keira—"

"How long?"

"Twenty-five years."

"Fuck."

He crouched beside her. "It's going to be all right."

There was a flash of fire in the dull eyes. It was a painful reminder of the old Keira.

"Don't patronize me."

He bit back a curse. Dammit. They didn't have time for this. She was sick, and exhausted, and in dire need of shifting.

"Keira, I don't know what the hell happened to you, but I can sense that your cat has been forced into hibernation. The only way to heal you is to get you into the Wildlands."

She licked her lips, her heart pounding so loudly he feared it would attract the natural predators of the swamp.

"I know I need it."

He inched closer, hoping the proximity of his cat could offer comfort. "But there's something that bothers you?"

"It frightens me."

"I'll take you to Parish," he promised. The two siblings had been closer than most since they'd been destined to be Hunters together. "No one will bother—"

"I can't." She reached out, her nails sinking into the flesh of his arm. "Not Parish."

Bayon frowned. "Do you remember him?" he asked.

"I…it's beginning to come back, but it's still fuzzy." She bit her lower lip, her fear palpable in the air. "Please, don't make me do this."

He tilted his head so he could hold her skittish gaze. "Easy, Keira."

"Not Parish."

"Then a Healer."

"No." Her nails dug deeper, the scent of his blood filling the air. "Only you."

"Honey, there's no way I can keep your return a secret." He tried to calm her rising hysteria.

There was a choked sound, as Keira turned her head to hide her expression. "I don't want anyone to see me like this. I'm broken."

A dagger being shoved into his heart would have been less painful than those low, traumatized words.

"No," he snarled, his body vibrating with emotion. "Keira, you're a miracle."

"That's not what they'll see. They'll want to try and fix me. Or worse, they'll lock me away."

"I would never let them hurt you."

"There's something else. Something…" She shook her head. "Please, Bayon, I'm not ready."

The brief flare of joy as his name unconsciously slipped from her lips was crushed by her heartrending plea.

"Shit."

Bayon wasn't modest. He had any number of talents, not the least of which was the ability to directly connect with the inner cat of his people. It was a rare skill that was particularly useful when dealing with a Pantera who'd gone feral. But he wasn't a Healer. Hell, his bedside manner would have him run out of the faction within the first day.

Unfortunately, Keira was depending on him.

For now he'd have to take on the role of caregiver.

He glanced toward the Wildlands, knowing he had to get Keira into the magic of their home. But how could he keep her presence a secret? Parish would scent her…

Parish.

159

Of course.

"The caves," he muttered. "Parish is busy organizing the Hunters, not to mention caring for his mate." He grimaced. Parish had hauled all of Keira's possessions to the caves where they'd played as children, refusing to dispose of them no matter how many years passed. "No one will notice you're inside unless they come looking."

She turned back to study him with an unsettling intensity. As if she were trying to determine if he could be trusted.

"You'll keep them away?"

He gave a slow nod. Parish and the others would kick his ass when they discovered he'd kept the stunning truth from them, but right now all that mattered was getting Keira home so she could be healed.

"Yes."

"You swear?"

"I swear." There could be no mistaking his sincerity and she gave a slow, hesitant nod. Then, moving until they were nose to nose, he held her gaze. "But once I release your cat, Parish will sense the bond. The only way to keep your presence a secret is to imprint myself on you."

Long ago, a Pantera parent could deny a potential mate for one of their children. The elders had forbidden the practice, but in olden days the purity of bloodlines had been far more important and there were families who were willing to condemn their child to a life separated from their destined mate rather than dilute their pedigree.

Of course, a Pantera male desperate to claim his lover couldn't be easily denied. They discovered a way to smother the family bond with their own scent. It was temporary, but it allowed the pair to avoid their family long enough to discover if they were truly meant to be mated.

Over time it had developed into a declaration of love between couples who weren't yet prepared to become fully mated.

Like humans becoming engaged.

She trembled, her face coated with a thin layer of perspiration. She was on the edge of collapse which was no doubt the only reason she didn't argue.

"Fine."

He lowered his head until his face was buried against the curve of her neck, his lips teasing her silken skin.

"Let me in, honey."

He stroked his lips to the pulse that thundered at the base of her throat, his tongue making a quick swipe over the flesh. Abruptly, his cat strained at the leash for more.

More heat. More skin. More Keira.

Christ. How had he survived even a day without this woman?

Patiently waiting until she'd tentatively relaxed beneath his touch, Bayon wrapped her in his arms. Once he was certain she wasn't going to panic, he tightened his hold, allowing his musk to wrap around her. It was the first time he'd tried to imprint himself on a female, but his most primitive instincts knew precisely what to do, triggering his male need to claim this woman.

She made a sound deep in her throat. Not rejection. But a low sound of hunger that tumbled him over the edge of a cliff he hadn't known he was standing on.

Without warning his mouth widened and he sank his teeth into the flesh of her upper shoulder, saturating her in his scent.

She grabbed his shoulders, sighing softly as the force of his claim flooded through her, wrapping her in a layer of protection. Bayon licked the tiny wound on her shoulder as she collapsed against him, trying to be as gentle as possible as he cradled her too-thin body in his arms and rose to his feet.

A savage anger exploded through him as he realized just how delicate she'd become. Had she been starved? Beaten? Sexually abused?

Dammit, he was going to hunt down the savages and make them scream for mercy.

Then he was going to roast them over an open fire and feed them to the gators.

Keeping well away from the patrols that guarded the borders, Bayon headed over the spongy ground toward the isolated caves at the far side of the Wildlands. Since Parish had taken them as his home no one had dared to trespass. Which meant there shouldn't be any stray intruders.

He could only hope the current leader of the Hunters was too occupied with his duties to return in the next few hours.

The moon was bathing the towering cypress trees in silver as they reached the solid land, heading toward the low rise of hills where the entrance to the caves was hidden by the thick shrubs.

Forced to bend low to keep from smacking his head on the outlying rocks, Bayon shuffled forward until he at last reached the surprisingly large inner cavern with a high, dome-like ceiling and a shallow stream on one side.

The cool, thankfully dry air wrapped around them as he headed directly to the tunnels at the back of the cavern. He felt Keira shiver and he pressed her closer to his chest, choosing the tunnel that led to the furthest end of the series of caves.

He could hear the splash of the waterfall before he hit the circular end of the tunnel. Then, stepping around the curve, he came to a halt, savoring the sight of the water tumbling off the edge of a natural opening in the ceiling to pool in the deep basin in the center of the cavern.

It was that pool that had attracted the young Pantera, their cats joyously climbing the narrow ledges that lined the walls before shifting into their human forms to splash in the fresh water.

Now the children had all grown up and there were no cubs darting through the droplets of water that shimmered in the moonlight or shouts of laughter as young boys tried to capture the interest of the girls.

The thought abruptly reminded him that he had to contact Parish. Someone had to return to tracking the bastards who'd attacked Ashe and her baby.

"I remember this place," Keira whispered softly, her gaze on the waterfall as Bayon gently lowered her so she could stand beside the pool.

Bayon tugged her to face him. "Look at me, Keira."

The eyes that remained unnervingly dull lifted to meet his steady gaze. "What?"

"It's time for me to call your cat."

He heard her swallow, her eyes too large for her pale face. "You won't let anyone take me?"

"I'll protect you," he pledged, his fingers cautiously cupping her chin. "No one is ever going to hurt you again."

Tilting her head back, he peered deep into her eyes and spoke the ancient words of power.

A heat prickled in the air, the magic a smothering power that slammed into Keira with a force that sent her to her knees, as a pained sound wrenched from her throat.

Bayon grimaced, hating the knowledge that he was forcing her into an involuntary shift. It was a gift that he used when a Pantera was severely injured in their human form and needed to transform into their cat to heal. Or if the cat had become feral, unable to recall their humanity.

It wasn't something he did lightly.

Transformation was supposed to be a private, joyous event. For him to compel a shift was uncomfortably close to stealing a person's free will.

Keira tumbled to the side, then, with a burst of swirling colors, her human form was altering, the muscles thickening and the fur coating her once smooth skin. Bayon continued to speak the low words of command, his hands held over her as her eyes abruptly glowed with power and the cat emerged with a roar of long-suppressed fury.

Sheer relief flooded through him as he took a careful step backward, giving the cat plenty of space. After being forced into hibernation for so long there was no telling what she might do now that she was wakened.

The golden eyes studied him with a predatory hunger, but clearly too weakened to pounce, she instead displayed her massive teeth before curling on the hard floor and lowering her beautiful head to her paws.

Bayon backed out of the cave, giving the cat enough privacy so she could rest in peace, while remaining close enough that the human part of her knew she was being protected.

God almighty.

He pulled a cell phone out of his front pocket. He carried two. One that was his private phone with all the bells and whistles. And one a burner phone that couldn't be traced.

He chose the burner. He didn't want anyone realizing he'd returned to the Wildlands.

Parish answered on the first ring.

"You have them?"

Bayon grimaced. The Hunter wasn't going to be pleased with what he had to say.

"I tracked them to a home just one block north of the schoolhouse in Melton. They'd taken off but there's a good chance they'll return. If not, Talon should be able to follow their trail." Bayon winced at Parish's brutal reprimand at not having stayed on the hunt for the intruders. "I have a lead I want to investigate. It's important." There was another furious chastisement that included Parish's opinion of idiots who couldn't follow orders and the threat of Bayon's manhood being removed by a rusty knife. "Trust me, *mon ami*, you'll be the first to know when I have info I can share. Oh, and tell Talon that in the attic of the house he'll find a metal collar. I think it has some sort of toxin on it so he'll have to be careful, but he needs to bring it back for the Healers to study. It might be important. I'll be in touch as soon as I can," he promised before shutting off the phone and shoving it back into his pocket.

Parish was furious, but he wouldn't hesitate to send Talon back to the house. Which meant that Bayon had a few hours at least to concentrate solely on helping Keira. A duty that might not be his by blood, but was surely his by right.

Keira had always belonged to him.

Even if she'd been too damned stubborn to admit it.

———

Keira wasn't surprised that she dreamed she was in her cat form. It was how she hung on to what little remained of her sanity.

164

But the dreams had never been so tangible she could actually feel the sun slanting over her slumbering body, warming her pelt with a delicious heat, or hear the sound of splashing water playing like a symphony in the background.

She desperately tried to cling to the dream. She didn't want to wake to find herself in the cramped attic with the collar wrapped around her neck and the stench of the nearby humans making her want to hurl.

But there was something that felt like a rock digging into her ass, and a strange heat pressed against her back.

Slowly she forced open her eyes, tensing as she realized she wasn't in the cage. This was…a cave.

But not just any cave. Her favorite cave.

And she was most definitely in cat form, lying in the late morning sunlight.

Which meant she'd been asleep for hours.

Without thought, she was shifting back to human, whirling around to find a beautiful golden puma slumbering directly behind her.

Bayon.

The name came easily, her mind slowly beginning to clear as she breathed in his warm, musky scent.

Home. Dear lord. She was home.

Distantly she was aware that she was completely nude, the side effect of being forced into a shift, and that there were still large holes in her memories. But suddenly she was consumed with the need to prove this was more than a dream.

That she was really, truly saved.

"Bayon," she murmured softly, reaching to run her fingers through his soft pelt.

He was a magnificent cat.

Large, muscular, fiercely male.

She'd been overwhelmingly attracted to him from the moment he'd been old enough to join the Hunters. No shocker. Bayon started breaking female hearts before he ever left the nursery.

He was gorgeous, brash and too damned charming for his own good.

And as far as Keira was concerned, he'd also been firmly off-limits.

She told herself it was because he was too young for her.

All male Pantera were horndogs, or rather horncats, once they hit puberty, and Bayon was no different. When he wasn't training or on duty his only thought was getting laid. Keira hadn't had any interest in being another notch in his bed.

Not when she'd had far more mature lovers who could ease her needs.

The sort of lovers who understood her position as the leader of the Hunters, and never crossed her barriers.

Bayon wouldn't have recognized a boundary if it bit him on the ass.

But a part of her had always known that was an excuse to shut down his persistent pursuit of her.

Deep inside she'd been a coward.

In hindsight it was easy to see.

Bayon was too bossy, too demanding, too…everything, to be a comfortable partner. And for a woman struggling to maintain her alpha status, it'd been easier to slam the door on the fragile bond she could sense trying to form between them than to struggle against Bayon's natural tendency to dominate.

Now, however, she didn't give a shit about complications or politics or any other stupid reason she shouldn't give into her needs.

Her cat had been without touch far too long, and her female knew exactly which man she wanted to ease her hungers.

On cue, Bayon lifted his head, his eyes more gold than green when he was in his cat form, warming with a genuine pleasure as he shifted in a flurry of magic.

Keira shivered beneath a blast of lust as the cat was replaced with a large, delectable male dressed only in a pair of faded jeans. Oh, shit. His chest was even broader than it had been, and tattooed with tribal markings that flowed down the side of his lean waist.

He'd hardened over the years. Matured into the lethal warrior she'd sensed from the beginning. But there was still a twinkle of the boyish charm deep in his eyes.

Irresistible.

She growled low in her throat as she kneeled directly in front of him, shoving her fingers into the satin gold of his shoulder length hair.

"Welcome home, honey," he murmured, his voice still thick with sleep.

Acting on pure instinct, Keira leaned forward to kiss the lips that she'd fantasized about in the privacy of her bed. Instant, molten heat flared through her. Oh god, he tasted so good. Male spice and pure power.

She moaned as nerve endings she hadn't felt for years sparked to life. Her fingers tightened in his hair as his lips parted in ready response, a tantalizing musk filling the air with the scent of his arousal.

"Christ, I missed you," he muttered against her lips.

Her desire flooded through her, the need to be close to this man so intense it was painful.

"Touch me," she pleaded, arching her back so she could press the tips of her aching breasts against his chest.

A moan was wrenched from his throat, but even as his hands cupped her hips, he was lifting his head to study her with a wary expression.

"Keira?"

With a shove, she had him flat on his back. Quickly straddling his hips, she allowed her hands to explore the smooth terrain of his chest.

"I need to feel your touch," she said in husky tones, her breath hissing through her clenched teeth as he spanned her waist, before his fingers skimmed up her sides to cup the small mounds of her breasts. "Yes," she said in approval, leaning forward to spread a path of kisses over the silken heat of his skin, pausing long enough to lick a flat nipple. "More."

He shuddered, his erection thickening to press against the zipper of his jeans. Deliberately Keira ground herself against his bulge, her pussy growing wet. She needed that hard cock deep inside her.

Now.

His slender fingers teased her nipples with exquisite expertise, his touch sending shockwaves of pleasure through her shivering body. She released a shaky breath, craving him with a force that defied logic.

There was a flash of heated gold in his eyes as his cat responded to her touch, but even as a purr of approval rumbled through her chest, Bayon tensed beneath her.

"Wait, Keira," he growled.

She nipped his collarbone, hard enough to draw blood. "No, don't stop."

With a muttered curse he surged to the side, reversing their positions until she was on her back and he was perched on top of her.

Keira might have protested if it didn't feel so damned good to have his weight pressing against her trembling body. Her legs were spread to allow his lower body to rest between them, his fully erect cock pressing near her precise point of pleasure.

Bayon scowled. "What's going on?"

Her gaze dropped to admire the bulging muscles of his biceps, oddly disturbed by the searching question in his eyes.

She didn't want to think. She wanted to feel.

"You're the last man who needs an explanation for what's going on," she said, refusing to dwell on the number of females who'd enjoyed Bayon's touch. The thought was far more painful than it should be. Then she stiffened, struck by a horrifying fear. "Unless you're mated?"

His scowl deepened. "Christ, no."

Sheer relief had her reaching up to frame his face in her hands, tugging his head downward.

"Then kiss me."

He made a sound deep in his throat as he allowed his mouth to crash into hers, kissing her with a raw hunger that demanded capitulation. A capitulation Keira was eager to give.

So long as it was on her terms.

Angling her hips so his cock pressed directly against her clit, she bit the tongue he shoved into her mouth, before sucking it with a rhythmic insistence that had him moaning in sheer male need.

Her fingers skimmed over his bronzed face, taking an amazing delight in the hard angles and planes. He wasn't pretty. He was too male, his features too bluntly carved. But he had a compelling beauty that enthralled her.

Taking her time, Keira memorized the prominent line of his cheekbone and the sensuous curve of his lips. During the brutal years she'd been held captive, she'd discovered that she had no regrets for the things she'd done, but she had plenty of regrets for the things she hadn't done.

Things like this.

She stroked the line of his stubborn jaw, relishing the rough stubble of his beard as she rubbed herself against the delicious hardness of his erection.

Bayon growled, then with a last thrust of his tongue he wrenched his lips free to bury his face in the curve of her neck. He bit into her flesh with enough pressure to send white-hot lust jolting through her.

She hissed in pleasure. Yes…oh yes. She needed this.

Running her hands down the impressive width of his back, she grabbed the waistband of his jeans, impatiently trying to tug them down.

"Off," she muttered in frustration.

"Wait." With a harsh groan, he arched back to stare down at her flushed face. "Keira."

Her hands skimmed to the front of his jeans, struggling with the snap. "What?"

"Stop."

She frowned, wrapping her fingers around the massive erection that pressed against his zipper.

"Why?"

His pained groan echoed through the cave. "Because twelve hours ago you didn't even remember me."

She abruptly turned her head, pretending an interest in the nearby waterfall. "I was…confused."

She could feel the heat of his gaze searing over her profile. "And now you're not?"

"I know what I need."

"And what's that?"

She reluctantly turned back to meet his demanding gaze. "I need to know you're real," she breathed. "That *I'm* real."

"Shit." His face twisted with an agonized regret, then before Keira could guess his intent, he was seated on the ground with her trembling body cradled in his lap. "I have you," he murmured as she instinctively tried to escape his hold, pressing his cheek to the top of her head. "And I'm not letting go. Not ever again."

She should have been pissed. This was supposed to be a hot, sweaty bout of sex that would ease the hunger she'd had for this male for years and prove once and for all that she was out of the damned cell.

No fuss. No muss.

Just a glorious knowledge that she was able to do exactly what she wanted.

But as swiftly as her desire had exploded, it altered to a different, but just as savage need.

Comfort.

The feel of Bayon's hand softly stroking up and down her bare back. The warm, familiar musk of his cat. The sound of his heart beating beneath her ear.

She snuggled against him, feeling the magic of the land seep inside her.

It should have added to her comfort.

The magic had healed her cat. It soothed the damage done to her human form by the damned collar. And with every passing second it was repairing the damage to her mind.

All fan-fucking-tastic things, if there wasn't something buried in the depths of her brain that was wigging her out.

Something she wasn't prepared to deal with. Not yet.

"No one knows I'm here?"

"No," he swiftly assured her, nuzzling his face in her hair. He was such a cat. "But you realize they're going to skin me when they find out I didn't tell them you're alive?"

She grimaced. It wasn't fair to force Bayon to choose between protecting her and his loyalty to fellow Hunters, but the suffocating dread that enveloped her didn't give a shit. And for now she wasn't strong enough to battle through it.

"I'm not ready," she muttered.

Thankfully Bayon didn't press, perhaps sensing she was still dangerously fragile. "Can you tell me how you disappeared?" he instead demanded.

She paused, trying to sift through the memories that were a strange patchwork of perfect clarity and murky confusion.

Now that she was home, she could clearly remember her childhood playing in this cave with Parish. And the day she'd taken command of the Hunters. And even eyeballing Bayon when he was too occupied to notice her fascinated survey.

But the second she tried to concentrate on the events leading up to her kidnapping, her brain began to sputter and shut down. Like a computer with a virus.

"It's still fragmented," she admitted, her voice tight with frustration.

His hand continued to run a soothing path up and down her spine. "We thought you were dead." He was forced to halt and clear his throat as he relived the day of her disappearance. "Parish could sense you were being attacked, then suddenly his connection to you was severed. He searched for you for months, but his cat was convinced you were dead."

She hissed with dark fury, knowing her death would have tormented her brother. It wouldn't be enough for Parish to mourn her passing. No, he would've made certain he carried the full weight of guilt for having failed her.

Damn, but she wanted to make those bastards pay for what they'd done.

"I think they had some sort of black magic that blocked my connection to my cat," she said.

"That's what Raphael said when he was ambushed."

Keira tilted back her head in surprise. "Raphael was attacked?"

"Yeah, just outside the borders." Bayon's expression was guarded, as if he were hiding something from her. "He was shot with a dart by a human who was tattooed with a raven in front of a full moon."

Pain ripped through her head as a shard of memory pierced through the black hole that surrounded her kidnapping.

"The Mark of Shakpi," she breathed, squeezing shut her eyes as a wave of nausea threatened to overwhelm her.

CHAPTER THREE

Bayon cursed as he felt Keira tremble in distress.

Goddammit. The last thing he wanted to do was cause this female more pain, but they had to discover if her disappearance had anything to do with the attack on Ashe. For all they knew the bastards were already plotting another assault aimed to kill the vulnerable human and her precious baby.

Now he feared he pressed the still-weakened Keira too far.

"Keira." He urged her head against his chest as he reached behind him for the blanket he'd been laying on. Gently he tucked it around her naked form. "Are you—"

"I'm fine." She sucked in a deep breath. Then another. "Just give me a minute."

"Take your time," he murmured softly, savoring the feel of her in his arms.

Yeah, she was only there because he'd been the one to rescue her, but his cat didn't care. It only knew that he'd waited for an eternity to have this woman curled in his lap, her head resting over his heart.

Then, as if to remind him of just how little right he had to hold her so tight, she opened her eyes and forced herself to share what she recalled of her kidnapping.

"I remember I was meeting with Sean."

His muscles clenched at the reminder that she'd chosen a mere mortal to warm her bed while slamming the door in his face.

"Your human lover?"

She lifted her head from his chest, studying his rigid expression. "He wasn't my lover."

Bayon frowned. "No?"

Her lips thinned at the disbelief in his voice. "No, he approached me at The Cougar's Den one night. He said he'd heard rumors there was a new gang in the area who were spending a lot of time in the bayous."

Bayon hesitated, reeling beneath her blunt confession.

Shit. Did she have any idea how often he'd tormented himself with the thought that her last hours had been spent with her human lover instead of with the family who would have protected her?

And now he discovered that she'd lied to him...he gave a sharp shake of his head.

"He knew what you are?" he demanded. Most humans were convinced that the Pantera were no more than a myth. A belief that the Pantera were happy to encourage.

"Yes, and that we'd be interested in the strangers," she said. "I asked him to try and infiltrate the gang and get us information." She shuddered at some unpleasant memory. "He was willing, for a price."

His gaze narrowed. "What price?"

Again with the thinning of her lips. "Not the one you're thinking."

Bayon grimaced. His age-old jealously was making him behave like an ass. And why? She'd just revealed that she'd used Sean as an asset to discover information, not to be her playmate, hadn't she?

Maybe it was because at the time she'd gone to such an effort to make him think she was in the midst of a passionate affair.

"You just pretended to be lovers so you had a reason to meet him?"

"Give the cat a gold star," she muttered.

He bent down to nip her nose. "And to piss me off?"

The flush staining her cheeks revealed he wasn't wrong. "Not everything is about you, Bayon."

"Says who?" he teased before pulling back to meet her wary gaze. "So what happened?"

She frowned, her eyes shadowed with a fear that he desperately longed to erase.

"I remember he cornered me as I was leaving The Cougar's Den one evening. He told me he had information I needed to hear, but he was scared to tell me where we could be overheard. He wanted to meet me at our secret location the next evening."

"And you agreed."

"Yes, I had no reason not to trust him. Although I did notice there was suddenly something off about his scent. It was—"

"Sour?" he completed for her.

She gave a startled nod. "Exactly."

Which meant they were definitely connected to the same idiots who'd attacked Raphael and Ashe.

Dammit.

How long had their enemies been spying and plotting on them?

And why wait until now to strike?

Questions he had no answer for.

Bayon's cat snarled with the need to be on the hunt.

"He must have decided the enemy had more to offer than we did," he growled.

"Maybe." The shadows in her eyes darkened. "I assume that I went to meet him."

"Keira." He cupped her cheek as she was shook by a violent tremor. "What is it?"

"I can't remember, but it's something important," she breathed, the acrid tang of her fear suddenly thick in the air. "Something that's a danger to the Pantera."

Genuine concern squeezed his heart as he sensed her rising hysteria. "Shh. Don't try to force it."

She shivered, abruptly trying to push him away as her fear threatened to consume her. "Now you're a Healer?"

Bayon wished to hell he was. Maybe he'd know what to do to help her work through the stress of her forgotten memories.

All he could do was offer a distraction.

With a speed that caught Keira off guard, he had her flat on her back, and his heavier body pressing against her.

"I'm all Hunter, honey," he assured her, unleashing the hunger that was a constant ache deep inside until the musk of his arousal filled the cave. "And one of the best despite your lack of faith in me."

Her eyes flashed with the golden beauty he remembered, the very center a starburst of exquisite emerald.

"I never doubted your skills as a Hunter, Bayon," she snarled, her anger overwhelming her fear. "Not ever."

"Just my skills as a lover?"

She sucked in a sharp breath. "Bayon—"

"I need to find Talon." With a fluid movement Bayon was on his feet and heading toward the nearby tunnel. He'd meant to distract her. Not open old wounds that for him had never healed. But for a brief, savage moment she'd been the old Keira and he'd been the old Bayon, and he'd wanted to claim her more than life itself. "I'll bring back lunch."

"Bayon...wait."

———

It took some time, but Bayon eventually tracked Talon to The Cougar's Den, a seedy bar owned by the Pantera and built on the edge of the swamps in a small town called La Pierre.

The younger Hunter, with dark gold hair threaded with copper highlights and eyes a pale gold rimmed with jade, had obviously just arrived. His boots were coated with dust and his LSU Tigers sweatshirt was marred with something that smelled like ash.

"Well?" Bayon demanded as he joined his friend at the long bar at the back, gesturing to the bartender for a cold beer. "Did you find the house?"

Talon grimaced, downing a shot of his private stash of tequila he kept in a silver flask. "They burned the place to the ground before we could get there."

"Shit." Bayon took a long drink of his beer, frustration burning in the pit of his gut. Their enemies might be mere humans, but they were managing to stay a step ahead of the Pantera with monotonous regularity. How the hell was that possible? "Any tracks?"

"Yep. They led us to a hidden airport."

Airport. Bayon slammed his bottle onto the wooden counter. Not even someone with the finely tuned senses of a puma could track his prey through the air.

"Then they're gone."

Talon reached out to give Bayon's shoulder a comforting squeeze. "Raphael is using his contact with law enforcement to try and trace the owners of the land as well as any FAA filings from the area. Someone has to have a pilot's license." The golden eyes glowed with the hunger of his cat. "Once he has a name I'll be all over them."

Bayon bit back the urge to remind Talon that they needed at least a few of the bastards left alive.

Talon could be bloodthirsty, but he wasn't stupid.

"How's Ashe?" he instead asked.

"Holding her own." Talon lowered his voice. Not everyone in the bar was Pantera. In fact, Ashe's mother was quite possibly seated just a few stools down. "For now."

Bayon grimaced. "Has anyone heard from Jean-Baptiste?"

Talon snorted. "You know as much as I do. Probably more."

"Which isn't nearly enough." Bayon abruptly shoved himself to his feet. He really fucking hated the sensation that they were all being shoved around like pawns on a chessboard. "We need answers."

Talon lifted his brows at the savage edge in Bayon's voice. "Why are you taking this so hard, *mon ami?*"

He curled his hands into tight fists, glancing toward the pool tables where a group of male Pantera were knocking balls around with an obvious lack of interest. Instead their gazes roamed over the handful of humans before moving toward the door of the club, as if expecting violence to erupt at any minute.

"Can't you feel it?" Bayon muttered.

"Feel what?"

"Evil." Bayon shivered, abruptly overwhelmed by the need to be with Keira. Crazy, considering he'd left the cave because he had to get away from her. But then, that was pretty much the story of their volatile relationship. "I have to go."

Ignoring the calls from the gathered Pantera to join them for a beer, Bayon left the bar and headed directly toward a nearby restaurant that reeked of stale grease and fried onions. The stench was enough to make his cat shudder in distaste, but he grimly walked to the front counter to pick up the order he'd called in before entering town.

After he'd paid, he clutched the paper bag and headed back to the caves with a speed that made the native wildlife duck for cover. Even the gators had enough sense to remain out of the path of a Pantera on a mission.

Leaping over the fallen logs and narrow channels clogged with water lilies, Bayon tried to concentrate on how he could assist Raphael in tracking the missing kidnappers. He didn't have personal contacts in the human world, but he was a Hunter who understood prey.

Once the men had returned to the house to discover Keira gone, they would have instantly realized their location was no longer secure. That discovery would no doubt have triggered a pre-planned escape, including torching the house. But they couldn't have disappeared without help.

Which meant cell phone calls. Bank transfers. New identities.

Things that he was certain were already being tracked down by the Geeks, the faction of Hunters who used technology to protect the Wildlands and to trace their enemies.

They were as dangerous as any warrior.

The various methods of locating the bastards shuffled through his mind even as his attention kept sliding back to the female who'd been so miraculously returned to him.

Christ, he'd mourned her for so long. It'd been a constant hole in his heart that he'd hidden beneath his image of a horny puma on the prowl.

Was it any wonder he'd been reeling since he'd found her in that cage?

One minute the overprotective part of him wanted to wrap her in cotton wool until he was convinced that she was completely healed, and the next his cat was snarling with the primitive urge to claim her so she would never, ever be taken from him again.

Scowling at the tangled emotions he hadn't felt in twenty-five years, Bayon entered the Wildlands from the deepest part of the swamp and headed directly for the caves. Once at the entrance he paused to make certain that no one else had been in the area before crouching low enough to enter without banging his head. Then, with a feral smile, he followed the intoxicating scent of Keira to the back cavern.

She was seated near the waterfall, her fingers playing in the pool of water as the sunlight crept through the opening in the ceiling, bathing her in a golden glow.

The breath was wrenched from his lungs as he took in the dark satin of her hair that tumbled down her slender back and the delicate profile that was so painfully familiar. How often had he studied her striking beauty from a distance? How often had those female features haunted his dreams?

His gaze swept downward. She'd found her clothes that Parish had kept boxed in one of the caves, and was wearing a pair of low-riding jeans and a cropped top that offered a tantalizing glimpse of her slender waist.

His cat snarled in approval, the hunger that he'd kept tightly suppressed blasting through his defenses as he prowled forward.

Keira was home. Physically, at least, she was healing.

And she was his.

That was all his cat needed to know.

The man part of him would continue to worry about the bastards who'd stolen her. And why her memories refused to return. And why she feared revealing her presence to the others. But the cat…

Yes, he was satisfied.

Or he intended to be satisfied. Once he had Keira beneath him, screaming his name in pleasure.

Very, very soon.

Keira was lost in her thoughts, but her head jerked up as he crossed the smooth stone floor, her hand automatically lifting to catch the paper bag he threw in her direction.

"I thought you might be hungry."

"Starving," she admitted, peeking inside the bag before lifting her head to study him with a guarded expression. "You remembered?"

With one pounce he was on the ledge of the pool, not bothering to hide his arousal as the scent of her warm musk wrapped around him.

"Everything," he admitted, no longer willing to pretend she was just an old friend who'd come home.

Her once-bold gaze was skittish as she pulled out one of the greasy burgers and consumed it in two bites.

"You said something about Parish being mated?" she asked.

Bayon smiled. He didn't doubt her interest in her brother. Or his new mate. But he also recognized a distraction when it was thrown in his face.

"It's recent." He allowed his fingers to trail over her lower back. "Very recent."

She demolished another burger, but she couldn't disguise her shiver of pleasure. "Who's the lucky female?" she choked out.

He traced the hem of her shirt. "Julia. A human doctor."

Finished with her food, she tossed aside her bag and sent him a startled glance over his shoulder.

"Human?"

"Trust me, no one was more shocked than your hard-ass brother," he admitted. "After…you disappeared, he blamed the entire human race." His fingers teased the sensitive dip at her lower back. "For a while I thought I was going to have to cage him to keep him from going on a bloody rampage."

The emerald starburst in the center of her eyes smoldered with a hunger that matched his own.

Not that she was about to admit the truth. Stubborn feline.

"Do you approve of this Julia?" she asked.

He shrugged. "We don't know much about her, but she saved Ashe's baby, so she's got my vote of approval."

"Ashe?" Keira frowned in confusion. "Baby?"

As concisely as possible, Bayon revealed the stunning news that Raphael had not only mated, but that Ashe was expecting the first Pantera babe in over fifty years. As well as the fact that they'd recently been attacked.

"A baby." Her smile was filled with genuine joy. "Oh my god."

"This child might be the savior of the Pantera, but only if we can protect the babe from our enemies." His own expression was grim. "I was tracking the bastards who attacked Ashe when I found you."

She turned so she was facing him. "Have they been captured?"

"Not yet." He grimaced. "They torched the place and took off."

Without warning, she surged upright, her cat eager to be on the hunt. "I'll find them."

Bayon reacted without thought. One minute he was perched beside the pool, and the next he had knocked Keira flat on her back and was lying on top of her rigid body.

"Like hell, you will," he snapped.

A dangerous gold flared in her eyes as her cat reacted to his display of dominance. "Maybe you've forgotten that I'm the one who gives the orders," she snarled.

He pressed a finger to her lips, halting her furious words. "Oh no, honey. There's a new sheriff in town."

She shook off his hand, her eyes narrowing. "What the hell does that mean?"

"I don't take orders from you. In fact, for the next few hours I intend to give them."

She snorted, unimpressed. "And you expect me to obey?"

His slow smile was filled with wicked intent. "I not only expect you to obey, I expect you to plead for more," he explained.

If looks could kill he'd be dead on the spot.

"Don't make the mistake of treating me like one of your bimbos," she managed to warn between gritted teeth.

She was beautiful when she was jealous.

Eyes glowing with emerald and gold fire. Her hands pressed against his chest, her breasts heaving as her cat struggled to be released.

He held his upper weight on his elbows, allowing his hands to slide beneath the too-revealing shirt.

"What would you know about my bimbos?"

"They weren't a secret." Her voice became a low rasp as his fingers found the swell of her breasts. "There used to be bets placed in the dining hall about how long the latest would last and who would be next to crawl into your bed."

"And it never occurred to you that maybe all those stories were more myth than truth?"

"Yeah, right."

She tried to sound skeptical, but he didn't miss her tiny groan of pleasure as his fingers grasped the nipples already beaded in anticipation. He tugged them with enough force to make her hiss with a growing hunger.

"I may not be a virgin, but—"

"Understatement of the century."

With an impatient motion, he yanked off the tiny top, cupping her swollen breasts with a gentle reverence.

"But my reputation has been highly exaggerated."

She groaned, her claws extending to prick the skin of his chest. "I doubt that."

"Why?" he muttered, distracted by the spectacular sight of her rosy nipples that begged for his kiss.

"Because you flirted with every female in the Wildlands."

"Did you sleep with every male you flirted with?"

"Fine." She cleared her throat. "What about the females you kept in New Orleans?"

Bayon lifted himself until he could shuck off his boots and jeans before kneeling between her legs as he wrenched his T-shirt over his head.

"There were no females."

Chapter Four

Keira shuddered, lifting herself on her elbows to regard the man kneeling between her legs like an ancient conqueror.

She should be pissed.

She was an alpha. Men didn't toss her on her back and have their way with her.

Not unless they wanted their throats ripped out.

So why was she lying there like she was some helpless kitten?

Perhaps it was because she was so damned consumed by her hunger for this male she couldn't think of anything but getting that hard, bronzed body on top of her.

Or perhaps it was because she was struggling to accept that he wasn't the testosterone-driven playboy she'd believed for so long.

"Then why did you let people think you had an apartment in New Orleans where you kept your latest lover?" she husked.

A golden glow spread through his pale green eyes as his cat studied her with a restless need.

"Because I didn't want a bunch of curious cats pushing their noses into my business."

She frowned, struck by an intense need to know what Bayon had been hiding. "Is it some secret?"

He hesitated, as if debating whether or not to confess the truth. Then he gave a small shrug.

"My mother was a born Nurturer," he at last said.

Keira nodded. Bayon's mother was beloved by all Pantera. "I remember her being in charge of the nursery," she said in fond tones. "I don't know how many times she kissed my boo-boos or slipped me a chocolate chip cookie when the other girls teased me for not playing with dolls like the rest of them. Your mother will always have a special place in my heart."

His blunt features softened with love. "In all our hearts."

"I don't understand what this has to do with New Orleans."

"When the Pantera stopped having children, the nursery was closed." He grimaced. "My mother was...devastated."

"Of course she would be," Keira breathed, wishing she'd made the effort to realize how difficult the past years had been on the Nurturers.

"I feared that she was losing her will to live, so I found a project that would keep her occupied."

"What project?"

"I opened an orphanage in New Orleans." His lips twisted as her eyes widened with shock. "It seemed like the perfect solution. My mother has endless love to share with the human children."

"Oh." Her heart melted. She'd always known Bayon was special. This only proved just how special. "Why the hell did you keep it such a mystery?"

"I did it for my mother," he said. "There was no need for anyone else to know. Besides—"

"Besides what?"

His gaze strayed toward her naked breasts. "Besides, I wanted you to believe that I had a harem in New Orleans."

"Why?"

"You know why."

She did. It was the same reason she'd pretended that Sean was her lover.

Stupid games designed to keep barriers between them.

But now the truth had torn down those walls, and left them both unable to deny the raw, savage need that pulsed between them.

Slowly her gaze lowered to take in his massive erection that seemed to grow even larger as she studied it with an undisguised desire.

"You're playing with fire, honey," he breathed, lowering himself to sprawl beside her, the heat of his naked body like a furnace.

"This is crazy."

"Not as crazy as denying what we both want." His cat glowed in his eyes as he reached for her hand, pressing it against his dick. "Feel what you do to me."

"Bayon."

Unable to resist temptation, she wrapped her fingers around his erection, exploring down to the heavy testicles before slowly skimming back up to find the broad tip that was already damp with his seed.

He shuddered, exposing his claws to slice her jeans and then her tiny lace thong into tatters. She parted her lips to protest the destruction of her clothing, only to have a groan escape as he cupped her bare ass, his fingers squeezing her flesh in a promise of pleasure to come.

"I let you keep me at a distance for too long." He peered deep into her eyes. "I'm not letting you do it again."

She forced herself not to look away. There would be no more hiding. "Do you know why I was afraid to let you near?"

"Because I wasn't going to let you neuter me like you did your other lovers."

She deliberately gave his cock a slow pump, taking full pleasure in the fine layer of sweat that suddenly glistened on his bronzed skin.

"It was because I feared you would undermine my authority as the leader of the Hunters," she bluntly confessed. "I had a hard enough time being taken seriously as an alpha without you distracting me."

"I might have tried," he admitted, his lips curving into the boyish grin that was lethal to the female heart. "But I have faith you would have sliced off my balls if I'd become too obnoxious."

Clever, clever cat.

He knew precisely what to say.

And how to touch, she acknowledged, as his fingers moved from her ass to trace the curve of her waist.

"My need for dominance doesn't bother you?" she pressed, knowing his answer was important.

Her cat would never be happy in a subservient role.

"Let's say I'm willing to compromise," he said, the rasp of his breath filling the air. "I don't always have to be on top."

Without warning his hands gripped her hips, rolling her until she was lodged on top of him. Tiny jolts of bliss speared through her as her already damp flesh was pressed to his thick cock.

"Oh hell," she moaned.

"No more denying what's between us, Keira?"

She met his gaze that blazed a brilliant gold.

She'd fought this moment for so long. Ever since she'd sensed this cat was destined to be more than just another lover.

She couldn't fight any longer.

"No more," she whispered.

His hands skimmed to cup her breasts, his cat watching her with a sensual intensity.

"Admit that you want me," he prodded, his fingers squeezing her nipples with a pressure that was on the right side of pain.

Oh…yes.

"I want you," she breathed.

"Bayon." His voice was thick with need. "Say my name."

"Bayon."

He smiled with satisfaction. "Now show me what you want."

She planted her hands on either side of his shoulders, lowering her body and tilting her head to the side in open invitation. With a growl of approval, Bayon sank his teeth into the tender curve of throat where it met her shoulder.

The same spot he'd used to imprint himself.

She shuddered, rubbing against his hard erection as his elongated fangs pressed into her flesh.

"Wait." He clamped his hands on her hips, holding her still as his lips kissed the tiny wounds on her throat. "You aren't going to freak out once you're mine, are you?"

She gave a lift of her brows as she trailed a finger over his chest. *Once you're mine.* The words should be terrifying.

Instead they were oddly erotic.

After twenty-five years of brutal isolation, where she'd been cut off from everyone and everything she cared about, she understood exactly the precious gift he was offering her.

Never again would she be afraid to open her heart to love.

"I could ask you the same question."

He hissed in pleasure as she scraped her claws lightly over his upper chest, dangerously close to breaking his skin.

"This is all I've ever wanted, but you're still recovering."

"My memories might still be fuzzy, but otherwise I'm recovered. The bastards tortured me by keeping me locked in the damned cage and using that collar to control my cat." She held his gaze. "But they never touched me."

"Fuck." His breath rasped through the air. "I'm going to skin them alive for what they did to you. Hell, I've already promised myself I'd chop them into pieces and feed them to the gators. But, I was so afraid—"

She nipped his bottom lip. "I'm fine. And I know what I want."

"Good."

A moan was wrenched from her throat as he allowed his lips to travel over the curve of her breast, at last latching onto her aching nipple.

Her eyes squeezed shut as raw, undiluted pleasure raced through her. The heat of his body. The rough stroke of his tongue. The silken brush of his hair against her chin.

She'd been starved of touch for so long.

Now she savored each touch, each caress as if it were her first.

"Oh...god, yes."

He used the edge of his teeth to tease the very tip. "You like that?"

"Harder," she whispered.

"Like this?"

He clamped down until her back arched in delight. "Perfect."

"You're perfect." His mouth moved to torment her other nipple, lapping and nipping until her fingers dug into his shoulders. "Competent. Smart. Willing to kick ass when necessary."

She trembled, his soft words as much a turn-on as his skillful touch. Oh hell, she was being burned alive.

Perhaps a more girly-girl would want the first time with her potential mate to be a slow, romantic seduction, but Keira had never been that sort of female.

She took what she wanted.

And she wanted Bayon with a force that threatened to overwhelm her.

As if sensing she was tumbling out of control, Bayon studied her with a gaze that made her heart skip a beat.

It was a gaze that spoke of need and lust and…sheer male possession.

Framing her face in his hands, he pulled her down to kiss her with an aching sweetness. Keira sighed. When she was younger she'd devoted endless hours to fantasizing about this man and his kisses, but nothing could have prepared her for the reality.

Her hands explored the corded muscles of his chest. His skin was warm, silken. The perfect temptation for her cat, and with a moan of need she gave in to the urge to spread kisses over his face before licking her way down the strong column of his throat.

"I like the taste of you, Bayon," she whispered as she continued to tease him with tiny nips and nibbles

"I'm supposed to be tasting you," he growled, his hands clutching her hips as he sought to retain control.

Such an alpha.

"I'm on top this time, remember?" she whispered, moving steadily lower.

"I…oh hell, woman."

"Do you want me to stop?"

"Keira," he rasped as she reached the rippling muscles of his lower stomach.

"Mmm?"

"You stop and I'll never bring you back another greasy burger," he ground out.

"Such a demanding kitty."

She gave a throaty chuckle, deliberately rubbing her breasts against his rigid body as she kissed her way to the tip of his massive erection. They both gasped at the electric sparks ignited by the friction of their naked skin. Damn, but this felt good. Her claws flexed, pinning him to the ground as she took the broad head of his cock between her lips.

His shout of pleasure echoed through the caverns, the musk of his cat spicing the air. She stroked her tongue over the tip, lapping the bead of pre-come and purring at the taste of him. Yummy. Widening her lips, she sucked him deeper into her mouth.

Bayon's hips arched upward, his breath hissing through his clenched teeth as she took her time to savor every impressive inch of him, scraping her teeth down the throbbing shaft before using her tongue to trace a thick vein back up to the tip.

"Wait." He threaded his fingers through her hair as she took him deep enough to feel the head of him at the back of her throat. "Christ, honey, I need to be inside you when I come."

With a tantalizing lack of speed she lifted her head, freeing him from the suction of her mouth with an audible pop.

He cursed, tugging her by the hair to urge her up his body. Keira growled in glorious anticipation.

It'd been so long since she'd felt such stark, uncomplicated desire. Hell, she wasn't sure she'd ever felt *this* kind of need before. Her every nerve was buzzing with life, sensitized to the point that she thought she might combust.

"Bossy and impatient," she murmured. "I was just getting started."

Without warning he grasped her hips and jerked her into place, stealing her breath as the fierce jut of his cock settled in the damp heat between her legs.

She sighed, the persistent throb in her pussy rejoicing as the wide tip of him slipped just inside her body. But instead of shoving himself home, he clutched her hips and regarded her with smoldering eyes.

"You can play all you want next time," he said in thick tones. "But Keira, I've waited for you all my life," he rasped. "I can't wait another second."

God almighty, she was in trouble.

189

"Bayon."

"Now…my turn for some tasting," he informed her, drawing her toward his waiting lips. "I want you begging before I'm done."

With a smile that held a wicked promise, Bayon branded her lips with a kiss of pure hunger. The taste of his cat on her tongue sizzled through her, setting off explosions of pleasure.

Then, spreading kisses over her face, he at last stroked his tongue down the length of her arched neck. Keira's fingers dug into his shoulders as he tugged her upward, catching the tender tip of her nipple between his teeth. She gave a soft purr as he nipped her sensitive flesh, her head tilted back at the insistent bliss darting through her. He turned his attention to the other breast, deliberately urging her desire to a fever pitch.

She needed to get him inside her.

Immediately.

But Bayon wasn't finished tormenting her. Even as she struggled to slide onto his waiting cock, he was ruthlessly tugging her up to her knees. She cursed, glancing down to watch his mouth explore the clenched muscles of her stomach, his tongue darting out to send a shiver of searing lust through her.

She moaned, her heavy lashes lowering as his extended teeth scraped over the curve of her hip and down the inside of her thigh.

Okay, she'd let him play alpha. Just this once.

Then his seeking lips found her moist pussy and any logical thoughts were destroyed. Oh, this was so fucking good.

Barely remembering to breathe as his tongue stroked the highly sensitive flesh, she speared her fingers in the thick satin of his hair.

There was something a bit naughty about straddling him as he expertly tongued her, although she intended to become a whole lot naughtier before the day was over.

Still holding her hips, Bayon found her clit, gently sucking as the magical pressure began to build.

"I knew there was a reason I called you honey," he rasped. "You taste so sweet. Cream and honey, my favorite."

"Oh god, Bayon, I'm close," she gasped.

"Yes," he muttered, guiding her back so he could position her over his straining erection.

Then, slowly he penetrated her damp channel.

Keira purred as she pressed herself ever deeper. She'd known he was large. Hell, she'd had him in her mouth. But she hadn't realized what it would mean to have that delectable hardness stretching her to the limit. Now she groaned in fierce approval. She could become addicted to the sensation of being speared by such a large cock.

Oh, yeah.

Size really did matter.

Spreading her knees, she allowed him to sink even deeper inside her, smiling with wicked satisfaction when he hissed in approval. She liked to reward excellence. And Bayon was truly a master at pleasing a demanding female.

Savoring his slow, steady pace, Keira at last placed her hands on his chest, holding his gaze that had gone cat-gold. With one swipe, she deliberately allowed her claws to pierce his skin, marking him from his collarbone to just above his nipples.

His roar of shock shook the air, vibrating through her as her cat stretched toward her mate.

"Mine," she breathed.

"Mine," he panted. "Forever."

Lifting herself until the tip of his cock was nearly at her entrance, she sharply plummeted downward. His hips jerked off the ground, his snarl of pleasure sweet music to her ears.

Keira chuckled, euphoria at the sensation of being bound to this male bubbling through her like the finest champagne.

This cat meant to be hers for all eternity.

How could she ever have tried to push him away?

Refusing to dwell on how close she'd come to losing this strong, loyal, astonishingly compassionate man, she concentrated on the sensation of Bayon's deepening thrusts, her soft pants filling the air as her muscles clenched in preparation for her impending orgasm.

Bayon tightened his grip and buried his face in the curve of her neck. Then, still pumping into her at a furious pace, he sank his claws into her lower back, marking her at the same time he catapulted her into a shattering climax.

Keira quivered in ecstasy, convulsing around him as he gave one more thrust and cried out with the violent pleasure of his own orgasm.

CHAPTER FIVE

Bayon wrapped Keira tightly in his arms as they sprawled beside the pool, lazing in the fading rays of sunlight that peeked through the narrow opening at the top of the waterfall.

Mate.

The word seeped into his soul, filling the empty void that had made him feel half alive for far too long.

This female completed him in a way that defied explanation.

Nuzzling the soft skin of her temple, he sensed the instant her mind cleared of the sensual fog that had held her enthralled. Lifting her head, she eyed him with a guarded expression.

"Well, that was—"

"Marvelous, stupendous, the best sex you've ever had?" he helpfully supplied.

She licked her lips, sending a jolt of raw lust through him. He'd just had the best orgasm of his life, but his cock was already hardening for a second round.

"Unexpected," she said.

He frowned, a sudden stab of fear piercing his heart. "You don't regret becoming my mate, do you?"

Her brows lifted in genuine surprise. "God, no. It's something we should have done a long time ago."

"Yes, it is," he muttered, relief searing away the knot of dread in the pit of his stomach. Keira had battled against their mating for so long he hadn't been entirely confident she might not bolt in horror when she realized she'd actually done the deed. "So, what's bothering you?"

"I feel selfish."

"Selfish?"

"Our people are in danger." The emerald in her eyes darkened with concern. "You should be out on the hunt for our enemies, not pandering to my needs."

His hand cupped her bare ass, pressing her against his thick shaft. "I like pandering to your needs."

She narrowed her eyes. "Bayon."

With a chuckle he kissed the tip of her nose. "Trust me, Keira, everything possible is being done," he assured her. "When Talon has located a name or an address I'll return to the hunt."

Her still-pale features tightened with a surge of emotion. "I need to help."

Bayon had known this moment was coming. Keira was too dominant to willingly remain in these caves.

"Keira."

She stiffened, clearly preparing herself for his protest. "What?"

"You're not ready."

"Be careful." There was a golden flash of danger in her eyes. "Just because we're mated doesn't mean you can start giving me orders."

The scent of angry female puma filled the air, but Bayon wasn't just another Hunter who relied on brute strength. His mother had taught him that keeping his prey off guard was always preferable to direct confrontation.

It worked the same with a powerful woman.

"I may be occasionally dense, but I'm not stupid," he assured her, his fingers absently trailing up the curve of her spine. "I have no intention of giving you orders. I was trying to point out that until your full memory returns you're a liability."

She hissed at his blunt words, but even as her lips parted to inform him that he was a total jerk-wad she snapped them shut, grudgingly accepting he had a point.

"You're right," she at last managed to rasp. "We can't be sure what they did to me. I could be programmed to betray the very people I've sworn to protect."

Bayon held her gaze. It might be shitty to use her loyalty to her people to keep her from charging after her kidnappers, but Bayon knew he'd have to use every trick he possessed to handle this female.

She was cunning, strong, and utterly independent, and she would walk all over him if he wasn't careful.

"For now it's more important that you try to piece together how you were kidnapped," he murmured softly. "That might lead us to someone who can give us info on the bastards."

With a sudden shove, Keira was out of his arms and seated on the edge of the pool with her arms wrapped around her knees.

"I've tried," she muttered.

Taking care not to startle her, Bayon moved to sit beside her. He was painfully aware that while his mate was physically healed, there was still a part of her that was dangerously fragile.

"Do you think they had a method of erasing your memories?"

"No." Her gaze was locked on the droplets of water that sparkled like diamonds, as if they held some clue to her missing memories. "I think it's me."

"You?"

"I think there's some reason I'm blocking the memory."

His gaze skimmed her fragile profile. Keira's personality was so forceful it was easy to forget just how delicately she was built.

"Then we wait until you're prepared to face it."

She gave a sharp shake of her head. "No."

He growled low in his throat. Damned stubborn feline.

"Keira—"

She turned to meet his annoyed glare, her expression one of grim determination. "Listen to me."

He didn't want to. He wanted to tell her that it was too dangerous. But one look into the shadows that lurked in her eyes and he knew that Keira didn't need a protector. Not now. She needed to know he would support her.

"I'm listening," he said.

"For the past twenty-five years I've been forced to feel helpless." She shuddered, the days of being locked in the cell still raw in her mind. "It nearly destroyed me."

Bayon reached out to brush his fingers over her pale cheek, his heart squeezing with pain. Only a Pantera with Keira's mental strength could have survived.

"I get it, honey, I really do."

She grabbed his fingers and pressed them to her lips. "Then you understand I can't just sit here waiting. I have to *do* something."

He grimaced. "Do what?"

"I don't…" She surged upright, her hands clenched at her side. "Wait."

Bayon straightened much more slowly. "I'm not going to like this, am I?"

"I want to retrace my steps."

It took a second to understand what she was suggesting. "You mean the night that you met with Sean?"

"Yes."

"Why?"

"It might jog a memory."

He gave a slow nod. It wasn't a bad plan. And as much as he hated the thought of allowing this female to leave the protection of the caves, the memories she was suppressing might very well be necessary to tracking down their enemies.

"It's been twenty-five years," he cautioned. She was desperate to feel as if she were actively involved in hunting those who had tortured her, but he didn't want her to get her hopes up too high. "The human world has changed."

She tilted her chin to an angle that said 'don't screw with me.'

"I have to try."

"Fine." Strolling forward, Bayon grabbed her by the waist and tossed her over his shoulder. "But first, a bath."

She gave a startled squawk. "What are you doing?"

196

He waded into the water, smiling as he caught the scent of her rising arousal. "You're my mate."

"Yeah, I got the memo." She reached around to rub the marks on her lower back that had healed to silvery lines.

"It's time you take up your wifely duties," he informed her, reaching the middle of the pool and lowering her to her feet.

"Really?" Her stern expression was ruined by the sparkle of amusement in her golden eyes. "And what wifely duties do you expect me to perform?"

He turned, the warm water lapping around his waist. "You can begin with washing my back."

He heard her laugh before she was pouncing from behind and pushing his head under the water.

"Or I could just drown you and find a mate to wash *my* back."

His cat purred, relishing her playful response. This was the Keira from their childhood. The female who'd stolen his heart.

Underwater, Bayon flipped to swim between her spread legs, breaking the surface behind her.

Before she could turn, he pinned her arms to her side and hauled her against his bare chest. Then, with a growl he sank his teeth into the side of her neck.

"Mmm." The taste of sweet female musk exploded on his tongue, and with one tilt of his hips he slid his cock deep into her welcoming heat. "My wildcat."

Keira flexed her claws, digging them into the mossy ground beneath her paws as she stood at the entrance to the caves.

Standing so still she appeared a part of the shadows, she simply absorbed her surroundings. The damp breeze. The scent of rich earth and vegetation. The tangible tingle of magic that touched everything in the Wildlands.

Home.

This place wasn't just where she lived. It was a part of her that was as necessary as breathing.

Her brief moment of contentment was shattered by the distant scent of her brother as he headed toward the village.

Shit.

She battled back the surge of grief at their continued separation.

When Bayon had carried her into the Wildlands, she'd been panicked at the thought of meeting Pantera.

Any Pantera.

She had no explanation. Just a ruthless fear that refused to be dismissed.

Now she understood that her continued reluctance to reveal herself to Parish had nothing to do with that strange sense of dread.

She'd adored her younger brother from the moment their mother had placed him in her arms. He'd been a quiet, intelligent baby with an intense stare that could intimidate grown men.

A born leader.

And a born protector.

He'd smother her with the need to keep her safe.

And she couldn't risk him trying to block her search for the truth.

Not when she sensed the very future of the Pantera might depend on her discovering why she'd been kidnapped.

A low roar that assured her the coast was clear thankfully intruded into her dark thoughts. Pausing long enough to make sure she was fully focused, Keira moved with a swift grace through the underbrush. She'd been the one to demand the opportunity to search the cabin where she'd been kidnapped. The last thing she wanted was to prove she wasn't prepared.

She joined Bayon, who was waiting for her across the nearest lily-clogged channel. Like her, he was in cat form, a beautiful golden creature with golden eyes swirled with pale green. She rubbed her head affectionately against his thick neck before turning to trot across the boggy ground.

They moved in silence, but Keira didn't need to hear Bayon telling her that he was frustrated as hell by her insistence on retracing her steps. The sharp-edged scent of his temper rolled off his body in fierce waves. Still, he was wise enough keep his opinion to himself, even when they reached the edge of the Wildlands and shifted back to human form.

They were both dressed in black jeans and black sweatshirts to blend into the night, and both had strapped small firearms to their upper thighs. They could easily kill with their bare hands, even when in their human forms, but they didn't know how she'd been overpowered by mere humans.

A little extra firepower seemed a sensible precaution.

Heading directly north, Keira grimaced as they were forced to skirt around a large bog filled with brown sludge that smelled like rotting eggs.

Christ, how had the nasty quagmires that had started to form at the edges of the Wildlands over fifty years ago spread so far?

The realization spurred her to a faster pace. She had no idea if her kidnapping had any connection to the destruction of the marshland, but the sooner she and Bayon could track the bastards down, the sooner they could start beating the answers from them.

They'd traveled several miles before Bayon at last broke the silence. "Where are we going?"

"It's not far." She glanced over her shoulder. "Trouble keeping up?"

Despite his lingering frustration, he flashed a wicked grin. "I like the view from behind."

Of course he did.

She shook her head, slowing until they were walking side by side. "Tell me about your orphanage."

He looked embarrassed, clearly unused to discussing his generous gift to his mother and the human children.

"It's not large. Only six to ten children at a time." He gave a dismissive shrug. "Most of them need temporary shelter while their parents are in rehab."

They ducked beneath the low-hanging branches of cypress. "They're fortunate to be in the care of your mother."

"They are," he agreed without hesitation. "She's a very special lady."

"True. Of course, she spoiled you shamelessly."

He widened his eyes with faux innocence. "Who could blame her?"

She chuckled, leaping along small islands to cross a wide channel. Once on relatively stable ground, she turned to watch Bayon as he moved with elegant beauty at her side, his gaze constantly searching for hidden enemies.

"I always assumed you would prefer a woman who was more a Nurturer than a warrior," she abruptly admitted.

He turned his head to capture her gaze. "I adore all women, but I always knew my mate would have more spice than sugar."

"Really?"

"Oh yeah."

She sniffed at his smug male expression. "And how did you know that?"

"Because I'd met you."

She stumbled over a hidden branch, her heart slamming against her ribs at his simple, absolutely perfect explanation.

Damn but the cat knew how to make a woman melt.

"You—"

His brows lifted as she struggled for words. A once in a lifetime occurrence.

"What?" he prompted.

"Astonish me," she said softly. She lifted her hand to touch his face, only to come to a sudden halt as she realized they'd reached a familiar gate that was now rusted and nearly hidden beneath a tangle of clinging ivy.

She frowned, studying the thick layer of moss and cow lilies that covered the ground. "There was a path here."

Bayon kicked the gate, watching it tumble to the ground. "It looks abandoned."

"I want to get closer."

He placed a hand on her shoulder, his expression tight with concern. "Let me scout the area first."

She leaned forward to nip his bottom lip. "You go left, I'll go right."

He released a rough sigh before pressing a frustrated kiss to her lips. "Stubborn."

Yep. She was stubborn as hell. But she was beginning to realize that Bayon was the one man who possessed enough self-confidence to allow her to be powerful, while refusing to let her bully him.

The perfect combination.

With a short nod, he turned to melt into the shadows, his movements as silent as hers as they swiftly searched the dense foliage that surrounded the rapidly decaying cabin.

Finding no sign of recent activity, she returned to the front of the cabin, studying it with a growing sense of familiarity.

The tin roof was rusted, and the paint peeling from the wooden planks, but she had a vivid memory of the small wooden structure with its white shutters and shallow, wraparound porch.

"It's clear," Bayon murmured as he moved to stand at her side, his brows drawing together at her obvious preoccupation. "Keira?"

"I remember," she said softly.

"Remember what?"

"Coming to this place."

She shivered as she had the mental image of walking up the once-cleared pathway, her mind distracted by thoughts of the next week's rotation of guards she'd been working on rather than her surroundings.

There hadn't been any premonition of danger.

Not until too late.

Another shudder racked her body, threatening to steal her fragile courage until a warm arm wrapped around her shoulders, tugging her against a solid male chest.

"I'm here," he promised in low tones. "And I'm not going anywhere."

Absorbing the strength he offered, Keira sucked in a deep, steadying breath and allowed the memories to flow through her mind.

"I was early. I'd gotten Parish to cover my duties." Her head tilted back to study the thick canopy of trees that nearly blocked out the sky. "The moonlight was just beginning to peek through the leaves as I walked up the steps."

Still holding her tight, Bayon led her up the sagging steps, his gaze scanning the darkness for hidden dangers.

"Did you smell anything?" he asked.

"Yes." She gave a sharp nod. "Humans. But that wasn't unexpected. The cabin was used by the local gator hunters." Her nose flared as she abruptly recalled the weird, sour scent that had surrounded the cabin. "And the same stench I'd caught on Sean the night before."

They stepped past the door that had rotted off its hinges and into the cramped kitchen. Bayon frowned as he moved across the floor to study the interior of the cabin. There wasn't much to see. On one wall was a row of rotting cabinets that hung at a drunken angle. Below the cabinets was a short countertop that was chipped and covered in layers of dust with a sink at the end. On the other side was a sofa and chair that had been invaded by a growing population of rodents. In the middle was a kitchen table, and at the far back a door opened to a bedroom that was barely big enough for a narrow cot.

Bayon turned back to stab her with a narrowed gaze. "Show me where he was waiting."

Keira pointed toward a spot directly in front of the empty doorjamb. "Here."

"That close to the door?" he pressed.

She paused, shuffling through her memories. She'd walked across the porch and yanked open the door. She'd been startled to discover Sean standing directly in her path.

"Yes."

"Why?"

She frowned at her mate's persistence. "I don't understand."

"He wasn't expecting you until later." Bayon waved a hand around the cramped interior of the cabin. "Why was he standing at the door? Did he hear you arriving?"

Oh. Keira paced the floor, struggling to clear away the murkiness that made it nearly impossible to recall exactly what had happened. The door had opened, and Sean had been standing there...

Wait. He hadn't just been standing there, he'd been pressing against the door.

"He tried to keep me out," she muttered.

"Because there was something he didn't want you to see?"

She continued to pace, her heart suddenly lodged in her throat, and her palms damp with sweat as she pressed past the fog in her mind.

Yes. She'd shoved open the door and then forced her way past Sean, more annoyed than worried by his strange behavior. And then…

Then she'd been overwhelmed by the strange smell. It'd assaulted her nose until she'd nearly vomited.

That was when the back door had opened and two men and a woman had stepped from the bedroom.

One male had been a human. He was large, with a bald head and a tattoo of a raven in front of a full moon on his neck.

But the other two…

She hissed in pain, dropping to her knees as the memory slammed through her.

"No. Not something," she forced past her gritted teeth. "Someone."

CHAPTER SIX

Bayon crouched down, wrapping his arms around his mate's trembling body. "Keira, are you hurt?"

With an obvious effort, she lifted her head to reveal her too-pale face and golden eyes dark with some inner torment.

"Pantera," she managed to rasp.

"What?"

"There was another human here with Sean," she said, shivering as she struggled to share the memory that had clearly traumatized her. "And two Pantera."

Bayon frowned. "They were being held hostage?"

She slowly shook her head. "No."

"They weren't…" He grimaced. "Dead?"

"They were alive," she assured him. There was a pause before she managed to spit out the words. "And working for the humans."

Bayon sucked in a startled breath, his cat roaring in protest. For over fifty years the Pantera had been battling an unseen enemy, but never once had they considered the possibility that the rot might be coming from within the Wildlands.

"Shit."

"It was the Pantera who overpowered me," Keira said, her eyes as dull and bleak as when he'd first found her in the cage.

"Traitors," he growled in disgust, inwardly promising to destroy the bastards who'd been willing to torture one of their own people for personal gain. "Did you recognize them?"

"Vincent and his mate, Savoy."

It took a second for Bayon to place the names. Then he made a sound of surprise as he recalled that the two Pantera had worked with his mother.

"They're both Nurturers, aren't they?"

Her jaw tightened. "Yes."

"This makes no sense," he muttered. The two were gentle creatures who'd devoted their lives to caring for the Pantera young. "Why would they join with our enemies?"

With a sudden surge, Keira straightened and turned toward the door. "I intend to ask them."

He grabbed her arm. "Wait, Keira."

She glared at him in frustration. "I've waited twenty-five years."

"I know, honey," he soothed, his fingers brushing her pale cheek. "But if they see you then they're going to bolt. We need to have Parish arrange enough Hunters to take them into custody without the chance of them escaping." His expression hardened. "Or hurting someone else."

She blew out an exasperated sigh. "You're right."

Her immediate ability to put her personal lust for vengeance aside for the benefit of protecting her people was only one of the reasons that this female had been such an effective leader.

"I'll have to reveal that you're alive," Bayon warned, pulling his cell phone from his front pocket? "Are you ready?"

There was only a brief hesitation before she was giving a firm nod of her head. "It's time."

"Okay."

He punched the number on his speed dial, but before Parish could answer Keira was gently taking the phone from his hand, a rueful smile curving her lips.

"Let me."

He lifted a startled brow. "You know how to use it?"

She shrugged. "I've seen my idiot captors using them. How hard can it be?"

"I'm not going to fight you for the privilege," he assured her. They both knew that Parish was going to kick his ass for not immediately informing him that his beloved sister was alive.

"Wait here."

She left the cabin and was halfway down the path when Bayon heard Parish answer his phone. He grimaced as the male Pantera's tone transformed from impatience to shocked disbelief to a joy so pure it made Bayon's heart twist with regret that he'd forced the male to suffer even one second longer than necessary.

"Christ, he's going to fucking kill me," he muttered, watching as Keira ended the call and then gestured for him to join her.

"Let's go," she urged, her earlier anguish replaced by a fierce impatience to confront her kidnappers.

He was swiftly at her side. They jogged down the overgrown path and leaped over the fallen gate.

"He's going to capture the traitors?"

"He's already on the hunt. He'll meet us at the Den," she said.

Bayon was momentarily puzzled before he realized that Parish wouldn't want anyone to know they'd discovered traitors among the Pantera, at least not until they could be certain there weren't any others.

And there was the added benefit that the prisoners couldn't shift while away from the Wildlands. They were far less dangerous in human form than in puma.

They headed directly for La Pierre, skirting the edges of the Wildlands. Bayon kept a careful watch on their surroundings, prepared to attack anything or anyone who lurked in the shadows.

For the moment, he had to assume everyone was an enemy.

Even a Pantera.

It was a realization that wounded the heart of his cat.

"At least a couple questions have been answered," he muttered.

Keira ducked beneath a low-hanging branch before glancing in his direction. "What are you talking about?"

"I now know how the enemy entered the Wildlands undetected, and how they found Ashe so easily."

"And why my mind was so reluctant to remember what happened," she snarled. "I could accept the treachery of humans, but not Pantera."

Bayon shook his head, hating the knowledge that they would have to eventually reveal the betrayal of Vincent and Savoy to the rest of their people. A damned shame. It was destined to destroy the trust they'd always had in one another. At least until the danger had passed.

Whether it could ever be rebuilt was something that was in the hands of fate.

"I'm not sure any of us will be able to accept that we could be betrayed by our own people," Bayon muttered.

They slowed their pace as they reached the edge of the swamp and stepped onto the road that marked the edge of the town. Ahead of them the neon sign hung outside The Cougar's Den, but even as they stepped toward the wooden building built on heavy stilts, a dark-haired man was sprinting across the road and wrapping Keira in a smothering hug.

"Keira," Parish breathed, glaring at Bayon over her shoulder. "You, I will deal with later."

———

Keira smiled, despite the fact that she was being clenched hard enough to crush the breath from her lungs.

She was surrounded in the heat and scent of family, her cat purring in bone-deep satisfaction.

"Are you real?" Parish asked, his voice thick with emotion.

She rested her head on the solid width of his chest. "I'm real."

"I've dreamed of this moment a thousand times only to wake and find that you were still gone. Goddamn, I've been so alone."

"Not so alone anymore." She lifted her head with a smile. "I hear you've mated."

207

His bleak features abruptly softened with blatant adoration. Keira would never have believed it of her brother if she hadn't seen it for herself.

"My Julia. She completes me."

"I get that," Keira agreed, glancing toward Bayon, who had stepped away to give them privacy for their reunion. A low growl had her sharply turning back toward her brother. "Don't start," she warned, her eyes narrowed.

Parish gave a bark of laughter as she slipped back into her role as older sister, unwilling to take shit from her brother even if he did have several inches and a hundred pounds on her.

"Keira," he growled. "I've missed you."

"Brother," she breathed before forcing herself out of his arms and glancing toward Bayon.

Later they would have a proper reunion. Now they had to concentrate on protecting their people.

Moving to her side, Bayon regarded Parish with a grim expression. "Do you have the traitors?"

Parish jerked his head toward the building. "Inside."

"Are they still alive?" Keira demanded.

A humorless smile stretched Parish's lips, the promise of death in his eyes. "For now."

"Good." Keira headed for the back steps of the building, her murderous fury heating the air. "I want some answers."

"Keira."

She ignored her brother, taking the steps two at a time.

"You're wasting your breath," Bayon murmured before he was jogging to catch up with her.

A portion of her tension eased as he lightly placed a hand at her lower back. Just having Bayon near returned the courage she'd feared had been stripped from her twenty-five years ago. A steel door opened and a male Pantera offered her a slow nod of respect before escorting them into a secret chamber hidden behind the shelves of the storage room.

None of the humans drinking in the front bar had any idea there were meeting rooms, a high-tech surveillance room, and two large guest rooms for Pantera separated from them by a sound-proofed wall.

They found Vincent and Savoy on their knees, both stripped naked with iron shackles around their wrists and ankles.

The two Pantera were both older than Keira. Vincent was built on solid lines with brown hair and dark gold eyes while Savoy was a tiny female with reddish hair and eyes the color of spring grass.

Standing behind them, Talon held a gun toward the back of their heads, despite the prisoners' mutual appearance of utter resignation.

No one was taking chances.

Talon, who had still been in training when Keira had been kidnapped, straightened his shoulders and snapped a salute.

"Welcome home, commander."

"Just Keira now," she insisted, glancing toward her brother who entered the room to hold his loaded gun at the prisoners. "I'm absolutely confident that Parish has done a brilliant job and I intend to concentrate on tracking down the son of bitches who kidnapped me." Her attention turned toward the kneeling Pantera. "Starting with these two."

"They're all yours," Talon murmured, taking a step back.

Vincent slowly lifted his head, his face gaunt and his eyes shadowed with guilt. "Please, forgive us."

Parish made a sound of disgust, but Keira leaned forward, needing answers. "I want to know why."

"We didn't know—"

"Stop," Keira snarled. "I don't want excuses, I want answers."

Vincent licked his lips, glancing toward his cowering mate. "Savoy was one of the first females to fail in becoming pregnant. It was…" He halted to swallow the lump in his throat. "Difficult."

"I tried everything," Savoy timidly offered, her once beautiful face lined with regret. "The old herbal remedies, human drugs, even artificial insemination when it became available, but nothing worked. At last I went to see a voodoo priestess in New Orleans."

Keira narrowed her gaze. "And she told you to kidnap me?"

Savoy shook her head. "No. She promised she had a potion that could ensure my fertility, but only if we agreed to help her people."

Bayon pulled a dagger from the sheath at his lower back, running a finger along the lethal edge.

"What people?" Bayon demanded.

Vincent curled his lips in disgust. "They were humans."

Bayon continued to stroke his finger along the dagger's blade. "What help did they demand?"

Sweat beaded Vincent's face. "They wanted to study the Wildlands."

Keira scowled. "What?"

Vincent grimaced. "They said that they were ecologists who were afraid that there was some disease that was attacking our homelands. They were certain they could help if they had access to study the places where the magic was still strong."

Bayon snorted. "And you believed them?"

"Yes," Savoy breathed, tears in her eyes.

Keira folded her arms over her chest, in no mood to offer sympathy. Maybe they'd been driven to desperation at their inability to conceive. Nurturers had an inbred need to care for others. But unlike Bayon's mother, who'd devoted herself to human children who needed her love, they'd thought of no one but themselves.

She didn't believe for a minute that they hadn't been well aware they were putting the Wildlands at risk.

"Then why keep it a secret?" she snapped.

Vincent flinched. "They said they'd approached the elders with an offer of assistance only to be denied because of the elders' belief that humans are inferior to Pantera."

Bayon's low growl vibrated through the air. "So you brought them through the borders and allowed them access to our deepest secrets and vulnerabilities?"

"We thought they wanted to help," Savoy said.

Keira grabbed the woman's chin, forcing Savoy to meet her gaze that burned with the memory of twenty-five years of hell.

"No," she ground out. "You allowed your own selfish desire for a child to blind you to your betrayal."

Tears streamed down the female's pale face. "I'm so sorry."

Abruptly dropping her hand, Keira straightened. Beating them to a bloody pulp wouldn't give them the answers they needed.

Unfortunately.

"What else did you do for the bastards?" she demanded.

"Nothing. I swear," Vincent said, clearly trying to draw her attention away from his sobbing mate. "When we didn't conceive we were determined to break our agreement with the priestess. She sent us a message to meet with her at the cabin, but there were human males there who threatened to expose us if we didn't keep our promise. Then—"

"Then Keira appeared and we panicked," Savoy finished for him.

"We only meant to disable you long enough for us to escape." Vincent held Keira's gaze, silently pleading for her understanding. Yeah. When hell froze over. "But the humans put a metal collar around your neck and told us that they'd kill you if we didn't continue to bring them into the Wildlands."

Parish stepped forward, his anger a tangible force in the air. "You should have come to me."

"We couldn't," Vincent insisted. "They swore that as long as we did as we were told that Keira wouldn't be hurt. Otherwise—"

Keira made a sound of disgust. "And you just trusted their word?"

"Of course not." Savoy licked her dry lips. "They sent us pictures of you each week. They claimed it was to prove you were still alive, but we always understood that it was a warning that you were still in their clutches and that your life depended on us fulfilling our end of the bargain."

There was an explosion of curses from Bayon and Parish, but Keira kept her attention focused like a laser on the traitors.

"Even if you knew I was alive, you couldn't have possibly known they weren't torturing me."

Vincent cleared his throat. "The collar."

Keira scowled at him in confusion. "What about it?"

"I had a chance to study it while we were in the cabin," he admitted in a strained voice. "It was made of an unfamiliar metal alloy, but I could detect a magically-enhanced toxin coating the inside of the collar."

Shit. Bayon's suspicions had been right. There was something about the collar that had been poisoning her.

"That doesn't explain why you assumed I wasn't being abused."

"The toxin was potent enough to cripple you, which meant it would be lethal to a human. Even touching your skin would have made them extremely ill."

Keira grimaced. Now she understood why they'd gone to such trouble to avoid all physical contact. Even when they took her to the bathroom, they'd kept their distance, using the electrical shocks to warn her of the dangers of trying to escape.

And, of course, they couldn't risk removing the collar. Not when they couldn't know for certain how swiftly her strength would return.

Not until they were ready to kill her.

She shied away from the thought that the nasty Roger might have been contemplating raping her dead body.

She shuddered. She had no forgiveness for the two traitors. Not when they'd left her at the mercy of those animals.

"They might not have raped me, or beat me with their fists, but they tortured me every day I was in that cage."

Vincent lowered his gaze. "I'm sorry."

Feeling her tremble, Bayon stepped close enough to wrap her in the comforting scent of his cat.

"Did you ever watch to see what they were doing?" he demanded of the two.

Vincent gave a slow shake of his head, his shoulders slumped in defeat. "They claimed they were taking samples, but I fear they were performing some dark ritual."

"They have to be the ones causing our homelands to rot," Parish growled, his gun pointed directly between Vincent's eyes. At that short distance it would be a lethal shot. "Did you tell them of Ashe's pregnancy?"

Savoy made a low sound of distress. "No, they already knew."

"But you told them where she would be?" the Hunter persisted.

Vincent gave a jerk of his head. "Yes."

"Fuck."

Keira lightly grabbed Parish's wrist, keeping him from squeezing the trigger. They were all battling against the primal lust for revenge. For now they had to put the welfare of the Pantera ahead of vengeance.

She held Vincent's wary gaze. "How many other traitors are there?"

The older Pantera frowned at the question. "None that I know of."

Talon slapped the back of his head. "The truth."

"That is the truth," Vincent rasped, a spark of gold smoldering in his dull eyes. His cat might be cowed, but it wasn't dead. "We never spoke of our bargain with any other Pantera."

"Shit." Bayon exchanged a frustrated glance with Keira. "There could be a dozen and we would never know."

"There's a way," Savoy said in soft tones.

"Tell me," Keira commanded.

"The priestess demanded that we be marked to prove our loyalty," the older female admitted.

Keira lifted her brows. "What mark?"

"The soles of our feet."

Together Keira, Bayon and Parish moved to stand beside Talon, all of them studying the outline of a raven that had been branded onto the meaty flesh of their heels.

Keira shuddered. It wasn't the full Mark of Shakpi, but Vincent and Savoy should have suspected that it represented their ancient enemy.

Parish sent her a questioning glance, clearly asking permission to take control. She gave a discrete nod. She hadn't just been trying to avoid confusion among the Hunters as to who was their leader when she said she was happy to let Parish remain in his position of authority.

It would take her time to fully recover from her years of being held captive by the humans. And just as importantly, she was determined to track down every bastard who'd been responsible for attacking their homeland and make them suffer.

"Talon, you need to find a way to begin searching for that mark without letting anyone know what you're doing," Parish commanded the younger male Pantera.

"Are you shitting me?" Talon protested. "I can't start randomly inspecting people for a brand without making them suspicious."

"Just do it."

"Christ."

Talon rolled his eyes, but obediently headed toward the doors. Keira was one of the very few who'd ever been a match for Parish when he was in full commando-mode.

Vincent cautiously reached out to take his mate's hand. "What will you do to us?"

Parish nodded a head in her direction. "Keira, it's your choice."

She shrugged, the brutal need for revenge fading beneath the sight of Savoy's cowering body.

The two would have to be punished; maybe they would even be condemned to death. But that was something that would be decided after the danger to the Pantera had been effectively destroyed.

"Take them to the elders," she ordered.

Parish arched a dark brow. "No one would blame you if you want to—"

"No." She leaned against Bayon, absorbing his strength as her knees threatened to collapse. It was going to take a few days for her to fully regain her strength. Until then, she had utter faith she could depend on her mate. It was a knowledge that banished the last of her bitterness. The past was the past. It was her future with Bayon, and the future of her people, that mattered. "Just before Bayon arrived, one of my captors let slip the fact that my time in the cage was coming to an end. He believed that whatever they were plotting was about to happen. And that they were going to succeed."

Bayon rubbed a comforting hand on her lower back. "They never gave a hint what that plot might entail?"

"No." She pointed toward the traitors. "But they might have information we need."

"Fine." Parish gave a grudging nod, his lust for blood still lurking in his golden eyes. Shoving the gun into the holster at his waist, he reached to grab the two kneeling traitors by their hair and jerked them to their feet. "Let's go."

She watched as her brother hauled Vincent and Savoy from the room before snuggling against Bayon's chest, breathing deeply of his familiar scent.

"Are you all right?" he asked, wrapping his arms around her as he laid his cheek on top of her head.

She smiled, kissing the strong column of his neck. "I will be, once we have answers."

"We will," he said without hesitation. "The Pantera are nothing if not stubborn creatures."

"True," she agreed.

For now, a shadow continued to hang over the Wildlands, but she fiercely held onto the belief that someday soon they would defeat their mysterious enemies and the magic would once again heal their land.

And their people.

Bayon rubbed his cheek against her hair. "Can we go home now?"

She planted another kiss on his neck, needing to be alone with her mate. "The caves?"

"Actually I thought you might stay with me." He lifted his head to study her weary face. "At least until we can decide where we want to live."

Her hand pressed against his cheek, her gaze drinking in his male beauty.

She'd been an idiot to ever doubt her ability to be with an alpha male. Bayon didn't threaten her independence.

He only made her stronger.

"I don't care where we go as long as we're together."

His eyes held a love she felt to the very depths of her soul.

"For all of eternity, honey."

JEAN BAPTISTE

By
Laura Wright

Chapter One

The Suit looked like shit.

Jean-Baptiste stood with his back to the window of the Medical facility, and watched the blond male pace back and forth in front of a large cypress. The leader of the Diplomatic Faction had always given off a controlled, unruffled vibe, but as the sun died around them in a glow of pale orange fire, Raphael's true state of mind was revealed. His clothes were wrinkled and hanging off his tall, lean body. The skin on his face was pulled tight over the bone, his eyes looked exhausted and sunken and desperate, and his hands were clenching and unclenching as he stalked from one end of the lawn to the other.

"You need to release your cat, Raphael," Jean-Baptiste said, the irony of his words clawing at his guts, while the Nurturer inside of him—the one who was an expert on mental issues for the Pantera—pressed on. "When our minds grow weary with stress, our cats are trained to take over, give our human side a break. It's how we survive, how we're built."

"Can't," Raphael muttered.

"I get that you want to guard your mate, but your cat can be just as effective."

Raphael just shook his head.

Damned stubborn shifter. It seemed to be a personality flaw all Pantera males suffered from. "You won't be able to remain in your human form the entire pregnancy without losing it."

"You don't understand." The words were curt, and flung at Baptiste like they were coated in alligator dung.

Jean-Baptiste didn't have a female—and it was looking more and more like he never would—but he knew how puma males were when something was wrong with their mate. The levels of crazy ranged from "manageable" to "batshit." But for Raphael, and what he was dealing with, it might very well be "rocket ship to the moon" time. His mate, Ashe, carried the fate of the Pantera within her womb, and if she had truly been attacked inside the Wildlands as Bayon had claimed...

A low growl erupted from Jean-Baptiste's throat, but he shut it down instantly. The last thing he needed right now was to allow his cat even one claw out of its cage. Even if it was to sniff out the bastard who'd had the balls to touch a Pantera's pregnant mate on Wildlands soil. But the fantasy of catching and carving a long and deep "*P*" across the intruder's chest was the kind of revenge Baptiste and his cat were hungry for.

"Bayon tell you what I want?" Raphael asked, his voice stripped of emotion as a breeze kicked up off the bayou, rustling the Spanish moss coating the Cypress.

Baptiste nodded. "Wish I could help."

"You can."

"Sorry, *mon ami*." *I've got problems of my own to deal with.*

"This isn't a request, Baptiste."

"Maybe you're forgetting, Raphael, I'm not Diplomatic Faction."

"I don't forget. Anything."

"Then you know I don't report to you."

"True." Raphael stopped pacing and turned to glare at Jean-Baptiste. "But what I'm proposing isn't exactly official Pantera business."

Baptiste's brows shot together, and the skin on his neck, where he'd gotten inked a few days ago, started to burn.

"In fact," Raphael said, his voice dropping as his gaze checked right and left for Pantera in the area. "I don't think either one of us would want it to be."

The urge to spring at the male, drop his frail-looking ass to the ground, ripped through Jean-Baptiste. But he'd grown used to the feral cat inside of him, and he forced patience into his already sour gut.

"I know you've been dealt a handful here," he said coolly. "I respect that. Hell, I'm as concerned about what's happening with Ashe as any Pantera. Maybe even more so. I'm a Nurturer after all." He heard the bitter note in his own voice. "But I don't have time to travel—"

"Why? Because you just got back?"

A flash of alarm moved through Jean-Baptiste, and he eased away from the window and started toward the male. He never talked with anyone about his personal trips into New Orleans. The fact that the leader of the Suits knew something like this was alarming at best.

"Was it a new piercing?" Raphael said, standing his ground as the male drew near. "Or did you get inked again?"

Baptiste's jaw tensed. *Play it off, Shifter. Don't let him see one shred of your unease.* "Didn't know there was a problem with a puma who appreciates body art," he said with a casual shrug.

"Not the art. But…maybe the reason behind it?" Raphael's nostrils flared, and once again he checked to see if they had an audience. When he found the lawn behind Medical deserted, he turned back to Jean-Baptiste, his voice low. "I know about your little problem."

Nostrils flared, Baptiste stopped a foot from the Suit. Inside his body, his cat screamed and clawed to get out. It wanted to attack. It wanted to rip the voice box from the male standing before it with all kinds of accusations swimming in his green eyes. But the only thing Jean-Baptiste allowed the feline to display was a cool, confused purr. "No clue what you're talking about, *mon ami*."

Undeterred, Raphael continued as though he hadn't heard anything at all. "Just don't know how it started. Or when. Few weeks ago? A month?" His eyes locked with Jean-Baptiste. "Considering how many tats and holes you have in that body of yours I'd say you've been trying to push down the fact that you have no control over your cat for some time now."

The words sank so deep Jean-Baptiste didn't have time to suppress his animal's reaction. With a terrifying growl, he grabbed the male's shoulders and rushed him like a linebacker. "Who the fuck told you?"

he snarled, saliva forming in his mouth as Raphael's back hit the trunk of the cypress.

"Perks of being a Suit," Raphael said through gritted teeth, his green eyes flashing gold fire. "I have connections outside the Wildlands. That piercing there," he jerked his chin forward, "through your eyebrow—the one coated in malachite—well, it was done by the brother of one of my spies' girlfriends."

Baptiste's eyebrow twitched. So did his lower lip—the one with the twin silver rings through it. He'd been betrayed. By a foolish, foolish soon-to-be dead human male. He forced a dark laugh. The sound was hollow. "Proves nothing."

"I don't think so," Raphael said. "Malachite is inside every tattoo and piercing you have."

He was going to cut the tongue out of that human before he killed him. "I like the mineral, that's all," he said. "It helps me to heal faster."

Raphael sniffed, his expression glib. "I'm sure it does. But it's also the very mineral that's purported to ground a cat inside the body. The elders use it as punishment to cage a wild puma." Raphael's gaze narrowed. "And I hear the Nurturer shrinks also use it on patients who can't control their mind or their feline."

Dead, fetid air sat inside Jean-Baptiste's lungs as he gripped the male's shoulders. Every inch of his skin had gone tight around the muscles and bones, and his canines and claws were starting to emerge. The desperate need to kill this male, end his questioning, his accusations, his impossible truth, was almost unbearable. So he did the only thing he could do.

He released Raphael and walked away.

"Any other time and I'd be all about helping your ass," Raphael called at his back. "But today my one and only concern is my mate."

Stopping at the window, Jean-Baptiste stared through the glass at that mate. *Ashe.* She was completely still, lying in the bed, and she looked as pale as a frog's belly.

"Go to that voodoun you visit," Raphael called to him. "The one who recommended the malachite and every tattoo that's on your body, and bring her here."

Fucking loose-tongued human better enjoy his last few days of breathing. Baptiste didn't turn around. "Impossible."

"Make it possible."

"She won't come. She's terrified of the magic of the Wildlands."

"You'll make her come. Because if you don't, the Pantera—starting with the elders—will know your secret."

"Blackmail," Baptiste uttered coldly. He glanced over his shoulder at the Suit. "You've fallen pretty damn far down the well, Raphael."

The male's eyes blazed gold fire. "I'd fall on a fucking blade for my Ashe and our cub."

Jean-Baptiste stared at him, let the words and their weight sink in as the sun sank into the calm waters of the bayou beyond. The air around them crackled with tension and heat. They couldn't remain here, speaking like this for much longer. Soon the Pantera would be out, their cats playing after sharing meals with their families or Factions.

"Why do you need the voodoun?" Jean-Baptiste asked. "You have the human doctor. Or was the attack more serious than Bayon let on?"

If it was possible, Raphael's skin pulled even tighter over his bones, and his eyes grew dark with fear and rage. "Ashe was injected with something. She's not conscious, and she's been...taken over by...I don't know..."

"What?" Jean-Baptiste asked.

Raphael shook his head. "Some kind of dark force."

Holy shit. "A possession?"

"We don't know." The Suit's voice broke. "We don't know."

"And the cub...?"

"The cub has a strong heartbeat. That's all they know."

Jean-Baptiste exhaled on a curse, ran a hand through his hair. He was surprised at the sudden and deep concern he and his cat felt for the new and important life inside Raphael's mate. And yet, despite the hell he was experiencing as of late, he was first and foremost a Pantera. He wanted his kind to survive more than he wanted his next breath.

"What the hell is happening to us?" he whispered blackly. "The Wildlands, the pumas, the magic?" His question wasn't meant for Raphael, for anyone in particular, but the male answered it anyway.

"I don't know. But it's growing worse."

Jean-Baptiste turned to face the male. "The borders aren't holding."

"We must act, Baptiste."

"I'll go tonight. But I will have your word, what we've said here tonight is never mentioned again."

Raphael nodded. "Done."

"I'll report back if there's a problem. Otherwise, I'll see you in the a.m." Jean-Baptiste started to walk away, but Raphael called him back.

"One more thing."

Turning, Jean-Baptiste hissed at the Suit. "Trying to keep my cat caged here, and it's not your biggest fan right now."

"You're not going alone."

"Come again?"

"I'm sending a Suit with you."

Baptiste shook his head. "No. I do this alone or not at all."

"I need to have backup there, a top negotiator, in case your voodoun becomes a problem."

"We agreed to keep this between us," Baptiste growled. "No one else can know."

"She doesn't know." Raphael moved toward him. "She thinks she's on assignment, bringing back someone to help Ashe."

"My voodoun could tell her—reveal our connection."

The Suit reached the window. He glanced inside, ran his hand down the glass, then fisted it and cursed. "That's your problem. Mine is in there fighting for her life and the life of our cub." He turned to glare at Jean-Baptiste. "The cub who might very well be the savior of us all."

Jean-Baptiste growled. "Who's the Suit?"

"The newest member of the Diplomatic Faction, Genevieve Burel."

"No," Baptiste stated flatly.

"You don't even know her."

"I've heard about her, and with my cat so unstable and ready to pounce on anyone who even slightly irritates me, taking her to New Orleans would be a batshit move."

"She's brilliant!"

"She's a pain in the ass! A prickly, buttoned-up, nose-in-the-air pain in the ass," Baptiste returned hotly.

"Good. Then she'll make sure the journey is a success."

He growled. "Either that or my cat will take her down before we even leave the Wildlands."

———

Genevieve Burel placed the perfectly folded shirt inside her shabby overnight bag and gently slid the zipper closed. Her critical gaze moved over her room, taking inventory: the neatly made bed with the quilt her mother had made for her when she was a cub; the ancient chair that couldn't hide its desperate need to be re-stuffed; the scuffed wood floors she'd spent hours trying to sand; and the dusty pictures and photographs that hung on the faded walls.

She exhaled heavily. She'd just cleaned an hour ago.

She slung her bag over her shoulder, then headed into the hall and down the stairs, careful not to grip the loose banister too firmly. On the small table that met her descent, the vase of Louisiana Iris she'd picked that morning were struggling to remain upright and full of color. The shockingly purple flower grew inside the magical borders of the Wildlands all year long, and was her grandparents' favorite. In fact, it was their mating day flower. Genevieve tried to pick some every day, but the bloom was becoming harder to find.

Scooping up the vase, she entered her Grands' bedroom with a bright smile. The room had once been the parlor, but Genevieve had converted the large space into a bedroom after her mother and father left the Wildlands six months ago. It was easier for her grandparents to get around, and despite how the ancient and errant magic was slowly depreciating the house and its furnishings, Genevieve had done her best to make the room clean and comfortable.

"Finished with your dinner?" she asked the pair, placing the vase down beside their bed. "I hope it was all right. You know I'm not so great with the stews."

"It's was perfect, Bé," her nearly bald Paw-Paw said, giving her hand a squeeze.

"Yes, indeed," her pink-cheeked Maw-Maw agreed, grinning. "Your culinary skills are far more advanced than you think they are."

Genevieve laughed, her cheeks warming. Her grandparents were the sweetest, dearest creatures in the world, and she didn't know what she'd do without them.

"You leaving now?" Paw-Paw asked.

Genevieve nodded at the pair who were cuddled up in bed together, as they were most days now, the covers pulled to their waists as they sipped their tea. "Shouldn't be more than a night, if that."

"We'll be fine," Maw-Maw assured her with a broad grin. "Lena's coming. You know we adore that girl. Even if she is a Hunter," she added with a wink. "So take all the time you need."

Paw-Paw nodded. "That's right. Our Bé's an important Diplomat now."

"Not that important," Genevieve said. "And never too important to take care of my favorite Grands."

"We're your only Grands, Bé," Paw-Paw said with a chuckle.

Genevieve met his soft chuckle with one of her own, but inside, her heart did that squeezee thing that made her feel like tears could appear at any moment if she wasn't careful. Her Grands didn't understand what was happening around them, just that Genevieve's parents had decided to forge a life outside of the Wildlands. They saw the house crumbling of course, felt their bodies crumbling, too, but didn't think—or refused to think—it could be more than just age and wear.

Genevieve knew better.

Where the magic inside their home, infusing their ancient blood, had once been impossibly strong, now it waned. The crackle of energy no longer permeated the air, and every item inside, every being, lacked luster. Genevieve's parents might have chosen to run instead of "dealing with the shame of one of the ancient families being rejected by their magic," as they'd put it. But Genevieve was determined to stay and fight, care for her Grands, and figure out why the weakening magic along their borders was moving inward. And why, according to the elders, hers was the only dwelling affected.

She bent down and gave each one a kiss on the cheek. They smelled like chamomile tea and soap and gentle memories.

"I'll see you tomorrow," she said. "And no telling Lena to spike your sweet tea. I've already warned her about that trick."

While Paw-Paw snorted and grumbled, Maw-Maw cupped Genevieve's face before she could get away. "Will you laugh at this old Pantera female if she says to have a good time? Maybe a little fun on your journey?"

"No laughing here," Genevieve assured her before straightening up.

"I mean it, Bé."

"Yes, ma'am."

As Genevieve walked out of the room, Maw-Maw called after her, "If anyone needs to cut loose and have a good time, it's you!"

Placing her bag on her shoulder again, Genevieve headed for the front door. She loved her Grands more than anything in the world, and she knew they had her best interests at heart, but they didn't understand how vitally important it was that she remain focused, controlled, and completely and utterly unflinching in her goals and assignments. Especially now. Unbeknownst to Raphael and the Suits, she was destined for the elders' inner circle. Working alongside the three ancient females. It was a coveted position, a great honor, and it was in her blood. Many of the females in her line had worked under the elders. Even her mother had been selected as a candidate before her fear of shame had run her off.

Genevieve wouldn't be that weak.

She headed out the door and into the warm bayou evening. *Breaking loose and having a good time?* Her Maw-Maw's words echoed in her ears. Unfortunately, those two suggestions weren't even on her radar.

"Miss Burel?"

In one second flat, Genevieve's thoughts died and her entire body went up in flames.

Standing on her rickety porch, with the chipped white paint and the sweet double swing, was the owner of that deep, demanding baritone. Genevieve stared at him like a mole who had just seen the sun for the first time. Hot, blinding and impossible to turn away from. She was sure she had never met him before. She would have remembered if she had. Her gaze moved over him. Yes. This male in dark blue jeans and a worn, black leather jacket wasn't someone you walked past without either staring, double-taking or running into a tree. He was so tall his head grazed the roof of the porch, and so broad across the chest, the white T-shirt he wore strained against all that muscle. But it wasn't just his size and fierce manner that had her skin vibrating with awareness, or the thick, dark hair, or the light dusting of stubble around his mouth—or, god, even those incredible liquid amber eyes that equally mocked and studied her. No. It was the brightly colored tattooed skull interwoven with tribal markings that covered his collarbone and ran up the length of his neck.

And the piercings.

Air seemed to gather in her lungs and stay there. Her mouth was uncomfortably dry. She couldn't stop staring. At the metal barbell poking through his left eyebrow, and the two thin, silver rings fastened to his lower lip.

Besides the individual black birth markings each Pantera had, she'd never seen anything like this on their males. She wanted to rush at him, place her hands on the skin of his neck and trace the colored lines, inspect them, study them. But instead, she backed up toward the closed front door, protective not for herself but for the two vulnerable Pantera inside. Was this indeed the Nurturer, Jean-Baptiste, who Raphael had assigned her to? Or someone else? Someone who wished her harm? After all, the Wildlands had been infiltrated, and everyone was being cautious.

That eyebrow with the metal lifted. "Raphael told you I was coming."

It wasn't a question. She suspected he wasn't the type who asked a lot of questions. At least she knew he wasn't the enemy. Not the kind she needed to be worried about anyway.

She stuck out her hand. "I'm Genevieve Burel."

He didn't touch her, just glanced at her hand, then dragged his gaze back up to her face. "I know."

Heat warmed her cheeks at his slow and obvious perusal. Males didn't look her over this way. Inspect her. At least if they did, she'd never noticed it before.

"Right." She dropped her hand. "And you're—"

"Jean-Baptiste," he finished for her.

"Yes. It's a pleasure to meet you, Mr. Baptiste."

A brief flicker of what she believed to be amusement crossed his features. "You sure about that?"

"Pardon me?" His tongue had darted out and swiped at the twin rings of silver on his bottom lip. Her mouth filled with saliva and she gripped the strap of her overnight bag until her knuckles turned white. What the hell was going on with her? She'd never felt so flustered in her life.

This is not acceptable. For a Suit, a Pantera or a female. But especially not for a disciple of the elders.

"I'm asking," he pushed away from the porch railing and moved toward her with sensual, cat-like grace, "if you're sure it's nice to meet me. Because frankly, Miss Burel, your face and body language scream the opposite."

Body language? She touched the pearl buttons at her throat, and tried to control the sudden outbreak of sweat under her arms. Lord, this was three shades of irritating. "I assure you, Mr. Baptiste," she said, clearing her throat. "My body does not scream." *Wait. Did that come out right?*

His eyes narrowed. "That's too bad."

No. It hadn't.

"What I mean to say is that I'm focused on our mission." She cleared her throat again and tried to look him directly in the eye without her legs feeling funny. "Getting in and getting out." *Oh Christ, that wasn't much better.*

His eyebrow—the one with the metal barbell through it—raised a good quarter inch.

They needed to go, leave her porch, the Wildlands, get to New Orleans, complete their task, bring it back to Raphael, and never have contact again. Or at least never speak to each other again. Never look at each other again. Specifically *her* looking at *him*. And at that mouth. Those tattoos. Wondering where they disappeared to. How far down they traveled—

"Ready?" he said, interrupting her thoughts. Her incredibly inappropriate thoughts.

"Absolutely," she said, wishing she could slap her own face without it looking odd, and possibly a little insane. "Shall we shift?" she asked, moving past him and down the steps. God, he smelled good. Leather and something completely indescribable, yet almost debilitatingly mouthwatering. "At least until we hit the border. I know the magic will refuse us once we're on human soil."

"We're not heading to New Orleans on foot, Miss Burel," he said, suddenly appearing beside her. "That would take too long. And I want this trip over as quickly as possible."

She made the mistake of turning to face him again. The sun had set completely now, and twilight ruled lavender and gray around them. The evening bayou breeze moved through his shoulder-length dark hair, batting at his dark, fearsome face. As petite as she was, Genevieve had never felt intimidated by anyone in her life. She was a strong, hard-nosed female who dealt in reality, who knew what she wanted and went after it. The fears and insecurities of her heart never made it past their respective barriers. But under this male's imperious, scrutinizing, sexually-fierce gaze, she felt like a small, tasty woodland creature who knew she was on borrowed time if she remained out in the open.

"If we're not running," she said finally. "How do you propose we get there? Did your voodoun acquaintance arm you with a generous supply of fairy dust or something?"

His eyes flashed with heat under the cool light of the bayou moon. "No fairy dust, Miss Burel. Just a *ride*."

Genevieve's legs threatened to buckle at his words—*no, just that one word*—and her mouth opened but nothing came out. Struck dumb by a great, inked-up beast of a Pantera male. She'd never been so ashamed of herself.

With a slash of a grin, Jean-Baptiste turned and started down the path. "Come along, Miss Burel. I promise I won't go any faster than you can handle."

CHAPTER TWO

The female beside him would be smoking hot if it weren't for all the buttons, zippers and pins, Jean-Baptiste mused, racing down Route 90, his cat eyes stunningly sharp in the dark. Sitting bone-straight in the passenger's seat of his 1967 Jaguar Roadster convertible, her milky white fingers splayed on her wrinkle-free lap, the small, fantastically curved, wondrously-busted Suit was the very picture of prickly put-togetherness.

Except for all that honey blond hair trying to escape the confines of an overly tight bun.

Fuck, he hoped the bun lost.

"Too fast for you, Miss Burel?" he called over the breeze.

"Not at all, Mr. Baptiste," she returned, her eyes forward, her expression tight.

"What about for your cat?"

"She's also quite content."

She. Jean-Baptiste's brows shot together, and his fingers wrapped around the steering wheel just a hair tighter. He'd never heard a Pantera refer to their cat as he or she before, and damn if it wasn't intriguing as hell.

"Do many Pantera have cars outside the Wildlands?" she asked, her eyes on the road in front of them.

"There are a few of us."

"Us?"

"Car enthusiasts. We like to buy and restore. Keep them in private garages in and around La Pierre." He touched the dash. "This one was a real piece of shit when I took her on."

Genevieve turned to face him. Her eyes were wide with surprise. "You fixed up this car yourself?"

"Rebuilt the engine, but it was mostly body restoration." That moonlight overhead was really working on her, he mused, and the wind whipping threads of blond hair about her face. She looked like a goddamn angel.

"You did an amazing job," she said. "It's beautiful."

Shit, Female. So are you.

"How many Pantera are in this car club of yours?"

"Around ten. Something like that. It varies from year to year."

"All males?"

His mouth twitched. "No. There are two females," he said. "Both Hunters. Both crazy for Mustangs."

"And is one of them your mate?" she asked.

His gaze cut back to her. She was staring at him, all prim and proper. He wanted to toss out a smartass remark like, '*What do you mean, one?*' over the rush of bayou air, but this female didn't seem like the type who'd find his brand of humor funny. In fact, she'd probably be insulted.

Damn, she really was just as Xavier had described her.

The Geek had told Baptiste all about Genevieve Burel, the supposed genius recruit he and his tech brethren had tried to bring on board the wannabe Faction last month. Rumor was she killed at decoding, and the Geeks had really pushed for her to give it a try. But after a couple of weeks, she'd bailed. The stories of her starched-collars, imperious attitude and one-word answers, however, had become legend.

"I have no mate, Miss Burel." Jean-Baptiste let his gaze travel down her skirt to the sexy legs beyond. He might be willing to take on her imperious attitude if those legs were wrapped around him, and the starched collar removed.

Or ripped away, courtesy of his canines, he thought with a wicked grin.

"So, this woman we're going to retrieve," she said tightly. "She's just an acquaintance of yours?"

"Something like that."

"A friend?"

The wind turned cool around them. "She's not my mate or an object of my imprint, if that's what you're asking."

"I'm not trying to get personal with you, Mr. Baptiste."

"Clearly." Spotting his exit, he banked the wheel to the right sharply. "Since you don't even seem to know my last name."

The sudden movement made Genevieve jerk, and she reached out for something to steady herself. What she got was the door handle on one side and Baptiste's thigh on the other. "Again," she said yanking her hand back. "Not getting personal."

But the movement came too late for Jean-Baptiste. And his cat. Her palm, her nails, had gripped him like a hungry lover, and his cock was now turning to steel behind his zipper.

"I only want to know more about the subject we're to obtain and transport," she said. "Collecting data. That's all."

Holy fuck, he mused. This female might be prickly and buttoned-up. She might be cold as dry ice on the outside. But her blood ran hot. Molten lava hot. He'd felt her sensual burn through his jeans, and the strike had awakened his already restless puma.

"I take my work seriously, Mr. Baptiste," she continued.

"I can see that," he uttered, his gaze narrowing as he headed for the Vieux Carré.

"I don't have time to waste."

"Why? You got a hot date later?"

He hadn't meant to say it. After all, he was pretty sure she repelled all things humorous, and when she glanced over at him, pinned him to his seat with a glare so fierce her pale blue eyes resembled twin icebergs, he knew that assessment was spot on.

"You know," she said tightly, "I was hoping you'd be more of a Pantera."

The hard-on in his jeans, combined with the growling cat inside him—not to mention the unwanted sexual interest he was sporting for this female—caused him to abandon any shred of manners he might still have possessed. "Oh, I'm all Pantera, baby," he said with a husky growl as he took the Toulouse entrance. "If you don't believe me, I can pull over to the side of the road and show you."

She wrinkled her nose. "That's disgusting."

"No, that's the truth."

"If you were truly Pantera you wouldn't be making inappropriate comments when there is so much at stake—when the life and health of Raphael's mate and cub are in danger."

He turned onto Bienville, sharp and quick, and didn't acknowledge her squeal of concern. She was starting to piss him off. Which, along with the attraction, was a pretty shit combination. "Don't pretend to know the behaviors of our kind, Miss Burel. Pantera instinct, character and function are my department. You are as green as the moss that grows along the banks of the bayou. A student, an observer, barely out of your training pants—sent along to make sure I follow the rules. Which I won't." He raced up the street, getting hit with the scents of night-blooming jasmine and a hundred restaurants. "Now. I didn't ask for company. But I got stuck with it. So, my prickly little puma, you're going to have to deal with inappropriate and whatever else I toss your way."

He was surprised when she uttered a very calm, "Or?"

"Or I get uncooperative and difficult to control. I know this is your first big Suit gig." He stopped at a crosswalk, waited for a passing pedestrian or two. "You don't want it to go badly, right?"

She was staring straight ahead, her jaw tight, a flood of color creeping up her neck. She looked damned good in pissed-off pink. And he was a jackass for noticing.

"Raphael should've been more forthcoming about you," she said tightly.

No, he shouldn't have. "What did he say?" He hit the gas, made a sharp right and headed down Chartres Street.

Genevieve's gaze scrolled over the crowds streaming in and out of the restaurants and galleries to her right. "That you're a Nurturer. An expert in the field of brain study. Brilliant and…" Her eyes darted toward him, and she snorted. Actually snorted. "*Serious.*"

He wasn't sure why, but her easy censure bothered him. "And you think I'm not serious, Miss Burel?"

"With all that you've demonstrated so far, no."

"You think because I crack a joke, I don't understand the magnitude of what our people are facing? Or because I come on to a hot female, I'm not swimming in concern for Ashe, and rage for whoever has dared to betray us?"

"That's exactly what I think," she said quietly. "And don't call me *hot* again, unless you want a nosebleed."

Jean-Baptiste was silent as he pulled up in front of Isi's place and killed the engine. The pale pink shotgun house was pretty unassuming, except for the massive blood-red shingle that read, THE CARE AND FEEDING OF VOODOO, and underneath it, *Isi Rousseau.* But Jean-Baptiste knew the depth and intensity of the magic that lived and breathed inside, and he never underestimated it. Beside him, Genevieve turned to get out of the car, but the sudden click of the locks halted her.

She whirled around, her expression stony. "Problem?"

His eyes moved over her face. Pale, perfect skin, a mouth that invited hot, hungry kisses, and a severe attitude that was supposed to ward off all male attention, but somehow managed to turn Jean-Baptiste into a brain-dead, lusty, adolescent Pantera male.

Problem?

Fuck, yeah.

"Believe it or not, Miss Burel," he said with barely contained aggression. "I would do anything to help the Pantera, to help Ashe and the cub. And I am. You have no idea." He stabbed at the lock, growled softly as it released. "Let's go."

As Genevieve walked past Jean-Baptiste into the dimly lit shop, she once again reminded herself of the rules of this game she was playing. Make sure the voodoun didn't get anywhere near the Wildlands, while acting as though that very journey was her one and only goal.

All she knew was that the elders believed this human to be detrimental to the Wildlands, to Ashe and the child. And that was all Genevieve needed to know. The elders were not to be questioned. After all, they were the essence of Pantera, the wise ones and the ultimate protectors. They and their judgment were valued beyond all things.

"Remember, Miss Burel, I do all the talking," Jean-Baptiste said, following her past a row of books, crystals, voodoo love dolls, and potions, all backlit by a mass of blue-flamed candles. "Isi's not going to be happy about this."

Isi. Very pretty, Genevieve thought. *Exotic.* "Why's that?"

"Let's just say that the Wildlands' magic and her own don't mix well."

Lucky for me. "How would she know that? Has she been to the Wildlands?"

"She's been to the border."

Genevieve's insides hummed, and she glanced over her shoulder. Tall, broad, eyes wary, tattoos and piercings glistening eerily in the candlelight, Jean-Baptiste looked like the sexiest demon alive. "Alone? Or with you?"

"Curb the questions, Miss Burel," Jean-Baptiste said coolly. "And don't forget you're here in a diplomatic capacity only."

"I know why I'm here," she returned.

Did the elders know about this? The voodoun at their borders? Was that their reasoning for keeping her out? Did they believe she had something to do with what happened to Ashe?

"Well, well, Baptiste," came an almost otherworldly voice near Genevieve's ear.

Startled, Genevieve whirled around to find one of the most extraordinary-looking women she'd ever seen. Not near her ear as she'd believed, or felt, but standing a full ten feet away in front of a cobalt blue curtain. For a second, Genevieve couldn't put her thoughts together. She blinked several times. A sudden blast of incense impaled her nostrils, and her head grew fuzzy and slow. She reached out for something to steady herself, but there was nothing.

"Isi." She heard Jean-Baptiste's voice behind her, his tone thick with warning. "Cut it off."

"But it's so much fun," she nearly whined.

"Now," he growled.

The scent of incense died away, and the haze inside Genevieve's brain vanished. She drew in air, and had the most extraordinary urge to turn around and run. But her feet were planted to the floor, and her eyes pinned to the woman.

Isi.

She was dressed in skin-tight jeans, black heels, and a sleeveless red top that showed her flat stomach on one end and her firm breasts on the other. She had short, jet black hair with blue streaks running through it, a tattoo of a rose wrapped around a candle that ran from just under her right ear down to her shoulder, and a diamond piercing in each nostril. Genevieve's mind felt murky as hell, but even so she knew that this was the kind of woman Jean-Baptiste probably went for. A real kindred spirit, complete with ink and metal. And she wondered if he had lied about them being more than just friends.

"Hello there." She shoved away the urge to fiddle with her top button and walked straight for the woman, her hand outstretched. "I'm Genevieve Burel. Diplomatic Faction for the Pantera."

Her expression stony, the woman ignored Genevieve and her hand, and pushed past her. Genevieve watched. Heels clicked on the stone floor and hips swayed as Isi made her way to Jean-Baptiste. Goodness, the woman moved like she knew how to work her body at all things.

When she reached him, she instantly brought her hand up to his neck. "Looks good."

"I think so," he said.

She ran a finger down the cord of muscle in his neck. "Healed and ready for another?"

He grinned. "Always."

The fuzzy head thing was gone, but something else—something far more worrisome—moved through Genevieve as she watched this woman. Isi's hands moved over Jean-Baptiste's body as if they had eternal permission to do so, and her voice practically licked at him, it was so intimate.

Were they lovers? And if so, why had Jean-Baptiste not disclosed it?

"I need to speak with you," he said to the voodoun, his voice grave.

"Problem?" Isi asked.

He nodded.

Isi glanced over her shoulder at Genevieve. "Another foolish female fall in love with you, Baptiste? Must we administer a reverse spell?"

"No," he said with a smooth chuckle. "Nothing like that."

"No, nothing like that," Genevieve returned with barely disguised irritation. More for herself than for them. She was getting real sick of this back and forth, pseudo-flirtatious, weirdly possessive behavior she was feeling and exhibiting. Her future, and her family's future, rested on this pick-up and delivery. Or preventing it, and that was all she was going to be focused on for the next twenty-four hours.

"Miss Rousseau," she said tightly. "As I said before, I'm here for the Pantera. To assist Mr. Baptiste in making sure you—"

Jean-Baptiste interrupted sternly. "I got this." He took Isi's arm and ushered her down the candlelit aisle. His eyes were hard, his mouth too. "If you'll excuse us, Miss Burel."

"I absolutely will not!" Genevieve called after him, far more passionately than she'd intended. "This wasn't the arrangement."

She heard Isi grunt, and ignored it.

"We're supposed to do this together, Mr. Baptiste," she continued, going after them.

"Mr. Baptiste?" Isi said with a husky laugh. "What the fuck is that about?"

His expression fierce, Jean-Baptiste guided Isi through the curtain, whispered something in a terse tone, then re-emerged.

"I warned you, Miss Burel," he said, halting her progress. "I don't follow rules. Especially ones that were decided upon without me."

She stared up at him, hated how fast her heart was beating. "I don't care about any of that. I have a job to do. Raphael sent me—"

"Raphael sent you as a backup. In case I didn't get the job done." His voice dropped. "And I always get the job done, Miss Burel."

Instead of muscle and bone, it felt like water suddenly resided inside her legs. And his scent, that heady, masculine, animal-like aroma, was forcing itself inside her nostrils, battling for dominion with the remnants of Isi's head-screwing incense. This was impossible, she thought with deep irritation.

"Now," he continued in a soft, deadly voice, "You're going to remain out here, while I have a conversation with my...*friend*."

"That's not fair," she growled. "Not how this was supposed to go."

His eyes flashed amber fire. "Life is made up of the unfair, Miss Burel. Learn to accept that and you'll never face disappointment."

"Disappointment is my elixir, Mr. Baptiste. It gets me going, fires me up, turns me on." She tried to yank herself back, but she couldn't seem to curb her tongue.

"Well then, expect to be highly aroused for the next twenty-four hours."

She could hardly breathe as they stared at one another. Dark hair fell over his cheekbones, a few stray wisps brushing against the two hoops in his lower lip. Her eyes traveled down to the full, lush flesh. What would it be like to kiss him? How would she do it? Would it hurt him if she tried to get the tip of her tongue inside, spear one of those small rings? Tug on it? Ease him closer?

A soft, male growl pierced the thick air between them, and Genevieve's brain lurched back to the 'on' position. Oh, Christ. What was wrong with her? The things she was saying...the way she just openly stared at him, challenged him. The female who was all set to enter a life of service with the elders—a life where she would have no mate, no sex, no intimacy—was openly lusting over the very Pantera male she had to outwit.

This was bad.

Jean-Baptiste's eyes narrowed, and he pulled back sharply. "I'll be back in five minutes. Look around. Maybe you'll find something you like."

Too late.

"Or maybe you'll find some happiness. Isi puts that in the gray bottles, I believe."

What the hell was she doing? Genevieve thought shakily as she watched him walk away and disappear behind that blue curtain. Why was the top button on her blouse digging into her throat, irritating her, begging to be bitten off, when it had always lain so comfortably against her skin?

And why had her mission of making sure the voodoun never entered the Wildlands suddenly expanded into the disjointed goal of never allowing the dark-haired woman to put her hands on Jean-Baptiste again?

She turned to a table of potions, released a heavy breath, and started picking up random bottles. Forget happiness. There had to be something here that returned sanity to a clearly insane mind, and calm to a body that had never experienced the true meanings of the words *lust* and *possession* until just a few moments ago.

CHAPTER THREE

"Have you lost your fucking mind?"

Jean-Baptiste eyed the petite woman with the foul mouth, quick wit and fiercely sharp brain. "You know I have."

Isi smacked the seat of the leather recliner in front of her and huffed, "Then get your ass under Derek's needle again because there's no way in hell I'm stepping foot back in the Wildlands."

"Derek," he uttered blackly. "That idiot's cat food."

"What?"

"When I see him again, he's dead."

"Oh, Jesus," she muttered, pulling on a pair of gloves. "What happened?"

"The guy you hired to perform magic-laced tats can't keep his mouth shut. He told one of our spies, who informed the leader of the Suits just what goes in my ink and metal."

Isi sighed, picked up some tools and dropped them in the autoclave bag. "I'm sorry. Seriously. I'm sorry. But if that's what you're looking for from me—a Wildlands house call—I can't do it." She gave him a pointed look. "Don't you remember what happened the last time?"

Damn right, he remembered. It was a week after he'd realized he had a problem, that his cat wasn't behaving. He'd popped a few capsules of the malachite drug he gave his patients, testing to see if it grounded the feline inside his body once again.

It had.

But not for long.

He'd known right then he needed something permanent. Knew that if he didn't want to be caged liked the very ones he treated, he'd have to hide it. He'd heard about Isi, her incredible magical abilities, and tried to get to her. But even though Pantera couldn't shift outside the borders, his cat had. Twice. And had nearly taken down a couple of tourists in the process. In the end, he'd slunk back to the Wildlands and begged Isi to come to him.

The attempt hadn't turned out well. For either of them.

"You got sick," he said, trying to play down the truth as he watched her shove the autoclave bag inside the machine.

She snapped the latch, then turned to glare at him. "What I got was the equivalent of seasickness on land, times ten. I could barely stand, keep anything down." She shuddered in remembrance. "I don't care what the reason is or how dire it is, I'm not going."

Jean-Baptiste sighed, crossed his arms over his chest. "How much?"

"What?"

"How much? We'll pay. Even in stones, minerals…whatever you want. I know you've been dying to get your hands on all that ancient shit below the surface of the Wildlands' soil."

Baptiste saw a flicker of excitement light her eyes, then a shroud of fear quickly overtake it.

"No."

"Isi. That could've been a one-time thing."

She pointed to the curtain. "You have to go. I have a client coming."

For one brief second, Jean-Baptiste thought about putting up a fight, scaring the shit out of the human who was coming to see her, offering her more than just cash or crystals. But he knew her. Knew what worked and what didn't. Fear played her hard and often, and if he was going to get what he wanted, negotiation wasn't the way.

Unfortunately, the *way* was probably going to get him despised, hunted and, more importantly, cut off from the ink and metal his body and his feral cat desperately needed.

Anger simmered below the surface of Genevieve's skin as she watched the two males greet each other in the lobby of the swank Hotel Fils de France. At first, when Jean-Baptiste had walked out of the voodoun's shop and headed for his car, Genevieve had assumed she'd just become the luckiest female in the world. Isi had said *no* to the trip, and the inked Nurturer hadn't put up a fight. She'd be home by midnight, she'd thought smugly, and standing before the elders at dawn.

Her cat had practically purred along with the engine of his Jag.

Then he'd made a call, and two minutes later they'd pulled into the valet line of a beautiful French Quarter hotel. Before she'd even gotten a word out, a question, a demand to know just what the hell was going on, another male had pulled up beside them in an equally gorgeous car and they'd all walked inside together.

"I appreciate this, Michel," Jean-Baptiste said in a low, almost conspiratorial voice as they entered the sumptuous, violet-hued lobby.

"Anytime, *mon ami.*" The suit-and-tie male was extraordinarily handsome, with a skull-shaved head, shockingly broad shoulders, and piercing green eyes that seemed to move over every inch of the hotel and its patrons. "How are things at home? How is the human female recovering?"

Baptiste's voice dropped to a growl. "You've heard."

Michel nodded. "We're working on it from our end."

"Any leads?"

"I'm afraid that's classified," he said, his gaze coming to rest on Genevieve. Though his eyes remained watchful, his mouth relaxed into a very charming, confident smile. "I recognize a fellow Suit when I scent one. And you, *ma chérie*, smell like magnolia flowers and twilight on the bayou."

Genevieve felt a sudden shock of heat hit her cheeks, and she wanted to kick herself. She wasn't appreciating this new and embarrassing side of her nature. *For goodness' sake,* handsome males were a dime a dozen. So were compliments.

He reached out. "Michel."

244

She shook his hand. It was warm, strong, and, knowing his profession outside of the Wildlands, probably able to kill her with just the tiniest of efforts. "No last name?" she asked him.

"Oh, now you're into last names?" Jean-Baptiste muttered.

Genevieve ignored him.

Michel drew closer. "I find I don't need one."

"How convenient."

His grin broadened. "And your name, *chérie?*"

"Genevieve," Jean-Baptiste supplied with more than a trace of annoyance.

Green eyes raked over her. "Beautiful name for a beautiful female."

A low, fierce growl echoed throughout the bustling lobby, and both Michel and Genevieve turned to look at Jean-Baptiste. The male looked ready to rip Michel's head from his body. His eyes were narrowed into slits, his nostrils flared, and if she wasn't mistaken, his canines were a hair longer than they should be outside of the Wildlands.

As a bellboy passed them, followed by a giggling young couple, Genevieve turned back to Michel and said quickly, "Thank you. But I'd say I'm more of an impatient, annoyed, and confused female at the moment."

Michel's gaze remained fixed on Jean-Baptiste. "Are you the cause of this, *mon ami?*"

"Probably," the male uttered, his tone so near to menace it actually made the hair on the back of Genevieve's neck lift.

With a soft chuckle, Michel pressed something into Jean-Baptiste's hand, then clapped him on the shoulder. "You have the entire top floor. The owner is a good friend. Anything you want, it's taken care of." His gaze flickered toward Genevieve, then back to Jean-Baptiste. "And I apologize. I didn't know."

Jean-Baptiste nodded, then inhaled deeply, seemingly trying to get himself under control.

"Know what?" Genevieve asked, staring at the key in his hand. This had better be a joke. And if it wasn't, there had better be a cab waiting outside. Hell, if she had to, she could run home.

When neither Michel nor Jean-Baptiste answered her, she looked up. There were plenty of humans milling about the lobby, checking in, but the Pantera spy was gone—as if he'd never been. Panic flared within her, and she turned in a slow circle looking for him. "Where did he go?"

"Come along, Miss Burel."

She whirled back to face Jean-Baptiste. But he wasn't there either. He was heading for the elevator.

"Hey!" she called after him.

He didn't respond, though several hotel employees looked her way.

"We're not staying here!"

"You don't have to do anything, Miss Burel," he called back. "The front door is that way. Just let Raphael know I'm on it."

"On what?" *Dammit.* She ran after him, bypassing three giggling, stumbling, women who had clearly been out enjoying their evening cocktails. "Your voodoun friend said no, didn't she?"

"She did."

"Then there's nothing else we can do."

"I'm giving her some time to calm down, think."

"Think about what?"

"Giving up a little easily, aren't we, Miss Burel?"

"What?" Her heart stuttered. "Of course not."

When they reached a bank of elevators, Jean-Baptiste ignored the gathering crowd and walked straight past, to another, smaller elevator at the far end of the hall. He held his key up to a strip of metal, waited for the keypad to turn red and beep, then glanced over his shoulder at her. Dark brows lowered over amazing eyes. He studied her. "Isn't it your job to step in if I can't get the job done?"

"I thought you always get the job done, Mr. Baptiste."

That elicited a wry grin before he stepped into the waiting elevator. "I think I'm starting to like that name. I'll speak to Isi again in the morning."

Morning? "Are you actually suggesting we stay here all night?"

"In or out, Miss Burel."

Dammit. She couldn't go back to the Wildlands without him, and she couldn't let him talk Isi into coming. She needed time to think. She needed time to—

246

"Goodnight, Miss Burel."

Guess she wasn't getting it.

She lurched forward and slipped inside the elevator just as the doors closed.

———

To Jean-Baptiste's vexation and possible ruin, the female who'd just entered the elevator brought not only her ire and concern into the luxurious leather and suede box with her, but her particular brand of body heat. And the warm, honey-like sensation was quickly fusing into his skin, turning him—and his cat—into a hungry, sensual predator.

He leaned back against the wall and hissed. The last thing this mission needed was an underlying sexual attraction, and yet he'd steered it there too many times to count. Wanting what he shouldn't be wanting. The prickly Suit female. *And* he'd displayed his desire and possessive instincts for her in front of another Pantera male. *Fuck.* Michel's flirtation had been innocent.

His gaze slid over Genevieve, taking in her stunning body and beautiful face. He grunted. Who was he kidding? Nothing a Pantera male did was innocent when it came to their females. Michel had been completely and frustratingly into her, and Jean-Baptiste didn't blame the randy bastard one bit. Genevieve Burel was the most desirable female he'd ever laid eyes on, and the fact that she was wrapped up too tightly for anyone, including him, to see just how true that assessment was, made it all the hotter.

"Was this planned from the beginning, Mr. Baptiste?" she asked in a tight voice, her eyes locking with his across the elevator.

"What's that, Miss Burel?"

"The sleepover?"

His body twitched. "There was always a possibility our mission would take more than a few hours." He crossed his arms over his chest and regarded her. "Something you're clearly aware of as you brought a bag with you. So, what are you really asking?"

She swallowed tightly and shrugged. "Just want to know if there's something more going on."

"Like what?"

She gave him a sharp look. "You're really going to make me say it?"

His mouth twitched. "Yes, I think I am."

She took a deep breath. "Are you trying to seduce me, Mr. Baptiste?"

Just the query alone had his heated blood ratcheting up to blistering, and his fingers flexing with the need to rip clothing from skin. This female was making him crazy, and he wasn't sure exactly why. She was beautiful and sexy and intriguing, but it was more than that. He pushed away from the wall and moved toward her. Her scent wrapped around him, infusing his skin, permeating his nostrils with every step. Michel had been right. She smelled like flowers and twilight, and it pissed him off to no end that the Suit had been the one to notice it first.

Her eyes grew wide with his approach, and she drew back, her shoulders hitting the smooth suede walls of the elevator.

"Seduction is a fallacy, Miss Burel," he said, coming to stand before her. "A way to diminish your own wants, deny what your body needs, refuse responsibility for taking what belongs to you." He couldn't help himself. He inhaled deeply. Then cursed. "If your mouth is ready, your eyes are pleading, your hands are itching to grab and grope, and your pussy is hot and wet and turning the cool air around you into steam, then its mutual. And if it's not? A simple *no* is all it takes for an honorable male to back the fuck off."

The elevator was moving upward like a goddamn snail, yet Genevieve's breathing was rapid.

He watched as her tongue slipped from her mouth and swiped at her bottom lip.

"I could do that for you," he whispered. "I want to."

Her eyes lifted to connect with his. White fire swimming in bayou blue. God, she was gorgeous. Debilitatingly so.

"And you want me to, don't you, Miss Burel? You want me to lick you?"

Her nostrils flared, and a soft whimper escaped her throat.

"I'll admit it. Don't think I can stop myself." *Or my cat.* "I've wanted to taste you since the moment I saw you." He leaned in, near her ear. "And not just your mouth."

Her sharp inhale made him growl. And the scent of her arousal grabbed hold of the innocent waft of magnolia flowers and the bayou at twilight and shoved them aside, claiming Jean-Baptiste's nostrils, and making his cock swell painfully.

"The door," she whispered in a pained, breathless voice.

"What door?" he uttered, running his nose across her cheek.

"Behind you."

Her skin was so damned soft. He knew it would be soft in other places, too. Her belly, her lower back, behind her knees, between her thighs…

"We're here," she continued almost painfully.

Fuck.

He eased back, his teeth grinding together, his entire body rigid with a hunger he knew he shouldn't be encouraging. His cat was already scratching to get out, get at her, and the feline didn't give a shit where it showed up and who it took out these days. With the way this female was staring at him—with longing and fear and sexual curiosity in her sleepy eyes—he wouldn't be able to control the wild cat if it broke free.

"What now?" she whispered, her eyes drinking him in.

"We could take another ride," he uttered. *Goddammit.* He was an idiot.

She nodded slightly.

"Or we could get off here." He grinned. *Dangerous, foolish, bastard.*

His words, and their double meaning, weren't lost on her, and she blushed furiously, prettily. He wondered if she grew pink all over when she was teased.

His eyes flicked up, past her blond bun, to see the open elevator and beveled glass door of the suite a few feet ahead. There was nothing he wanted more in that moment than to remove each one of those hundred or so buttons on her shirt, and stare, then touch, then feast on what was beneath. But he wasn't going to be that big of a selfish prick. Even if he could keep his cat caged long enough to taste her, he could never be the male for her. He could never offer her a mating. And she was the kind of female who would not only require it, but who wholeheartedly deserved it.

He growled softly, grabbed her hand and her bag, and led her out of the elevator. Xavier had been right about two things: her intelligence and her starched collars. But besides that, the male didn't know shit. This female was not only hot and sexy, but she was intriguing and innocent. And if Jean-Baptiste had been the male he was before, the one with unmarked skin, an optimistic attitude and a cat he could cage with only a thought, he would've dropped to his knees and asked Genevieve Burel to consider his imprint. Shit, maybe even consider him as a mate—and the only male who would ever be allowed to see and explore the soft, sexual playground she hid beneath all that fabric.

CHAPTER FOUR

Genevieve encircled the hotel suite's sumptuous living room furniture for the fifth time, her cell phone pressed to her ear. Her skin was still humming from the elevator encounter with Jean-Baptiste, and her mind refused to drop the memory curtain on his face, his eyes, those lips. She didn't understand what was happening to her, and why she didn't seem capable of releasing it, forgetting it. He was gorgeous, yes. Had a body so long and heavy with muscle that she felt tiny and nondescript in comparison. He wore that dangerous, mysterious, don't-get-too-close attitude like a second and very sexy skin. But she was a smart female. Logical and thoughtful. She had a job to do. A future to procure. A home and family to save and protect. And no male—not even the very captivating Jean-Baptiste—was going to get in the way of that.

No matter how much her body begged her to think otherwise.

"Dammit," she grumbled, then yanked herself back to reality as the female on the other end of the line questioned her outburst. "No, no," Genevieve said quickly. "Nothing to do with you. Everything's fine, and I'll be home in the morning. I promise."

"Don't make promises you can't keep, Miss Burel," came a sharp, masculine growl behind her.

Genevieve startled, jabbed at the off button.

"Canceling that hot date?" he continued.

251

"I told you, I don't have a…" Her words died away, never to be found again, as she turned around and her eyes focused on the drool-worthy specimen before her.

Standing in the bedroom doorway, only a white towel wrapped around his lean hips, was Jean-Baptiste. Clearly he'd just come from the shower because his hair was wet and slicked back from his face, and a few water droplets clung to the heavily tattooed skin of his hard chest. Her gaze ate up every inch, every marking, every color. She'd seen the skull and tribal ink adorning his neck and collarbone, but beneath that, covering his broad shoulders and down both massive biceps, were two gold and black pumas baring their teeth. Artistic lines of green and blue seemed to move beneath their paws, like water and grass, like the bayou.

Her perusal continued inward. His pectorals were free of ink, but one nipple was pierced, and down at the very base of his ripped abdominals the word Pantera was scrawled in cat-scratch markings.

For one brief second, Genevieve nearly demanded he turn around. God, she wanted to see his back, wanted to see what kind of tattoos had been inked into his smooth, tanned, thickly muscled skin.

But then her sane mind returned.

"I thought that was my room," she said, gesturing behind him.

"It is."

"And my shower."

He sniffed with irritation. "I have a bathtub."

"And that's a problem?"

"I don't do bathtubs, Miss Burel." His eyebrow lifted. "Unless I have company."

She might have had her sane mind back, but her body was still completely and totally refusing her call for control. Her legs were doing that made-out-of-water thing again, and her skin was pulling tight around her muscles. She could do nothing to stop it. This strange, new compulsion to attack.

Lust and deep sexual interest had never played a part in her life. She'd been too busy with establishing her career and caring for her Grands. And lately, refusing to be angry with her parents for acting cowardly and taking off, leaving her to deal with the dying magic inside their home. Sure, she'd found males attractive. But wanting them? Needing to feel their skin? Taste their lips? Run her fingers through their hair as she growled and begged them for all things dirty?

Not until now.

Until Jean-Baptiste.

Her stomach clenched. This…this attraction, this lust, this hunger, this desire to run at him and lick her way down his throat, chest, abdominals, hipbones…

It was going to ruin her if she let it. Working alongside the elders required full focus, a vow of chastity, and a gold star with this mission. She could not allow herself to be swayed.

"So, who was that on the phone?" he demanded.

Genevieve started toward him. If she could just get past him, get into her bedroom and close the door…

"I was just letting my family know I'm all right."

"They worry about you?"

"Of course." She moved around the leather couch.

"You don't seem like the kind of female who would make a parent worry."

Unlike you, Mr. Baptiste. "I'm afraid I don't know what that means."

His mouth curved into a wicked smile. "Yes, you do."

She stopped before him, waited for him to move aside. But he didn't. "You have very strong opinions about who I am, Mr. Baptiste. I'm curious to know where that comes from. Are you listening to rumors, or simply judging a book by its cover?"

He looked her up and down. "Which one would bother you more?"

"I'm not sure."

"You should be sure, Miss Burel. Because one is understandable, the other is not."

"And which one are you?" God, he smelled good. Like soap and hungry puma.

His eyes lifted to meet hers. "Let's just say we all make judgments based on appearances."

So, he'd heard rumors about her? Who the hell was talking about her? And what were they saying?

"You may think it's understandable, but I don't judge others," she said, trying like hell to control her breathing. He was just so close. His clean scent, and all that naked, heavily inked, heavily muscled skin was making her dizzy. If her legs buckled and she fell, would he catch her? Maybe she should try it and see.

"Come now, Miss Burel. Don't pretend you didn't take one look at me, at this," he pointed to his lip, "and these," he brushed a hand across his shoulder, "and decide I'm bad news."

Lucky hand. Lucky, lucky hand. "I'm not going to deny it," she said primly. "But I think my judgment in this case was right on."

His eyebrow—the one with the metal—jacked up.

Her eyes locked with his. "You *are* bad news, Mr. Baptiste."

"I've done nothing to you, Miss Burel."

Nothing except make me question the direction of my future. Nothing except make me forget again and again why I'm here.

He reached out then, and touched her hair, snagged a piece that had long ago escaped her miserable bun, and wrapped it gently around his index finger. "You have beautiful hair. Feels like silk in my hand."

"Thank you." *God, what else could she say?* Her heart slammed against her ribs.

His eyes narrowed on the crown of her head, at her bun. "I have this irrepressible urge to take it down. I want to see what all that pale gold looks like floating around your face, kissing your neck, playing against the pale skin of your shoulders."

Her chest tightened. Her breasts and nipples, too. "You mean against the fabric of my shirt."

He shook his head. "No, Miss Burel. That's not what I mean."

Her stomach clenched with awareness, and below her waist, between her unsteady legs, she felt the heat in her sex turn liquid. Her lips parted and she started to pant. The button at her throat once again constricted her breathing, and she touched it with her fingers. Maybe she could undo just one button…

A knock at the door startled them both.

"Dammit." Growling with true menace, Jean-Baptiste stalked past her.

Genevieve took the opportunity to make a break for her room, for safety, for a place to get her head on straight.

"You get *that* door," she called after him. "And I'll get *this* one."

The last thing she heard was a great whoosh of air as Jean-Baptiste hauled back the thickly beveled glass, then snarled at whoever stood on the other side.

———

He'd put clothes on.

He'd even set the table.

But as he stared across the black marble at Genevieve, all he wanted to do was strip them both bare and take her on top of the china.

She was drinking a beer. That's all she was doing. But it was the way she was doing it that was making his cock stand up tall and scream for an exit inside his jeans. Her long, pale fingers were wrapped around the bronze, pony neck, and her lips were sealed against the wet rim as she swallowed.

Fuck, he was in trouble.

His cat snarled and spit inside his chest in agreement.

Stay put, you bastard.

Never in million years would he have pegged this female for a beer drinker. Possibly a margarita. Wine, maybe. Shirley Temple, more like.

She looked up then and caught him staring. She gestured to the full plate in front of him with that nearly drained Bayou Bock in her hand. "You're not eating."

Very observant, Miss Burel. I'm too busy watching, lusting, and trying to keep my cat caged and my steel prick from exploding.

"I'll get to it," he muttered.

"Well, don't wait until it gets cold," she admonished. "It's amazing. Best étouffée I've ever had. It was nice of your spy friend to arrange this." She cocked her head. "Michel, wasn't it?"

"Something like that," Jean-Baptiste said, not liking the Suit's name on her lips. "And he's not being nice. Males don't think that way. *Pantera* males don't think that way."

She paused, fork halfway to her mouth. "Really?"

"We stalk, claim and possess, Miss Burel. We're natural predators. We see something we want, and we go after it." He stabbed his fork into the center of the catfish and came up with a steaming chunk of white flesh. "He was trying to impress you."

She looked thoughtful for a moment, then grinned. "Well, if he really wanted to impress me he would've had them bring beignets and coffee along with this étouffée."

"I'll let him know for next time," Jean-Baptiste said, then stuffed the fish into his mouth.

"You will?" she asked, slightly taken aback.

"No."

She laughed. Then took another bite of her food and groaned happily. "What do you think of the catfish? I like it spicy, don't you?"

Did she have to keep taunting him unknowingly? Christ, he could practically feel the malachite leaching from him. "Just like mama used to make," he said.

"Really?"

"No." He glanced up. His face broke into a smile that mirrored hers. Damn, he couldn't help himself. "She's not much of a cook. How about yours?"

That smile suddenly died. "She was." She started picking at her rice.

Shit. "I'm sorry."

She shook her head. "It's okay. It's just me and my Grands now."

"You live with your grandparents?"

She nodded.

Was that who she was on the phone with? And why did that belief, that hope, fill him with far too much relief?

"Do you live with your family?" she asked.

"No. Haven't for many, many years." He took another bite of fish. "They're Nurturers. Very important. Very brilliant. Very consumed with their work."

She nodded her understanding. "So no family dinners."

"Not since I was five."

She studied him for a moment. "That bothers you, doesn't it?"

He shrugged. "You know, what kid doesn't want his family crowded around a table, barking at him to sit up straight, to stop making disgusting noises, eat his peas?"

She laughed. The sound was like fucking church bells. "Most kids don't want that, Mr. Baptiste. To be bossed around."

"Sure they do." He put down his fork. His eyes locked with hers. "They may gripe about it, but they want it. They want the structure and the boundaries and someone to take control so they don't have to. All that strictness and nitpicking—just means someone loves you enough to give a shit."

Her mouth fell open, but she didn't say anything. She just stared at him, her eyes boring a hole in his head.

"What?" he said.

"You."

His chest squeezed with tension. And maybe the thing beating rapidly inside it, too. "What about me?"

"Never judge a book by its cover?" She shrugged, her eyes glowing a little. "Never again."

He nodded. "Back atcha, Miss Burel." He tipped his beer bottle in her direction, and she instantly scooped hers up and gave his a solid clink.

"And who knows?" she said, after taking a quick swig. "Maybe you'll have it."

His brows knit together. "Have what?"

"A cub to boss around at the dinner table."

His gut tightened. "Odds are against it, don't you think? Fifty years and counting."

"There's Ashe."

"She human."

"So, go get yourself a human."

This time, it wasn't just his gut that tightened. It was every damn part of him. Even his fingers curled around his fork. "I don't want a human."

257

"How do you know?"

"I know."

"Maybe you just haven't met the right—"

"What are you doing, Miss Burel?" he said, placing his fork on his plate.

She shook her head, her eyes uneasy, taken aback by his gruff response. "What do you mean? I'm just talking—"

"Do you want me to go out and find a human? Really?"

She started chewing her lip. "I don't understand what you're—"

"Yes, you do. " He leaned forward, his meal completely forgotten now. "Acting naive is almost as grating as believing you've been seduced." His eyes narrowed on her gorgeous face and his voice lowered almost conspiratorially. "Tell me, Miss Burel. Can you continue to sit here, across from me and pretend there's nothing going on? Nothing between us? Eat and drink and talk about our families and our history when all we want to do is answer the real questions on our minds?"

She looked startled, and her cheeks flushed.

"What does she taste like?" he continued. "How would his arms feel around me? Would she like it slow and deep, or completely and totally out of control?"

"Oh my god," she uttered hoarsely.

"I don't think I can pretend, Miss Burel." He stood up. "Never been any good at it."

"Sit down and eat. Please."

"No."

"It's getting cold."

"I'm not hungry," he growled.

She closed her eyes for a brief moment and whispered, "Neither am I."

"Then what the fuck are we doing?" With a roar of lust-fueled ire, Jean-Baptiste swiped at the food on the table, sending it crashing to the ground. He heard Genevieve gasp, but all he wanted to do was get to her. He jumped onto the table, then leapt down on her side. His puma pacing inside his chest, he had her in his arms before she even had time to fully register what had happened.

"What *are* we doing?" she uttered, panic-stricken.

"Exactly what we both want."

"I can't…"

"You already are," he returned, lifting her up, placing her on the table.

"I should go to bed," she whimpered. "And we should forget this ever happened."

"What you're going to do, is keep your eyes open and brace yourself. After I take your mouth for a good long while, I'll be working my way down to all the bits and pieces you keep so tantalizingly and irritatingly covered."

Her eyes widened, but she whispered the only word that mattered to him in that moment. "Okay."

"Don't be afraid, Miss Burel. This won't hurt a bit." He ran his teeth over his lower lip, tugging at the silver hoops. "Unless you want it to."

CHAPTER FIVE

Heat, tension and anticipation barreled though Genevieve as Jean-Baptiste tugged her to the very edge of the marble table, then splayed her legs with one of his powerful thighs. The table that had once held their dinner, she thought inanely—the dinner which was now somewhere on the floor. Maybe on the walls, too.

But did she care?

No, she did not.

He took up residence in the empty space between her legs, so big, so imposing, his hands plunging into her hair, and his gaze roaming over her with such predatory hunger she broke out in goose bumps. Clearly, this male was accustomed to taking what he wanted—no questions, no invitations—and Genevieve was stunned to realize just how sexy and irresistible she found that.

His nostrils flared as he breathed her in, and his fingers pressed into her scalp. He looked on the verge of attacking, and for one brief second, Genevieve swore she saw his puma push through his skin, saw his canines drop and his eyes flash gold.

But then his mouth covered hers, his body pressed against hers, and she forgot everything.

He feasted upon her like a starving male, his tongue plunging into her mouth, demanding a groan, a moan, a cry of his name, and she gave him all three. It was the most perfect, lusty, mind-blowing, sensual kiss she'd ever experienced, and she wanted more. So much more.

Everything above and below her waist ran hot and suddenly frantic, and she curled her arms around his neck and clung to him as he took her mouth in kiss after kiss of perfect ocean waves; wet and pliant and drugging. She could feel the smooth metal of his lip piercings pressing into her skin, and it made her crazy with desire. She dropped her head back, forcing him to release her, just enough so she could run her tongue across the cool silver.

A sexual growl escaped Jean-Baptiste's throat, and he tried to nip at her, lap at her tongue. But she wouldn't allow it. She grinned wickedly, hungrily, and drove her fingers up into his dark hair, cupping his scalp. God, she felt out of her mind. Irrational. Uncaring about anything except this, him, her. Is this what lust was? The desperate need for another? Wanting him, needing him, as badly as you needed air or sunlight? Because truly, Genevieve had never wanted anything or anyone more in her life.

His eyes locked on her then, but her focus was entirely on those hoops. She'd thought about them so many times since they'd met. Now she was going to know.

Slowly, gently, she let her tongue probe inside the first ring. Then, just a hair inside the second. She heard him curse under his breath, felt his arms leave her hair and grip her hips. He yanked her closer, and she felt his cock pulse against the apex of her thighs. Her breathing turned ragged, and her mind went blank except for one thing, the one impulse she knew she couldn't shake.

She curled her tongue around the silver rings and tugged.

It was as if she'd unleashed a wild animal. With that one simple movement, Jean-Baptiste's face went from a sensual hunger to a mask of fierce, feline possessiveness. He glared at her. Snarled at her. Sweat broke on his brow, his eyes flashed burnt gold and he looked ready to attack.

Maybe she should've been scared. Or at least, cautious. But when she eased her tongue from the rings, she grinned.

"Lie back," he growled at her. "Now."

Her heart slamming against her ribs in a rhythm of total thrill and desire, she let him guide her; one arm under her shoulder blades,

LAURA WRIGHT AND ALEXANDRA IVY

one pressing at her hip, until she was completely stretched out on the black marble dining table. The room was lit by soft electric lights, and the pale gold walls etched in black created an intimate, opulent, feel.

"Knees up, Miss Burel," he commanded, his voice a rough snarl of desire.

Every inch of Genevieve was shaking. From fear, from the delicious unknown, from unbearable anticipation, from overwhelming need. Jean-Baptiste's hands found the edges of her skirt and not so slowly, or so gently, pushed the fabric up all the way to her waist. Liquid heat pooled into Genevieve's sex and trickled down her thigh. She knew he could see it, but she didn't care. She felt no shame. Only a desire to move, to demonstrate how badly she wanted this—wanted him.

His eyes flashing gold, Jean-Baptiste found the waistband of her underwear and curled his fingers around it. Genevieve bit her lip and groaned. *Do it*, she urged him, arching her back, canting her hips. *Do it now before I lose my mind. Or my will.* But instead of pulling down the damp, pale blue silk, he grabbed hold of it with his teeth, and ripped them right off of her.

"Now this is what I was hungry for, Miss Burel."

He eased her thighs even farther apart, then shouldered his way between them.

"So pretty," he whispered. "So wet. I can see your clit pulsing, Miss Burel. It calls to me, begs me to take it in my mouth and suckle."

The muscles inside Genevieve's pussy clenched, and her nipples tightened beneath the soft fabric of her bra.

Jean-Baptiste dropped his head and strung kisses across her hip-bones; slow, hot kisses, the silver hoops gently scraping against her flesh. Genevieve stilled, her breath little pants interspersed with swallows of saliva. She'd never been kissed there before, but she'd fantasized about it too many times to count. A male's head between her legs, his fingers gripping her inner thighs almost to the point of pain as he slid his hot tongue through her wet folds.

"So pink and swollen," Jean-Baptiste whispered, his fingers easing her lips apart, one brushing over the sensitive bud of her clit. "As your sex cries, rains down, down, into a true river of pleasure."

"Oh, god," she uttered, wanting to drag herself up, see what he was doing—watch him. But she just felt too dizzy, too heavy.

His breath…it was close…so close and warm against her pussy as he circled her clit gently with his finger.

"Please," she moaned, begged, her hips lifting, straining for more, for everything.

"Soon, Miss Burel," he whispered, his mouth so close now she could feel the cool edges of his lip piercing against her opening. "I just want to see how tight you are before I eat you."

And with that, he drove his tongue up, so deep inside her pussy Genevieve cried out. Her hands tensed and her nails scratched against the marble at her back. She couldn't stop herself, couldn't slow herself. She writhed and pumped, the feeling so shockingly perfect, she believed in that moment that she might go mad if she didn't have this—him—twenty-four hours a day for the rest of her life.

He eased out, lifted his head and locked eyes with her. "You, Miss Burel, are the sweetest, most tempting thing I've ever had on my tongue."

She stared at him, panting, her entire body on fire, her hips thrust up in a silent plea. "Please don't stop," she whimpered.

He chuckled wickedly, his eyes so gold they looked on fire. "Oh, Miss Burel. I'm just getting started. It's a feast I plan to savor."

His head dropped then, and his tongue made one long sweep from her pussy straight up to her clit. Crying out softly, Genevieve closed her eyes, and gave up everything from her past and everything in her future to accept this incredible, perfect, pleasure-filled moment.

Her thighs trembled uncontrollably as he licked her, as he made slow circles around her tight, hot bud. She made sounds from somewhere otherworldly, deep in her chest, her throat. And when his lips closed around her clit, when he started to suckle, his head lifting and lowering rhythmically, stunningly, she came apart.

"Jean-Baptiste!" she called out, her head thrashing from side to side against the cool, hard marble. "Yes! Please, yes!"

A fearsome growl escaped his throat, and he forced her legs even wider apart, burying himself even deeper as he started flicking her clit with his tongue. Over and over, back and forth, so fast, she felt tears behind her eyes. She bit down on her lip to halt them, her head pounding, her heart slamming so hard inside her ribs she was sure they were getting bruised.

Everything inside of her, every pain, every hope, every secret burst like an emotional and physical dam, and she was nothing but raw lust and unapologetic need. As his tongue worked her, and his growls and groans intensified, Genevieve came. She came so hard she couldn't breathe, pressing her mound against his mouth and rough chin as she writhed and convulsed, circling her hips, squeezing her muscles as she took wave after wave of orgasm.

Before she was even replete, before the breath held inside her lungs had a chance to escape, Jean-Baptiste lifted her boneless frame into his arms and stood. "I'm taking you to bed, Miss Burel."

"Wait," she said breathlessly, clinging to him.

"What is it?" His tone was rough and impatient and fierce. "I don't think I have it in me to discuss or flirt. If I don't fuck you this very instant, my cat will destroy my insides and I'll take care of the rest."

"I'm not Miss Burel," she whispered.

"What?"

"Not right now," she said, her drowsy eyes opening to meet his blistering amber gaze. "Not tonight. Not when you're inside of me. Do you understand?"

His nostrils flared and he nodded. "Genevieve," he snarled hungrily as he headed for his bedroom. "Beautiful, provocative Genny."

———

Jean-Baptiste stalked down the hall, removing as many pieces of clothing as he could. His. Hers. Fuck if he knew or cared. He just wanted them skin to skin as quickly as possible. He'd never felt this frantic, this desperate to connect, to feel, to know a female.

And it scared the shit out of him.

The lights were out in the bedroom, but the moon shone bride-white and brilliant through the open balcony windows. Enough for him to see her incredible face, her hungry eyes. And when his thighs hit the edge of the bed, when he gathered up the comforter, tossed it to the floor and laid her out on her back, her golden skin against stark white sheets, her exquisite body.

He growled as he settled her against the mattress. He'd done pretty damn well in stripping her. The bun was no more, and the shirt was gone, pearl buttons no doubt leading a pathway from the living room to the bedroom like opalescent breadcrumbs. All she had on now was her bra and that skirt he'd yanked to her hips on the marble table. The skirt that was nearly ripped from hem to waist.

Shit. He'd get her a new one.

He'd get her twenty new ones.

His eyes clung to her curves, her mouth, her wide, eager gaze as he yanked off his jeans and T-shirt. When he saw her hands disappear behind her back, working the clasp on her pale pink bra, he loomed over her, growling.

"That's my job, Genevieve."

Her hands stilled and her eyes flipped up to meet his. "I like that. The way you say my name."

Something hot and liquid moved through him, and it had nothing to do with sexual desire. Jean-Baptiste dipped his head, slid a canine inside the front of her bra and tugged. There was a quick pop and Genevieve gasped. Both silky pink cups flew to opposite sides, revealing a pair of the most spectacular breasts he had ever seen.

His mouth started to water.

"And I like that, too," she said breathlessly, her gaze raking over him; his face, neck, his chest. "And these," she continued, putting her hands on his forearms, moving up, over his pumas, tracing the lines of the water and grass. "Did they hurt?"

He shook his head, jaw tight. He was poised above her, his muscles straining, his skin vibrating, his cock so hard it could drill granite. He'd never wanted anything more. To be inside this female, so deep he lost himself. So wet, he drowned. So enveloped, all thought and anxiety bled from him.

"Maybe I'll get a tattoo," she whispered.

Fuck. He spread her legs with one thigh and demanded, "Where?"

Her gaze slid from his neck to his eyes. "I don't know. Any suggestions? My back? My hip? My ankle? My inner thigh?"

"Oh, Genny," he breathed, dropping his head, nuzzling the underside of her breast. "You have such beautiful skin. So perfect."

He lapped at one dusky pink nipple and she gasped, wriggled beneath him.

"I think the only mark you should have on your body is mine."

Her eyes slammed up to his. "What?"

He grinned. "You heard me. And you know what I meant by it."

He dipped his head again, but this time he took her nipple into his mouth and suckled it deep. A groan escaped her throat, raw and hungry, and her back arched off the bed. God, she tasted so sweet. He was never going to be able to forget it, forget her. His cat was right there with him, wanting the same thing. Snarling, threatening to emerge if it wasn't satisfied.

For one brief second, Jean-Baptiste felt the feline at the surface of his skin, felt the beginnings of a shift, but then Genevieve reached for him—her hand sliding between her bodies, her fingers wrapping around the trunk of his cock—and the puma growled and retreated back into its cage.

While she stroked him languidly, possessively, Jean-Baptiste turned to her other plump breast and suckled that one, too. He drew the fiercely tight nipple deep into his mouth until she cried out, until she squeezed the head of his dick—until pre-come rushed from both their sexes.

He knew the words he'd uttered to her had been impulsive as hell. The offer, the claim to mark her. But it had also been real and true, and had come from deep within his guts. How the fuck had he managed to meet the one female in the world who was meant for him? It was a goddamn miracle—and one he wasn't about to turn away from. Maybe he wasn't the best male for her. Not now. *Not yet.* But he wanted to be. He'd find a way to be.

As he circled her nipple with his tongue, then flicked it sharply up and down, back and forth, she moaned and gasped and writhed beneath him. Her thumb played with the pre-come at the head of his cock as he trailed his hand down over her ribs, to her flat stomach, to her hipbones and into the smooth curve of her sex. When he felt the fire, the molten lava between her legs, he nearly came.

"Sweet, Genny," he whispered against her breast. "You're creaming, *ma chérie*. Your thighs, your hot pussy and my sheets are drenched." He ran his teeth over her nipple. "Just the way I like it."

"Jean-Baptiste, please," she said breathlessly, wriggling against his wrist, wanting his hand, needing to be filled. And when he thrust two fingers up inside her slick, tight channel, she screamed his name again.

Tight, wet heat gripped his fingers, and he moaned and lifted his head. Her eyes were glassy and large and pinned to his face. Her lips were parted and she was panting.

Shit, he wouldn't last at this rate. One drive into her pussy and his cock was going to explode.

He took her mouth in a series of hungry, possessive, painful kisses as he growled against her lips, and his fingers pumped inside her slowly and rhythmically.

"Please, Jean-Baptiste," she murmured, nipping at his bottom lip as she wrapped her legs around his waist. "Please come inside me. I need to know. I need to know how you feel."

I need you.

The realization, the absolute truth in that thought, thundered through him, and he eased his fingers out of her, grabbed his stiff cock and pressed it against the plump, pink folds that guarded her slick pussy. He glanced down, saw the way her flesh hugged the head of his dick, beckoned him inside, creamed around him in anticipation.

And then she jacked up her hips, taking him inside her just an inch or two.

Jean-Baptiste felt his mind retreating and his body taking over.

Mine.

You belong to me.

He slid his hands beneath her hips, cupped her ass and lifted her, letting her body take him, one inch at a time until he was buried inside of her. Her eyes dropping closed, her face tensing and her throat releasing groan after groan, Baptiste guided her back and forth, her pussy fucking his cock. It was the most perfect feeling in the world, and he knew in that moment that if anyone tried to come between them, if anyone even looked at this female with lust in their eyes, he would attack to kill.

He eased her hips to the mattress, released her, only to spread her legs wider. He placed his hands on her inner thighs and started thrusting.

She cried out. "Yes! God, yes!"

"Your pussy is milking me, Genny," he said through gritted teeth. "It's like blisteringly hot ocean waves all the way down my cock, *ma chérie*. I don't know how long I can last."

She was gone, her head thrashing from side to side on the mattress. Jean-Baptiste pulled out, just partway so he could see her, him, their connection. Her dusky pink lips were wrapped around his cock, coating him in her sweet juices. Christ, if he could lick her and fuck her at the same time, he would.

His head dipped and he closed his lips around one luscious tit. As he pumped inside of her, he drew on that nipple, flicking it with his tongue. Inside her pussy, the honey sweet walls were spasming, electric currents and waves of wet heat.

"Jean-Baptiste!" she cried out, stiffening beneath him.

He battered her womb, suckled her nipple deep, as she came. With every thrust, he growled. With every new wave of orgasm, he cursed. With every roll of his hips, he claimed what had belonged to him the moment she'd walked onto that porch and eyed him warily, that god-damn blouse buttoned up to her chin.

She wasn't buttoned up now, he mused, fucking her so deep she cried out again. She was bare. Skin glistening with sweat, stomach muscles flexed, ripe breasts bouncing with every thrust, neck and jaw tense, lips parted as she breathed heavy and lustful.

She was his.

And when her slick channel convulsed for the third time that night, when she reached up, ran her fingers over his nipple, and tugged at the metal running through it, he exploded.

Pounding into her with utter and complete abandon, his body shaking and his balls tightening, he came, so hard and intense he felt something impossible overtake him. *No.* Not overtake him. Retreat inside him.

The cat.

He thrust up inside her one last time, and stayed there, buried against her womb, her warmth. Then he rolled them both to the side, and, breathing heavily, wrapped his arms around her and pulled her close. His heart was slamming against his ribs; his mind going nuts. He found her gaze. Her eyes were the bluest he'd ever seen them. And soft and satisfied and…dare he say, happy?

But inside himself, a miracle was taking place. The out-of-control, barely caged cat that he'd been trying to keep hidden for so long was purring. *Fuck.* The feline was nearly asleep. His tats and his piercings, and the malachite had never even come close to making him feel like this. Like her.

Genevieve.

His beautiful, sweet, and debilitatingly sexy Genny.

She controlled his cat.

———

Genevieve ran her hand up his arm, over the bulging muscle, over the growling pumas to his shoulder and neck. He was too beautiful.

Oh, god. What had she done?

What blissful, amazing, mind-bending act had she given into? Begged for? Wanted again, even now.

Jean-Baptiste was right. Seduction was a lie, an excuse—something you used to protect yourself from the vulnerability of asking for what you wanted.

She released a breath, her eyes connecting to his under the haze of moonlight streaming in through the window. Here she was, curled around this spectacular male, his arms protecting her, his gaze fiercely possessive, his cock still stiff and pulsing inside of her. And she never wanted to move again. Her throat felt suddenly tight. How was she ever going to walk away and forget this, forget him? How was she going to continue her quest and her mission when the sun rose the next day? Make sure Isi remained where she was, and then return to the Wildlands and a life that could never include him? Them? This...

His brows moved together in a frown of concern. "Genny?"

She pulled eye contact and buried herself deeper against his chest. "Don't go," she whispered into his skin. "I want to stay like this a little while longer."

Jean-Baptiste chuckled softly, his hands running down her back to cup her ass. "A little while? Oh, *ma chérie*. We have all night."

No, Jean-Baptiste, she thought sadly, letting her eyes drift closed and her breathing soften. *We only have one night.*

CHAPTER SIX

Leaving the warm bed and sweet, soft body of his female had been the hardest thing Jean-Baptiste had ever had to do. But it would pay off. In a grand surprise he hoped would please her, and show her that her first impression of him—*bad news*—was inaccurate.

Even at two a.m. the French Quarter was packed, in full party mode everywhere he looked—brimming with revelers. Everywhere but Isi's shop. Jean-Baptiste slid the Jag into a vacant spot in front of the house and killed the engine. Black and quiet. This wasn't like her. Midnight to five a.m. were her prime working hours. Either she was avoiding certain customers, or straight-up avoiding him.

She'd have known he'd return, that he wasn't going to accept one quick shut down about coming to the Wildlands. She'd have known he'd try again. And she'd be prepared.

Jean-Baptiste evaded the front door, and circled around to the back. He wanted the window that led straight into the body art room, the one they'd spoken in earlier. The room he knew best.

He swung himself up into a nearby tree, then silently crept to the edge of a thick branch and reached for the latch on the window. But before his hand even made contact with the chipped white paint, the scent of something pungent shot into his nostrils. Whatever it was stung like hell, and made his brain go slow and fuzzy.

"Was this head trip meant for me?" he muttered with irritation. "Or someone else?"

For anyone who wishes me harm.

The words blasted into his head, a near explosion of sound, and Jean-Baptiste whirled around, hissing as he reached for the red powder he carried in his pocket. She was somewhere above him, high in the tree, and though he couldn't see her, he could scent her. Granted, if this had happened a few days ago—shit, a few hours ago even, before Genevieve had eased and stroked his feral cat—Isi's magic would've pulverized him, made his cat so insane he'd have been debilitated. He'd have fallen out of the tree, clutching his head and begging for the pain to stop.

But times had changed.

"You know I don't want to hurt you," he said into the darkness, gripping the powder in one hand, swinging up onto another thick tree branch with the other. "But our kind is in serious trouble. Our borders are compromised, our magic is dying far faster than we realized, there's been an attack inside our lands, and the first Pantera cub conceived in over fifty years might not survive."

"What's wrong with you?" Isi said, her voice strangely far away, though her scent remained immobile. "You seem...different. More powerful."

"The cat's caged, Isi."

He heard her gasp. "What?" Then curse. "I want to help you, okay?" she said, her voice fearful and all over the place now. "But I just can't."

Jean-Baptiste took a deep breath and calmed his insides. "I'm afraid you must."

His instincts were sharper than they'd been in years, and his nose had always been first rate. In under three seconds, he leapt to the top branch. He caught her gaze, her shocked expression just before he opened his hand and blew the red powder straight into her face.

"Damn you, Baptiste," she uttered, her eyes rolling back in her head, her body swaying. "I can't...I'm not meant to be there..."

She passed out. But before she fell, Jean-Baptiste pulled her into his arms and held her close, then dropped easily from branch to branch until they hit the ground. As he headed around the side of the house and toward his car, he growled softly. He didn't relish in the fact that he was taking this female into the Wildlands against her will, but these were desperate times.

Not just for the Pantera.

But for him.

———

Genevieve awoke to rich, yellow beams of sunlight, the earthy scent of coffee, the delicious feel of Jean-Baptiste's warm, thickly muscled body against her back, and the breath-stealing intrusion of his steel-hard cock slowly pushing inside her.

She instantly arched her back, groaning as she gave him better access. Jean-Baptiste brought an arm around her waist and up to grip her shoulder. As he filled her, inch by wondrous inch, he pressed down on her shoulder, sending him as deep as possible.

Grinning, her entire body flaring with heat and hunger, Genevieve let her eyes drift downward. Jean-Baptiste's other hand had slipped between her legs and was working its way to her sex. The muscles inside her pussy clenched in anticipation, and she wasn't sure if she wanted to keep her back arched or swing her hips forward. But before she could even pull another thought from her already-fuzzy brain, she felt his teeth on her shoulder. Growling, he scraped gently over her skin as his fingers slipped into her wet pussy lips.

After that, it was impossible to do anything but give in and let her body react and respond.

Thrusting inside of her, nipping at her shoulder, circling her plump clit, Jean-Baptiste hit all the right spots, and Genevieve moaned and fisted the sheets and moved with him. God, being filled by him, taken by him, felt so right. Like the perfect breeze off the bayou, the perfect day when everything goes just as you planned it—the perfect kiss from the one male on earth who sees past your buttons and starch and into your splayed heart.

"Genny," he uttered roughly. "Just the thought of being inside you, so deep inside your tight pussy, is enough to make me come." He cursed and bit her shoulder again. "But the reality…Christ, it's like a drug. A drug I never want to come off of. A drug I will never let anyone else near—"

He pinched her clit. Lightly. But it was Genevieve's undoing.

She moaned, arched her back even farther, circled her hips over and over, feeling the volcanic rush of impending orgasm spread through her. And when he did it again—pinched her sensitive bud, a little harder this time—she screamed and came apart in his hands.

It was too much for Jean-Baptiste. He roared into the beams of sunshine cascading down upon them, gripped her, nipped her, and as she bucked wildly in his arms, he gave her three hard, deep thrusts before he came inside her, before he filled her with hot, milky seed, before he gathered her up and held her impossibly close.

It seemed like hours, days, maybe even weeks before either of them moved again. Before they even stirred. They lay still and sweaty as the sunbeams were temporarily overtaken by clouds, then returned, brighter and warmer than ever.

Then Genevieve purred and rolled in Jean-Baptiste's arms until she faced him. She draped her leg across his powerful thigh and stared. Sweat agreed with him. So did sex. His eyes were glowing. His dark hair fell around his neck, the tats, his jaw. And his mouth was a dusky, well-worked-over, crimson color. She wanted him again.

"Yes, Miss Burel?" he said, his eyes flashing with heat.

She grinned. "I smell something amazing."

"Well, thank you."

She laughed. "No, not you."

"Not me?" He plastered on a frown, which frankly only made him look sexier. "Then it must be the beignets and coffee."

"You're kidding?" Her heart pinged and she came up on her elbow. "You did that for me?"

He reached down and gave her backside a playful slap. "Just trying to impress you, Miss Burel."

She loved being called Genny, especially when he was inside her. It was soft and gentle and intimate. But she had to admit there was something that made every inch of her skin tingle when he called her Miss

Burel. "I can't believe you went out just to get me coffee and beignets. Where are they? I need them now."

He laughed. "Easy, *ma chérie*. I'll get it. I'll be serving you. Feeding you. Though, with how late it is, the coffee might be a little on the cool side."

"Late?" She looked around for a clock, but didn't see one. How late was it?

"Nothing to worry about." Jean-Baptiste growled, kissed her thoroughly, then flipped the sheets back and sat up. "And the beignets are only part of the surprise."

"Really?" The time was momentarily forgotten as she caught sight of his smooth, broad back and the spear tattoo running up the length of his spine. God, he was truly mouthwatering. "Are you spoiling me, Mr. Baptiste?" she purred.

He glanced over his shoulder, gave her a heavy-lidded, highly sexual grin. "All day, every day, Miss Burel."

Heat rushed through her. "Tell me."

"I took care of our little problem."

Confusion intermingled with the heat inside her and she came up on her knees. "What do you mean?"

He stood, lifted an eyebrow. "Isi is in the Wildlands."

Genevieve's lips parted, but nothing came out. No breath, no gasp, no words. Even though the sun was shining outside the glass doors, the room suddenly took on a gray cast, and inside Genevieve's brain, electric shocks of fear and warning detonated.

No. He couldn't have…*she* couldn't have…

"I took her there myself," he continued, standing gloriously naked before her. "It's done, *ma chérie. Our mission is complete, and we can stay here all—*"

"*No!*" The word came out harsh and fearful, and Genevieve wasted no time in scrambling off the bed. "Oh my god. Oh my god." *What time is it? How long did we sleep?*

"Genevieve? What the hell's wrong?"

Everything. God, how could she be so stupid? So careless? How could she have allowed herself to forget the point of this trip in a one-night-of-meaningless-fun sinkhole? Shit, the one road to her future…

What the hell time was it?

"Genevieve," Jean-Baptiste said again, this time with a growl attached.

"It's over," she said, grabbing clothes out of her bag and throwing them on.

"What's over?" His voice was low, wary.

"My career. My shot." *Finding a way to fix the broken magic in my family. Where was the damned clock?*

"What are you talking about? Raphael's thrilled."

She hastily toed on her shoes and zipped up her bag. "I have to go. Right now. I have to go." *I have to see if I can repair this damage. Beg the elders for a second chance.*

"I thought this would please you. I thought…" He ran a hand through his hair. "I'll call for the car."

"Don't worry. I'll take a cab. I can get back on my own." She wouldn't make this mistake again. She'd swear it to them.

"Okay, this is bullshit." Jean-Baptiste was at her side in a second, naked and tense, grabbing her by the arms. "Look at me."

She stilled. She didn't want to. God, she didn't want to. When she looked at him, bad things happened. Bad things that masqueraded as amazing, wonderful, perfect, future-killing, things. But her eyes slid up anyway. And as she met his gaze, saw the confusion and the heat and his desperate need to understand her, her heart squeezed. And her mind whispered traitorously. *Love?*

"Is this about bringing Isi in yourself?" he asked. "Wanting to impress Raphael? First assignment kind of thing?"

"No."

"Then what?"

She shook her head, bit her lip.

"You need to talk to me."

"I have to go."

"Not yet."

"You don't get to hold me here," she said, her throat tight. "I want to go."

276

"You want *me*," he said, his face a mask of hunger and heat.

Oh, god.

"You want me, Miss Burel. Say it."

"Of course I want you!"

"Then stop this. This ranting. This fear." He released her shoulders and took her face in his hands. "I'm here with you, Genny. Don't you understand that? You know how I feel, what I want—what I'm offering. My life is yours now. It's insane and too fast, but it's right. We both feel it. All I want to do is be with you, care for you, protect you." His eyes searched her. "Whatever the problem is, I can fix it. Just tell me. Talk to me."

She shook her head, her throat raw and tight.

"Yes," he assured her. "It's what males do for their females."

Never in her life had someone looked at her this way. Wanted her this way. Utterly and unabashedly. And yet, she couldn't embrace him. She'd chosen her path, made her commitment to the elders. And you didn't go back on that. Not unless you wished to incur their wrath. Her family needed her now. And as she'd found out with her parents, running off, giving in to selfish choices, wasn't going to solve the problem of the busted magic attacking her family.

His voice deepened to a possessive growl. "I've claimed you, Genny. I nearly marked you with my teeth a moment ago, for fuck's sake. And if we'd been inside the Wildlands, if I'd had access to my puma's claws, I would have."

She gasped then, her eyes going wide. All that he'd said when she was in his arms, beneath him, in front of him, crying out his name, came back in a rush. Yes, he'd offered for her and she'd allowed her mind to dismiss it. Pretend it never happened so she could enjoy the little bit of heaven she'd wanted so desperately. But now, looking up into his fierce, darkly handsome face, she could no longer dismiss it. The beautiful, perfect offer, and the ugly truth.

"No one can claim me, Jean-Baptiste," she said with such deep regret it was palpable. "I'm not a Suit. Not anymore. I work for the elders. I can never be this way with you again. And I can never be your mate."

CHAPTER SEVEN

Dusk was settling over the bayou, soft and quiet and milky. The massive sable puma watched the one he wanted above all others scamper off into the trees, her nearly white gold pelt acting as a beacon, a spotlight. He wanted to run after her, block her path, growl at her, hiss at her. At least until she listened to reason, maybe dropped to her belly and let him curl up beside her again, lick her fur. But Genevieve Burel was determined to get to the elders, plead with them to forgive her and allow her back into their fold. And Jean-Baptiste had decided to let her.

He turned in a circle, snarling softly. She'd lied to him. And yet, how could he be angry with her? He'd lied to her, too.

He opened his mouth to scent her one last time, pull the sweet, delicate fragrance of her and her cat into his nostrils, then took off in the opposite direction. He'd give her twenty-four hours to come to her senses, listen to herself, her body, and her cat. Twenty-four hours to realize they belonged together. Twenty-four hours to come to terms with the fact that the elders were her past, and Jean-Baptiste was her future. Then he was going in.

Clock starts now, Miss Burel.

He yowled at a few black puma Hunters on patrol near the edge of the yellow cow lily-strewn bayou. They returned his call, and he continued on, weaving in and out of a stand of oak, catching the scents of Hunters and Suits among the pitcher plants and wild bee balm as he headed for town. Though his heart hurt like a motherfucker, he wanted to check on Ashe, Raphael, and on Isi. See what progress was being made. See if the voodoun was awake and plotting his demise.

The village was buzzing like the cave-top hive he'd stumbled upon as a cub when he broke through a patch of anise shrub. Must be close to evening meal, Jean-Baptiste thought, heading down one of the side streets. The Pantera pumas were all shifting into their human forms, waving goodbye to friends, rushing out of shops, making their way toward their residences. Baptiste spotted the clinic ahead and picked up speed. A few pumas, still in their cat forms, jumped out of his way, hissing, but Baptiste didn't slow. Already up the steps and inside, he headed for his office, a place he'd hardly been in the last few months. He'd claimed to be either ill or working from home. He hadn't wanted to risk a problem with his cat. But he didn't have that problem anymore, did he? he mused, bursting into the lab. Not since Genevieve.

His lip curled and his cat purred. Damn, he missed her already. Maybe he should've insisted on going with her to see the elders, letting the three ancient females know just to whom their new recruit belonged. But he was trying not to be a possessive bastard. Trying to let her come to the realization that they belonged together on her own.

Of course, he wouldn't wait long.

Twenty-four hours.

Tick. Tock.

"Come to check on your voodoun?"

His cat's fur prickled and he turned around, eyed the party behind him. Raphael and two of the Pantera's best physicians entered the lab, the latter wearing pale blue coats and looking very concerned.

Baptiste shifted instantly, loving the new and precious feeling of control he now had over his animal.

Raphael's tired, green eyes narrowed with the new, quick and easy act. "Well, this a new development."

Not confirming or denying the Suit's assessment, Jean-Baptiste walked toward them. "The voodoun. She awake?"

"She is," Angel said dryly, his night-black eyes and white short hair a startling contrast. "Awake and pissed."

Grabbing the stack of charts from Angel's hands, CJ headed for her desk. "I think the last time I checked in on her, she was planning your death."

Just as he'd expected. "Weapon of choice?"

The red-haired female glanced up from her charts. "A little of everything. She was talking blades when we examined her. Then a very dull saw when we took blood."

They'd done a full work-up? Christ, she was going to be spitting fire. "Did you give her anything?"

"Just some anti-nausea meds. She was pretty green when she woke up. But the meds seemed to have given her some relief."

"Has she seen Ashe?" Jean-Baptiste asked.

Raphael growled before anyone could answer. "She's refused."

Damned, stubborn woman. "I'll talk to her."

"You need to do more than talk, Baptiste," Raphael said, closing the gap between them, his nostrils flaring. "You need to convince her to come and see Ashe, help her, cure her—"

"Raphael—" he began.

But the leader of the Suits was too far gone now. Rage and fear and misery coated his skin, was the air he breathed, directed every move, every thought.

He cocked his head to one side and flashed Baptiste his fully-descended canines. "Because if she doesn't help my female and cub, I won't be able to stop myself from killing her."

———

"The voodoun is here?" came the soft hiss. "In the Wildlands?"

"Yes." Genevieve sat before the elders, her chin lifted, but her insides twisting and turning with dread and grief and desire for the male she'd left back in the bayou. The three ancient, female Pantera, who existed in their puma state, were coated in mist, and sat in the three points of a triangle on the wide, cypress bridge that extended across the calm, moonlit bayou.

"You failed to stop her," said Wilu. The brown cat's words were not a question.

Genevieve nodded. "I know."

"What is your excuse?" Gaya asked, the blue-gray cat's matching eyes thoughtful.

I was asleep. I was in bed with a male.

I fell in love.

Her shoulders falling, Genevieve shook her head. "I can only claim inexperience."

The third elder, Tyee, rose to all four paws and started toward Genevieve, her white fur, thick and lush. "Do you wish to rectify your failure, Genevieve?"

"I wish to apologize for it," she said quickly.

The cat shook her head, her pale blue eyes narrowed. "It's not enough if your goal is to be one of our students. An elder yourself someday."

Warring emotions swam in Genevieve's blood. This was it. Her choice, her decision, and she had nothing but excuses. They wanted her commitment to a cause she believed in wholeheart-edly—a cause that could stop the decline of magic both inside her home and out—and she was hesitating. But could she truly give up seeing Jean-Baptiste again? Never being touched by him? Kissed by him? Even the idea, the thought, damaged her heart.

She was weak.

"It's no loss, Genevieve," Gaya said pleasantly. "Just as your mother before you, it seems that you may not be suited for such an honor."

The words had not been meant to bruise. The elders only spoke in facts, truths, hard as they might be to face. But Genevieve winced all the same.

"I don't believe that," she said, her chin lifting.

"Your passion is elsewhere," Wilu said, her bright yellow eyes cling-ing to Genevieve. "As is your focus. Perhaps you wish to find a mate."

"No," Genevieve said, shaking her head, even as her brain screamed, *I already have!*

Tyee stopped before her, leaned in and touched her black nose to Genevieve's hand. "Perhaps the magic inside your home wanes because your belief in the elders wanes."

Her heart lurched. "Never!"

The white puma dropped her head. "You have disappointed us, Genevieve Burel."

"Wait—"

"You are released."

Before Genevieve could say another word, all three elders vanished from the bridge, leaving only a thick mist curling above the bayou.

———

"You can forget my shop exists. No more ink. No more metal. I don't care if your cat chews your dick off, understand?"

Standing in the middle of the lab, a six foot, black-haired linebacker of a Hunter guarding her back, Isi glared at Jean-Baptiste. Arms crossed over her chest, blue-streaked hair wild around her face, the woman looked ready to murder him, and he didn't blame her one bit.

"How are you feeling?" he asked.

She flipped him off. "Don't pretend you give a shit."

He shook his head. "Not pretending. I do care. I just care more about the survival of my species. And this woman who carries the first Pantera cub in fifty years is being threatened by something. From the inside out, Isi. I swear to god, I wouldn't have gone to these lengths, been a complete asshole, if it weren't dire."

"You had no right to do what you did, Baptiste," she said. "I don't owe you or them anything."

He nodded. "That's true."

Her teeth ground together. "But..."

"But, shit, Isi. It's a baby."

She stared at him for several long seconds, then slowly started to shake her head. "I don't know what you think I can do for her."

"Just take a look, see what you think." He walked toward her.

"Do I even have a choice here?"

"Course you do."

"Don't try to play nice now, Baptiste," she warned as he approached. "I'm not forgiving you."

Jean-Baptiste grinned. He'd always enjoyed their almost sibling-like banter. "No forgiveness," he said, reaching out and pushing down a patch of her wild hair that was sticking straight up. "But maybe if I need the ink or metal again…"

She slapped his hand away. "I told you. Hell. No."

"Come on, Isi. You know you find it fascinating—"

He stopped speaking, his nose catching the most wondrous, most delectable scent in the world. Instantly, his body went hot and hard, a hungry growl vibrating in his throat.

His nose didn't make mistakes.

Not when it came to his female.

Miss Burel was near.

Chapter Eight

Violence had never called to Genevieve until now. Until she stood in the doorway of the clinic's lab and watched Jean-Baptiste touch the voodoun's hair. Her lip peeled back and her canines started to drop. She wanted to spring, release her puma, race across the floor and leap onto the woman, claws out. But hurting Isi, or even displaying her nearly debilitating jealously, wasn't why she was here. Trying to prove her worth to the elders and her commitment to the Pantera by removing the woman from the Wildlands without incident was.

Jean-Baptiste stepped away from Isi, and turned around to face Genevieve. If it was possible, he looked even more fiercely handsome than he had a few hours ago when she'd left him in the forest. His amber eyes were glowing with warmth and the metal in his lip winked at her.

She swallowed the saliva that had pooled in her mouth.

"It's good to see you, Miss Burel," he said. "And much sooner than I had anticipated. Have you come to tell me your dealings with the elders are done?"

His voice enveloped her, made her insides melt, made her cat purr. She growled and shook her head. "I've come for her."

Isi raised one eyebrow.

"And what do you plan to do with her?" Jean-Baptiste asked evenly, coming to stand in front of the voodoun.

"Take her back. She doesn't belong here. She doesn't want to be here." She looked at Isi then, tried to push back the desire to rip the diamond studs from the female's nose with her teeth. "Isn't that right?"

"By *here* do you mean the Wildlands?" Jean-Baptiste asked. "Or beside me?"

She turned to him and growled. "Of course I mean the Wildlands." But inside her guts, and her heart, the latter seemed a far bigger concern at the moment.

Foolish female.

"I think I have some of that anti-love elixir with me," Isi uttered dryly. "It's yours if you want it, Baptiste."

Genevieve whirled on the female and hissed, "Shut up."

Once again, Isi's eyebrows rose.

Jean-Baptiste started toward Genevieve. "The elders want her out of the Wildlands."

She lifted her chin. "That's right."

"And you've come to do their bidding." Those liquid amber eyes pinned her where she stood. "Do you even know why?"

"Of course I do. They believe her to be detrimental to our land, to Ashe and the child. They know what's best for our kind, Jean-Baptiste. They always have. They've always protected the Pantera." *It's why I've admired them so much. Why I've given up my life to be in their service.*

Jean-Baptiste didn't agree or disagree, just kept coming toward her. "Do you think it's wise to take on a job without knowing the reasons behind such a belief? What if they're wrong? Or misinformed?"

"They're the elders," she said as if that was the only explanation necessary. "They know all."

"I don't believe that. If they knew all, why is it we still can't breed? Why do we still have pools of dying magic on our borders?"

Genevieve just stared at him. She'd had the same thoughts, the same questions, and had pushed them from her mind. Wasn't it traitorous to question the elders?

"Isi could be the one person to help Ashe," Jean-Baptiste was saying. "Help the cub."

"And what if she's not?" Genevieve said softly, her head growing fuzzy as his scent pushed into her nostrils. "What if she does more harm than good? That could be behind the elders' motives. They could know something about her we don't."

Jean-Baptiste's gaze was fierce. "Something they refuse to name?"

"They are the Pantera!"

"No. *We* are the Pantera. All of us."

"Baptiste." It was Isi. She'd grown suddenly pale, and she moaned softly. "Can we do this? Now. I'm not feeling so great again."

"You don't have to stay here," Genevieve called to her. "You can't be held against your will."

"Dammit, Genevieve!" Jean-Baptiste roared.

But Genevieve wasn't listening. "I can take you back myself."

"No," Isi uttered, coming forward, reaching out for Jean-Baptiste. "I'll see her."

As soon as Isi's hands made contact with his arm, Genevieve lost it. The elders didn't exist anymore, neither did her weakness and pride. And claws appeared where her hands used to be. Instinct possessed her and she stalked forward, her eyes narrowed on the voodoun, her cat pushing through her skin.

"Stop, Miss Burel," Jean-Baptiste warned.

"Take. Your. Hands. Off. Him." Genevieve barely recognized the guttural, feral voice coming out of her mouth.

Isi groaned, and Jean-Baptiste turned to the guard. "Hiss, bring Isi to Raphael. Now. I'll be there in a minute."

His eyes watchful of Genevieve, the male went to the voodoun and took her arm, led her from the room. When the door to the lab closed and they were alone, Jean-Baptiste rounded on Genevieve.

"I'm not going to pretend I don't love you snarling and scratching to show not only me, but yourself, just how mated we truly are. But I'm not going to allow you to take Isi, Miss Burel—"

"It's Genevieve," she snarled.

"Not yet, it's not," he returned.

She froze, and behind her narrowed eyes she felt tears form. She missed him. How was that possible? In such a short time? His touch, the softness in his voice when he said her name, her nickname…

"Talk to me," he said, moving closer. "Do the elders have a hold over you? Are they blackmailing you or threatening you?"

She shook her head.

He gathered her in his arms. "Then what the hell is going on? You don't feel a desire for this work, for them. Your desire belongs to me now."

Goddammit, she hated his words. Hated them because they both echoed the elders', and because they were true. She nearly crumpled right there.

"Why, Miss Burel?" he pressed.

Her head dropped back and she locked eyes with him. "I love the Pantera. I only want to do right by them. The elders…" she began miserably. "I've always believed they were the answer to our longevity, our happiness and our peace. They are the ultimate problem solvers. And I'd hoped, once I was in their service, that they'd help me find the answer to my problem."

"What problem is that?"

Telling him the truth was far more difficult than she'd imagined. It made her feel oddly vulnerable. "The magic isn't just waning at our borders anymore, Jean-Baptiste." She swallowed hard. "It's broken free. It's fading inside my house. Inside my Grands. Maybe even inside me. Has been for several months now. My parents ran away instead of facing it, trying to find out how to stop it. I couldn't do that."

Jean-Baptiste was silent as he digested what she'd just told him. His gaze moved over her face, his brows pinned together, his mouth set in a grim line. He looked confused, possibly even angry.

Was he mad because she'd lied to him? Or was he disgusted at what was happening inside her house? To her family? Did he see her as weak now?

"This is unbelievable," he uttered, shaking his head.

Her heart lurched and she felt sick to her stomach. She couldn't stand to have him look at her with disgust and censure. Or listen as he told her he'd made a mistake—they weren't mates, and he didn't want to claim her.

She wriggled out of his grasp. "I have to go." She shouldn't have told him. Shouldn't have opened her heart.

"Wait. Your family's magic is gone?"

"I won't bother you again," she said, turning, hurrying toward the door, "Or your voodoun.."

"Genevieve!"

Before Jean-Baptiste could say another word, Genevieve ran out. Down the hall, she thought she heard him calling to her, but the sound was drowned out by her quick shift into her puma.

Jean-Baptiste tore out of the room after her. Christ, what a screw up. Both of them. So destined, so in love with each other, so desperate to find a way out of their strange predicaments so they could be together. Yet all the while keeping secrets. Pointless, harmful secrets. This was it. No more. They were both coming clean, leaving the past behind and turning to each other for help, for a future, for the truth.

But when he passed Ashe's room, her open door, and heard Raphael's pained voice leach out into the hallway, he slowed.

"What the hell does that mean?" the Suit demanded. "Is she okay? The cub? Fuck, I hate that I can't do a goddamn thing for her."

"What's wrong?" Jean-Baptiste came to stand in the doorway, his gaze hitting on every person in the room. Doctors, Isi, Raphael, and Ashe, asleep and pale on the bed. The small space was packed.

"The cub..." Raphael stuttered, glancing over his shoulder. The male sat on a chair beside the bed, Ashe's hand in his own, looking like death warmed over.

"The cub is healthy," said Dr. Julia, Parish's new mate. She reached down and took the pulse at Ashe's throat.

His eyes completely sunken, Raphael said, "But it's growing faster than a normal fetus."

"Our pregnancies are always faster, aren't they?" Baptiste said, his eyes lifting to Angel.

The male doc nodded, but quickly amended, "This seems to be more in line with a feline gestational period. I've never seen it before."

Shit. "When is she due?"

"Three months."

Momentarily dumbfounded, Baptiste turned back to Raphael. The male looked ready to explode, lose his mind, maybe collapse. Baptiste prayed to god Isi could do something, because if she couldn't, if Ashe didn't make it, he feared not only what the loss would do to the leader of the Suits, but to the Pantera as a whole.

"I see no signs of distress with the cub," Dr. Julia said, switching out a bag of fluids. "And though the child is developing quickly, it looks healthy. Ashe's vitals are strong. She should be fine—*if* we can stop whatever's holding her mentally."

Every pair of eyes in the room turned to Isi. And the woman shrank slightly under the weight of their hope and fears. Pale as the reeds beneath the water of the bayou, she nodded at them. "I'll try. I need time though. Time to study her, see the way she moves, smells, makes noises in her sleep—"

"Maybe you can do more than that," came a female voice behind Baptiste.

Walking into the room, Dr. CJ held up a file, her face a mask of tension.

"What are you talking about?" Raphael demanded.

CJ looked intently at Isi. "Your blood tests came back."

The woman flinched. "So? Did you figure out why I feel like puking every time I'm near or inside of the Wildlands?"

"No." CJ glanced at Julia, then at Angel, then back at Isi. "But I did find out that you and Ashe share DNA."

Isi's pale skin turned gray. "What?"

"You're related."

A soft groan echoed throughout the room. Everyone looked back at Isi. But the sound hadn't come from her. Jean-Baptiste's gaze slid to the bed, and to Ashe, covered in wires and tubes.

"No," Isi was mumbling, drawing back, fearful now. "That's impossible. I have no family."

"Blood doesn't lie, Voodoun," Dr. CJ said crisply.

"Oh, my god," Julia called, rushing to the bed, her stethoscope already in her ears. "Raphael. Look."

Isi looked over at Jean-Baptiste. "There's a mistake. I don't have family. They screwed something up—"

"You," came a breathy, pained sound.

Jean-Baptiste tore his gaze from Isi, and turned to Ashe. Her face was as pale as skim milk, her lips were dry and a dull pink, her body was still prostrate and hooked up to a ton of meds via a ton of tubes, but her eyes…holy shit, her eyes were open and pinned on Isi.

"*Ma chérie,*" Raphael said, his voice shaking as he took her hand and kissed the palm. "My love. Oh, thank god."

But Ashe didn't seem to recognize Raphael or his voice. She stared transfixed at Isi, her lips parting once again. "You," she uttered hoarsely. "I know you."

Chapter Nine

"Something's wrong with our Bé."

"Definitely."

Sitting cross-legged on her Grands' bed, Genevieve glanced up from her cards—a nearly full house—and caught them both staring at her, their own cards all but forgotten.

"Come on, tell us," Maw-Maw cooed.

"Yes," Paw-Paw said. "What happened on that trip, sweetheart?"

She'd been home for less than an hour, and in that time her Grands had done nothing but study her and grill her about her trip. Who was on it with her, why was she home so late, was that expression on her face an indicator of success or hardship?

"Nothing," she told them again. "Everything's fine."

Paw-Paw snorted. "We may be ancient, Bé love, but we know you better than anyone. Something went either very wrong on that trip." He turned to his wife and grinned. "Or very right."

Heat surged into Genevieve's cheeks, and she tried like hell to keep the image of Jean-Baptiste's face, body and mouth from entering her mind. But she failed. Seemed she was doing a lot of that lately.

"Oh, my blessed knees," Maw-Maw began, leaning forward so Genevieve could see the female's entire hand. Straight flush. "You met yourself a male, didn't you?"

"No," Genevieve said quickly, the word sounding phony even to herself. "I went to work. Nothing happened." *God, what a bald-faced lie.* "There was no one—"

"Is he handsome?" Maw-Maw asked.

"Who cares about that," Paw-Paw put in. "Can he be a good partner? Is he strong and fearless?"

A knock on the door not only stalled the conversation, but startled Genevieve.

"Genny!" called a male voice outside.

Genevieve's heart dropped into her stomach. Hell, maybe it had even burrowed itself into the mattress. What was he doing? Why would he come here after everything she'd told him? After how he'd reacted?

"Genny!" he called again. "Come out here or I'm coming in!"

Her gaze jerked back to her Grands. They were both reclining against the headboard of their bed, white down comforter to their chests, wide eyes and even wider grins plastered to their faces.

"Sounds handsome," Maw-Maw said.

"Sounds strong," Paw-Paw put in.

Oh, my god. This was humiliating. "I'll be right back," Genevieve said, scrambling off the bed.

"Take your time, Bé ," Paw-Paw called after her.

"We're not going anywhere," Maw-Maw added with a tinkling of laughter.

Her heart slamming against its cage of ribs, Genevieve hurried to the front door and burst outside. Jean-Baptiste was leaning against the porch railing. Just like he had when they'd first met. Except tonight, he didn't have on the leather jacket. Just jeans and a T-shirt, which showed off his sexy ink and hills of muscle to mouthwatering perfection.

"What are you doing here?" she asked, her mouth so dry the words nearly came out a squeak.

He cocked an eyebrow at her. It was the one with the metal through it, and she fairly sighed with desire.

"If we're to be officially mated I won't have you running from me every time there's an issue," he said, pushing away from the railing.

She backed up to the door. He followed.

"Who says we're going to be mated?" she asked breathlessly.

"I do." He touched her face, smiled. "And you do."

"You don't want to get involved with this, Jean-Baptiste."

"With what? The dying magic inside your home?"

She flinched.

"Genny, you're right about the troubles having crossed our borders. But it hasn't just attacked your family."

For a moment, Genevieve wasn't sure she'd heard him right. What was happening inside her home, to her Grands…was he saying they weren't alone?

"How do you know this?" she asked, looking at him intently, making sure she heard every word of his reply.

His thumb brushed across her cheek. "Because the magic is dying inside of me."

"What?" she said on a gasp.

"Or it was. Until you came along." His eyes pinned her where she stood.

She shook her head. "I don't understand."

"My cat has been out of control for a while now. It refused to remain caged. Even outside the Wildlands."

"Oh, my god."

"That's why the tats and the metal. I had malachite put into each to ground my puma. It was barely keeping me sane." He leaned in then and kissed her. Softly, sweetly, lovingly. "But you, my wonderful, beautiful Genny, have tamed us both."

Another wave of confusion, of shock, barreled through her. "That's not possible."

"I wouldn't think so either, unless I'd felt it." He kissed her again. "But love and chemistry, desire and respect can work miracles it seems." And again. "We're made for each other, Genny."

The knocking inside her heart, the heavy beats, the fear and worry and sadness, began to ease. He loved her. He wanted her. Despite everything.

Or maybe because of it.

"The elders told me it was just my house," she said, a strange and powerful rush of strength running through her. "They lied."

"Maybe not. Maybe they don't know about me, or if there are others who are suffering in silence and shame." His eyes grew serious. "But it's time we as a species talked about this. What's happening to our land, to our cats, to our people. So we can work together to find an answer."

Genevieve's chest swelled with pride. It's what she'd wanted from the elders. Being part of something bigger then herself, something that would help the Pantera, herself and her Grands included. Jean-Baptiste was right. The only way to find the reason for the dying magic, both on their borders and now inside their lands, was to work together as a species.

As the Pantera.

"Come, Mate," he said on a growl.

"You haven't even kissed me yet," she teased, the blood in her body surging with a now-familiar heat. "A little premature, don't you think?"

He grinned, and the look nearly made her legs turn liquid.

"Inside, Genny," he said. "We may be mated in our hearts and our bodies, but I'm going to ask permission from your Grands." He grimaced. "Hope they don't find me too scary."

She grabbed the back of his head and pulled him down for a kiss. "They'll love you. Just like I do."

He kissed her hard and hungry for several seconds, then eased back. He pulled open the screen door and was about to follow her in when his phone rang. He took a quick glance at the screen and cursed.

"Sorry, *ma chérie*," he said. "It's Raphael. And after what just happened in the clinic, I need to get this." He stabbed the button. "What's up, Raph?"

Genevieve watched him, silent as he listened to the Suit on the other end—the Suit Genevieve hoped would take her back into the fold. When Jean-Baptiste hung up, the happy, sexy, charming male who'd just kissed her dizzy and stupid was gone. In its place, stood a wide-eyed, teeth-bared male on the verge of shifting. Growling, cursing, he shook himself. Within seconds, he returned to his human form.

"Jean-Baptiste." She touched his arm, worried and a little fearful. Not of him, never of him, but of what he'd just been told. "What's happened?"

His eyes lifted to meet hers, and black ire glistened among the amber. "Not only is Ashe awake, but the ones who are responsible for her attack are in custody." His voice dropped to a dangerous pitch. "It seems there are traitors among us."

TALON

By
Alexandra Ivy

PROLOGUE

LOUISIANA
1988

The house hidden in the tangled undergrowth just south of Bossier City was one stiff breeze away from total collapse.

Built from logs that had warped in the humid Louisiana weather, the cabin had a thin sheet of rusted tin and the windows were framed by rotting shutters. Even worse, the front porch had sagged at one end, giving it the appearance of a cheap funhouse.

Not the first place any man would select for his wife to give birth to his twin daughters.

But what choice did Chayton have?

With a muttered curse, he paced through the thick grass that left a damp film of dew on his knee-high moccasins. With the blood of the Chitimacha tribe flowing through his veins, Chayton felt most comfortable in soft leather pants and a vest that had been beaded by his mother. His glossy, dark hair was worn in a braid that fell to his waist, and his lean face was dominated by a prominent nose and eyes so dark they looked black. His bow was loosely held in one hand, with a quiver of arrows strapped to his back.

He was always on guard.

Ever since the vision had forced him to go on the run with his pregnant wife.

A familiar fear speared through his heart at the memory of that fateful day.

He'd been in the Wildlands at the request of the elders. He was one of the very few humans ever allowed in the remote sanctuary of the mystical Pantera. At first it had been his position as a shaman that had allowed him entry. Like his father before him, he'd had the ability to touch the spirit world.

It was a gift that gave him a much longer life span than most humans and the strange talent to detect the faction of an unborn Pantera baby. They called him when a female was close to delivering her cub to foresee whether it would be a Diplomat or Hunter or Healer. The Pantera began training their young from the cradle. Or at least they'd called him until the Pantera stopped having cubs.

That should have been the end of his connection to the Wildlands, but during one of his visits he'd stumbled across a talent that had only been a distant rumor among shamans until he'd manifested the gift.

He could do more than a catch a hint of the future of a Pantera.

He was an actual seer.

His predictions were often vague and sometimes impossible to interpret, but they were accurate enough that he was summoned to the Wildlands when the elders were debating a decision that would affect their people. Surrounded by the magic of the Wildlands, he would call upon the powers of his ancestors to be blessed with a glimpse of the future that could help lead the Pantera in the right direction.

It was a power he used only when the need was great.

Opening pathways to the ancestors was not only dangerous to him, but could occasionally allow malevolent spirits to escape into the world of men.

A damned shame he hadn't said no when the elders had called for him again six months ago. But then he'd never seen a vision that was so clear. And certainly never one so intimately connected to himself.

His dark thoughts were thankfully cut short as the midwife stepped onto the porch. A small, dried up prune of a woman, she was known by the locals as JuJu.

"It's done," she said in clipped tones, wiping her hands on a bloody apron wrapped around her thin body.

She had the bedside manner of a rattlesnake.

Chayton stepped forward. "My wife?"

"Weak, but she'll live."

"And the babes?"

"Both are healthy." The woman stuck out a hand gnarled by age. "You have my money?"

Chayton reached beneath his vest to pull out the precious money that he'd earned by selling the pelts of animals he hunted. He didn't dare take a job that would force him to fill out paperwork.

Paperwork could be traced.

He held up the money. "Your word that you won't speak of this birth," he growled, his eyes hard with warning. "Not to anyone."

A cunning expression touched her dark, leathered face. "It will cost you."

"Fine." Chayton added another fifty he couldn't afford. "Your word."

"You have it." JuJu snatched the money and poked it into the pocket of her apron. "Do you want to see your children?"

"Yes."

Chayton took a step forward only to come to a horrified halt when he heard a female voice speak from the nearby trees.

"We all wish to see the children."

In one fluid motion he had an arrow in his bow and pointed toward the strange mist that flowed forward.

"Stay back," he snarled, his gut twisting with dread as the mist lightened to reveal three females who moved forward with grim intent.

The elders.

He'd only seen them in their puma forms, but away from the Wildlands the females were forced to take human shape. Still, it was almost impossible to make out anything of their features as they deliberately used their powers to manipulate his mind. Once they left, no one would be able to describe more than slender, female figures and a choking power that made it difficult to breathe.

Fighting through his clouded thoughts, Chayton prepared to attack. The bitches would die before harming his babies.

Preparing to take his shot, Chayton was caught off guard as he was hit from behind. Knocked to the ground by two large men, he felt the bow knocked from his hand. Then, once his arms were painfully pinned behind his back, he was jerked upright.

A glance to the side revealed his worst fear.

Two dark-haired men with eyes that glowed gold in the fading light. Pantera Hunters.

The elders waited until they were certain he was under the control of the Hunters before turning toward the stunned midwife.

"Take us to the children," they commanded in unison.

"Yes." Clearly under the influence of the elders, the midwife turned to walk back into the shack, her eyes unfocused.

The mist shimmered as the elders followed JuJu, making a gesture toward the silent Hunters.

"Bring him."

With a rough shove, Chayton was forced up the stairs and across the porch. A few more shoves and he was through the barren front room and into the back bedroom.

His breath was ripped from his lungs as he caught sight of his wife lying in the middle of the bed, a threadbare quilt covering her trembling body, and her pale hair damp with sweat. In her arms she clutched two tiny bundles wrapped in the blankets that Chayton had received from his mother as a birthing gift.

Her thin face turned in his direction. The past months hadn't been kind to Dixie. She'd thought marriage to him would mean a fine house and a position of honor in the small town of La Pierre. Instead she'd been forced to endure a difficult pregnancy living off the land like his ancestors.

Her eyes widened with confusion. "Chayton? What's going on?"

"Which child was born first?" the elders demanded.

The midwife reached to pluck one of the babes from Dixie's arms, pulling down the blanket to reveal the small birthmark on the child's collarbone.

"This one."

Shock rippled through the room as all eyes locked on the dark mark that marred the milky white skin. Even Chayton felt a twinge of unease.

"Ravens," the elders breathed.

The Mark of Shakpi.

No. It was just a birthmark. It was human nature to try and see a shape in what was nothing more than a blot.

Using his captors' distraction to his advantage, Chayton jerked free of their hold and lunged to take the baby from JuJu's arms.

"No," he rasped.

Dixie reached to grab the hem of his vest. "What are they doing?"

There was a low hiss from the elders. "The child is fated to destroy our homeland," they said.

"What?" Dixie's voice was shrill with fear. "She's just a baby."

Chayton clutched the baby to his heart. It was the first time he'd been allowed to cradle the sweet weight in his arms, but he'd loved his daughters from the moment he'd sensed that Dixie had conceived.

There was nothing he wouldn't sacrifice to protect them.

Including the future of the Pantera.

"We don't know that's what the vision meant," he rasped.

"What else can it mean?" the elders demanded, quoting back the words that had fallen from his own lips. "The blood of the Shaman's firstborn shall carry the taint of Shakpi, releasing her powers upon the lands of the Pantera."

He shook his head, stepping back. "You called me because your magic is already faltering. How can a newborn child be responsible for that?"

"Who is to say?" He had an impression of seething frustration just below the surface, although the elders continued to block his efforts to see beyond their magic. He was more immune than most humans to the mystic powers, so the fact they were able to keep him from seeing into their faces was annoying the hell out of him. Or maybe it was just a reaction to the fact they wanted to kill his daughter. "Perhaps we have failed in our duties," the elders continued. "Or perhaps time has weakened the bonds of Shakpi's prison."

"You would sacrifice the life of a babe on vague words that could mean anything?" He edged backward, sensing the door was only a few feet behind him. "Or nothing?"

"We must protect the Wildlands."

"A little late for your concern now, isn't it?" he charged.

There was a ripple of shock among the Pantera. "What do you mean?" they demanded.

Chayton lifted his chin. He'd had time to think over the past six months. He now realized that the elders had known all along how dangerous it was for him to open a direct doorway to the world of the dead. Which was no doubt why they left the task to the rare humans capable of manipulating the magic instead of trying to find a Pantera to perform the dangerous ceremony.

"You forced me to travel too often to the ancestors in your obsession to control the fate of your people, and allowed something evil to be released," he accused.

The air heated with the anger of the elders. "It's true we have discussed the possibility that Shakpi has used your journeys to the spirit world to infect you and now through you, your child."

Fury raced through Chayton. "Your arrogance created this disaster, and yet you would use an innocent baby to try and cover your asses."

There was a hiss of disbelief at his accusation before the elders moved toward him. "The sacrifice is demanded. Give us the child."

"Sacrifice?" Dixie clutched the younger twin in her arms, her face flushed. "Chayton, tell me what is happening."

The mist shimmered, as if annoyed by Dixie's interruption. "Sleep," they muttered.

Instantly Dixie fell into a deep slumber, the babe still tightly held in her arms.

Chayton bit back a curse at the sight of his wife's ready response to the command of the elders. Then, without warning, he was struck by a sudden, crazy plan.

His magic was limited, but he did have a small trick taught to him by his own father.

As the attention was turned toward the sleeping Dixie, Chayton reached into his pocket for the small flint he always carried. Then, concentrating his thoughts on the chiseled quartz, he felt it grow hot in his hands. Desperate, he poured every ounce of magic he possessed through his fingers and into the flint, waiting until the stone was searing his skin before he tossed it in the direction of the elders with a low word of ancient power.

On cue, the flint exploded into a searing white flame.

The elders cried out in shock while the two Hunters rushed to beat out the very real fire.

Instantly, Chayton was through the door and heading out of the house. He'd leaped off the porch and entered the nearby woods before the Hunters were on his trail.

Under normal circumstances a mere man wouldn't stand a chance against the lethal Pantera.

Even in their human forms they were stronger, faster, and their senses far more acute.

But Chayton wasn't just a man. He'd been trained by his father to become one with nature, allowing him to flow through the difficult terrain with a fluid ease. More importantly, he was far more familiar with the area than his trackers.

Choosing a route that would take him through marshy land so he could disguise his footprints as well as hide his scent, he ran as fast as his legs would carry him for a full hour. Only when he was certain the Hunters weren't about to tackle him from behind did he pause to carefully unwrap the blanket from the child in his arms.

Briefly he was distracted as the babe opened her eyes, regarding him with a solemn gaze that revived his flagging strength.

He was going to do everything in his power to protect his daughter.

With that thought, he pulled a dagger hidden inside the legging of his moccasin. Then, ignoring that trusting little gaze, he made a tiny cut on her foot. The babe let out a startled cry, but thankfully drifted back to sleep as he used the blanket to wipe the few drops of blood. He tossed the blanket into a nearby channel of water before making a much deeper cut into his forearm, swiftly smearing the blood on the mossy bank.

If he had any luck at all, the Hunters would believe he'd been attacked by an alligator or killed by some other predator.

If not...

He gathered the babe in his arms and took off.

If not, then he would keep running until the day he died.

Chapter One

THE WILDLANDS
2013

Moonlight glazed the lush foliage in silver as Talon crossed the boundary into the Wildlands. He stopped to take a deep breath, the magic in the air bubbling through him like the finest champagne.

Shit, he'd been gone too long.

Four weeks and two days to be exact.

He grimaced. He hadn't expected Parish's order to hunt for the traitors to lead him away from the Wildlands. It'd been enough of a shock to accept that there could be Pantera in their sanctuary who were willing to betray their own people. Hell, Parish had denied it even when the evidence was right in front of his face.

But after locking away Vincent and Savoy, and beginning his search for Pantera with the Mark of Shakpi branded on their heel, he'd learned that two Geeks had gone on the run, slipping away without leaving word with their families.

Talon had been in instant pursuit, at last tracking them to a cramped apartment in Baton Rouge.

A grim smile touched Talon's lean, starkly handsome face. He'd been pissed that he'd been forced to waste a month of his time tracking down the bastards, and even more infuriated that he might miss the upcoming Dyesse Fete—the celebration of the birth of the Pantera, and the most important holiday in the Wildlands.

Since the Elders had begun to notice the stagnant pools of decay at the fringes of their land it'd been feared that the tradition would die away. Just another sign that the Pantera were hovering on the brink of extinction. So it was hardly surprising that they each waited with baited breath each summer for the bloom of the purple water lily that would trumpet the beginning of the festival.

Still, when he'd entered the apartment he'd forgotten all about the endless days pursuing the traitors.

He'd located the mother lode.

Fake IDs, lists of addresses, and several papers written in code that would have to be deciphered. There were also three laptop computers that the tech wizards could use to gain information.

Talon had gathered it all, including the two male Pantera, before heading home.

Now he just wanted to return to his rooms at the communal Hunter house and collapse.

Giving the chains he held in his hands a tug, he moved through the thick undergrowth, not bothering to glance over his shoulder at the men who were leashed by heavy collars laced with malachite.

They'd given in to the inevitable without a fight, barely speaking on the trip back to the bayou.

That was fine with Talon.

If the Pantera didn't need the information the bastards could provide on why they'd become traitors and who was ultimately responsible for trying to destroy the Wildlands, he'd have happily killed them and left them to rot in Baton Rouge.

To him, loyalty and honor meant everything.

How could you call yourself a Pantera if you weren't willing to put the welfare of your people ahead of your own, selfish needs?

They'd reached a narrow canal choked with water lilies when Talon came to a sharp halt. His brows, the same shade of dark gold threaded with copper highlights as his hair, snapped together over his eyes that were a pale gold rimmed with jade.

He could sense a large number of Pantera rushing in his direction. Never a good thing.

Tightening his grip on the chains, Talon was preparing for an attempt to rescue the traitors when a familiar cat the color of rich caramel with glowing gold eyes leaped gracefully over the canal to land directly at his side.

Instantly he relaxed.

Raphael, the leader of the Suits, had been like a father to Talon after the death of his parents in an airplane crash thirty years ago. Despite the fact that they were only distantly related, and Talon's faction was Hunters, not Diplomats, Raphael had been the one to visit the school where Talon was being trained in his duties. Whether it was to cheer him on during his athletic competitions or to kick his ass when he'd snuck into the nearby town, La Pierre, and left an alligator in the mayor's bathtub.

Raphael had also been the one to take him to The Cougar's Den and get him cross-eyed drunk when the cute little female he'd been chasing decided to dump him for another male.

Talon trusted this man above anyone else in the world.

There was a shimmering swirl of color before Raphael shifted into his human form, dressed like Talon in faded jeans and T-shirt.

A tall man with chiseled muscles, Raphael had a golden beauty that had driven females wild. At least until he'd stunned them all by arriving back at the Wildlands with a mate who was already carrying his young.

It was a miracle.

As long as they could keep Ashe and her baby alive.

Which was why Talon had been sent to track down the traitors.

"Welcome home, Talon," Raphael murmured, his lean face too pale and his golden eyes shadowed with the brutal fear that was threatening to destroy him.

"Why the welcome committee?" Talon demanded.

"We need to speak." Raphael's tone was flat. A sure sign his emotions were on the edge of a meltdown. He snapped his fingers and Sebastian appeared at his side. The Suit was a bronze-skinned male with glowing hazel eyes and a chiseled body that proved he didn't spend much time sitting behind a desk. His tawny hair was threaded with gold and brushed his broad shoulders. "Take the prisoners to the elders."

Talon tossed the chains toward Sebastian who curled his lips to growl at the cringing prisoners. Next, Talon shoved the backpack that held the computers and file folders into the Suit's hand.

"These need to go to Xavier," he said, referring to the brilliant head of the Geeks. If anyone could coax information out of the computers it would be Xavier.

Sebastian gave an unnecessary jerk on the chains, leading the prisoners away just as Raphael nodded his head toward a thick grove of cypress trees.

"This way," the Suit commanded.

Following in Raphael's wake, Talon studied the tense set of the older man's shoulders and the manner in which he turned his head from side to side, as if searching for hidden enemies.

"This speaking doesn't involve dungeons and chains, does it?" Talon muttered, not entirely joking.

Raphael sent a puzzled glance over his shoulder. "We don't have dungeons."

Talon grimaced, shoving his way past the veil of Spanish moss to step into the small clearing in the center of the trees.

"We didn't when I left, but things are clearly changing," he pointed out in dry tones.

"Unfortunately," Raphael agreed, restlessly pacing over the spongy ground.

Talon rolled his weary shoulders, sensing he wasn't going to see his bed anytime soon. "What did I miss?"

Raphael turned to meet his worried gaze. "You were already on the hunt when Jean-Baptiste returned with the female voodoun."

Talon nodded. He'd known the male Healer had gone to fetch the human female, but he'd been headed out of the Wildlands before Jean-Baptiste returned.

"Did she help Ashe?"

"I believe so."

"Thank the goddess," Talon breathed, relief shuddering through him.

Raphael's mate carried the future of the Pantera within her fragile womb. The knowledge that they'd allowed their enemies close enough to put her and the babe in danger laid heavily on all of them.

"Don't give thanks yet," Raphael warned.

"Why?"

The leader of the Suits scrubbed his hands over his face. Talon wondered when he'd last slept.

Probably not since Ashe had been attacked and infected with some potent toxin.

"I need to start at the beginning," Raphael growled.

"Here." Talon pulled out his silver flask filled with Don Julio tequila and tossed it toward his friend. "Tell me."

Raphael took a drink, grimacing as the expensive tequila slid down his throat. "As I said, Jean-Baptiste brought Isi to the Wildlands." Another grimace. "Much against her will."

Talon arched a brow. "She's prejudiced against the Pantera?"

"No. For some reason the Wildlands make her ill."

The Wildlands making someone ill? That was weird.

"I've never heard of that before," Talon said. "Of course, I don't have enough interest in humans to know what makes them sick."

"None of us have."

Talon shrugged. He didn't really care if she was sick or not. Nothing mattered but Ashe and the baby.

"Did she have a potion for Ashe?"

Raphael turned to glance at the heavy layers of moss that kept them hidden from the rest of the swamp, sending a chill of fear down Talon's spine.

Was he afraid someone was trying to spy on them?

Were there more traitors?

Shit.

"Actually her mere presence seems to give Ashe strength," he at last said, his voice low.

311

Okay. That seemed a good thing.

So why wasn't Raphael happier?

"I don't understand," Talon admitted.

Raphael returned to his pacing. "The Healers suspect that the toxin in Ashe's blood is targeted to attack the babe. It's taking every ounce of her strength to protect her child."

"That makes sense," Talon said. He'd already heard the poison was manifesting itself like a possession, with an intelligent design to destroy the baby. "What does the female have to do with it?"

"Having her near appears to…" Raphael searched for the word to describe the female's effect on his mate. "Steady Ashe."

"Steady?"

"It's almost as if she gives Ashe more strength."

Talon frowned. He didn't doubt the power of the voodoun. The spiritual world was a powerful force. But he'd always thought they needed potions and spells and rituals to weave their magic.

"She helps by being in the same room?" he demanded.

"She helps just being in the Wildlands."

Talon shook his head. He didn't like the thought that the female could somehow tamper with Ashe by her mere presence.

It was one thing to stir up a potion. Or even do one of those mysterious rituals they seemed to love.

But this…it was strange.

And he didn't trust strange.

"Do the Healers know why?"

Raphael's expression tightened, his eyes glowing gold with the power of his cat. "They're divided."

"Why do I sense I'm not going to like this?"

"Because you won't," Raphael said bluntly, halting his pacing to meet Talon's wary gaze. "Isi is Ashe's sister."

Talon blinked, his brain struggling to process the words.

"Sister?"

"Her *twin* sister."

Twin sister. God almighty.

"I thought you said Ashe's only relative was a drunkard mother," Talon said.

"That's what Ashe had always been told."

Talon narrowed his gaze, his vague unease solidifying into ruthless suspicion.

"And now this Isi claims to be her long-lost sister?"

Raphael shook his head. "No. The DNA revealed their connection."

The scientific proof of the two women's biological connection did nothing to ease Talon's distrust. Hell, it only made him more skeptical.

"That's one hell of a coincidence," he muttered.

"Yeah, that was my thought." Raphael shoved his fingers through his hair. "And it gets worse."

Talon rolled his eyes. When were things *not* getting worse?

"Great."

"The elders are convinced that Isi is some prophesied agent of doom."

Talon made a sound of disbelief at the cheesy, sci-fi description. He might even have laughed if it hadn't been for Raphael's grim expression. He had a feeling a laugh would earn him an ass-kicking even worse than the time he'd set up a moonshine still in the caves and sold the potent liquor to his classmates. How was he supposed to know he'd brewed the alcohol so pure it would make them sicker than dogs?

"Now you're just screwing with me," he instead growled.

"I wish I was," Raphael muttered. "The elders claim that Isi and Ashe's father was the Pantera Shaman."

It took a minute for Talon to recall the human who had once been called on by the elders to reveal the faction of an unborn Pantera. There were also rumors he'd had visions of the future.

It'd been years since Talon had last seen him.

He at last managed to dig the name from his memories.

"Chayton?"

"Yes."

"Didn't he die?"

Raphael grimaced. "The elders assumed he had."

313

Talon made a sound of disbelief. The elders rarely made mistakes. Or maybe they just never admitted to them.

"Go on," he urged.

"They said that Chayton had a vision that his first born child would destroy the Wildlands," Raphael said, a hint of pity in his voice for the man who must have been devastated to reveal that his own daughter was born to be a force for evil.

Talon was far less sympathetic. He wasn't a firm believer in prophecies. There were too many ways they could be interpreted to offer a blueprint for the future.

But if the first born child was a danger to his people, he damned well intended to stop her.

"Isi was the first born?"

Raphael gave a sharp nod. "After the vision, Chayton took his pregnant wife and fled to the north of the state. The babes were just being born when the elders tracked them down."

"They intended to sacrifice the child." The words were a statement, not a question.

The elders weren't the sort of females to wait and see if something might become a problem. They were firm believers in preemptive strikes.

"They did, but Chayton managed to distract them long enough to slip away," Raphael revealed. "The Hunters found traces of blood and a baby blanket, but no sign of the Shaman. When Dixie returned to La Pierre with Ashe the Elders kept a close guard on Dixie expecting Chayton to try and contact her if he remained alive. When the years passed with no word from the Shaman the Elders assumed he and the babe had died."

The Shaman had to have been extremely talented or extremely lucky to have escaped the elders for so long.

"Ashe knew nothing about her father?" he asked.

"No." Raphael narrowed his gaze, as if daring the younger man to call his mate a liar. Yeah. Talon was more likely to stick his head in the mouth of a gator. "The elders obviously tampered with Dixie's mind, forcing her to believe she only had one child and that her husband abandoned her."

Talon shuddered. Mind alterations on such a large scale could be extremely destructive to humans.

"Maybe it's not so surprising she turned to booze," he said. "What was the elders' response to Isi's arrival?"

"Cataclysmic." The lean features tightened. No doubt Raphael had been at the epicenter of that cataclysmic response. "They arrived at Ashe's room once the DNA results revealed her connection to Isi. Until that point they'd assumed that Isi's only threat was her connection to her voodoo shop."

Talon wasn't expecting that.

"They knew about her?"

"They've been keeping a careful watch on artists who specialize in tattoos with malachite."

Ah. Talon had to admit it was a reasonable precaution. The mineral was used to ground a cat inside a Pantera's body. Or for Nurturer therapists to soothe patients who couldn't control their minds or their cats. And, of course, the elders used it as punishment to cage a Pantera.

"Only a person with intimate knowledge of our cats would understand the magical properties of the mineral," he pointed out.

"There's also this."

Reaching into his pocket, Raphael pulled out his phone and flicked through the photos. Finding the one he was searching for, he turned the phone so Talon could see the image.

Talon leaned forward, easily determining the picture had been taken on the streets of New Orleans. It appeared to be a small store. The sort you could find in any narrow street or alleyway. The only thing to make it stand out was the blood-red shingle that read, THE CARE AND FEEDING OF VOODOO.

"I assume this is Isi's shop?" he demanded, not entirely sure what he was supposed to be seeing.

"Yes. And this is her vehicle."

Raphael zoomed the photo until Talon could see the white van parked in front of the store, the emblem of a spread-winged raven flying across a full moon painted on the side.

A low growl trickled from Talon's throat at the unmistakable Mark of Shakpi.

"Shit." He glanced up at Raphael's bleak face. "Do they intend to kill her?"

The golden eyes glowed with a dangerous determination. "Not as long as I keep them away."

Talon frowned. Raphael was usually the levelheaded one. The one who looked at every situation with a cool logic that was as annoying as hell.

Now, Talon couldn't help but worry that his friend was allowing his devotion to his mate to blind him to the potential danger of having Isi so near.

"Look, Raphael, I get that she's related to your mate, but if she's one of our enemies—"

"I don't give a shit if she's related or not," Raphael sharply interrupted. "Her presence is helping Ashe fight back the toxin."

Talon chose his words with care. Raphael was on the edge of snapping. He didn't want to be the one to tip him into a homicidal rage.

Not when he was standing only a few feet away.

"You're sure it's not some trick?"

"I'm not sure of anything." Raphael gave a low growl of frustration. "But know this, I'll do whatever is necessary to protect my mate and child."

Talon swallowed the words of warning that trembled on his lips.

They were a waste of breath as long as Raphael truly believed Isi was able to help his family.

"As we all will," he instead muttered, his tone grudging.

The golden gaze narrowed, the air prickling with the heat of Raphael's cat. "I hope you mean that."

"Why?"

"I have placed Isi under my protection, but I don't trust the elders," the older man bluntly confessed. "They're convinced she's the doom of the Pantera. They'll kill her if they get the opportunity."

That didn't seem like a bad plan to Talon. With Isi dead, then they could return to finding a less risky way to protect Ashe and the babe.

But his loyalty belonged to Raphael.

There was nothing he wouldn't do for the leader of the Suits.

"What do you want from me?" he asked.

"We haven't been able to do more than moderate Isi's illness."

Talon grimaced. "The Wildlands are probably trying to drive her out."

"It doesn't matter." Raphael waved a dismissive hand. "We had to move her to your parents' home."

Talon flinched, his eyes widening.

The pretty cottage that was hidden on the edge of the deepest marshes had been shut up the day that they received the news that Talon's parents had been killed in an airplane crash. Talon had moved to the Hunter house, and while he visited the cottage to perform the necessary upkeep, no one had actually stayed there for years.

He didn't keep it as some tragic temple to his dead parents. Or at least, not intentionally.

But he sure the hell didn't use it as a B&B for the potential doom of his people.

"You put her where?" he rasped, unable to believe that Raphael could be so insensitive.

Raphael met his accusing glare with a stubborn expression. He wasn't backing down.

"It's the most easily defended location," he pointed out, referring to the marshland that was deep and thick enough to keep out all but the most determined predators. "Besides, there's something in the house that eases her sickness."

Talon didn't care if it made her sprout wings and a halo.

"You're asking a lot, *mon ami.*"

Raphael shoved his phone into his pocket and folded his arms over his chest. He'd lost weight in the past month, but he was still big, tough and capable of twisting Talon into a painful knot.

"I'm not done," he warned.

Talon counted to ten.

"What?"

"I expect you to become her guardian."

317

Talon made a sound of shock. "Say that again."

The golden eyes narrowed. "You heard me."

He had. Unfortunately.

"Why me?"

"I trust you."

The words struck straight at his heart, and Talon threw his hands up in defeat.

"Fuck."

Chapter Two

For the first time in weeks, Isi felt warm. Not just 'wrapped in heavy blankets until she was nearly smothered' warm. But warm from the inside out.

And even better, the constant sense of nausea was gone.

Completely, utterly gone.

With a sigh she snuggled closer to the source of the warmth, breathing deeply of the intoxicating musk that was driving away the hideous illness that plagued her at varying levels of hell since she arrived in the Wildlands.

She didn't know what was creating the delicious scent, and she didn't really care.

She just wanted to wrap herself in the soothing sensations.

As if answering her prayer, a warm hand slid down her back, cupping her ass.

"Oh, thank god," she groaned as the touch sent heat rushing through her veins. "Don't stop. That feels so good."

"I haven't even started, darling," a rough male voice whispered in her ear.

Isi was jerked out of her lovely dream, belatedly realizing she was no longer alone. What the hell? She forced open her heavy lids, her breath squeezed from her lungs as she encountered a pair of glowing golden eyes rimmed in jade.

They were spectacular eyes.

Clear, cunning and lethally male.

And they were set in a face that was drop-dead, do-me-now gorgeous.

Wide brow, a narrow blade of a nose, high cheekbones and sensually carved lips.

A true masterpiece of DNA.

Still foggy from sleep, Isi felt a surge of female appreciation tingle down her spine.

That was the kind of face that made smart women do stupid things.

And enjoy every second of it.

A dark, enticing arousal stirred deep inside her, shocking Isi with the intensity of her response.

She might enjoy the sight of a handsome man in a purely artistic way, but she didn't immediately consider how quickly she could rip off his clothes and wrap herself around him.

It was at last the inhuman glow in his eyes that snapped her out of her growing obsession.

Oh, shit.

This wasn't a man.

He was Pantera.

And he was currently rolling until he was perched on top of her.

"Hello, darling," he drawled, his lips curling as he watched her expression tighten with a surge of angry suspicion. "If I'd known you were waiting in my bed I would have returned sooner."

She shoved her hands against his chest, not surprised when he refused to budge. Even through the thin blanket she could feel his lean body honed to sleek, chiseled muscles. The shove was just a distraction so she could knee him in the nuts.

It didn't matter how tough a man was, he had one glaring vulnerability.

With a well-practiced jerk of her leg, she aimed directly between his legs. "Get off me, you pervert."

There was a low snarl as the cat managed to block her debilitating strike, using his longer legs to pin her to the mattress.

"No need to play rough, darling." His tongue traced the shell of her ear, sending unwelcome jolts of bliss straight to her pussy. "Unless that's the way you like it."

She hissed in frustration, trying to deny the fact that her entire body was humming with a treacherous awareness.

God dammit. When a man held her against her will it was a reason for homicide.

Not melting into a shivering mess of aching hunger.

"If I was playing rough I'd already have kicked the hair off your balls," she muttered.

"My balls aren't hairy." He nipped the lobe of her ear, grabbing her hand to lower it toward the hardening length of his cock. "Do you need proof?"

"Hell no." She wrenched her hand free, punching him in the chest with a force that would have broken the rib of a human. "Who are you?"

"Your reluctant host."

"Host?" Isi scowled. Raphael had told her that the pretty cottage hadn't been used for years. Of course, he'd also told her she wasn't a prisoner, but every time she tried to leave he warned her that the mysterious elders were just waiting for an opportunity to kill her. After a month of being stuck in the bayou with a bunch of angry cats who considered her the enemy, she was reaching her limit. In fact, tonight might very well have tipped her over the edge. "This is your house?"

"It's my parents' home, but this is my bed," the male Pantera said. "Why did you choose it?"

"What?"

"There are four bedrooms." He studied her with an unnerving intensity. Even in the darkness she knew what he was seeing. Short, jet black hair with blue streaks, mussed from sleep. A pale face with delicate features that were dominated by a pair of eyes so dark they looked black. His gaze lowered to the tattoo of a rose wrapped around a candle that ran from below her right ear down to her shoulder, before lingering on the diamond piercing in each nostril. His expression remained unreadable, but there was no missing the thickening of the intoxicating musk that filled the air. "Why did you choose mine?"

Isi hesitated. There was no way in hell she was going to admit she'd been drawn to the room because it'd eased the sickness that was a constant companion.

Not when an awful, unbearable suspicion was beginning to form in the back of her mind.

"It had the best view," she at last muttered.

His lips brushed a searing path of temptation down her throat. "Liar."

Her heart slammed against her ribs and her pussy clenched in brutal need as his lips teased the pulse at the base of her neck.

Oh…hell.

Without warning, she was suddenly slamming her fists against his chest, desperately trying to wriggle from beneath his hard body. There was no way to disguise her stupid arousal from the man's freakishly sensitive senses, but she'd be damned if she'd lie there like an obedient doll.

"Get. Off."

Lifting his head, the man frowned in confusion as he tried to halt her attack without hurting her. "Settle down, female."

"Not until you release me."

He hissed as she raked her nails down his face, rolling to the side so she could scramble off the bed.

"Damn wildcat," he muttered, his gaze running a brooding path down her slender body covered by a pair of silk shorts and camisole top.

Instinctively she folded her arms over her breasts, more to hide the hardened points of her nipples than out of any sort of modesty.

Young girls raised in orphanages didn't have the privilege of being bashful.

"Tell me your name," she commanded.

He continued to sprawl across the heavy four-poster bed that matched the hand-carved furniture that filled the second story room.

He should have looked ridiculous in the cozy setting with handwoven rugs, walls lined with stuffed bookcases, and the echoes of a loving childhood, but he didn't.

He looked...at home.

A familiar pang of envy sliced through her heart before she was squashing the worthless regret.

Homes were places you kept your shit until you moved on to the next place. End of story.

"Talon," he said, his voice rubbing over her skin like rough silk.

Isi frowned. She had a vague memory of Ashe mentioning the Hunter who had been tracking down Pantera traitors.

"No one told me you lived here." She edged her way toward the door. She needed to be away from the disturbing cat. Far, far away. "I'll go somewhere else."

"Where?"

"Home." She didn't know what she was going to say until the word left her lips, but suddenly she knew that's exactly where she was going. She'd had enough of freaking Pantera and their soggy Wildlands. She belonged in New Orleans, running her shop. "Where I should have gone weeks ago."

"What about your sister?"

She shrugged, continuing to inch toward the door. "I can come back."

With a blur of motion, Talon was off the bed and blocking her path. "No."

Her jaw clenched as she was forced to come to a halt. "No?"

He planted his fists on his hips, the T-shirt stretched tight over the sculpted muscles of his chest.

"Raphael sent me here to protect you." He didn't bother to hide his anger at being stuck on babysitting duty. "I can't do that if you leave the Wildlands."

Her chin tilted. "Thanks, fur ball, but I've been taking care of myself a long time."

The golden eyes narrowed. "What is it with you and my fur?"

"I want it staying the hell away from me."

He prowled forward, his heat wrapping around her with sensuous pleasure. "You weren't so averse to me and my fur when you were clinging to me and telling me how good it felt."

She meant to hold her ground. She really did. But as he continued his ruthless path forward, she discovered herself retreating until her back was pressed against a tall bookcase.

Annoying ass.

"That was—"

He halted inches away, his hands lifting to grip the shelf on each side of her head. "What?"

"I was suddenly feeling better, that's all."

"Raphael mentioned it has something to do with the house," he said, his gaze lowering to the pulse that thundered at the base of her throat.

Isi grimaced. Yeah. She'd thought it was the house.

Until Talon appeared and the illness went from manageable to completely gone.

"Whatever," she muttered. "I'll feel even better at my own house."

He leaned down, his breath searing over her lips like a kiss. "Ain't. Gonna. Happen."

"It's not your decision."

"Do you think you would last one second without Raphael's protection?"

"So he keeps telling me." Her lips flattened with a stubborn determination. She'd allowed herself to be bullied into staying for weeks. Or at least she told herself she'd been bullied. Otherwise she would have to admit that she stayed for Ashe. An unacceptable explanation. "How do I know that's not just bullshit to keep me here?"

"Raphael doesn't have to use empty threats," Talon warned. "If he decides to keep you here, I guarantee you that you'll stay. One way or another."

She glared into the savagely beautiful face. "So when you said you're here to guard me, you meant I'm your prisoner."

"Raphael asked me to make sure you continued to help to his mate."

Oh, yes. Raphael had made it clear that he would move heaven and earth to protect his mate and child.

Which didn't make her jealous at all. Nope. Not at all.

"And what I want doesn't matter?" she snapped.

"No."

She gave a humorless laugh at his complete lack of apology. "Nice."

"It's the way it is."

"Fine." She dipped down to slip under his arm, heading toward the door. "I'm too tired to argue."

"Where are you going?" he demanded, once again moving to stand in her way.

"To another room."

"Why?" He had the balls to reach out and lightly grasp her chin, turning her head toward the bed dominating the room. "This bed is all toasty warm."

"You said this was your room."

His thumb brushed her lower lips, his touch sending a rush of arousal through her. "I'll share."

Her mouth went dry as the vivid image of being spread naked across the mattress as this man kissed a path from the top of her blue-streaked hair to the tips of her fuchsia-painted toes blazed through her mind.

Desire streaked through her, white hot and so fierce it made her knees week.

God, she had to get out of there.

"In your dreams," she said, the words sounding lame even to her.

His gaze followed his thumb as it traced the stubborn line of her jaw.

"We're stuck here together," he murmured, his voice husky with invitation. "We might as well enjoy our time."

She slapped away his hand before stepping around his body and heading toward the door with a grim determination.

Dammit.

She didn't know what was wrong with her.

The man was a damned cat. And worse, he considered her nothing more than an unwelcome duty.

"I'd rather sleep with a snake," she informed him, her head held high.

He waited until she was at the door before he called out to her. "Isi."

Reluctantly she glanced over her shoulder, refusing to acknowledge the impact of his golden beauty as he stood in a pool of moonlight.

"What?"

His eyes narrowed. "Raphael might need you for now, but I don't trust you an inch." His soft words sliced through her like a dagger. "Don't give me a reason to kill you."

She stormed from the room and down the hall, choosing the bedroom furthest away before slamming the door behind her.

The arrogant son of a bitch.

How dare he threaten to kill her after…

After what?

She gave a choked laugh, pressing a hand to her lips as the faint queasiness began to return.

After he'd offered to have sex with her?

No. It wasn't even sex.

It was a quick fuck with a stranger.

It was clearly time she returned to her own life.

Far away from the bayous and Pantera males who would be greatly improved by having their bloated heads stuffed and mounted over the nearest fireplace.

———

A thrill of excitement raced through Talon as he slid silently through the underbrush. In his cat form he moved with a silent grace that made certain his prey was unaware she was being hunted.

Isi.

His excitement turned to a darker, more enticing emotion as he caught the scent of magnolia.

The female wasn't at all what he'd been expecting.

Harbingers of doom shouldn't look like exotic butterflies, with raven black hair highlighted with brilliant blue, and black eyes that contrasted with pale, milky skin. Even the tattoo and piercings that should have made her look hard only emphasized her striking beauty.

A rare, exquisite creature that had made lust explode through him from the second he'd caught sight of her curled in his bed.

Of course, she did have the attitude, he wryly acknowledged.

But even the sharp tongue and don't-screw-with-me insolence fascinated him.

It made him want to break through the brittle facade to find the warm, passionate woman beneath.

And she would be passionate.

He'd caught the scent of her arousal. An arousal that matched his own.

She wanted him. Just like he wanted her.

Beneath him.

Now.

Realizing they were nearing the border of the Wildlands, Talon began to close the distance.

He'd heard her the second Isi had left her room to creep downstairs. She'd taken time to slip into the laundry room and grab one of the sweat suits that every Pantera kept in his home. Even though their clothing usually transformed during the shift, there were times when they were stressed, or injured, or too weary to maintain full control of their transformation. The sweats were bought in bulk to be disposable.

Then, she'd slipped from his house like a thief in the night.

Talon had allowed her escape.

He wanted to know where the hell she was going and who she was meeting.

Now it was clear that she'd been serious when she'd said she intended to go home.

With a silent burst of speed, Talon was circling around her, hidden by the thick vegetation. He felt a brief flare of confusion when he caught sight of her pale face and the hand pressed to her lips as if she was struggling against the urge to vomit.

She was far sicker than she had been at his house.

And for some stupid reason the realization sent a stab of fury through his heart. As if the thought of her in distress was painful to him.

With a low growl he crushed the unwelcome suspicion, instead pouncing forward, concentrating on his shift from cat to human as he carefully knocked Isi to the mossy ground.

An explosion of magic burst through his body, making him shudder as his bones and muscle realigned.

An exhilarating sensation.

But not nearly so exhilarating as the feel of her slender curves pressed beneath him.

"Going somewhere, darling?" he drawled, running a searching gaze down her body to make certain she hadn't been hurt in the fall.

Not that he should care, he fiercely told himself.

He'd warned her what would happen if she tried to flee.

Still, he couldn't entirely shake his aggravating aversion to seeing her in pain.

Isi's eyes widened in fear before she realized exactly who was pinning her to the ground. Immediately her fear altered to pure fury.

"Shit." She wriggled beneath him, her face losing its pasty shade of green as his musk began to fill the air. "Stop leaping on top of me."

Sweet sparks of arousal tingled through his blood as she writhed against his swelling cock, the intensity of his pleasure wrenching a low growl from his throat.

Lowering his head, he pressed his nose to the curve of her throat, breathing deep of her magnolia scent.

"I wouldn't twitch a single muscle if I were you," he warned.

Her muscles tensed, her heart pounding so loud he could hear the frantic beats. "Why?"

"Because chasing you has turned me on." Unable to resist temptation, Talon sank his teeth into her silken flesh, not hard enough to draw blood, but enough to satisfy the cat inside him who abruptly wanted a taste of this female. Lust thundered through him. "Do you want to run some more?"

She slammed her fist against his back, her entire body trembling. But not with fear. Or anger.

"I just want you to leave me alone," she rasped.

"Liar." His voice thickened as the intoxicating scent of her cream teased at his senses. Her pussy was already wet and ready for him to penetrate. His cock twitched, anxious to fulfill her need. "I excite you."

Another blow to his back. "You're pissing me off, fur boy."

He licked a path down her throat, his cat prowling just below the surface, as if unnerved by the intoxicating flavor of her skin.

"Then why do you smell like sex?" he demanded.

"Because you're delusional," she muttered, making another bid for freedom.

"Dammit," he snarled, lifting his head to glare into her wide eyes. It was one thing to taunt her with his awareness of her arousal. It was another to realize that he was perilously close to ripping off her clothes and fucking her right there. He might be a Pantera, but he wasn't an animal. "I told you to stay still."

"I don't take orders from you..." Her words trailed away as he pressed a hand to her forehead, his gaze searching her pale face. "What are you doing?"

"You were sick," he said in abrupt tones, temporarily distracted from his potent lust.

She frowned. "This whole place makes me sick."

"Now you're better."

Something flickered in her eyes. Something she was trying to hide from him.

"We're close to border."

"No." He gave a slow shake of his head. "You were better in my home. And now you're better because I'm holding you," he reasoned out loud. Then the truth struck him. "It's me," he said, watching as the flush of color stained her cheeks. "I make you better."

She glared at him in frustration. "God, could your ego get any bigger?"

He leaned down to nip the tip of her nose. "Admit it."

"No."

"Why not?" His lips twisted as his lust returned in full, painful force. Christ, his cock was pressing so hard against the zipper of his jeans he was afraid it might bust through. "I'll admit your scent is driving me out of my fucking mind."

"Talon."

He hissed, heat exploding through him as he allowed his lips to trail over her cheek to the edge of her mouth.

"Say it again," he urged.

She trembled, her hands spread against his back as she forgot to fight him. "What?"

"My name." He used his tongue to trace the lush temptation of her lower lip. "Say it again."

"Talon."

"I like to hear it on your lips," he said, kissing the line of her jaw before heading down the silken skin of her throat.

Her nails bit into his shoulders as she arched in pleasure beneath him. "What are you doing to me?"

"Darling, I'll do anything you want," he muttered, forgetting where they were and, more importantly, who she was.

Nothing mattered but the sharp-edged hunger that clawed at him whenever he was close to this female.

He reached the neckline of her sweatshirt, impatiently using his chin to push it aside so he could trace her collarbone with his lips.

"Oh," she breathed, rubbing against the thick thrust of his erection.

He growled, about to reach down and yank off the loose bottom of her sweats when his gaze caught sight of a tiny mark at the bottom of her collarbone.

It was like being doused in icy-cold water.

One second all he could think about was the savage need that was pounding through his body, and the next he was pushing himself upright and shoving shaking hands through his tousled hair.

"Shit," he rasped.

She raised herself onto her elbows. "What?"

His gaze remained glued to the birthmark that marred the perfect ivory of her skin. "A raven."

She flinched. As if he'd physically struck her.

"It's not a raven, it's a birthmark."

"The symbol of evil." The words left his lips before he could consider their impact on Isi.

Hell, he was a Hunter, not a Suit.

"Evil?" Isi surged to her feet, grabbing a hefty stick off the ground to swing toward his head with a magnificent fury. "Get out of here, you son of a bitch."

Angry with himself for having forgotten he intended to treat this female as the enemy, and potentially putting his people in danger, he turned to walk away.

He needed some distance to pull his head out of his ass and start thinking clearly.

Or at least try to ease his raging hard-on.

"Gladly," he snarled, headed back to his parents' cottage.

The branch went whizzing past his head, grazing his ear. "And stay the hell away," she shouted.

Turning his head, he sent her a last glare. "You leave the Wildlands and the elders will kill you. Make no mistake about it," he growled.

She flipped him off. "Bastard."

Talon stormed away.

For the first time he felt like a bastard.

CHAPTER THREE

Isi woke with a weary groan to find the late morning sun pouring through her open window.

Momentarily disoriented, she pushed herself to a sitting position, glancing in confusion around the room painted a cheery yellow.

What the hell? This wasn't the room she'd been using for the past month.

It took a minute before the memories from the night before slammed into her.

Talon.

The bastard.

Talon the Bastard. Yep. That suited him to perfection.

Shoving herself out of the bed, she stomped her way to the attached bathroom.

Last night she'd hovered at the edge of the Wildlands for over an hour before the sickness had driven her back to the cottage. Her every instinct had warned her to return to New Orleans and take the first bus the hell out of town, but she wasn't entirely sure that the threat of the elders wasn't real.

Finally she'd had no choice but to return to the cottage where there was some measure of relief from the constant sickness.

Although not as much as there had been during the night, she realized as she quickly showered and pulled on a robe. Which could only mean that Talon was no longer in the cottage.

Good, she savagely told herself, entering the room he'd taken over, to gather her clothes and take them to her new, painfully sunny room. She'd rather be sick than have to endure his repulsive company.

Pretending she actually did find him repulsive, Isi pulled on a pair of jeans and skimpy top that hit just below the gentle swell of her breasts. She smiled with a grim defiance as she realized the top was cut low enough to display her evil birthmark. Then, spiking her blue-streaked hair, she headed out the door and to the clinic where her sister continued to fight for her life.

Acutely aware of the cats who trailed behind her at a discreet distance, she followed the narrow path that led from the isolated marsh to the village, keeping her head high.

She'd learned from day one that her presence in the Wildlands attracted unwelcome attention.

Some curious, some hopeful, but most filled with a predatory hunger that assured her they were just waiting for the opportunity to rip her to shreds.

Not the nicest neighbors a girl could have, but sadly they weren't the worst.

She'd run away from the orphanage when she was barely fourteen to live on the streets of Chicago.

Tough to top that.

Reaching the clinic, she entered the wooden structure through a side door and headed directly to her sister's room at the back of the building.

Unlike human hospitals, there was no stench of antiseptic or disinfectant. Instead the air was laced with the scent of healing plants and potions as well as the exotic musk that was unique to each Pantera.

There was also a decided lack of sterile white walls and linoleum floors. In this clinic the walls were paneled in rich cherry wood with floors covered by handwoven rugs.

Pushing open the door to her sister's room, she stepped inside, not surprised to find Raphael sitting beside the bed.

The male refused to leave his mate's side unless it was a matter of dire urgency.

Rising to his feet at Isi's entrance, Raphael motioned for her to take his seat beside the bed.

"Good morning, Isi."

She hurriedly perched on the edge of the chair, always a little on edge around the man.

He might have sworn to protect her, but he was clearly ready to snap. She didn't want to be around if something happened to Ashe.

"How is she?" Isi asked, focusing on the dark-haired woman lying in the wooden bed, covered by a hand-stitched quilt.

"She's holding her own," Raphael said, the weariness in his voice drawing her gaze to his haggard features.

Christ, he looked like he hadn't slept in days.

"Why don't you go rest?" she offered. "I'll sit with Ashe."

There was a brief hesitation, as if he was debating whether or not to trust Isi alone with his beloved mate. Then, obviously realizing he was near collapse, he gave a reluctant nod.

"I'll be just down the hall."

The Pantera leaned down to place a gentle kiss on his mate's lips before turning to leave the room and gently closing the door behind him.

Alone with the female they claimed was her sister, Isi studied the pale, perfect features that held only a faint resemblance to her own. Over the past month she spent a part of each day with Ashe, usually watching her sleep, although there were times when the other woman would wake long enough for a short conversation.

Still, Ashe remained more a stranger than a member of her family.

Which suited Isi just fine.

Concentrating on her sister with a fierce intensity that didn't allow any stray thoughts of *Talon the Bastard*, she was aware the second Ashe's lashes twitched and her hand unconsciously reached for her mate.

"Raphael?"

Isi leaned forward, lightly grasping the outstretched hand. "It's Isi."

The thick lashes lifted to reveal beautiful brown eyes. "Sister."

Isi stretched her lips into an uncomfortable smile. "That's what they tell me."

Ashe gave Isi's fingers a squeeze. "I always wanted a sister. Didn't you?"

Isi hid her shudder.

When she was young she'd learned that the only way to stay alive was to stay on the move and avoid attention. Something that would be impossible with family or friends.

Having a sister was a burden she couldn't afford.

Still, Ashe was studying her with her big, hopeful eyes. It would feel like kicking a puppy to admit the truth.

"I…" She struggled for words that would offer comfort without being an outright lie. "Wanted not to be alone."

"Yes." Ashe gave a weak nod of her head, looking impossibly beautiful despite the pallor of her skin and the shadows beneath her eyes. "I've always been alone. Until Raphael."

Isi frowned, perplexed by the soft words. "I thought you lived with our mother?"

Ashe wrinkled her nose. "Dixie wasn't much of a mother. She spent most of her time and money at the local bar." She hesitated before asking the question that had obviously been on her mind. "What about our father?"

Isi stiffened. "What about him?"

"Did you know him?"

"No." Isi felt a familiar stab of rage toward the man who had abandoned her when she needed him the most. "He dumped me at an orphanage in Shreveport and disappeared."

"Did you ever search for him?"

Isi scowled. Like she'd waste one precious second of her life on the worthless sperm donor who'd impregnated their mother?

"Why should I?" she demanded. "If he wanted to be with me he wouldn't have tossed me away like a piece of trash."

Ashe placed a hand on her swelling stomach, the gesture revealing her instinctive urge to protect the child growing so rapidly in her womb.

"Now you know he had no choice."

Isi abruptly released her sister's hand and rose to her feet. She'd done her best to pretend the elders' claim of her birth was nothing more than a fairy tale.

LAURA WRIGHT AND ALEXANDRA IVY

And she'd been remarkably successful.

Of course, she had a lot of practice at pretending the nasty things in her life didn't exist.

"Do I?" she muttered.

"You don't believe the elders?" Ashe asked.

Isi moved to gaze at out the window that offered a view of the clearing where the Pantera gathered for their meals.

There was no denying it was a beautiful sight, even for a girl who'd never spent more than an hour away from the city.

The long tables covered in green cloth set among the lush flowers and cypress trees. The unexpected wooden statues that were tucked among the azaleas to provide charming glimpses of native art. The nearby lake that sparkled in the lazy sunlight.

It was a land crafted by magic.

A magic that was fading.

And they wanted to blame her.

"Would you, if you were me?" She gave a humorless laugh, her voice edged with a bitterness she couldn't hide. "You get to be the beautiful princess who saves the Pantera while I'm the evil twin who offers nothing but destruction."

She heard Ashe's soft gasp of remorse. "Isi, I'm sorry. I didn't think—"

"Look, it's not like I give a shit," Isi interrupted the soft words. Hell, the only thing worse than being tagged as some sort of Antichrist was pity. The mere hint gave her hives. "Only suckers believe in prophecies."

"You're not evil."

Hidden behind her well-perfected wall of indifference, she turned to meet her sister's sympathetic gaze.

"Well, I'm not good," she said. "And it doesn't bother me at all."

"I mean what I say," Ashe insisted, clearly as stubborn as Isi. She smiled wryly. At least they had one thing in common. "You're not evil."

"Great." Isi shrugged, just wanting to be done with painful conversation. "If you could convince the crazy cats in charge I'm one of the good guys, I'll be on my way back home."

Ashe reached out her hand, her expression filled with a wistful yearning that tugged perilously at Isi's heart.

"We'll figure this out," she promised. "Together."

Isi instinctively backed away. She wasn't ready to give Ashe what she so obviously desired.

A sister.

"Yeah. Whatever." She continued to back toward the door. "I have to go."

Ashe dropped her hand, her gaze searching Isi's face. "You look better."

Isi came to a reluctant halt. "I was. Now…" She swallowed her words. There was no way in hell she was going to admit that there was something about Talon that eased her illness. "It doesn't matter."

Ashe bit her lip, her lids already beginning to droop. "I'm worried I'm draining you of your strength and that's what is making you sick."

Isi shrugged. "Don't sweat it, I'm tough."

Her sister struggled against the rising tide of weariness. "Isi—"

"I'll come back after dinner."

Isi slipped from the room, but lingered until she was certain her sister was deeply asleep.

It wasn't that she cared whether or not Ashe might feel alone. Or need something before Raphael returned.

It was just…

With a muttered curse, Isi headed out of the clinic and straight to the cottage.

This entire place was making her nuts.

NEW ORLEANS

Talon ignored the closed sign clearly displayed on the door of the voodoo shop. He wasn't a man who let pesky barriers stand in his way when he wanted something. Still, he was civilized enough to use his lock-picking skills to deal with the door rather than just kicking the damned thing open.

Glancing up and down the narrow street, he slipped inside and shut the door behind him. There would be witnesses to his B & E, of course. The specialty shops that lined the streets weren't so busy that the proprietors weren't aware of what was going on in neighboring stores. He could only hope they'd wait to see if he tried to walk out with a bag of loot before they called the cops.

Halting just inside the door, Talon immediate realized he wasn't alone.

Despite the heavy scent of incense that hung in the air there was no missing the smell of two human males. Or the sour stench that marked them as enemies.

Walking past the rows of leather-bound books, crystals that came in every size and color, ceramic pots that were filled with Isi's potions, and voodoo dolls, Talon silently paced to the body art room at the back of the store.

He hesitated at the open doorway, scanning the brightly lit room for hidden danger.

There wasn't much to see. The walls were covered with a variety of tattoo patterns and framed pictures of happy customers. There were two narrow massage tables covered with white paper, and rolling cabinets that held the paraphernalia needed by the tattoo artists.

No hidden closets or cupboards.

And best of all...no exits.

Curling his nose at the strange odor that clung to those humans who carried the Mark of Shakpi, Talon turned his attention to the two men who had yet to notice his arrival.

Idiots.

One was seated at the end of a table. He was a young, blond-haired man with the hard muscles of a dedicated bodybuilder. He had a dozen tattoos running up his arms and around his thick neck, but he wasn't at the shop for another.

No. The second man who was standing in front of him was holding a small metal rod with a flat piece of metal at the end.

A branding iron.

And Talon would bet his left nut it had a raven design on it.

A stupid, sharp-edged disappointment sliced through him before he was sternly reminding himself that he'd come to Isi's shop precisely because the elders suspected Isi was connected to their enemies.

What else had he expected?

With a shake of his head he forced himself to concentrate on silently stepping into the room. The men might be mere humans, but Raphael had discovered that their enemies had weapons that could weaken a Pantera and make their cats dangerously vulnerable.

"Am I interrupting?"

With a flurry of curses both men jerked their gazes toward the doorway.

The blond on the table was the first to recover. "Hey, this is a private—"

"Fuck," the one with the branding iron breathed. He had lanky black hair, a narrow face that had a rat-like quality, and brown eyes the color of mud, but there was an intelligence in his gaze that was missing from his companion. "Run."

"I don't think so."

Talon stood in the doorway, bracing himself as the blond pulled a knife and charged forward. He waited until the man was in striking distance, grabbing the arm holding the knife and using the attacker's own momentum to his advantage as he spun and slammed him face first into the doorjamb.

Having momentarily stunned his opponent, Talon spoke directly into his ear.

"Drop the knife and sit in the corner like a good boy and you might make it out of here alive," he offered.

Possessing the tedious belief that his size made him the toughest guy in the room, the blond wrenched his arm free and swung the knife toward Talon's face.

"Fuck you."

Dodging the blade, Talon grabbed the man's bloated head and with one efficient twist broke his neck.

He'd given the moron a chance to live.

Allowing the dead man to drop to the floor, Talon turned his attention to the slender, rat-faced man clutching the branding iron as if it could protect him.

Talon stepped forward, a lethal smile curling his lips. "We need to chat."

"I don't know who the hell you are, but—"

"Don't lie," Talon overrode the arrogant bluff. "I've seen you with Raphael."

"Yes…" A cunning light glowed in the mud eyes. "Yes, that's right. I'm Derek and I spy for him. He's going to be pissed if you blow my cover."

With a blur of motion, Talon was standing directly in front of the man, the tip of his dagger beneath his chin.

"Here's the deal," he said in soft, lethal tones. "You've been working with Suits. I'm a Hunter. Do you know what that means?"

The man licked his lips. "No."

Talon allowed his cat to glow in his eyes, watching the man with a hunger that would terrify any human.

"It means that my job description is tracking down enemies and killing them." He allowed the dagger to pierce the man's skin. "I don't negotiate. I don't heal. I don't nurture. I kill. And I do it very, very well."

"Fine," the man hissed, his expression sullen. "What do you want?"

"Answers."

"To what?"

"Who do you work for?"

"Isi," he answered without hesitation. "She owns this joint."

Talon clenched his teeth, pretending his cat wasn't snarling in disbelief. What did his cat know about human treachery?

"She trained you to brand traitors with that mark?"

Something flickered in the mud eyes. A warning that he was about to lie.

"She—"

"The truth or I'll start cutting off body parts." He lowered the dagger to press it against the man's dick. There was nothing like threatening to take an idiot's manhood to put him in the mood to share. "Starting here."

A layer of sweat coated the man's face, but his expression remained defiant. "No. The bitch has no idea what's going on."

Talon's grip tightened on the handle of the dagger. Did he believe the man?

Actually...he did.

Derek might pretend to be a tough guy, but at his core he was a coward.

If he could try to throw blame on Isi to cover his own ass, he would.

Refusing to dwell on the surge of relief that rushed through him, Talon nodded toward the iron rod still held in Derek's hand.

"Then who gave you the brand?"

"I made it myself." He lifted it to reveal the raven on the bottom. "Like it?"

Rage blasted through Talon.

These son of a bitches were destroying his homeland.

His people.

He wanted answers. Then he wanted to rip the bastard into tiny, bloody strips.

"It's as offensive as you are," he snarled. "Where did you learn to create the symbol?"

The man licked his lips, no doubt sensing Talon was just waiting for an excuse to kill him.

"I was approached by a voodoo priestess while I was in jail for a minor disagreement with my ex-wife," he said.

Voodoo priestess would match what Vincent and Savoy had told Bayon.

"What was her name?"

The man shrugged. "I don't know."

Talon lifted the dagger to press it beneath Derek's chin.

"Don't screw with me," he growled.

The man hissed in pain, but he was smart enough not to try to pull away. "I'm serious. She called herself Lady Cerise, but when I tried to find her later no one had ever heard of her. She must have used a false name."

"What did she say to you?"

"She paid my bail and told me she had a job for me," Derek admitted. "She gave me a card with the symbol of the raven flying across a full moon, and the address. Then she left."

"What was the job?"

"I went to the address that was an old warehouse where I met a group of men who promised an endless supply of money if I did what I was told and didn't ask too many questions."

Talon narrowed his gaze. Even with the threat of death, he was surprised Derek would so easily answer his questions.

He'd sensed the man was a coward, but surely he had to worry his fellow traitors would discover he squealed?

"For doing what?"

The man glanced toward the branding iron clutched in his hand. "My primary job is to brand the new recruits, but I do whatever I'm told to do."

"How did you end up in this shop?" he demanded, needing to know his connection to Isi. Why? He scowled, refusing to answer the question. "Was it because of her birthmark?"

Derek blinked in genuine bafflement. "What birthmark?"

"Never mind," he growled, aggravated he'd even asked the question. "Why did you choose this shop?"

"It was Lon."

"Who?"

"The alpha dog of our little crew." Derek's lips curled in disdain. The loser clearly had an allergy to authority. Typical. "He wanted me here to keep an eye on Isi."

Talon slid the dagger toward the man's throat, his eyes glowing as his cat snarled for blood.

"Why?"

Derek stiffened, the stench of his fear making Talon grimace. Still, his expression remained insolent.

"Lon wanted to know where she was and who was visiting the shop."

"He wanted to know about the Pantera?"

"Lon wasn't specific. He wanted me to keep a log on everyone who entered the shop." The mud eyes darkened with frustration. "I assume they were hoping someone would contact her, but they didn't share the information with me. I was just an insignificant peon."

Talon studied Derek's rat face. "And that's it?"

He gave a lift of one shoulder. "For me."

"What about the others?"

"There are some who sneak into the Wildlands and perform some hokey ritual," Derek said, unaware of Talon's burst of fury. Those hokey rituals were destroying his home. "And others who spend most of their time traveling around the world."

"Recruiters?"

"No." Derek arched backward, as if trying to remove his chin from the sharp edge of Talon's blade. "Like I said, they're looking for someone."

Talon was instantly intrigued.

If his enemies wanted this person, then it was imperative the Pantera got their hands on him first.

"You have some idea who this person is? Man or woman? Human or Pantera?"

Bitter envy twisted the man's expression. "That info was above my pay grade."

Talon made a sound of impatience. "Where is the warehouse?"

Derek abruptly spit in Talon's face, using the momentary distraction to yank out the gun he'd had holstered at his lower back.

Talon belatedly realized why the man had been so eager to answer his questions. He'd simply been trying to keep Talon distracted long enough to get out his weapon.

"That's enough questions," the man roared. "Die, you fucking animal."

"Not today."

With a speed the human couldn't hope to match, Talon wrenched the gun from the man's hand, and with one swing of his arm he'd knocked Derek off his feet to crash head first into the wall.

The man landed heavily on the floor, blood flowing from the cut on his forehead. He was injured, but Talon could hear the steady beat of his heart.

Grimly he forced himself to turn and leave the room, closing the door behind him.

There was nothing he wanted more than to cut out the man's heart and feed it to the gators, but he was a Hunter who understood that sometimes the best way to catch his prey was to use bait.

Once Derek woke up, his first instinct would be to return to the Mother Ship.

Or in this case, the warehouse where Lon and his crew were hidden.

Talon intended to make sure the bastard was followed.

Pulling his phone out of his pocket, he hit speed dial. "I need a surveillance team in New Orleans. Oh, and there's a stiff to clean up."

Chapter Four

Isi was standing in the kitchen with pretty white cabinets and a black and white tiled floor, trying to work up enthusiasm for dinner, when Talon strolled through the back door.

Immediately she glanced toward the granite countertops for something to throw at his head.

The ceramic cookie jar would make a satisfying projectile, but it probably wouldn't cause much damage. While the knives stuck in a wooden block would draw blood, but only if he couldn't dodge them.

Highly unlikely.

She was debating between the coffeemaker and the blender when he prowled forward to toss a white paper bag on the polished oak table that matched the china cabinet filled with family heirlooms.

"Here."

She glared at him, hating the fact that her body was already reacting to his presence.

Not just the easing of her nausea that had become progressively worse during his absence, but the immediate awareness that shivered through her.

God. How could her nipples be hardening beneath her sweatshirt and her pussy already be dampening in preparation for his hard, uncompromising entry?

Okay, he was gorgeous.

A tall, stunningly handsome warrior with a lean, sculpted body and eyes that appeared more jade than gold in fading light.

She was mad as hell at him, but her body craved him as if...as if he'd used one of her love potions on her.

In a desperate effort to ease the destructive tide of lust that was as unwanted as it was unexpected, Isi pointed toward the white bag.

"What is it?"

He leaned forward, pulling out the plastic bowl and removing the lid. "Gumbo."

Isi's eyes widened as the mouthwatering smell teased at her nose. There was only one place that made gumbo that smelled like heaven.

"That's my..." She cut off her words, unwilling to reveal any part of herself to the ruthless Hunter.

"Favorite?" he murmured, moving to the cabinets to open a door and extract a spoon. Returning to the table, he put the spoon in the bowl of gumbo before glancing at her rigid form with an unreadable expression. "I know."

Her frown deepened.

She knew the Pantera could screw with humans' minds, but she'd never heard that they could read people's thoughts.

"How?"

His lips twisted. "I was just leaving your shop when a female stormed up to me demanding to know where you were and why she hadn't heard from you."

"Emile." The older woman owned the restaurant across the street from her shop, and not only made the best gumbo in all of Louisiana, but she watched over Isi like a mother hen. Isi's heart clenched with sudden fear. "What did you do to her?"

"I told her that you had been ill and that I was taking care of you." He pointed toward the bowl. "She insisted that her gumbo was necessary to your healing."

Isi shook her head in disbelief.

Even dressed in a pair of faded jeans and well-worn LSU T-shirt Talon looked like a dangerous, potentially deadly predator.

"She believed you?"

"Why wouldn't she? It's the truth." He pulled out a chair. "Eat."

She sucked in a deep breath, savoring the scent of seafood and rice in rich broth. It smelled incredible, but her stomach rebelled at the mere thought of indulging in such a spicy meal.

"I don't think I can."

His lips flattened. "Don't be stubborn. I can sense your hunger."

She folded her arms over her rumbling stomach, hoping that it was the physical hunger he sensed and not the heat that had nothing to do with the steamy bayou night.

"I can't keep it down," she muttered.

"Ah." Comprehension flared in the golden jade eyes. Then, astonishingly, he held out his arms. "Come here."

She took an awkward step backward. "No way."

"Stubborn," he breathed, moving around the table and prowling toward her.

Her ass hit the edge of the counter, halting her retreat.

"What the hell are you doing?" she rasped as he continued forward, not stopping until he was pressed tight against her.

He wrapped his arms around her, lowering his head until she was surrounded in the heat and musk of him.

"Making you better," he murmured.

"Don't…" She forgot what she was going to say as the nausea eked away, replaced by a warm sense of pleasure. Even the throbbing pain at the base of her skull disappeared. "Oh, dammit," she growled, dropping her head against his chest. She knew she should be fighting. The man had called her evil, for christ's sake. Asshole. But it felt so damned good.

Sucking in a deep breath, she concentrated on the delectable musk that seeped deep inside her, chasing away the last of her sickness.

Not that she wasn't acutely aware of his hand that rubbed up and down her back with a shockingly tender motion. Or his warm breath that brushed her cheek. Or even the hardening thrust of his arousal that pressed into her lower stomach.

But for now, it was the glorious sensation of well-being that made her sigh in pleasure.

"Can you eat now?" he asked.

"Yes."

Without warning, Talon scooped her off her feet and carried her toward the table. Then, instead of putting her down, he sat on a wooden chair and tucked her in his lap.

"Talon—"

"Shh." He reached for the bowl of gumbo, placing it directly in front of her. "Eat."

Once again she knew she should fight.

This new and improved Talon was obviously some trick.

She didn't believe for a second that he actually gave a shit if she were suffering.

But it'd been weeks since she'd actually had an appetite and the gumbo smelled so damned good.

Why not enjoy her dinner?

She had plenty of time to be pissed at him after she ate.

Grabbing the spoon, she scooped out a massive bite of the gumbo, shoving it into her mouth with an unashamed lack of female manners.

She groaned as the taste of crawfish and exotic spices hit her tongue. "Oh, god." She hurriedly scooped more of the gumbo into her mouth. "It's heaven."

Talon remained silent as she worked her way through her meal, his hand continuing its soothing path up and down her back and his gaze locked on her face. Isi did her best to ignore him. Well, as much as any female could ignore a six foot two puma shifter with the face of a fallen angel and a blatant sensuality that rubbed against her skin like plush velvet.

Eating the last bite, Isi managed not to lick the bowl—barely—and dropped the spoon onto the table. Then she heaved a deep sigh of satisfaction, savoring the sensation of being full.

"I could put that look on your face," Talon's dark voice whispered in her ear, one hand cupping the back of her neck while the other grasped her hip, pressing her against his thick cock. "In fact, I already did."

She narrowed her gaze. So now they were going from pretending he was some sort of nurturing saint to the smooth seduction routine?

"You're so full of shit," she muttered.

He nibbled a path down the line of her jaw, his hips lifting so he could rub his erection against the soft flesh of her ass.

"But you want me."

She shivered, need thundering through her body. Yes, she wanted him. Dammit. It was taking every ounce of her self-control not to turn so she was straddling him, pressing herself against the length of his cock to ease her ruthless need.

But she'd spent the entire day convincing herself that she wasn't going to give *Talon the Bastard* another chance to humiliate her.

He'd called her evil.

He believed she was fated to destroy his people.

She'd had enough people in her life judging her without ever knowing a thing about her, thank you very fucking much.

"Why were you in my store?" she demanded, needing to remind herself she couldn't trust this Pantera any farther than she could toss him.

He gave a low growl, his fingers tightening on her neck before he blew out a frustrated sigh and reached into his pocket to pull out his cellphone.

With a flick of his finger, he brought up his photos, choosing one that was clearly taken in front of her shop.

"This," he said.

She frowned in confusion. "My van?"

His finger touched the emblem painted on the back panel. A raven flying across a full moon.

"This is the symbol of Shakpi," he murmured. "Our enemy."

She stiffened in his arms. Even expecting the blunt accusation, she flinched.

"I didn't paint the van," she muttered before she could halt the words.

"I know," he said with surprising certainty, tossing his phone on the table. "Your employee Derek designed it."

She sent him a startled glance. How the hell did he know about Derek?

"Yes. He said it would bring in more customers. I just liked it because—" She lifted her hand toward her birthmark only to drop it as she recalled his assurance that the blemish was a physical manifestation of her evilness. She shrugged. "I thought it was cool."

He held her gaze, his hand moving to lightly trace the dark spot on her collarbone. "Because of this."

His touch blazed through her like a wildfire, scorching her nerves until they were unbearably sensitive.

Which only pissed her off.

She didn't want Talon to be the one man who could make her crave his touch. To make her so hungry she could barely think.

At least...she *shouldn't* want it to be him.

"So you went to my shop looking for my tails and horns and pitchfork," she muttered, her nipples hardening in anticipation of his touch. "Did you find them?"

"I found Derek," he admitted, leaning forward to replace his fingers with the destructive touch of his lips. "And he confessed you weren't involved with the traitors."

She shuddered, her gaze locked on the savage beauty of his face as he used his tongue to trace the distinctive birthmark.

"And yet you don't trust me," she husked, barely able to breathe.

His fingers slipped into the short strands of her hair, tugging back her head so his lips could explore the satin length of her neck.

"I don't trust my judgment when you're near."

She tried to squelch the moan that was wrenched from her throat. "What the hell is that supposed to mean?"

"The prophecy says you're destined to destroy me." His fingers skimmed from her hip to tease the bare skin of her lower back. Then, as his teeth nipped the sensitive spot where her neck met her shoulder, he moved his hand to discover the ribbon that laced together the back of her tiny top. With one tug her silky fabric was falling down to expose her bare breasts. Talon hissed as he pulled back to admire his handiwork, the jade that rimmed his eyes darkening with a brutal hunger. "But when I look at you all I see is how desperately I want you."

"Talon," she breathed, unable to disguise the edge of yearning that thickened her voice.

His fingers tightened in her hair. Possessive. Demanding.

"Say it again." It was an order, not a request.

"Talon."

Isi was lost in the unyielding heat of his eyes, feeling as if she were slowly melting beneath the potent heat of his desire.

What the hell was wrong with her?

She better than anyone understood the need to protect herself from the monsters that filled her world. The pervs, the pimps and the users who were constant threats to young girls on their own.

So why now, when she was trapped in the Wildlands and surrounded by her enemies, was she so eager to make herself utterly vulnerable? She should be kicking some serious feline butt, not battling the urge to sink her hands in that thick, golden hair and kiss him senseless.

Of course, maybe she was looking at this from the wrong angle, she told herself as he dipped his head so he could use the very tip of his tongue to tease at her nipple.

Christ. Why not accept that she wanted this man, for whatever reason, and use him, just as he was no doubt using her?

If he intended to hold her prisoner, she might as well get a mind-blowing orgasm out of the deal, shouldn't she?

Not giving herself time to consider the numerous faults in her clouded logic, Isi reached down to yank her top off the rest of the way, before grabbing his T-shirt and performing the same service.

She trembled at the sight of his smooth, bronzed skin that was stretched tautly over the hard, chiseled muscles. His chest was broad and tapered to a flat stomach with a six-pack her fingers lingered to explore. He was sleek and well-toned without unnecessary bulk. And his hands...lord, they were magic as they cupped her breasts with a possessive touch that sent streaks of heat directly to all her most intimate places.

He was hard, male perfection top to bottom, and every place in between.

The bastard.

"This means nothing," she muttered.

"Tell yourself whatever you want, darling." A slow, wicked smile curved his lips. "But don't doubt for a second that I intend to give you a night you're never going to forget."

"Arrogant."

He nipped the tip of her nipple, making Isi's heart stutter in shock. How could the tiny pain send jolts of ecstasy through her?

"Confident in my ability to please you."

"You're so full of shit..." Her taunting words were completely ruined as his lips closed around the nipple, sucking her with an expertise that had her trembling with need. "Oh."

"Oh, indeed," he growled, moving his lips to her collarbone. "I fucking want to taste you all over."

His enticing musk invaded her senses, embedding itself so deep inside her that she feared it would remain a permanent part of her.

"What are you doing to me?" she muttered, her hands running a restless path down his chest.

His soft laugh brushed over her cheek as he reached down to grasp the button on her jeans, helping her wriggle out of them before tossing them across the room.

"Nothing you aren't doing to me," he muttered, arching back to run a searing gaze over her body now covered in nothing more than a red thong.

Isi shivered, the gold and jade gaze a near tangible force as it moved from the tattoo that ran the length of her neck to linger on her breasts that felt oddly heavy.

"Why does your musk make me feel better?"

His hands glided down to grip her hips, his lips tracing the curve of her breast.

"Actually, I don't have a clue."

"Can you use it as a—"

His hands gripped her hips, abruptly lifting her up so he could tug her to face him, settling her back down so she straddled his lap. A groan was wrenched from her throat as the hard line of his cock hit her tender clitoris, nearly making her come.

"A what?"

She struggled to think as he returned his attention to her aching breasts. "An aphrodisiac?"

"It can be." He tilted back his head to flash her a grin filled with wicked promise. "But trust me, I don't need an aphrodisiac to make you hot and bothered."

She dug her nails into the smooth skin of his shoulders. "Don't mock me."

He continued to tease her nipple, rubbing his cock with flawless precision against her. Oh…shit. It felt good. Violently, insanely good.

"Mocking is not what I want to be doing with you," he said, kissing a path between her breasts.

"Talon."

With a low groan, Talon lifted his head to claim her lips in a kiss that demanded complete surrender. Hunger blasted through her, searing away any hope of resistance.

"Before this night is over I intend to hear you scream my name," he husked against her lips. "Over and over."

She pressed against his erection in blatant invitation. "You talk a big game, but how do I know you can deliver?"

He chuckled, blazing a path of kisses down her throat. "Don't ever challenge a Pantera, darling. I might not ever allow you out of my bed again."

She instinctively shied from his possessive tone.

"I'll leave your bed whenever I want to," she warned, deliberately rubbing against his cock. She smiled at his violent shudder of pleasure. "And if you think you can manipulate me with sex, you'd better think again."

"Isi," he growled, his eyes narrowing. "Can you stop searching for an insult in everything I say?"

"I just don't want you assuming—"

His hands moved over her body, his mouth planting restless kisses between her breasts and down the quivering plane of her stomach.

"There's no assumption," he rasped. "Just you and me. Let yourself go."

Isi gasped when he grabbed her by the waist and before she knew what was happening, she found herself perched on the edge of the table with Talon kneeling between her spread legs. Leaning forward, he dipped his tongue into her belly button, a shocking bolt of pleasure aiming straight between her legs.

Holy shit. Talon truly was a Hunter.

He went straight for the kill.

She planted her hands on the table behind her, feeling as if she was being assaulted with sensations. The bold exploration of his hands, the moist caress of his tongue, the heady musk that stirred her senses.

It was like being tossed into the middle of a raging vortex.

"Just for tonight," she managed to rasp.

He lifted his head to stare at her with open amusement. "You won't budge an inch, will you, Isi?"

"Never." Way past the point of no return, Isi decided the only thing left was to give in to the inevitable. Running her hands up the curve of his neck, she plunged her fingers into his hair. "Now shut up and prove you're more than just talk."

Hell no, she didn't just go there.

What Pantera could resist a blatant challenge to his manhood?

Especially if proving his manhood meant taking this female over and over, until she was too sated with pleasure to move.

Of course, he would prefer if she wasn't watching him with that wary defiance, as if convinced he was plotting some nefarious means to hurt her. Not that he could blame her. He'd given her little reason to trust him.

Something that was going to change.

Gently spreading her legs wider, Talon allowed his hands to skim up her bare thighs, his gaze drinking in the sight of the tiny scrap of lace that was all that hid her delectable pussy.

His heart thundered as his fingers headed toward the sweet spot, feeling off-balanced by the intensity of his desire.

He expected the male part of him to be ready and eager to have sex with this female. Even when he was trying to convince himself she couldn't be trusted, he was battling his ruthless desire. But the hunger of his cat was unexpected.

He'd never had his animal so close to the surface during sex. It was intensely erotic to have his pleasure echoed within the cat.

He didn't question why his animal would be so intensely fascinated by Isi.

Not when he was already beginning to suspect the truth.

She hissed out a sharp breath as the power of his cat glowed in his eyes, filling the room with a golden light. Not that she was afraid. Not his foolishly brave Isi.

It was the same raw hunger that clawed at him.

"I need to taste you," he said thickly, his fingers at last reaching the edge of her thong. "I can't wait any longer."

Her eyes darkened, her hands tightening in his hair as he allowed a claw to form, slicing through the delicate fabric. His cat growled in pleasure as the satin fluttered to the table, leaving her bare to his avid gaze.

Damn.

She was beautiful.

His mouth watered as he slowly leaned forward, closely monitoring her reaction. As desperately as he wanted her, he was prepared to halt the second she revealed any hesitation.

She watched him from beneath lowered lashes, her face flushed with passion. Then, for one breathless second she tensed, her expression troubled. Talon swallowed a curse.

Isi had been forced to the Wildlands, and then bullied into staying.

He wasn't going to pressure her into sex if she had doubts.

But before he could pull away, she tightened her fingers in his hair and tugged him forward.

He met her smoldering gaze. "You're sure?"

"I'm sure." She gave a slow nod, her dark hair with its blue highlights shimmering like satin in the dim light. "Don't you dare stop."

He studied her for a long moment, waiting until he could see the frantic urgency smoldering in her midnight eyes.

Only then did he lean forward, at last allowing his tongue to stroke through her slick fold.

His eyes slid shut in pleasure.

Christ.

She tasted of magnolia and woman. Sweet, luscious cream and power.

Talon's cock twitched, pressing painfully against the zipper of his jeans.

He needed to be in her.

He needed to mark her. Not only with his passion, but with his musk. Hell, with his very essence.

The thought should have been terrifying. Instead, nothing had ever felt more right.

This female was precisely what he needed. Strong. Independent. But with a heart that was aching for the opportunity to love.

They'd both lost their families and deep inside they were both searching for a place to call home.

Something they could build together.

Isi, however, instinctively shied from his possessive animal instinct.

"Keep your cat leashed, fur ball," she muttered.

His hands grabbed the curve of her waist, holding her still as his tongue found her swollen clitoris.

"My cat is the least of your concerns, darling."

"You...oh, shit."

For once, she was speechless as Talon flicked his tongue over her tender nub, her hips rocking upward in a silent plea for release. Again and again he stroked through her damp heat, his cat snarling in satisfaction as he wrenched a low whimper from the stubborn female.

In this moment nothing was as important as giving her more pleasure than she'd ever experienced before.

"Isi, come for me," he commanded in thick tones.

She moaned, her body trembling as she hovered on the edge of climax. "No, Talon," she breathed. "I want you inside me."

Her soft plea sliced through him, and he reluctantly pulled back. As much as he wanted to taste her orgasm on his tongue, he wanted to please her more.

And if that meant waiting to give her an orgasm when he was buried deep inside her…then that's exactly what he would do.

Gritting his teeth, Talon rose to his feet, hastily yanking off his boots so he could dispose of his jeans. The taste of Isi lingered on his tongue, the scent of magnolias making his head spin.

Unaware of how close he was to the edge, or perhaps simply enjoying her power over him, Isi stared at the throbbing length of his cock, a hectic passion glowing in her dark eyes.

He reached to grasp her around the waist, hauling her up his body to claim her lips with an intensity that branded her as his.

"I can't wait," he muttered.

She deliberately wrapped her long legs around his hips, her smile smug. "I thought cats were known for their stamina."

"Hold on, darling." Talon lowered onto the chair, the tip of his cock at the entrance to her body. Then, with a slow, ruthless thrust he pushed himself into her damp channel, not halting until his balls were pressed tight against her ass.

"Oh, god…yes," she husked.

Running his hands up her back, Talon sucked the tip of her breast between his lips, relishing her low moan of pleasure. She fit as tight as a glove around him, making him tremble with the effort to wait until she was accustomed to his penetration.

"You feel perfect," he rasped. "Ride me, Isi."

Planting her hands on his shoulders, she lifted her hips, drawing him out to the very tip before slowly sinking back down, burying him deep inside her. Talon muttered a curse, his hands gripping her hips as he battled against the climax that was already building.

Dammit. She'd just challenged his stamina. There was no way in hell he was going to come before he was certain she was satisfied.

But never before had sex called to both the man and cat inside him.

Sweat gathered on his brow as he concentrated on the mesmerizing beauty of her midnight eyes. The wary suspicion was gone, the pupils dilated as she quickened her pace.

His hips lifted to meet her downward strokes, his growl of satisfaction filling the air as she leaned down to sink her teeth into the flesh at the base of his neck, drawing blood.

The air was saturated with the perfume of her arousal, her slender body bowing above him as she tipped back her head and lost herself in the pleasure.

"Talon," she cried softly, a desperate edge in her voice as her orgasm neared.

"Darling," he whispered. "Trust me."

"I…" She moaned in pleasure as Talon tightened his grip on her hips, driving deep into her with an unyielding tempo. "Yes, that's it."

"I have you, Isi," he swore, his hand cupping the back of her head and tugging her down so he could kiss her with savage pleasure. "And I'm never letting go."

Their tongues tangled, their bodies moving together at a frantic pace. Then, just when Talon feared he was going to explode, he felt Isi stiffen, her cry of completion muffled against his lips.

Talon felt his claws emerge, slicing through the lower skin of her back as her climax clutched at his cock, his hips slamming upward as he unleashed his passion in a flurry of wild hunger.

His cat howled in satisfaction as his orgasm burst through him, the violent jolts of pleasure radiating through his entire body.

Realization hit him at the same moment.

This woman was his.

His mate.

His destiny.

For all eternity.

CHAPTER FIVE

Talon managed to stagger up the stairs with a limp Isi in his arms, his knees still weak from the intense pleasure that had exploded through his body.

A part of him had wanted to linger in the kitchen. To lay her across the table and eat his dinner off the satin magnolia of her skin before sliding his aching cock back into her body and stroking them both to paradise.

But a more logical part of him understood they needed to talk before he indulged his ravenous hunger.

Not the least of which, he had to somehow explain that in the heat of their passion he'd marked her as his mate.

Yeah. That was going to go over well.

He grimaced, hoping she didn't slice off his balls in his sleep.

Oddly, he didn't question how he'd gone from considering her the enemy to accepting her as his mate with such ease.

His cat had known she belonged to him the second it'd caught her scent. It just took the male side of him a bit longer to figure it out.

Now both were in agreement.

Isi was his mate.

And somehow he had to convince her to accept him.

A task he'd made a hell of a lot more difficult when he'd accused her of being an enemy to the Pantera.

Entering his bedroom, Talon crossed to the wide bed and gently placed her in the middle of the mattress, crawling to lie beside her. Gently he pulled her into his arms, her weary head snuggled on his shoulder.

It felt…right.

Not only having Isi in his arms, but being in this cottage that had been empty for so many years.

It was almost as if he could sense his parents' approval.

Heaving a soft sigh, Isi tilted back her head, her exotic beauty shrouded in shadows.

"That shouldn't have happened," she muttered.

He smiled wryly. Those were the words he'd been waiting to hear since she'd collapsed in utter completion.

"Why?"

She struggled to reconstruct the brittle barriers that she kept between herself and the world.

"Obviously because I don't have sex with people who think I'm evil."

He slid a finger beneath her chin, easily becoming lost in the dark beauty of her eyes. "I don't think you're evil."

A hint of vulnerability touched her pale face. "Then what do you think?"

His thumb brushed her lower lip, his gaze lightly moving over the fragile features to the diamond piercings that shimmered on her nose. They only added to her unique beauty. As did her tattoos and even her birthmark.

They were the proof that this woman was as much a warrior as he was.

"I think that you were given a shitty start to life, but you've not only managed to survive, but to become an intelligent, competent woman able to create her own business," he murmured in soft tones. "And one who is courageous and loyal enough to be willing to suffer just to help a sister who was a complete stranger to you."

Her expression remained stubbornly defiant. "Nice, but we both know I'm staying because the elders want me dead."

He leaned down to snatch a brief, utterly carnal kiss. "Lie to yourself if you want, but you can't lie to me," he murmured. Over the past hours he'd started to understand the gentle female beneath the hard façade. "If it weren't for Ashe you would have disappeared the night you were brought to the Wildlands."

She sucked in a sharp breath. "Don't say that."

He frowned, easily sensing her distress. "Why are you so scared to admit your feelings?"

"Because feelings are for suckers."

He arched a brow. "Suckers?"

"They're anchors that weigh you down," she said, a sudden tension humming through her slender body. "To survive you have to keep moving."

Talon's heart squeezed, easily able to picture Isi as a little girl, lost and terrified in an institutional setting that taught her emotions were a weakness.

"Or you can depend on those who love you to keep you safe," he assured her, his hand running down her bare back to linger on the healing scratches that were proof of their mating.

She shivered, reacting to the tenderness of the mark. "I don't depend on anyone but myself."

"You can depend on me."

She pressed her hands to his chest. "No."

"Yes." He held her gaze, his expression fierce. "You feel it, Isi. Don't deny it."

The truth flared through her eyes...the knowledge that they were fated to be together.

Not that she was going to accept her destiny.

Not without a fight.

"And what about the elders?" she demanded, doing her best to throw fences up between them. "They believe I'm destined to destroy you."

He clenched his jaw. He didn't have an answer.

Not yet.

But he was damned certain that she wasn't any harbinger of doom.

The problem was how to prove it.

"How did you learn about the Pantera?" he abruptly demanded.

She shrugged. "Everyone's heard the rumors of the savage half-men half-beasts that live in the swamps."

"Most assume we're a myth," he pointed out. "But you specifically cater to my people."

The rigid tension began to ease from her muscles, her fingers drawing absent patterns on his chest. Talon trembled beneath her soft caress, his cat purring in contentment.

Christ, he would walk through fire just for her touch.

"I was always fascinated with mixing my tattoo inks with different materials," she murmured, seemingly unaware she'd completely domesticated him. "And the voodoo priestess who helped train me in creating my spells and potions encouraged me to use malachite. She was the one who introduced me to my first Pantera. Others followed."

Talon latched onto the obvious connection. "Was the voodoo priestess called Lady Cerise?"

"No." She stared at him, genuine fear flashing through her eyes. "How do you know that name?"

His hand lifted to cup her nape, gently rubbing his thumb along the side of her neck. "Your friend Derek was approached by her," he said. "That's how he ended up in your shop."

Her breath tangled in her throat, her eyes wide. "Shit."

Concern clenched his heart. Isi clearly felt threatened by the woman.

"Who is she?"

Isi shivered. "She first approached me in Baton Rouge. I was already a student of Esme, but Lady Cerise continued to come into the voodoo shop where I was working, claiming that she could teach me magic that would be far more powerful than my potions."

"You weren't interested?"

"There was something…evil about her." She narrowed her gaze, determinedly remembering his stupid reaction to her birthmark. "Truly evil."

With a deliberate motion he dipped his head down to stroke his lips over the dark mark on her collarbone, silently apologizing for having hurt her.

"So you declined her offer?" he murmured, his lips brushing her skin.

She heaved a rueful sigh, accepting that he wasn't going to let her keep him at a distance. Instead, she threaded her fingers through his hair as his lips moved to the fascinating spot where her shoulder met her neck.

"More than that," she said, her tone growing distracted. "I fled Baton Rouge when she took an apartment in the same building where I was living, and moved to New Orleans. She was seriously creeping me out."

"She followed you?" Talon demanded, grabbing her hand and lowering it toward the aching length of his cock.

Without further urging she wrapped her fingers around his hard length, stroking down to his heavy sack.

A smug smile touched her lips at his tortured groan.

"Yes, but she kept her distance so I did my best to ignore her."

"There must be something that she wants from you," Talon said, trying to put together the pieces of the dangerous puzzle.

He now knew that the enemy had been keeping track of Isi, and that they were searching for someone who was obviously important to their cause. He'd also made certain that the Suits had eyes on Derek who would eventually lead them to the warehouse where Lon and his crew were hopefully hidden.

Later he would send someone to New Orleans to search for the mysterious Lady Cerise.

Those were all steps in the right direction.

For now, he intended to concentrate on his new mate.

Her fingers began to pump up and down his erection with a steady pace, and he made a raw sound of approval.

"Lady Cerise isn't the only one to want something from me," she muttered.

With a strangled groan, Talon rolled so he was perched on top of her slender body, framing her face in his hands.

"All I want is your happiness," he swore, holding her wary gaze so she couldn't mistake his sincerity. "And I promise, no matter what it takes, that's what I'll give you."

Her lips parted, her expression a mix between wariness and a grudging hope.

"Talon."

"You know you're mine. You feel it here." He lowered his head to press his lips directly over her thundering heart. "And here." He moved to lick the tip of one tightly clenched nipple before spreading his kisses down the flat plane of her stomach. "And here."

"Oh god," she moaned, her legs instinctively spreading as he licked through the warm, delectable sweetness.

"And most definitely here," he rasped, thrusting his tongue deep into her body. She gasped, her body arching as she clenched the sheet beneath her. "Admit it, Isi," he urged, continuing to torment her as she remained stubbornly silent. "Tell me that you belong to me."

"I…" Her words broke off in a blissful sigh, her hands reaching to grasp his hair as he expertly tongued her to a swift climax. "Yes."

"Yes, what?"

"I belong to you."

He lifted his head, meeting her dazed eyes. "Forever."

———

Isi understood on a basic level that she'd lost her mind.

There could be no other explanation for the joy that bubbled through her as she lay entangled on the bed with her annoying cat.

Hers.

Talon was right.

She'd felt a connection to him before they'd ever met.

The scent of his musk had not only eased her illness, but it'd stirred a longing deep inside her that she hadn't fully appreciated until Talon had appeared.

It was as if her heart and soul had already realized that she'd found the man destined to break through her barriers to claim the lonely woman beneath.

Just the sort of corny, fairy-tale ending that used to make her gag.

As far as she was concerned, Disney was selling a load of crap to young girls.

And then Talon had crashed into her life.

The prickly, impossibly arrogant cat had done his best to piss her off from their first meeting.

So was it any wonder she was struggling to admit to her growing bond?

Not that Talon was going to allow her the time or space to come to terms with their intense, rapidly changing relationship.

He was leaning on his elbow, glaring down at her with a narrowed gaze.

"You said it," he accused. "You agreed you belonged to me."

She tried to be annoyed by his insistence. Unfortunately, she could barely form a coherent thought as she studied the spectacular beauty of his face. Christ. No man should have such stunning eyes. It was completely unfair.

"You can't hold a person responsible for anything they say in bed." She said, her voice pathetically weak. "That's the rule."

"Whose rule?" he demanded.

"Mine."

He leaned down until they were nose to nose, the light picking up the copper highlights in his hair.

"This is my bed and my rules. You said you belong to me, so you do."

She shook her head. She might have shoved him away if her body hadn't been too lethargic from her last explosive orgasm.

"You can't just make the decision."

Talon abruptly stiffened. Almost as if her words had struck a nerve.

"Actually, I should probably admit that..."

Isi arched a brow as he hesitated. Since when did arrogant, "I'm always right" Talon pause to consider his words?

"What?" she prompted.

"That I marked you."

She stared at him, waiting to hear the punch line. Surely he couldn't actually be saying what she thought he was saying.

"You mean...you *marked me*, marked me?" she demanded. "As in mating mark?"

His expression was somber as he ensnared her gaze, forcing her to accept that this was no joke.

"Yes."

She licked her dry lips. "What does that mean?"

"You know what it means." His hand slid down her spine, lingering at the sensitive spot on her lower back where he'd marked her. "You're mine."

Isi struggled to be pissed at his outrageous proclamation.

What right did he have to mark her?

She wasn't a piece of property he could just claim.

She was a thoroughly independent woman who had no intention of tying herself to another human being, let alone a Pantera.

But she wasn't pissed.

In fact, she had a disturbing suspicion that if she'd just let down her guard she would discover that his mark was the inevitable conclusion to their heated mating dance.

"Don't you think you should have asked me if I wanted to be yours?" she forced herself to demand.

His eyes were more jade than gold as he studied her face with a tenderness that made her heart pound in her chest.

"It's not a question of choice." His fingers lightly feathered over his marks of possession, the caress sending erotic jolts of pleasure through her. "At least not for me."

A surge of satisfaction burst through her before she could tilt her chin to a defiant angle. "And me?"

He held her gaze, his musk teasing at her senses like the finest aphrodisiac. "I would never hold you against your will, Isi," he swore. "Whether you decide to accept the mating is in your hands."

"And if I don't?" she challenged. "What happens to you?"

A raw, starkly painful emotion darkened his eyes. "I will continue to try and earn your love for the rest of my life."

Isi bit her bottom lip.

It was, of course, the absolutely perfect thing to say.

The bastard.

"Oh," she whispered.

His head dipped down to kiss her. Then he gave a sudden hiss, jumping off the bed and rushing to the window. "Shit."

Alarm blasted through Isi as she shoved herself off the bed. "What?"

"Put this on," he commanded, tossing her one of his T-shirts before reaching to pull on a pair of faded jeans.

Isi didn't argue, tugging the T-shirt over her head. It fell to mid-thigh, covering the basics.

Not that she really gave a shit what she was or wasn't exposing. It was obvious something bad was happening.

"Talon, what is it?" she rasped.

His face was grim. "Intruders."

Oh, hell. Her heart squeezed with fear.

"Human?"

"No." He headed toward the door of the bedroom.

"Where are you going?"

"To get rid of the trespassers."

Panic thundered through her as she chased after him, down the stairs and into the kitchen. She didn't have to ask who was out there. Talon wouldn't be so on edge if it was anyone but the elders.

"Not alone," she pleaded. "We have to call Raphael."

Never slowing his determined stride, Talon snatched his cellphone off the table and tossed it in her direction.

"You call," he said, sending her a warning glare. "And don't come out of this house."

"But..." She muttered a curse as Talon stepped out of the cottage, firmly closing the door behind him. "Dammit."

With shaky hands she pressed on the phone and scrolled to find Raphael's number. Within seconds she heard a familiar voice.

"What?"

"It's Isi," she said, her voice a raspy croak. "Come to the cottage. And hurry."

She placed the phone on the counter and headed to pull open the door.

Talon could toss out as many orders as he wanted, but she'd be damned if she was going to allow him to fight her battles.

She stepped onto the porch, her gaze moving to the two large, male Pantera in human form who bracketed a strange mist just inside the front gate. She felt a terrifying chill spear through her heart as the mist parted to reveal three female puma.

The three ranged in shades from brown to a pristine white, with different colored eyes. But they all shared the same aura of ancient power.

The sort of power she couldn't hope to battle.

The elders.

She gave a startled jump as they suddenly spoke. Not just because they combined their voices to speak as one, but because they didn't speak aloud. Instead she heard them in her mind.

"Step aside, Talon," they commanded of the man who blocked the pathway to the house.

The stubborn cat folded his arms over his chest. "No."

The mist trembled around the elders, as if astonished by Talon's refusal to obey. Odd. Isi had known him only a few days and she could have informed them that he had an allergy to being told what to do.

"The female must be sacrificed if we are to rescue our lands from destruction," they said in unison.

Isi wrapped her arms around her waist, glaring at the pumas. Bitches.

Talon growled low in his throat. "You don't know that her sacrifice will do anything to save the Wildlands."

"It was foretold."

"Prophecies can be interpreted to mean anything," Talon argued.

The elders regarded him with flat gazes, a sudden heat prickling in the air.

"Will you risk the future of your people to protect the female?"

His answer came without hesitation. "Yes."

Isi forgot to breathe, her gaze locked on Talon's broad back as he stood between her and the powerful females who wanted her dead.

Never had anyone stood up for her. Let alone risked their life to protect her.

God...Talon was willing to sacrifice his people.

The last layer of her protective barriers shattered as the bond between them settled into place, irrevocably binding them together.

There was the sensation of surprise before the voices of the elders echoed through her brain.

"You've mated her."

"Fate mated us," Talon countered.

Mated. Yes. The word was perfect for the bond she felt for Talon.

But even as she adjusted to the knowledge that her future was forever bound to the cat, a fierce fury was racing through her.

She'd been alone for as long as she could remember, and now, just when she had the opportunity to share her world with a man who she loved and a sister who needed her, the damned elders were threatening to snatch it all away.

"It changes nothing," they were saying, their gazes studying her with a grim determination.

"Fuck that," Talon snarled. "It changes everything."

"You will give us the female or you will die," the elders warned.

Talon shrugged. "Then I die."

"No."

The horrified denial was jerked from Isi's lips as she rushed down the steps to stand beside her mate.

Talon turned to glare at her with a smoldering frustration. "I told you to stay in the house."

She lifted a hand to brush her fingers through his silky hair, her heart twisting with a fear that had nothing to do with her own danger, and everything to do with this man who'd somehow become a vital part of her existence.

"I won't let them hurt you."

His expression tightened with a savage need to protect her. "Not your choice."

"Yes," she said softly. "It is."

"Dammit, Isi," he growled. "You're not alone anymore. We're in this together."

Together. A wistful smile touched her lips.

It was ironic. She spent her whole life avoiding relationships, certain they would demand a price she wasn't willing to pay. Now, when she was facing certain death, she realized that there was no price to love.

It didn't take.

It gave.

Everything.

"Not if it means watching you die," she said in husky tones. "Anything but that."

His cat glowed in his eyes, his emotions scalding the air with heat as the two male Pantera rapidly approached.

"Isi...no."

Her finger brushed his lips before she was turning to haul ass toward the side gate, glancing over her shoulder as she flipped off the elders.

"You want me? Then catch me, you bitches."

CHAPTER SIX

Talon was braced for the two Hunters who charged toward him, prepared to kill them if that's what it took to protect his mate.

It didn't matter that he'd trained with them. Or that they were only following the commands of the elders.

If they stood between him and the woman who was his other half then they had to die.

On the point of shifting, Talon was caught off-guard when the nearest Pantera halted, pointing a small crossbow in his direction.

What the hell?

He dodged to the side as the small bolt whizzed toward him, striking him in the upper thigh.

The weapon wasn't large enough to cause permanent damage, but Talon swiftly realized that he was in trouble.

Already a thick potion laced with malachite was pumping through his bloodstream, caging his cat and weakening him.

God. Dammit.

"Don't interfere, Talon," the voices of the elders thundered through his mind as they went in pursuit of Isi who'd already vaulted over the gate and disappeared into the marshes.

The two guards followed behind them, leaving Talon to collapse against the stairs of the porch.

Black fury engulfed him, his cat roaring in distress as the scent of his mate faded.

On hands and knees he tried to claw his way toward the gate, refusing to give up despite the knowledge that he'd never get to Isi before she was caught by the elders.

He would fucking drag himself across the entire country to get to his mate.

He'd managed to crawl halfway down the path when he heard a startled curse and Raphael was abruptly kneeling beside him.

"What the hell is going on?"

Talon reached out to grab Raphael's hand. "The elders…they have Isi. You have to save her."

"Shit," Raphael muttered. "What did they do to you?"

Talon struggled to lift his head, meeting Raphael's eyes that glowed with a luminous rage.

"Malachite," he managed to mutter.

With another round of foul curses, Raphael ran his hand over Talon's trembling body, at last locating the dart.

"This is going to hurt," the older cat warned, yanking out the dart before he used his dagger to cut a deep incision and sucking out the potion like it was snake poison.

Instantly Talon began to feel stronger.

With the source of the malachite removed, his natural immune system kicked into gear, beginning to burn away the effects of the mineral.

Forcing himself upright, Talon would have tumbled on his face if Raphael hadn't reached out to wrap an arm around his shoulders, hauling Talon against his side.

"Damn," he growled.

"I've got you," Raphael promised, keeping Talon upright as they headed toward the gate.

Talon's balance remained uncertain and his movements painfully stiff, but he grimly forced himself to keep pace as Raphael led them along the edge of the marsh, the older Pantera's expression intent as he remained locked on the trail.

Then without warning he came to a halt. "Dammit."

Talon clenched his teeth, the need to get to Isi pounding through him with a brutal insistence.

"What?"

Raphael grimaced. "The elders used their mist to mask their scent."

Talon closed his eyes, concentrating on his bond with Isi. "I can find her."

"You're mated?" Raphael demanded in surprise.

"Not now," Talon snarled. "We have to get to Isi."

"Fine. Where are they?"

"The temple."

Raphael gave a sharp nod and together they were headed toward the most sacred section of the Wildlands. Less than fifteen minutes later they approached the wide, cypress bridge that extended across the moonlit bayou.

It was said that the middle of the bridge marked the precise spot where the sisters Opela and Shakpi were born.

And where Opela had sacrificed herself to imprison her evil sister.

Tonight the foot of the bridge was brightly lit with torches. The pools of light surrounded the three elders who sat before Isi who'd been tied to a wooden pier. On each side of her was a male Pantera guard holding a large dagger. Not that they needed the weapons. Isi was not only bound and gagged, but she was barely conscious, with a large bruise already forming on the side of her head where she'd been hit.

Talon roared in outrage, desperately trying to shift so he could rip the bastards to tiny, bloody shreds.

"Stay back." The voices of the elders blasted through his brain, but Talon moved grimly forward.

"Talon." Raphael grabbed his arm, holding him in place. Then he turned to glare at the elders. "Don't do this."

"We have no choice," they replied in unison. "Look at the land. Even here, in this sacred place, the magic is fading."

Talon glanced toward the mossy ground, noticing for the first time that it had turned a sickly shade of brown. A part of him was saddened by the sight of the decay. He was as horrified as any Pantera at the thought that the Wildlands were endangered.

But in this moment, nothing mattered but rescuing Isi.

Raphael spoke directly to the elders. "My baby...the first Pantera in fifty years...will die without her."

The elders never allowed their attention to waver from Isi or the men who both lifted daggers to slice through Isi's forearms, the wounds deep enough to allow blood to drip down her arms and onto the ground.

Talon lunged forward, only to be halted by Raphael. He growled in fury, but the malachite still coursed through his blood, making him too weak to fight the larger Pantera.

"This is the only way to ensure the child will survive," the elders pronounced, hissing in disgust as Isi's blood hit the ground with a loud sizzle, scorching what was left of the dying vegetation. "There. You see. Her blood is toxic."

A shocked silence filled the air as they watched in varying degrees of horror as the blood continued to spread over the ground, leaving blackened earth in its path.

It was as if her blood held a wildfire that destroyed whatever it touched.

Chillingly aware of what was going to happen next, Talon fiercely called on his cat, overcoming the lingering malachite with grim resolution.

In a blur of power he shifted, lunging forward before anyone could react to his abrupt attack.

His roar shook the ground as he rammed into one of the guards who'd dare to hurt Isi, using one brutal swipe of his paw to knock him unconscious. Without hesitation, he was slamming into the second guard, catching him before he could shift and defend himself.

His teeth sank into the man's flesh, but before he could rip out his throat, Raphael was at his side, yelling directly into his ear.

"Wait. Dammit, Talon, look."

Slowly the words penetrated the red haze that filled Talon's mind with the need to kill, forcing him to release his prey and glance where Raphael was pointing.

Astonishment jolted through Talon, jerking him from his cat form to human. Instinctively he moved to stand as a barrier between Isi and the elders, his frantic gaze watching as the blackened earth trembled, as if a powerful force was surging from beneath the ground. Then tiny, tender sprouts of green began to break through the crusty dirt.

"It's starting regrow," he breathed. "She's healing the land."

There was the sensation of furious disbelief as the mist around the elders shimmered in the torchlight.

"It's her death—"

"Stop." Talon took his life in his hands by challenging the powerful females. "You see what's happening." He swept his hand toward the tender green shoots that were beginning to spread. "Are you going to let your stubborn belief that you're always right destroy our hope for the future?"

Raphael moved to stand at his side, his arms folded over his chest. "Talon is right. Until we understand what is happening, we can't risk destroying the female."

There was a long silence, as if the elders were arguing among themselves. Talon swiftly used their distraction to turn back to Isi, using a claw to slice through the ropes that bound her to the pier.

His heart clenched as she tumbled into his arms. She was barely conscious, her body trembling from a combination of pain and shock.

God dammit.

He'd failed her. She was his to protect, but he'd allowed her to be stolen from him and injured.

"Talon." Wrapping her arms around his neck, she buried her face in his throat.

He scooped her off her feet, cradling her against his chest. "I've got you, darling," he swore, his gaze locked on the elders. No one was taking her away. Not ever again. "And I'm never letting you go."

"You have made your point, Talon," the elder with white fur spoke in his head, taking the lead for her sisters. "Although we are not convinced she is harmless, there is enough doubt to delay her death until we have a greater understanding of what is occurring."

"I think I might be able to help." Stepping from the shadows at the edge of the sacred land, a male Pantera offered the elders a low bow. "May I approach?"

The elders spoke in unison. "Welcome, Xavier."

The tall, mocha-toned man with startling blue eyes moved gracefully forward.

Talon felt a leap of hope at the sight of the leader of the Geeks. If anyone had managed to coax the secrets from the computers Talon had brought from Baton Rouge, it would be this brilliant Pantera.

"What did you discover?" he demanded, ignoring the annoyance of the ancient females who clearly felt they should be in charge.

He didn't give shit who he had to piss off.

He was going to do whatever necessary to protect his mate.

Xavier walked forward, his gaze flickering toward the fresh green vegetation on the ground before moving to Isi who remained cradled in Talon's arms.

"I know who our enemies are searching for."

Talon felt a tingle of premonition inch down his spine as Xavier's dark gaze remained locked on Isi.

"Who?" Raphael at last demanded.

"Chayton," the Geek revealed. "Father of Isi and Ashe."

XAVIER

By
Laura Wright

CHAPTER ONE

Sweet freedom.

Pool cue in one hand, margarita in the other, Amalie strode across the dusty floor of The Cougar's Den.

Hot damn, she was emancipated.

Granted, it was only for three days and nights, but she planned to make the most out of every second. Clad in her tightest jeans, black high-heeled boots, and a white tank that showed off her young, Hunter's body and plenty of cleavage up top, she felt every male eye move over her as she passed.

Well, every male but one.

Stopping in front of the pool table, she dropped her cue on the playing surface and lifted her glass to her lips. Salty sweet goodness rolled over her tongue and down her throat. She wasn't a big drinker. Shoot, she wasn't a big anything. In fact, this was her first time in The Cougar's Den. For years, she'd heard all about it from the other Hunters. Listened as they regaled her with stories about drunken nights, hard-won pool games, hook-ups with hot males or females. While she went home.

Not tonight, she mused, draining her glass, then eyeing the bartender. Tonight she was cutting loose. Tonight she was going to know what it felt like to play hard, drink hard and just be a ready and willing single female.

"What do you say, darlin'?"

Mal glanced over her shoulder, spied the male who'd just spoken to her. He was tall, blond and human, and his mouth curved into a wicked smile. "Dance?"

She turned around and faced him. "I didn't know this place had a dance floor."

"They don't," he said. "Not yet anyway."

The male whistled to one of his buddies and the pair grabbed a few tables and pushed them aside.

He turned back to Mal and shrugged. "Nothing fancy, but it'll do. What do you say? I like this song and you're smoking hot."

Mal's heart fluttered in her chest. Sure, she was a kickass Hunter who was capable of bringing down several full-grown males with one hand tied behind her back—part of her training—but in the Wildlands no one ever talked to her like this. Looked at her like this. Like she was desirable and available. It felt so good.

Alcohol snaking through her blood, making her warm and bold, she followed him out onto the makeshift dance floor. The bartender had cranked up the music and a few other couples had already taken advantage of the space.

"Name's Beau," the male said over the music as he started to move.

Mal grinned as she sidled up close to him and started to sway her hips. "Nice to meet you, Beau."

"You too, darlin'." His eyes traveled down her body. "Never seen anything as sexy as you come in here."

"I'm sure that's not true," she said on a husky laugh, her head feeling deliciously fuzzy. "But I appreciate it anyway."

He laughed with her, his dark eyes glittering with interest. They were a handsome set of eyes, deep and soulful, and she could probably get lost in them if it wasn't for the breath-stealing, knee-weakening crystal blue orbs of a certain Pantera male in the room. Eyes she'd been lusting after forever.

Seeing those piercing, highly sexual eyes in her mind, and fueled by inhibition-killing margaritas, she turned her head.

Such a big mistake.

He'd only been in The Cougar's Den for maybe a half hour, but it was enough for him to cause a stir. Not like he could help it. Females just couldn't seem to catch their breath around him, and males were understandably intimated by his size.

Still swaying, Mal ran her hands up the sides of her body as she watched him at the bar. Eating up the metal bar stool he inhabited, Xavier was by far the hottest male specimen that had ever walked the earth. Over six foot four, and all powerful shoulders and broad chest, the gorgeous male looked more like a professional athlete than the head of the Geeks. His skin was the color of wet bark, and his features were sharp and fierce. His dark hair had just been recently cut, buzzed close to his scalp, making his amazing, crystal blue eyes pop. And every time Mal saw him, she had an irrepressible urge to rush at him, leap into his massive arms and attack his perfect mouth.

It'd been like that for the past seven years.

Oh, who was she kidding? More like ten.

As the male she danced with moved around her, Mal's gaze slid to the female who sat beside Xavier at the bar. Blond, petite and quietly appealing. *Why does Xavier have to go for the exact opposite of me?* she screamed silently, wondering if it was psycho to actually plot the woman's death while dancing with some random guy.

Then Xavier reached across the top of the bar and covered the woman's hand.

A shock of pain brought Mal's head around. Her gaze connected with Beau and his dark eyes and dreamy smile. "I need another drink."

He grinned. "I'll get it for you, darlin'. Just stay here and keep those hips swayin' and those hands runnin' up and down yourself. I'll be right back."

Why couldn't Xavier say things like that? Well, maybe not exactly like that. Maybe not so creepy and proprietary, but something that indicated that he saw her as a female and not his best friend's little sister?

She closed her eyes and moved seductively to the music. She felt someone come up behind her, definitely male, maybe Beau, maybe not, but she didn't stop to look. Tonight and for the next three nights, she just wanted to let go, give in, feel, be felt...

She needed a spanking.

Maybe more than one.

Xavier narrowed his eyes on the Hunter female who was gyrating on the makeshift dance floor, sandwiched between two greasy human males, while another ordered drinks a few feet down the bar. Did he blame them for going after her? Leering at her? Drooling like dogs? No, he did not. With her perfect body clad in way-too-tight clothes, hungry green eyes, and thick ebony hair flowing down her back, she looked like a goddamn sex kitten tonight, and he was going to pummel the bastard who'd let her out of her cage.

Where the fuck was Aristide?

Her brother—and Xavier's closest friend—never let his sister out of his sight, except when she worked as a Hunter. And even then, Xavier could count on the rest of the Pantera to watch her. They all knew how special she was. Important. The kind of female you put up on a pedestal and stared at.

Not fucking leered at.

His eyes narrowed into pinprick slits as he watched her rock the dance floor. How the hell had she learned to move like that? Her hips. Her ass. Her hands threading in her hair and running down her body.

Another jolt moved through him, but he forced it away. He always forced away those kinds of flashes when it came to her. Amalie was not just the last Pantera born, which made her untouchable in and of itself, but she was also his best friend's little sister. And the code of honor between males killed even the most desperate of attractions.

He stood, slipped the flash drive the woman beside him had brought with her into his jeans pocket. "You didn't have to disable the camera to get these shots, did you?"

The blond PI he'd hired to help in his search for Ashe and Isi's father, Chayton, shook her head. "No. But it was a bitch and a half to get up there, and *stay* up there while I located the serial number. Thank god some asshole got a tattoo last night. Gave me a solid hour."

The human female had found a hidden camera in Isi's voodoo shop, and had spent the past three days trying to get a few minutes alone with it. "Did you run the number?"

"It's some exclusive, expensive shit. There's a list of the high-end stores that sell cameras like that on your drive, but I couldn't get sales records. You're going to need a top notch hacker."

Good thing he was one, Xavier thought, his gaze sliding over to the dance floor again. A growl sounded in his throat. Amalie was grinding her hips against some human male like she wanted sex.

"My payment?" the PI said.

"Already in your account."

She laughed softly, almost seductively. "Gotta love a man who anticipates a woman's needs. Can I buy you a drink?"

"Not tonight," he said, his eyes still pinned to the Hunter female and the human drooling machines bracketing her. "But I'll be in touch."

He pushed away from the bar and headed through the small crowd to the dance floor. He should be gone by now, heading back to Geek headquarters, checking out the drive the PI had just handed him. After all, it was vital the Pantera find Chayton before their enemies did.

A good fifteen patrons were working it to the killer baseline of some rapper, and a few females tried to catch Xavier's eye and draw him into their circle. But he only had eyes for one female, and she was going back to the Wildlands immediately. To her home, and to her brother's care.

Eyes closed, full pink lips parted, long hair mussed, the female before him looked like she'd just come from her bed. Xavier drew close and wrapped his large hand around her slim wrist. Instantly, her eyes opened. At first, she seemed confused as she stared up at him. Then, as she registered not only his presence but his hold on her, she smiled.

"Hi, Xavier," she said. "Want to join the party?"

Shit. How many drinks had she had? Her speech wasn't slurred, but it was pretty damn close. "You're making a scene, Amalie."

"My name is Mal," she corrected him, her luscious jade-green eyes flashing momentary fire. "And I'm not making a scene, I'm having fun."

Three or four drinks of fun. He didn't say a word, just lowered his hand to close around hers and led her off the dance floor. Xavier knew she could fight him if she wanted to. The female was tough as hell. Smart, too. But she didn't. In fact, she squeezed his hand and moved with him through the crowd and toward the door. Maybe it was the alcohol in her blood? Could do funny things to the Pantera system.

Night was just settling in, but the warm bayou air of the day still remained, rushing over Xavier's skin as he stepped outside. As he turned Amalie to face him, his hands on her shoulders, he tried not to stare at how that same breeze affected her hair, sending it swirling about her face.

Her fucking perfect face.

Releasing her and sliding his gaze away, Xavier growled low in his throat. Thoughts like these were becoming too commonplace lately. He needed to find a way to get rid of them. Permanently. Or he'd have to get rid of himself being around this female, permanently.

Amalie cocked her head. "Are you growling at me, Xavier?" Her tone was all flirtation, warmth, intimacy. "Not that I'm complaining."

"How much have you had to drink?" he said tightly.

"Not nearly enough."

"Your Pantera scent is being strangled by tequila."

She shrugged. "Shit happens."

"Yes, it does," he said, moving closer to her. "Like you being here of all places. Does Aristide know you're here?"

Her eyes clouded over, and for a moment she just stared at him. Then she laughed and shook her head. "No, my jailer of a brother doesn't know I'm here. He's stuck in quarantine with that human woman, Ashe's sister."

Isi? The one whose blood had both damaged the Wildlands and had caused it to bring forth life?

And Aristide didn't tell me?

What the hell? Xavier mused darkly. Someone needed to be watching out for Amalie.

The door to The Cougar's Den burst open and one of Amalie's dance partners nearly stumbled out. When the greasy male spotted her, he grinned like a fucking wolf with prey in sight.

"You coming back in, darlin'?" he drawled.

"No," Xavier answered.

Amalie turned to give him a dirty look, then glanced back up at the human male. "In a minute, Beau."

Xavier growled at her. "I'm taking you home, Amalie."

Her gaze slid his way once again, and no longer was there even a hint of flirtation glittering there. "No, you're not. I'm here to have some fun. Just because you don't know the meaning of that word."

"I'll show you some fun," Beau said, loping down the steps toward them.

"I suggest you go back inside, Male," Xavier said darkly, though his gaze remained pinned to Mal. "We're leaving, Amalie. Say goodbye to your little friend here. Perhaps you can schedule a playdate for another day."

"Do you hear yourself?" she growled back at him.

"I do."

She stuck a finger in his face. "I'm not the young cub you and Aristide get to tell what to do anymore. I'm a grown female."

Xavier sighed, his nostrils flaring with irritation. Yes, unfortunately, she was. A female with curves designed to make a male anxious to breed. A face angels would be envious of. A husky voice that belonged near a hungry male's ear.

All attributes that shouldn't be allowed near this oily, drunken human.

"Say goodbye, Amalie," he said evenly.

"She doesn't want to say goodbye," Beau said with a grunt. "Do you, Amalie?"

"My name's Mal," she corrected.

Beau chuckled, his eyes pinned to her chest. "Hey, I'll call you whatever you want, Sexy."

"Oh, I like that." Amalie's gaze flickered Xavier's way, and she said something under her breath that sounded an awful lot like, "Why can't you ever call me that?"

Xavier pretended not to hear her. Just as he pretended to not be affected by the way she chewed her lower lip. He shook his head slowly. "You know I can't let this happen, Amalie."

Her hands went to her hips. "The funny part is that you actually believe that. Or is the funny part that you're still doing Aristide's job? I'm not sure. Wait. Maybe they're both funny."

The human moved closer to her, his eyes now trained on her ass. "I know some funny stories, Mal. I'll buy you a drink and share a few."

Xavier felt his insides flood with aggression. This male was about two seconds away from unconsciousness. Which would be a bad idea, as they were on human land. The last thing Pantera wanted to do was draw attention to themselves. But this idiot was really begging for it.

"I'm going to say this once more, *mon ami*." Xavier's eyes narrowed on the human male. He wasn't particularly tall, but what he lacked in height, he made up for with muscle. Not Pantera kind of muscle, but impressive for a human. Something to consider if things went bruised and bloody. "Go inside and find yourself another female. This one is not available."

"I'll decide if I'm available or not," Amalie said tightly. "You got some nerve, Xavier. Go home."

The human grinned, then slid his arm around Amalie's waist, yanked her close and licked the curve of her ear. "You tell him, Sexy."

The haze that had only a second ago glimmered in Amalie's smoky green eyes receded, and a flare of golden heat took its place. It was the sign her cat hovered at the surface of her skin. Her control was lost, courtesy of too much tequila. In under five seconds, she removed the male's arm from her waist, took his hand in hers and slammed it back into his face. Making a sound like air escaping a balloon, Beau slithered to the ground and remained.

Xavier's eyes flipped up to meet hers. "Was that necessary?"

She stumbled backwards a step. "He licked me."

"Grow up, Amalie."

"You won't let me." Her eyes locked to him. "You and Aristide."

Xavier's gut clenched. She had no idea how he saw her, how his skin ached every time she touched him – how he stood taller, prouder, every time her eyes were on him. And hell, she never would, if he could manage it.

"Then perhaps we should concentrate on sobering up." He reached for her hand. "We're leaving. Now."

She didn't try to pull away. "Careful, Puma. Or I'll drop you like I dropped Tongue-Boy there."

Xavier refused to reply to such absurdity. As he moved past her, he scooped her up in his arms and continued down the path toward the parking lot.

"Neanderthal," she spat out.

"Pantera," he corrected, trying not to think about how good she felt in his arms. How right. How natural.

"You don't have to carry me," she grumbled. "I know how to use my legs."

His jaw went tight at her words. So did everything below his waist. Fucking female. Fucking male brain for taking those innocent words and twisting them into a goddamn fantasy. "It'll take us all night to walk home," he said. "And something tells me you can't run in those come-fuck-me-boots."

She glanced up at him. "Is that what they're called?"

He didn't answer, didn't look at her either. She'd been too god-damn beautiful in the harsh fluorescent lights of the club. Under the glow of twilight, he was pretty sure she'd send certain parts of his anatomy skyward.

He didn't need that. Not tonight. Not ever.

Clearing the parking lot, he took off toward the dark protection of the woods. He was fast in his human state, but he ached to shift to his puma and really taste the wind.

"So, I guess you're my way home tonight," she said with a soft yawn.

His arms tightened around her. "Who brought you? How did you get to The Den?"

"I caught a ride."

"If you tell me with a stranger—" he began through gritted teeth. He felt her shrug. "He was only a stranger for the first five minutes." A low growl escaped his throat. Shit, he needed to break out the fur and the canines. "I'm going to take you home and tie you up until Aristide gets out of quarantine."

She snorted, then yawned again. "I'd like to see you try."

"Would you?"

He made the mistake of looking down at her. Trying to put the sweet weight of her body out of his mind as he moved was problem enough. Now he saw full lips, drowsy eyes, a strip of tanned stomach where her tank was riding up.

Fuck. Me.

"What about your date?" she said. "Isn't she waiting back at The Den for you?"

"That was business."

She snorted softly. "She didn't look like business. She looked like she wanted to do some licking of her own."

Xavier growled—not at the idea of the human PI, but with the recent memory of that greasy human male's hands on Amalie. His *tongue* on Amalie.

"What?" she asked, concern lacing her tone.

"If I didn't have to babysit you tonight, I'd go back to The Cougar's Den, scrape the human male up off the ground and remove his eager tongue from his mouth."

"I took care of it, Xavier."

"Yes. And you provoked it. Humans should not be played with. It's not good for us."

"Us or me?" she said softly.

Xavier didn't answer. Doing so would mean he'd have to examine his feelings for his best friend's sister. And he made it a practice never to do that. Instead, he picked up speed, racing through the bayou lands toward the border. Quiet, except for the sound of the breeze and the buzzing of the insects, reigned. Xavier had actually thought Amalie asleep when she moved in his arms and spoke.

"Xavier?"

Goddamn, her soft, yet husky voice wrapped around him. Squeezed the shit out of him. "Yeah?"

"When we get to the edge of the Wildlands…I don't think I can shift."

"The tequila?"

She nodded against his chest. "Sorry."

With a soft, protective growl, he pulled her closer to his chest. "Not to worry, Amalie. I'll carry you to the border, and my puma will carry you home."

CHAPTER TWO

The moon's filtered light followed them as they traveled the varied terrain of the Wildlands. Night was in full bloom now, bringing with it cool air and rich, earthy scents. Her arms wrapped around the thick neck of Xavier's cat, Mal reveled in the smooth cadence of his movement. She'd only ridden on the back of a puma once before. When she'd lodged a thorn in her foot after a hard-won race between a few Hunters last year. But it was nothing like this. Xavier's puma was not only large and powerful, it was quick and sharp and keen. And riding on his back, under the moonlight, seduced by the scents and the wind, made her wonder how it would feel to not only ride him, but to be ridden—

Her sensual thought was ripped from her mind as Xavier came to a halt in front of her small, sage green house. For a second, she just remained on his back, wondering why she hadn't noticed them entering the boundaries of town. Hadn't, at the very least, scented it.

She scrambled off of him, and, from the shelter of a rose-trellised archway, watched as he shifted from sleek black cat into devastatingly hot male. Her heart squeezed. Wearing jeans that stretched over heavily muscled thighs and a killer ass, and a black T-shirt that could barely contain his vast chest and bulging arms, Xavier made every female who came within a mile of him sigh. Tall, dark and fierce, he was sex walking. And added to it—Mal's favorite attribute of all—those incredible, icy blue eyes. Well, she just wanted to get lost in him and not be found for days.

If only he wanted that too.

Damn. Why couldn't he notice her? See her as the one female on earth who was perfect for him, would make him happy?

"Who's staying with you while Aristide is quarantined?" Xavier asked, following her up the path to her front door.

"No one."

He made a sound deep in his throat. It was a cross between a growl and a groan, and it made her insides flare with heat.

"Not acceptable, Amalie."

She glanced over her shoulder. "You realize I'm a grown female, right?"

His gaze, those shockingly blue eyes, traveled down her body. Then he looked away and hissed.

No. He didn't see her as grown.

Or wouldn't.

Irritation moving over and through her, she turned back and opened her front door with a hiss of her own. She was growing into quite the little masochist. Maybe it was time for that to stop.

She called over her shoulder, "Thanks for the ride."

But before she took a step inside, she felt him at her back, his massive frame pressed against her, his warm breath near her ear. "We're not done talking about this."

Without her permission, her skin went tight, and everything below her waist clenched. "I think I am. I'm tired and still a little drunk and I should probably go to bed."

"You can't stay here alone."

"Why not?"

He moved to her side, leaned against the doorframe. "It's not safe."

She laughed. "Are you serious? I'm a Hunter. Even you would be hard-pressed to get me on my back." When his eyes narrowed at her words, her laughter downgraded to an embarrassed chuckle. "You know, unless I wanted to be there."

His jaw tightened. "I know you can handle yourself physically, Amalie. What concerns me is shit like tonight."

"I went out and had fun like a bunch of other people do every damn day. What's the problem?"

"You had too much to drink and it affected your judgment."

Her judgment? She snorted. Shit, that had been compromised ten years ago when she'd seen Xavier with his shirt off for the first time. Summer on the bayou. Warm water, warmer evenings. Swim party for her birthday, and Xavier—the most perfect birthday present ever—came to hang out with Aristide. Of course, he hadn't even looked her way. Mal didn't even think he'd known it was her birthday. But she'd noticed him. Back then and every day since.

"My judgment is fine," she told him. "I won't drink as much next time, that's all."

He shook his head. "There's not going to be a next time."

She glared at him. Crush of a lifetime or not, Xavier was being a pain in the ass, aka a wannabe substitute for her brother. And that she wasn't going to put up with.

"Okay, we're done here. I'm going to bed." She pushed past him into the house, and stalked into the foyer. "Just lock the door before you take off. You know, so I stay safe and all."

Ten years, she grumbled. Ten freaking years she'd spent internally—and probably externally as well—swooning for this male, and he either couldn't see her as anything but Aristide's sister, or just didn't find her attractive. Ugh, that last bit stung, and she wondered how much longer this feeling, this need, was going to lay claim to her heart. Maybe she should make another trip into town. Not to The Cougar's Den, this time, but to that Voodoun's shop. Maybe inquire about a potion to kill her crush.

Feeling a rush of alcohol-infused heat take over her skin, she pulled off her tank and dropped it on the floor of the hall as she headed toward her bedroom. *Tomorrow. Tomorrow when she sobered up she was going to stop wanting the ridiculously beautiful Geek.*

She got halfway to her bedroom before a shocking smack of dizziness hit her. Stars glittered in front of her eyes, and she cursed and reached out for the wall. When her hands met nothing but air, panic gripped her heart. Then the floor rushed up to meet her, and her vision went utterly black.

———

Xavier's heart dropped into his balls as he caught Amalie before she hit the floor.

Christ, this female made him crazy, he growled inwardly, settling her into his arms. Flirting with him one second, pissed off at him the next. He pulled her close as he moved down the hallway. Yes, he knew she liked him. Had this lighthearted crush on him. And he'd be lying his ass off if he didn't admit to having his own attraction and problematic curiosity about her...how she might taste, how her skin smelled...

Fuck. He was going to hell. Or the Pantera equivalent: down beneath the Wildlands, imprisoned with Shakpi.

He was never going to act on that attraction. She was Aristide's blood, precious to the Pantera, completely off-limits.

Entering her bedroom, Xavier couldn't help but glance around as he made a beeline for the bed. Shit, the female acted so tough, but when it came down to it, she was all heart and fluffy white bed-spreads and flowered pillows. Hard on the outside, soft and sweet on the inside. His insides curled with desire at the thought.

Why did he find that juxtaposition so damned sexy?

With gentle hands, he placed her on the cool, white blanket, then sat down next to her. His gaze raked over her face. *What a fucking vision.* Dappled moonlight streamed in through the window to his right, spot-lighting her yards of rich, dark hair, beautiful face, pink mouth and long, supple neck. His traitorous gaze moved downward. The tank was gone, now a small, white puddle forgotten in the hallway. All she had on was a bra, and a skimpy one at that. And the creamy slip of lacy fabric barely covered her large breasts.

His mouth watered.

Rein it in, asshole.

The lids of her eyes moved, and she fisted one hand and moaned.

Xavier leaned in and brushed a strand of hair off her pale cheek. Trying not to focus on how soft her skin felt under the rough pads of his fingers, he whispered soothingly, "Everything's okay, Amalie. You're home. In your bed."

Her eyes fluttered open, and for a moment those smoky green orbs displayed extreme confusion. But in seconds, the haze dissipated, and she blinked, her teeth grazing her bottom lip. An action that once again had Xavier's skin tightening over his muscles.

"Xavier?"

He nodded. "How you feeling?"

She didn't answer him. Her eyes were pinned to his and her breathing grew labored.

"What?" he asked, concern moving through him. When she'd fallen, had he not caught her in time? Had she hurt herself? "What's wrong?"

"I'm not a cub."

Relief moved through him. This wasn't pain he was seeing in her eyes, but frustration. "I know you're not," he said.

"You all treat me like I am."

"No," he amended, his voice dark, quiet. "We treat you like you're special."

She flinched, then huffed out a breath and looked away, past him. "So I was the last cub born to the Pantera. Who cares? Why does that mean anything different than the second-to-last cub? Or the third? It doesn't make me special. It just makes me lucky."

Xavier didn't want to do this. Have this conversation. Especially not in her moonlit room, sitting on her bed. Granted, he understood the Pantera's affections and protective ways regarding Amalie, but his actions and reactions were less about her 'last born' status and more about his own barely controlled attraction. Truthfully, if she wasn't Aristide's sister, he wasn't all that sure he'd give a good goddamn about the Pantera's need to keep her sheltered.

"You should sleep now," he told her.

"I don't want to sleep." With a frustrated sigh, she came up on her elbows. "I want to be free. I want to live my own life. I want to be treated like something that can't be broken with just a simple touch."

"No touch is simple," Xavier said quietly. "Trust me."

"I don't want to trust you!" she suddenly exploded, sitting all the way up, tears welling in her eyes. "Goddamit!" She threw up her hands. "I want to know it myself! I want to feel it myself!"

"Amalie—"

"I'm a fucking grown female!" she cried, looking down.

"I know."

Her eyes snapped up to meet his. "Do you?"

His breath caught in his lungs. As much as she was beautiful when she was docile and flirtatious, she was nearly irresistible like this. So impassioned, so vicious, like she wanted to kiss the shit out of him, then knee him in the balls.

His gaze moved over her face, down the smooth column of her neck, then into her spectacular cleavage. Did he know she was a grown female?

Fuck yeah.

"Listen to me, Xavier," she fairly growled. "If I don't get *broken* soon, I'm going to lose my mind."

"Don't talk like that," he growled back, giving her a fierce look, his cock twitching.

"Why not? It's true. There's nothing wrong with wanting to be touched, wanting to go out and have a good time. Wanting sex."

Christ, she was killing him. "I'm warning you, Amalie—"

"Just because you don't see me as a grown female doesn't mean other males don't."

"No males will be getting within ten feet of you," he declared roughly.

"You can't say shit like that."

"I just did." He stood up. He had to rearrange. He had to get the hell out of this room, out of her airspace before he did something regrettable.

She looked up at him, her eyes deep and dark, her hair wild and falling over her shoulders and between her breasts. "Go home, Xavier."

He should. He really should.

In fact, he should walk out of this house and never come back. From now on, he and Aristide would meet somewhere else, anywhere else. And when Amalie's name was brought up, he'd pray for deafness.

Instead, he narrowed his eyes on the half-naked vixen sitting in a pool of white softness before him and said with deadly calm, "I'm not going anywhere."

One dark eyebrow raised. "*Pardonnez-moi?*"

"Clearly you can't be trusted on your own." He turned and headed for the door, calling over his shoulder, "While Aristide is gone, I'll be taking care of you."

CHAPTER THREE

Bastard.

Asshole.

God, she wanted to jump him.

Mal stared, watched Xavier's exit with hungry, greedy eyes. He looked so good from behind. Even if he was walking away from her.

With a sigh of self-disgust, she dropped back on the pillow and closed her eyes. Truly, it stung that Xavier was staying with her out of obligation—not out of want. Or desire. She'd thought, fantasized, about being alone with him for so long, and now here they were. Not making out as she'd hoped, but residing in two separate rooms, both clothed, both breathing normally, skin not coated in a thin layer of sweat...

She groaned and turned on her side.

And yet, no matter the reason, he *was* staying.

For three days and three nights.

She wrapped herself around her extra-long pillow and squeezed, a glimmer of something akin to hope and wonder moving through her blood. In her mind, she saw him. Emerging from the bayou, his beautiful brown skin wet, his muscles flexing, his dangerous blue eyes catching hers as he stepped onto the bank.

Naked.

Her skin hummed, and she grinned as old memories and new fantasies collided. She wanted to release this long-held need she had for him, but it just clung so tightly to her. He was perfect. The body of a Hunter, the heart of a Nurturer and the brains of a Geek. He was everything she'd ever wanted.

Well, with one exception.

He refused to see her as grown or sexual or even female.

I'll be taking care of you.

Her breasts tightened at just the memory of his deep, husky promise, and between her thighs, heat radiated. She was a strong female, passionate, and a truly capable Hunter. Rarely did she lose the prey she sought. And damn, she sought Xavier something fierce. She wanted his touch to be her first. Obligation or not, she'd already 'captured' him. Now she just had to make her gorgeous prey see what was right in front of him.

Hugging her pillow close, she drifted off to sleep with a confident, hungry smile.

———

I'm @ clinic. Quarantined w/Ashe's sister. Her blood being tested. Take care of Mal 4 me. 3-4 days, they think. Thx, mon ami. I owe u.

Seated on the couch in Aristide and Amalie's living room, two of his laptops open on the coffee table in front of him, Xavier read the text from his best friend again. The text he hadn't even known he'd gotten until one of his Geeks dropped off his phone, along with his laptops, at the house a few hours ago. The thing screamed at him. Gave him the finger. Threatened him with pitchforks, torches and the sharpened claws of a pissed off puma brother.

Goddammit.

Take care of her? Shit, it was like asking a forest fire to take care of a pile of dry brush. But he'd do it. Hell yes, he'd do it. Aristide was his best friend, true, but he was also family. It was Aristide and Amalie's parents who had helped Xavier's mother find her smile again after his father's death. The two Nurturers had always been there for him. For advice, a meal, a place to crash when he was being a hardheaded cub and his mom couldn't handle him. And he wouldn't betray them. Not with their own daughter, for fuck's sake.

His eyes slid to the screen on his right. Along with photos of Isi's shop, photos of the camera from several different angles and close-ups on the serial number, there was a list of high-end camera shops within a ninety miles radius that carried the model. For the past few hours, he'd been working the web on his second computer, seeing if any of the images from the camera had been uploaded. Then he could backtrack, searching the serial numbers embedded in the jpegs. But so far he hadn't had any luck. Looked like he was going to have to go through the records of each camera store.

His phone rang, and for a second he thought it might be Aristide. But one glance at the readout and he saw that the call wasn't coming from the clinic, but from Geek central.

"Xavier."

"You get anything?" Robby asked. The male Geek had started off as Hunter, but he'd quickly found his home with the other tech heads. Even took on the screen name "Robin Hood" because he was all about stealing information if it helped someone in trouble.

"Not yet," Xavier told him. "Going to have to do a little breaking and entering."

"Mmm, my favorite," he said. "Send me some, I've got a few hours to kill before bed."

"No. I'm going to bring Captain in on this one. I have another job for you."

"I'm not bringing you pajamas, so don't even ask."

Xavier snorted. "Not necessary. First off, because I don't wear them and second, because Danny brought me everything I need."

"Too much info, bro. The first part."

Chuckling, Xavier explained, "I need you to hack into the computer at Isi's shop, The Care and Feeding of Voodoo."

"Nice name."

"Don't start hatin', *Robin Hood*."

"Fuck you."

Xavier laughed.

"So, what do you want me to look for, bro?"

"Anything on the computer about Chayton, anything in her emails. Any correspondence with people who have interest in Chayton, or finding her father. Do the store's website, too. Any posts, questions, comments, that type of thing."

"You got it."

"I'm sure she has some kind of firewall up."

Robby laughed, said arrogantly, "Please."

"Take it down in under ten seconds and I'll let you stay on the Geek squad."

"Under five and I'm the new leader," Robby countered.

"Keep dreaming, bro." Staring at the screen, Xavier sobered. "I'm just afraid this guy's gone completely off the grid."

"Everyone's got a footprint, X. You know that."

"Well, lets hope so. I'll talk to you later."

"It is later, bro," Hood said with a grin in his voice before he hit the end button and killed the connection.

Tossing his cell onto the couch cushions, Xavier glanced at the time on the top of his screen. Five in the morning. Shit, he hadn't realized how long he'd been at it. Going hard and heavy for five hours straight. Maybe he needed a break. Maybe he needed a drink. Damn, maybe he needed...

Before the thought cleared his brain, his nostrils flared, scenting her arrival seconds before he heard her.

"What's all this?" Amalie said, moving toward him.

Xavier's entire body flared with heat, but he didn't acknowledge her presence until he closed both computers. "Work."

"More with the human woman?" she asked, her tone only mildly curious as she walked around the side of the couch.

"No, this cybertracking job was a solo all-nighter—"

The words died in his throat, and he inhaled sharply. *What the hell—*

His breath came out in a rush, and before he could stop it, his puma broke from his control and blazed to the surface of his skin. His hands balled into fists. His mind screamed at the cat to retreat. Never in his life had he experienced such a reaction. Such a wild, instinctual response. To anything or anyone. He didn't understand it, and quickly forced it back down, beneath his pounding heart where it belonged.

Panting, his eyes raked over the female standing in front of him. "What the hell are you wearing?"

"A towel." She looked at him like he was crazy. "And was that your puma I just saw? Flashing in and out of your features?"

He shook his head. No. That wasn't possible. He didn't do the uncontrolled cat thing. "I'm just tired, that's all."

"Then maybe you should get some sleep." She gestured down the hall, which meant she released the front of her towel with one hand.

Thank fuck she had two.

"Aristide's bed is available," she said, her dark eyes glistening. "And mine too, if you'd be more comfortable in a clean and fresh-smelling environment."

It had been said with halfhearted humor, but once again, the puma inside him rushed upward, flaring to life. What the hell was going on? He glared at Amalie, praying she and her barely clothed self weren't the cause. Hoping it was truly lack of sleep and maybe lack of food that was making him so edgy.

"Why are you in that goddamn towel?" he ground out.

She cocked her head. "Shower."

"In the living room?" he countered blackly. "Are you trying to make me crazy?"

Her brows lifted and a smile played about her lips. "Why? Would it work?"

"I'm male, Amalie. And you're…" His gaze traveled over her and he growled.

"I'm what?" she encouraged.

His eyes narrowed. "A devious brat."

She laughed. The sound pierced his skin and went straight to his groin.

"Shower's outside the house remember?" she said.

"Right." Goddammit. So, this was going to be a regular thing over the next three days? Showering? The untouchable goddess walking

403

around in skimpy towels, making him drool and growl and hunger for things other than food?

"I'm on patrol in an hour," she said. "Better get soaped up."

Stay the hell down, he warned his puma. "Next time wear a robe," he said as she started past him.

She paused, gave him a lopsided smile. "Why?"

"You know why, Amalie." His tone was like ice. Ice that wanted to be melted in a hot shower with a hotter female.

"You see me as family, right?" she challenged. "So what's the problem?"

He turned back to his laptops and opened them. "Go. Take your shower. Get to work."

She chuckled. "Have a good day, Xavier."

"Yeah, you too," he muttered to himself.

But she heard him, and called over her shoulder, "Oh, I will."

Xavier told himself not to turn, not to look, not to watch her move down the hall in that goddamn scrap of white cotton, but it was impossible. Like iron to a magnet, he ripped his eyes from the screen and glanced over his shoulder. With flared nostrils and a tight chest, he watched as her towel slipped down her back to her hips as she sauntered away, giving him a view of her back and the rise of her ass.

This time when his puma rushed to the surface of his skin, he let it.

Chapter Four

The sun was high in the sky as Mal sprinted along the west border, every so often opening her mouth to taste the air.

It remained.

Always remained.

The sour stench of human intruders. Problem was she couldn't find the source. She and her partner had been patrolling for six hours straight—and nothing.

Hiss came to an abrupt halt near the footbridge that curved over the small stream that jutted out from the bayou. With a shake of his auburn pelt, he shifted from cat to human male.

Coming up beside him, Mal shifted too. "What? Did you scent something?"

The rugged male Hunter, who wore his dark hair back in a leather thong, shook his head. "It's the same everywhere we go. Dying land, sour stench, but no clues. No intruders. I don't get it."

"They'll be back. Both human, and any more traitors we harbor." She gave him a tight grin. "Damn, I'd love to be the one who catches that prey."

Hiss's grey eyes flashed. "You and me both."

"I wonder if they're camping far enough outside the border to keep their scent quiet." Releasing a heavy breath, Mal shaded her eyes and looked out over the quiet bayou water. "Maybe we should go take a look."

A wide grin split the male's handsome features. "Go hunting across the border?"

"Maybe."

"Those aren't our orders."

She matched his grin and shrugged. "So?"

He laughed. "I like patrolling with you, Mal. Taking risks is important for a Hunter. Keeps us sharp. Keeps our instincts—"

"Oh my god!" Mal exclaimed, cutting him off, her attention suddenly diverted by something she saw out of the corner of her eye.

"What?" Hiss said, alert now. "What is it? Humans?"

Her eyes nearly bugging out of her head, Mal ran to the edge of bayou and waded a foot into the water. "Look."

Hiss followed her, shading his eyes as he searched the calm surface for whatever she was indicating. When his breath caught in his throat, Mal knew he'd seen it, too.

"I...I didn't think..." Hiss stumbled over his words. "*Merde*...with everything that's happened. With Ashe's sister, and her strange effects on the land...I didn't think we'd see it this year. I didn't think we'd see it ever again. What a miracle."

Her face growing warm with happiness and pleasure, Mal waded in deeper until she was forced to swim. Her clothes felt heavy in the water, but she didn't care. She couldn't believe it. She had to touch it.

"*Mon dieu*, do you scent it?" Hiss called from the bank.

Mal didn't answer. She was upon it now, its heady fragrance slamming into her nostrils. It made her insides vibrate, and her outsides, too. She reached out, palmed the large water lily that had only a moment ago been as white as the clouds overhead. Now, it was pale lavender, the color growing deeper and more vibrant with every moment that passed. She couldn't speak, she was smiling too hard.

The most perfect Dyesse Lily she had ever seen.

Even though they knew it was the time of year for the Dyesse Fete, they had all been secretly praying the celebration of the birth of the Pantera—and the most important holiday in the Wildlands—would actually come to pass. With the land's magic deteriorating at such a rapid rate, they'd wondered if any would remain.

Especially something so powerful and rare as the Dyesse.

She released the lily, and as she did, the two bracketing it started to change. By tonight, even the moon would turn a shockingly beautiful shade of violet. Laughing with unabashed happiness, she turned back to Hiss on the shore, and a silent understanding passed between them.

"I'm going right now," he called. "I'll tell Parish."

She swam toward him with fast, powerful strokes, hit the shore just as he shifted into his puma and growled his excitement. She did the same, shaking off the excess water that had transferred from her skin to the fur of her puma.

Hiss spoke inside her head. *You want to go with me?*

She looked up, growled. *To the fete?*

His puma nodded, smoky-grey eyes flashing with enthusiasm. *Good food, music, sparring matches. We were the first to spot the change. It's only right we celebrate together.*

Hiss was a friend, nothing more, but she liked him, felt comfortable with him, and god, it felt good to be asked. And, she thought with wicked intent, maybe good for Xavier to see. A grown male, a Hunter, wanted to take her to the most important night of the year for the Pantera—the night when unbridled mating was encouraged.

She grinned at the auburn cat. *Okay.*

Great! I'll pick you up around seven.

He turned and darted off into the forest, and Mal glanced over her shoulder, crying out into the fragrant air as she saw yards of Dyesse lilies turn purple on the calm surface of the bayou.

"I don't want to see him, Jax," Xavier said with an irritated growl. "I just want to talk to him."

The male guarding the door leading to the quarantine barracks shook his head. "Sorry, *mon ami.*"

"Look, the male's a good friend. I'm watching his house, his sister." A soft snarl accompanied that last word. Xavier ignored it. "I need a word."

"Can't help you. There's no outside communication unless this is an emergency." The male raised a pale blond brow. "Is this an emergency?"

Fuck. "No. It's not." He released a frustrated breath. "Fine. I'll see him in a couple of days."

"That's only an estimate," Jax said with a thin-lipped smile. "Could be a week. We just don't know."

Perfect. The news just got better and better, Xavier thought darkly. And more problematic. Three days under the same roof as that towel-wearing puma temptress was bad enough. How the hell was he going to last a week?

He gave the guard a curt nod, then turned and headed back down the hall. Maybe he could get someone else to watch her? One of the grandmothers…A low chuckle exited his throat. Yeah, that would go over well. She barely tolerated him. She'd make quick work of some sweet, old Pantera female.

"Hey, X."

Lost in thought, Xavier turned to see Raphael a few feet away. The leader of the Suits looked pretty shredded, like he hadn't slept in weeks, and was standing outside his mate, Ashe's, room, with a small group: Hunter leader Parish, Nurturer Jean-Baptiste and his mate, Genevieve, who Xavier knew from her momentary blip with the Geeks. They all turned to acknowledge him.

"Checking in on Aristide?" Jean-Baptiste asked. Being from the same faction, the Nurturer knew that Xavier and Aristide were tight.

"Something like that," Xavier said. Not keen on giving out details about his problem with Amalie, he quickly turned from the heavily tatted male to Raphael and changed the subject. "How is she? Your mate?"

The Suit's jaw went tight and he slid his green gaze toward the closed door. "She was better when her sister was around."

"The quarantine?" Xavier asked.

Raphael nodded.

Yeah, that thing was fucking with everyone's lives.

"But I'm hoping I can take her out for awhile," the Suit said. "Take her to the fete tonight."

"The fete?" Xavier repeated, momentarily stunned. He looked from Raphael to Parish. "Has there been a sighting?"

Parish nodded, his gold eyes flashing, his face splitting into a wide grin. "Two of my Hunters spotted a bayou of purple lilies about thirty minutes ago."

Amazing, Xavier mused. *And wonderful.* He'd been wondering if the Dyesse would occur this year. It had been a hope on everyone's mind.

"Can't wait to take Julia," Parish said with a growl. "Celebrate our fertility right."

Leaning against Jean-Baptiste's side, Genevieve laughed. "I'd be careful. Females, even humans ones I imagine, can be overly demanding on the Dyesse Eve."

Parish grinned wickedly. "I look forward to being chased and caught by my Doc."

"Are you ready to run, my love?" Genevieve asked her male with a teasing grin.

Growling, pulling the blond female closer to his side, Jean-Baptiste nuzzled her cheek. "I will never run from you, Genny. It's time wasted when you could be ravishing the shit out of me."

Everyone laughed, even Raphael. It was good to see, Xavier mused. The ghost of a male letting down his guard. But it didn't last long. He turned his weary gaze back on Xavier.

"I know you met with the PI. Did she have something of interest? How are things progressing with Chayton? Any leads?"

Though most of the Pantera knew about their search for Ashe and Isi's father, it was the Suit leader who Xavier was reporting to. The male had become the reluctant go-between for the elders.

"I went through a shitload of sales records today from several different camera shops," he said with a snarl of frustration. "I want to figure out where this camera came from and who put it there. I don't think it was our enemies or human tattoo artist, Derek." He shook his head. "But you know me, whoever it is, I'll get them."

Raphael cuffed him on the arm. "I know you will. And hopefully it will lead us to Chayton."

Just then, the door beside Raphael opened and Parish's mate, Dr. Julia, poked her head out. "She's asking for you, Raphael."

Instantly alert, Raphael gave them a quick nod. "See you later. We should all take the night off and celebrate our birth, and the magic that continues within us despite those who are trying to destroy it." He eyed Xavier. "Even you, X."

As Raphael disappeared inside the room of his mate, Xavier and the rest of the group offered quick goodbyes before disbanding. Walking down the hall toward the front doors, Xavier thought about the Suit's words. A night off to celebrate the birth of his kind. He wanted that. Wanted to be a part of that. But time was ticking away. He had to find out who had placed that camera, and he had to find Chayton before those assholes did. Before they found him and used him to wake Shakpi.

If Xavier did his job right, there would be many more purple moons to celebrate.

CHAPTER FIVE

Butterflies inside her stomach and ants crawling up her spine, Mal put the finishing touches on her makeup, then stood back and took a long, hard look at herself. Not bad. For a first attempt. Lipstick, eyeliner and mascara were definitely not her thing. In fact, she'd felt kind of clueless putting it on and had needed to use one of Xavier's computers to look up a tutorial on how to apply makeup without looking like a clown.

She grinned at herself.

Normally, she went all natural. The Hunter look: jeans, tank, boots, clean face, easy and ready to shift into her puma. But tonight, she really wanted to make some heads explode. Well, one head. One very gorgeous, very stubborn head.

She was just finishing up washing her hands when she heard the front door open. Her heart stuttered in her chest as she fumbled with the towel. This was it. The great reveal. Not only had she put on makeup, but her dark hair was brushed to a shine and hung down her back in gentle waves, and the ultra-feminine dress she wore didn't even remotely resemble Hunter gear.

"Honey, I'm home!" Xavier called, the dark humor in his tone obvious. "Where are you? I brought dinner. I'm warming it up." The mild crash of a pot hitting the stovetop rose above the sudden silence. Then, "Aristide said you don't cook, or you can't cook. I can't remember which."

With one last look in the mirror, she released the breath she'd been holding and opened the door to her room. She spotted Xavier right away. He was bent over the kitchen counter, staring at the screen of his computer, something heating up in a pot on the stove, a rugged blue flame shooting off sparks beneath it. She swallowed, smoothed the front of her dress and walked toward him.

"Which one is it?" Xavier called, still staring at the screen. "You can't cook or you don't?"

"Both," she said.

Courage, Female. You hunt bad guys and badass animal prey all damn day, and this male's reaction to your new look is making you sweat?

"But I won't be eating dinner," she added, moving toward him, her heart pounding in her chest. "Not here anyway."

"What are you talking about, Female?" he asked, tearing his gaze from the screen to look up.

When he did, when he saw her, when his eyes traveled from her shiny hair all the way down to her strappy sandals, a strange sound exited his lips. It was like a cross between a wheeze and a growl, and ended with a ferocious lip curl. She waited for him to say something, move. But he didn't. He just stood there, hands balling into fists, ice blue eyes turning frosty—and his puma vibrating beneath his skin.

Forcing her nerves aside, Mal strode toward him. "Puma got your tongue, Xavier?"

His gaze remained fixed on her as she moved. "What are you wearing?"

"That's the first thing you're saying to me? Seriously."

"Hell yes, seriously," he growled. "Deadly seriously."

She stopped directly in front of him and lifted her chin. "It's a dress, Xavier."

His nostrils flared and she felt his cat's heat radiate off his body. "And why are you wearing a dress?"

"I'm going out."

His lip curled, and he slowly shook his head. "You're not going anywhere. Not like that."

"Like what exactly? Dressed up? Looking hot?"

His eyes nearly bugged out of his head.

"I'll take that as a yes." She grinned, then turned in a slow circle in front of him. "I do look hot, right?"

His jaw was so tight, Mal thought it might shatter into a hundred pieces.

"Doesn't matter, Amalie," he said icily. "You're not going out. Not like that, and not alone."

She looked up at him through her lashes. Her curled and painted lashes. "I'm not going alone."

This time, he moved. Closed the distance between them in one stride. He was so tall, so broad. Fearsome and sexy. Why couldn't he just lift her up and plant a killer kiss on her eager lips? He was so god-damn frustrating. "I have a date."

"No." He said the single word without heat.

She cocked her head to the side and chewed her lower lip. "I'm not asking permission."

"Good, because you're not getting it."

Her gaze flickered past him, to the stove—to the raging blue flame. Something caught her eye; something bubbling out of control. "Your sauce, or whatever it is you're making, is burning."

Cursing, Xavier whirled around and rushed to the stovetop. Without thinking, he grabbed the handle of the pot, then cursed again when the metal burned his hand. He tossed the pot into the sink and slammed on the water.

Forgetting the irritation-slash-flirtation from a moment ago, Mal hurried to the sink and to his side. "Are you all right?"

"Fine," he growled, fisting his hand.

"Let me see it."

"It's nothing."

She grabbed his hand and forced his fingers open. "Stop being a stubborn ass." Angry red welts decorated his palm. "Let's get some cool water on it."

He didn't fight when she guided his hand under the faucet, but hissed when the water met his skin.

"You're mothering me, Amalie," he said on a growl. "I don't need it."

She looked up at him, met those crystal blue eyes that always made her weak. "Welcome to my world, Friend."

He snarled gently. "Last thing I'm trying to do is mother you."

"Then what is it? This thing you're doing with me?"

His nostrils flared as he stared down at her, and once again, she felt heat roll off him. Why couldn't he say it, she thought angrily. Why couldn't he admit there was something inside him that wanted to reach out and touch her?

"I could make this cub go away, Amalie," he said, his eyes on her mouth now.

"He's not a cub. He's a grown male, a Hunter."

"Doesn't matter."

"Matters to me, Xavier. I deserve to celebrate this holiday like all the other Pantera. Maybe even more so, being the final birth."

That silenced him.

At least until the knock on the door.

His head came up, his eyes narrowed and he growled with unabashed antagonism.

"Okay, no." Amalie dropped his hand, which was already starting to heal, and pointed a finger at him. "You're not going to interrogate him or threaten him or whatever."

His eyes still pinned on the door, Xavier gave her a lazy shrug. "If he's a true Pantera male he won't have a problem with that."

She gave him a warning glare before hurrying to the door. As she opened it, she felt him come up behind her. *Damned puma. Damned mother hen.*

Standing on the porch in a pair of black jeans and a white dress shirt, looking far handsomer than she'd ever seen him, Hiss grinned at her. "Wow."

Mal grinned back. "Hey, Hiss."

His gray eyes moved over her. "You look beautiful, Hunter."

"Yes, she does," Xavier said, moving out from behind to stand beside her.

Mal rolled her eyes. "You know Xavier."

Hiss tore his gaze from Mal and acknowledged Xavier with a nod. "How's it going, X?"

"Great. You?"

"Fantastic. You going to the festival?"

Mal answered before Xavier had a chance. "No. He has to work."

Shrugging, grinning, Hiss said, "Too bad," then turned back to Mal. "Ready? Because that moon is turning violet as we stand here."

She nodded, then stepped out onto the porch. "Have a nice night, Xavier."

As they walked down the path, Mal glanced back over her shoulder. She probably shouldn't have, but as usual she couldn't stop herself when it came to looking at the gorgeous Geek. Her heart trembled with what she saw. Cast in the dark lavender light of the Pantera moon, Xavier looked severe and sexy. And ominous. And hungry. He was standing in the doorway, his massive frame barely allowing the light inside the house to peek through, his piercing blue eyes trained on her. Vehemence fairly radiated from him. As she turned and headed for town with Hiss, she prayed that envy was the emotion that sparked that look. And if it was, that Xavier might finally do something about it.

———

He was an idiot.

But it couldn't be helped.

The air circulating within the Wildlands was ripe and heady with the scent of purple water lily. A strange, yet addictive aroma. The Pantera's birth lily—the first flower to grow on their new land back when Opela created them—was purported to have a magical property that infused the Pantera in happiness, warmth and, for those who were mated or wished to be, a sensual euphoria.

Fine for most, Xavier mused, heading down the shop-lined street toward the center of town. But not the type of magic he wanted his wild little kitten exposed to.

Not unsupervised at any rate.

After she'd left, side by side with the Hunter, Xavier had gotten a call from Robby. The Geek had found a couple of interesting instant messages on Isi's store computer. At first, they'd reminded Xavier of poetry. But after several listens, he'd recognized the strange collection of words as protection spells, and had given Robby the go-ahead to follow that IM trail.

I should be working the keyboard too, he thought darkly. Not tracking and spying. Hanging out in the shadows of one of the town's many produce stands, scanning the Pantera's merriment for Amalie, making sure she acted sane—and that her Hunter male escort acted like a gentleman.

Deep in the shadows of the empty stand, Xavier let his gaze travel over the square. Given the limited amount of prep time, the Pantera had created quite a spectacle. Purple and lavender flowers and ribbons were everywhere, on tables, strung from tree to tree. In one corner, a Cajun band—five Suits who had played last year—was kicking up some fine, foot-stomping music. And warring with the scent of water lily, some of the species' best cooks were working over open flames, creating culinary magic and sending it out to the masses who were at tables, both long and intimate, around the wood floor that had been laid out for dancing. As usual, the food was being served family-style, passed around from table to table. Xavier's belly growled as he scented rich gumbos and crawfish, meat pies, vegetables, bread pudding and fruit. When he spotted his favorite, alligator sausage, he nearly howled.

But it was the sound of laughter—a female's laughter—over the din that made that sound truly exit his lips.

His eyes scanned the square, the diners, dancers, even a small group of shifted Pantera, who were sport fighting a yard or two away from the band. *Where are you, Female? I hear your laughter*. He didn't like that the male Hunter had caused such a reaction in her—had caused that beautiful face to break into the most infectious fucking smile in the world. No one should be making her laugh. No one, but—

Before he could finish with *'but me'* the music changed. From rocking bluegrass to a slow, Cajun waltz. As if the calming sound brought on another level of clarity to his vision, Xavier turned to see the pair at one of the small tables set apart from the others. They were standing up, their plates cleaned, and were heading for the dance floor. His hand clasping hers, the Hunter male led Amalie into the small crowd of couples and took her in his arms.

Xavier's body went rigid.

Sure, she deserved this night. And yes, she should have some fun. But why did it have to be with this male? This male who seemed like a decent guy, not like that slobbering dog back at The Cougar's Den. This male who acted respectful, and looked at her like he genuinely wanted to pursue something after tonight.

Amalie could actually like this male, he thought with a twist to his gut. *Shit, Aristide could like this male.*

Without weighing the rights or wrongs of his actions, Xavier abandoned the shadows of the produce stand and headed toward the dance floor. He didn't want to be a prick. Didn't want to be a pushy bastard who claimed something he had no right to claim. But the desire to take Amalie from Hiss's arms was too strong to fight against.

Eyes pinned to them, Xavier moved easily and swiftly through the crowd. The song ended, and Hiss and Amalie were just stopping to clap when Xavier came up beside them.

"Mind if I cut in?" he said in the most forced polite voice in the world.

With a soft gasp, Amalie turned to look at him. Her eyes widened and she shook her head as if to say, 'Are you crazy?' He probably was, but he couldn't stop himself.

Hiss, however, grinned broadly. "Good to see you here, X. No one should be working tonight." Then he turned to Amalie. "I'll get us a couple of drinks, okay?"

"Thanks, Hiss," she said sweetly. But the moment the Hunter was out of earshot, she whirled on Xavier and spat out, "What are you doing here? Spying on me?"

"Yes."

She looked momentarily stunned by his honesty.

His eyes moved over her face and he closed the distance between them. "You look beautiful tonight." His arms went around her, and he started to move to the music. "Hot."

All the tension left her body and her face split into the most incredible smile he'd ever seen. "Thank you."

One dark eyebrow lifted as he amended, "Too hot."

Her mouth quirked. "Bastard."

He smiled and eased her closer. Her warm, soft skin beneath his palms, her gentle weight. She felt like heaven in his arms. And the scent of her mixed with the scent of purple water lily was acting like a drug on his control. Xavier's skin hummed with awareness, and in that moment there was nothing he wanted more than to pull her away from the crowd, ease her into the shadows where he'd once stood looking for her, and remove her pretty dress with his teeth.

Blood surged into his cock, making him hard.

No. Fuck, no. His mind was playing tricks. He couldn't have her. Not tonight. Not any night. But then again, neither could Hiss. He couldn't allow that either. No matter how nice and respectful the male was, no one else was going to touch her. He wouldn't allow it. Neither would his puma. A growl formed in his throat. The water lily's scent was capturing him, surely. What else could be the reason for these possessive thoughts?

"Come with me," he ordered, taking her by the hand and leading her off the dance floor.

"Talk about déjà vu," she said dryly. "Where are you going, Xavier? Hiss is coming back."

Ignoring her question, Xavier eased her into the shadows of the produce stand. Out of the corner of his eye, he saw Hiss, drinks in hand, searching the dance floor.

She isn't yours. Not now. Never ever.

Curling her around him, pressing her back to the faded-white walls of the stand, Xavier coiled over her and inhaled deeply.

Amalie stared up at him, her breathing labored. "What's wrong with you?"

Wrong? He nearly laughed. Shit, he was out of his mind. Drugged. Had to be. "I want to leave."

Irritation flashed in her green eyes and she made a move to get past him. "Then go."

But he placed a hand on either side of her and shook his head. "I want you to come with me."

She shook her head. "No."

"You got your touch," he whispered. "Your flirting. Your date."

"It's not enough. It's nothing. I want more."

A snarl escaped his throat and he leaned in close to her face, almost until they were nose to nose. "That Hunter touches you again and I'll hurt him."

Amalie growled at him and tried to back up, but there was nothing but wall. "What the hell is wrong with you?"

"I'm protecting you."

"From what? From Hiss? He's a good male."

"Don't say that."

"Then from what? Being held? Kissed? Those are normal things, Xavier."

His puma scratched to break free, and he nuzzled her nose with his own. "Dammit, Amalie."

"Come on, Xavier. Don't do this to me," she uttered, her tone pained. "Don't hold me, block me. It's not fair. Especially coming from you. Do you really expect me to go through life alone? Without being kissed? Staying a virgin—"

She never finished her thought. The word—no, the image—drove Xavier and his puma over the fucking edge. With a snarl of possession, he slid his thigh between her legs and covered her mouth with his own, kissing her long and hard and deep.

Oh, fuck, the taste.

Xavier's mind exploded into tiny fragments of desire. The taste of her was beyond what he'd ever imagined. Sweet and hot and liquid, and hungry. Fuck, so hungry. And he wanted to consume her. Fill his body with hers.

Her arms went around his neck and she moaned into his mouth. The sound went straight to his dick, and he nipped at her, suckled her lower lip, then kissed her passionately once again. Oh Christ, this was it. She was perfect. *His* perfect. The way she moved, touched him, molded to him—wanted him. He'd never be able to go back from here.

He'd felt her and tasted her now. Her heat and her desire belonged to him. How could he ever let another soul get close to her again?

And then her hands moved down to his shoulders and his back, her nails digging into his skin as her teeth bit at his tongue, and he lost all control. All that remained in the darkness, in the shadows, were two desperate, ravenous puma shifters. Groaning her name, Xavier crushed her against him, ravaged her mouth, pressed his thigh up harder against her sex, feeling the wet heat of her pussy. He wanted inside her, belonged inside her. He wanted to take her—lift up her dress, rip off her panties and fuck her right there. He didn't care who saw them. In fact, in that moment, he wanted spectators. Wanted every last Pantera male to know who Amalie belonged to.

The thought killed him. Stopped him.

As did the look in her drowsy, sex-hazed eyes when he eased back from her.

"Shit," he whispered so close to her mouth their breath co-mingled. She swallowed, her eyes trying to focus. "Xavier."

His name on her lips had Xavier's cock straining against the zipper of his jeans. His eyes cut left, past her ear. Hiss was still searching, irritation and concern playing about his features. "I'm so sorry, Amalie."

"Don't say that," she warned.

"Oh, fuck, this was a mistake."

"Or that."

He wanted to let her go, release her, but he couldn't make himself do it. Though Hiss hadn't seen them yet, he was drawing closer to where they hid. A low, terrifying growl erupted from Xavier's throat, and he knew that if the Hunter male got within a foot of Amalie right now, he might actually attack, maybe even kill him. He was that jacked up—that proprietary. His puma snarled and ripped at his insides, and to save himself, and possibly the Hunter male as well, he allowed it to break free.

He stumbled back, away from Amalie, and shifted into his cat.

"Xavier," she said, her voice threaded with heat.

He looked at her for one brief moment, saw her anger and hurt, and enduring lust, and let his puma snarl and hiss before turning and stalking away. From the party, the food, the music, the sexually-charged atmosphere.

And from the female he could never taste again—no matter how desperately he wanted her.

CHAPTER SIX

Furious and turned-on so badly she just wanted to go to her room and find comfort in her own hand, Mal burst into the house. Poor Hiss. He deserved an amazing female. Not some dope with a relentless crush. The Hunter male was gorgeous and honorable, and more than a few female eyes had covetously followed him around the fete tonight. He could've stayed—should've stayed—when she'd told him she wanted to go home. But he'd insisted on escorting her.

While Xavier had left her alone, panting, confused and pissed off. *Xavier.*

That goddamn male had ruined her. Truly. First when she had fallen in both lust and love for him on that birthday in the bayou, and now tonight, when he'd given her a moment of that fantasy, then ripped it away. No, not just ripped it away, but ripped it into shreds.

As she slammed the door and started down the hall, the memory of his hands on her, his mouth on her, mingled with his apologies and regrets. Fuck him, she didn't want it—neither one. Why couldn't he get that? She wasn't asking for a future or a promise or a mating. All she wanted was him.

For him to be her first.

The sound of running water curbed her emotional and frustrated thoughts momentarily, and instead of heading for her room, she turned down the hall toward the door that led to the outside shower. She knew who was out there, *in* there. With every step, every shaky breath, her hand curling around the door handle, she warned herself to stop and walk away. *Go into your room, take care of yourself and go to sleep.*

But like the cat she was, her hunger for prey—shit, for the prey of a lifetime—could not be quelled. For better or for worse, Xavier was her fantasy, her addiction, and he was in there, nude, wet, steam rising off his thickly muscled body. She had to see it. See him.

Without another thought, she pulled off her dress, panties and bra, and tossed them to the ground.

———

His hand wrapped around his cock, Xavier leaned against the rock wall, hot water pummeling his shoulders and back. He was such a fuck. Touching her, tasting her. He had no self-control and no honor. And he couldn't blame it on the fete or the moon or the purple lilies. That stunning need, that irrepressible want, it still ran through him like a vindictive snake in his blood.

Groaning, growling, he pumped himself from root to tip, trying like hell to see a blank screen on the lids of his eyes. But it was no use. She was there now. Imprinted. In that dress and out of it. Smiling at him, laughing, biting his lip as her nails dug into the skin of his back.

Come leaked from the tip of his dick and he ran his fingers over the head. But as he slid his palm back up his shaft, a warm hand suddenly closed around his and squeezed.

"Releasing some tension?" a female voice whispered seductively.

Xavier's head jacked up, his eyes slammed open and he released his hold on his cock. "What the hell, Amalie—"

She wrapped her hand around his shaft again and uttered, "Don't move." Then looked up at him with accusing eyes. "You kissed me tonight."

Her hand, hot and soft, held him with such possessive skill. He groaned, "Oh, fuck."

"That's not an answer, an explanation or an apology." Wearing nothing but a fierce, highly sexual smile, she tightened her grip on his cock.

Christ, he wanted to move, wanted to thrust into her hot, little palm. "It was a mistake, Amalie," he ground out, his heart slamming against his ribs.

"Maybe." She snarled softly. "Probably. But it happened, and I can't forget it. Can you?"

His cock turned to steel in her hand.

Feeling what she did to him—what just her words did to him—she grinned and started to stroke him. "I didn't think so."

Cursing inwardly, Xavier stared at her, his nostrils flaring with each breath he dragged into his lungs. Steam raged around them, but it did nothing to mask her nude body. Her insanely hot nude body. He'd imagined, fantasized about what she'd look like under her clothes, standing before him, stretched out on his bed, her arms above her head. But it was nothing to the reality. She was perfection. Her legs were long and tight with muscle, her small waist flared upward to strong, toned arms and luscious shoulders. But it was her chest, her large, heavy breasts that made his mouth water and his hands fist in anticipation.

"Why did you come home early, Amalie?" he said hoarsely, his gaze flipping up to meet hers.

Beautiful dark green eyes flared with emerald heat. "I got tired of playing games. Pretending. It wasn't fair to Hiss."

"Hiss." His eyes narrowed. "Did the Hunter male touch you?"

Her tongue darted out to swipe at her bottom lip. "The only one who touched me tonight was you, Xavier." She reached down with her other hand and cupped his heavy sack, rolled his balls between her fingers. "And it wasn't enough. In fact, it was a goddamn tease."

The muscles in his abdomen tensed and he groaned. "Fuck... You're going to make me come."

"Good." She drew closer to him, under the hot spray, her strokes to his shaft growing faster, tighter. "Tell me."

"What?" His body flexed in anticipation of climax, and he had to do everything in his power not to grab her hips and ram her up against the stone wall, fuck her blind—fuck her blissful.

"Tell me why you didn't want me with him," she said, her words a whispered demand.

He pinned her with a predatory stare and growled out, "I don't want you with anyone."

She leaned even closer, pumping him off as she brushed her pebbled nipples against his chest. "Why? Tell me why."

"No one's good enough for you, Amalie," he rasped, his cock growing harder, thicker.

"Not even you?"

He cursed and thrust himself into her fist. "Especially not me."

"That's bullshit," she said before dipping her head to his chest. "And you know it. Christ, you'd better know it."

She didn't say another word. Her mouth closed around his nipple, and as she stroked him, played with him, she sucked and scraped her teeth across his flesh.

Xavier was lost to what he knew to be right and wrong. What he believed she deserved. She had taken him over. She owned him. And there was no going back. He bucked, ground his hips, pistoning his cock into her soft, wicked hand as she stroked him fast. His balls tightened, filled with come, and he growled her name. His hips jerked, and hot seed burst from the head of his dick. As he came all over her hands and belly, she bit down lightly on his nipple, causing him to groan and curse, and utter her name. Over and over.

It took him only seconds to come awake, even with climax still shuddering through him. Hunger and need like he'd never known assaulted his mind and he had to have her or he was going to lose it. Snarling, his puma just millimeters below his skin, Xavier wrapped his hands around her waist and lifted her up, set her back against the shower wall, safe from the heavy spray.

"You just unlocked the puma's cage, Amalie," he said, his eyes pinned on her, his voice a dangerous, deep purr. "And he's hungry."

Mal felt a delicious unease move through her as Xavier lowered to one knee before her. She might be a virgin, but she was no innocent. She was Pantera, and the ways of mating were not hidden behind a curtain of immoral shame. They were offered as a way to connect, to love, to allow the puma a chance to feel human touch, and the human self a way to react with animal-like hunger. More than once, she'd come across couples in the forest, kissing, touching, even fucking, as she'd been on patrol. Normally, she'd left them to it, darted off in the opposite direction. But there had been a few times she'd stopped to watch. Hidden behind a tree, her heart pounding, her sex growing tight and wet as she observed what she'd wanted so badly.

What she'd saved for the male on his knees before her.

Xavier's ice-blue eyes drifted up her belly, to her ribs and breasts. He watched as her nipples beaded, as her chest rose and fell quickly with her excited breathing. She knew what he intended to do to her, where his mouth would go—his tongue—and as his hands wrapped around her ankles and raked upward, she moaned with anticipation.

Steam continued to rise and coil around them, protecting the moment. Xavier's eyes connected with hers then and she felt that hungry, fierce stare deep inside her sex. The greedy, eager muscles clenched, and her thighs trembled. She had to fist her hands to keep them from grabbing the back of his head and slamming his face into her pussy.

"So beautiful," he rumbled, looking at her. "Beautiful, beautiful Amalie."

Her heart squeezed with his words. He had no idea, no clue how long she'd waited to hear him talk to her that way. With both tenderness and sexual desire. It ripped her open, left her vulnerable, and she whimpered.

"Shh," he whispered, his hands lightly grazing her inner thighs as he trailed upward to her sex. When he reached her mound, he gently spread her lips wide and released a sensual groan. "Beautiful Amalie has a beautiful cunt."

It was as if Mal lost all brain function after that. As he dipped his head, ran his tongue from her opening up to her clit, she became one trembling, bundle of nerves. The feeling was too good, too overwhelmingly perfect to contain. Bracing her hands on either side of the shower walls, she watched him, his dark head between her thighs, his tongue lightly flicking over her clit. Groans escaped him, and he eased one finger inside her.

She gasped with instant pleasure. Her body had only ever known the thrust of her own fingers, and while that had felt good, this— Xavier's thick digit deep inside of her—was a thousand times better.

"Oh, Amalie," he growled against her swollen bud. "You are so tight. So hot. You wrap around me. Your sweet, honeyed walls tremble around me."

Mal's eyes closed and she let her head fall back against the stone, let the steam envelop her.

"That's right," Xavier said, easing a second finger inside her and pumping her gently. "Let me make you feel good, Amalie. Let me make you come so hard you scream. God, there's nothing I want more than to please you."

His mouth found her sex once again, and as he fingered her, deeper and deeper with each thrust, he suckled her clit, drawing on it, sending her to the purple moon and back. Her fingernails dug into the rock walls, and she whimpered and bucked against his hungry mouth as her arousal made his sexy jaw glisten.

Just when she thought she was going to explode, Xavier drew back and gentled his touch. His tongue swirled around her swollen, sensitive bud, flicking it back and forth until she gulped in air. But it was his purr that did her in, made her still, made her moan into the hot, steamy air. The vibration curled up from the back of his throat and hit his tongue.

The tongue that was pressed lightly against her clit.

With a pained, delicious cry, she fell apart under his mouth, her knees buckling, her thighs shaking. Pulling his fingers from her drenched sex, Xavier grabbed her ass, held her up as he kissed her shaking mound and licked her cream.

It seemed like hours before she came down, before her legs stopped trembling, before he stopped pleasuring her and rested his head on her abdomen.

"Xavier," she mumbled incoherently. "Take me to bed."

For several seconds, he remained silent. Then he released her and stood up. The pained and guilty expression on his gorgeous face combined with the wetness around his mouth, made her growl.

She wanted to lick him. Taste herself on him.

And then he cursed and shook his head, and ruined it for the both of them.

"Goddamn you." Her heart lurched. "You want me. I know you do."

"That's not the point," he ground out.

Her gaze searched his. "Do you think this was a mistake?"

"Oh, Amalie."

"Do you?" she demanded, feeling suddenly naked and cold and vulnerable.

"It shouldn't have happened." He looked away, his jaw as tight as the rest of him. "Fuck me."

"Yes. Fuck you."

Enough. This had to be it. This had to kill her goddamn crush once and for all, right?

Wrong, her heart whispered as it clenched miserably.

She pushed past him, stumbled out of the shower and into the fragrant night air. Tears blurred her vision as she rushed into the house and headed down the hall. What an idiot. What a stupid, foolish female. Maybe he was right. Maybe she was still a cub. Because only a cub would harbor a crush for so damned long. Only a cub would react this way: hurt and miserable, yet desperate for more. A grown female would take her orgasm and walk away satisfied.

She slammed the door to her bedroom, and headed for her bed. She was cold and wet beneath her covers, due to the fact that she hadn't dried off. But she didn't care. She just wanted to cry in peace.

She didn't hear the door open, didn't hear Xavier pad across the floor. She only sensed him, scented him, when the mattress dipped with his weight, and he curled up behind her.

"Don't ever say *fuck you* to me," he whispered into the curve of her ear.

She swallowed a sob. "Why not? You deserve it."

"Maybe, but it hurts me. Cuts me deep, Beautiful."

Swiping the tears from her eyes, she growled and rolled around to face him, connect with those killer blue eyes. "How can you say that? When it's you who's hurting me. Every time you reject me. Every time you say this is a mistake—that *we're* a mistake."

"I have to say that," he ground out, his eyes flaring with sudden and passionate heat. "Shit, Amalie." He reached out and brushed her hair off her cheek, then kept his palm there. "If I take you to bed, if I mate you, I'll claim you. Do you understand me?"

Her insides tensed. *Claimed.* She stared at him.

His eyes bore into hers, and he growled. "You'll be mine, goddamit."

"I want to be yours," she said, shaking her head. "Tonight, tomorrow, for the next three days—"

"No, Amalie," he cut her off, his tone deadly serious. "You'll be mine for a lifetime."

His words silenced her, made her chest ache and her mind race with thoughts, memories and wishes. She wasn't sure how to feel. She didn't want him to fuck her and stick around out of obligation. And wasn't that what he was saying? That if he slept with her, he'd feel obligated to claim her?

"Xavier, I'm not asking for anything more than this," she began. "Three days of this. I'm not asking for a commitment, a mating—"

He cut her off again, but this time with a deep, hungry kiss. It was so intense and toe-curling, Mal couldn't stop herself from moaning and snuggling in closer and wrapping her arms around his neck.

When he broke the kiss, his breathing labored and his eyes dilated, her body and her puma purred.

"This isn't about you asking, Amalie," he said with animal-like ferocity. "This isn't even about what you want—though fuck, I want to give you everything. It's about me. My regret in all of this is that because I've given in to what I want, what I'm hungry for, I don't think I can ever let you go. And if I fuck you, if our bodies connect, you will not be able to walk away from me. I won't allow it. You'll be mine. Forever. Always. No one will look at you without me growling at them. No one will touch you without getting their paws ripped off." He reached around her, grabbed her ass and hauled her tight against him. "Even now, with your cream on my tongue, down my throat, inside of me, I don't know if I can let you go."

Staring at him, her mouth open, Mal felt as though both her head and her heart might explode. "Xavier…"

"No, no," he uttered hoarsely, his hands raking up her ass to stroke her lower back. "Not tonight, Beautiful. No more tonight. Just let me hold you while you sleep. Let me feel your warmth, your skin against mine."

CHAPTER SEVEN

Light shocked the backs of Xavier's eyes as he came awake. He could count on one hand the number of times he'd slept all night—been able to sleep all night. Normally, his mind was so thick with ideas, moving too rapidly as he built codes and cracked codes, that he couldn't calm himself enough to sleep well.

But last night had been different.

He growled softly, reveling in the heat and sweet scent of the female curled up into him, her back against his chest and groin. Nothing had prepared him for the depth of desire he'd experienced on his knees before her in the shower. The surge of possessiveness. Even as he held her now, even as his cock filled with blood and grew hard against his belly, he felt it.

Mine.

The haze of sleep still within him, Xavier lowered his head and kissed the back of her neck. She had the most beautiful skin, softness over lean muscle. He was about to follow the line of her backbone with his mouth, all the way down to the curve of her sweet ass, and into heaven once again, when his smartphone rang out from the living room. He wanted to ignore it. He even lifted his hand toward the door and flipped it off, but he knew it could be news about the camera's owner, perhaps even news about Chayton. They were counting on him—Raphael, Ashe, the elders, the Pantera—he'd given his word.

With a quick kiss to her shoulder, promising himself he'd be back beneath the sheets before she even woke up, Xavier left the warmth of her bed and padded out into the hallway.

He swiped the phone from the top of the couch, pressed the answer button and muttered in an irritated voice, "Yeah."

"Shit, X." Captain's laughter rang out on the other end. "Wrong side of the bed?"

Right side. Perfect side. "What's going on, Cap?"

"I have something for you. Got your computer open?"

Rounding the couch, Xavier had both computers open, and his cell on speaker before he even sat down. "Go."

"Tracked down the store that sold the camera," Captain said, his voice booming through the speaker Xavier had attached to one of the computers.

Xavier could hear the male working the keyboard hard and fast. "With the serial number?"

"Yep."

"Show me."

Instantly, both the camera shop website and a copy of the receipt popped up on his screen. Xavier enhanced it while Captain explained, "This place stores their records digitally, which is a space saver, but there was a weakness in their backup files I used my genius to exploit."

Xavier snorted at the male's smugness. "No address?" he asked, his fingers moving over the keyboard a mile a minute.

"Whoever bought it paid in cash and in person."

"Fuck me."

"No, no, bro. Here's the part you're going to love." His puma grin was practically audible. "Maybe it'll even pull you out of the shit-tastic mood you're in."

"Doubt it." He forced his mind to focus. Not on the bed and the warm, wet naked female within it, but on his work.

"Our camera owner emailed the store," Captain told him proudly.

"No shit."

"A service problem. Seems the camera's battery life wasn't as long as promised."

This was good. Damned good. He'd been hoping, but so far the leads had gone dead. Could their target have actually left a digital fingerprint for them? "You trace it?"

"Yeah. No luck yet. The trail keeps bouncing all over the globe. Whoever we're dealing with has definitely got an encrypted router on his PC—or whatever computer he or she is using."

Xavier grinned as the email address popped up on his screen. "Could we possibly be dealing with a techie here?"

"I don't know. But either way, this is your department now. No one cracks code like you, *mon ami.* It's fucking art."

"Thanks, brother. Soon as I get a location I'm going to check it out in person, see if this human can lead us to Chayton. I'll be on the cell if you guys need me."

Captain paused, then sniffed. "Tracking offline and on foot? Isn't that a Hunter's job?"

"Why, yes, it is," came a female voice behind him.

Xavier whirled around, growled at the intruder. The very sexy, nearly naked, intruder. She was standing in the doorway of her bedroom, wearing only a tank top that barely covered her shaved mound. Blood surged into his dick, and even though his fellow Geek couldn't see shit through his phone, Xavier felt possessive ire barrel through him.

"Gotta go, Cap," he muttered to the male. "I'll be in touch."

Xavier didn't even wait for the male to reply, just hit the off button and stood. "You should've stayed in bed."

"Why? Were you planning on coming back?"

"Hell, yes."

As her mouth curved into a wicked grin, her gaze drifted down his body, lingering on the thick erection pressing against his lower abdomen. "Too bad we have to go. Get to work."

The word *we* wasn't lost on Xavier, and he shook his head. "Not happening, Beautiful."

433

She leaned against the door, the action causing the edges of her tank to lift, giving him an unobstructed view of her glorious pussy.

His mouth watered. God, he wanted to taste her again. Spread her thighs and send his tongue up inside her slick, hot channel until she screamed.

But that spot in hell beside Shakpi was growing closer by the second.

"I'm one of the best trackers in the Wildlands, Xavier," she said, her eyes searching his now.

"I'm going outside of the Wildlands, Amalie," he countered.

Her kitty cat grin widened. "Perfect. We could use a break."

"From the Pantera or from each other?"

"I'll leave that answer to you." She crossed her arms, grabbed the edges of her tank and pulled it over her head. Naked, her nipples hardening, her eyes still pinned to him, she tossed the white strip of fabric at him. "You could always leave me here. Alone." She laughed softly. "Or not."

Come leaked from the head of his dick, and a growl escaped his throat. "You play dirty."

"Oh, Xavier," she purred, "you have no idea."

She would be the death of him. Or maybe the life. He wasn't sure which option worried him more. But either way, it wasn't going to get examined in that moment. He was too worked up, and she was too tempting.

"Fine," he ground out. "Put on some goddamn clothes before I fuck you against that door."

"Promises, promises," she called as she turned around and strode back into her room.

———

Her arms wrapped around Xavier's waist, she reveled in the feel of his back against her chest and the motorcycle's engine between her legs. It wasn't as hot as riding on his puma, but it was pretty damn close.

Getting dressed and leaving the house, and the Wildlands, had taken supreme effort on both of their parts. But the reminder of why they needed to go on this mission, search out any clues to Chayton's whereabouts—find the human male before their enemies did—had sobered their desire.

The heat of the day grew thicker as they drew closer to Lafayette. Insects hit the plastic visors of their helmets, and Mal wished she'd worn something lighter than a black leather jacket over her blue tank. Xavier's friend had tracked the IP address to two possible locations. A coffee shop in Lafayette and a cabin in the swamps. They'd gone to the coffee shop first. The owner had been friendly enough, but hadn't given them anything major to go on. Seemed folks with laptops were in and out of the shop all day long. The human male explained that he recognized some of them, didn't know others, but he rarely got intimate enough with anyone to glean personal information.

Now, as the day started to wane into late afternoon, they were headed for the cabin.

"Wrap your arms tighter around me, Amalie," Xavier called back to her as he took a curve with practiced skill.

"I'm not going to fall off," she shouted.

"Who said anything about you falling off?" He took one hand off the bars and used it to press her arms closer. "I just like the feel of you."

She grinned and rubbed her chin against his shoulder. Fantasy or reality. For three days or one. It just didn't matter. She'd never felt so happy. "I won't forget you said that," she called to him.

He growled back, "Good."

After another stretch of curves, one hill and a bumpy-ass bridge, Xavier finally slowed and pulled onto a road marked, 'Swamp Estates. Private Property.' As they kicked up crazy amounts of dust on the dirt pathway, Amalie couldn't help laughing.

"What's so funny?" Xavier asked as they entered a small parking lot and slid into one of many empty spots.

"Estates is really pushing things," she said as he killed the engine and got off the bike. "Rustic cabins is way more like it."

435

Xavier glanced over his shoulder at the ten or so cabins dotting the swamp's lip in the distance. "Never underestimate the subliminal powers of marketing, Beautiful." He turned back to face her, his eyes flashing. "Sometimes to accept what we're given in this life, to be content with it, we have to amplify or change its value."

Good god, was it possible that she loved this male even more for his incredible brain than his knee-weakening body? She studied him. And tried to pretend she hadn't just used the word 'love' in her mental query regarding how she felt about him.

"Have you ever done that?" she asked. "Changed the value of something you had to accept?"

"Sure."

Her heart stuttered. "When?"

He didn't answer right away, seemed to be mulling something over in his head. Then he glanced past her to the road they'd just traveled, and scrubbed a hand over his face. "When my father died."

It was something she'd known about, had heard about, but they hadn't been close enough to talk about back then. She hoped they were now. Or getting there. She fought the urge to reach for his hand. She didn't want to do anything to stop him from opening up to her, being vulnerable. "How did you amplify that? Or change its value?"

With a tight exhale, his gaze slid back to meet hers. "I got to have two families."

It took her all of five seconds to glean his meaning, but it made her gut ache. His family was Aristide, maybe even her. And he'd crossed a line he hadn't wanted to cross. "I understand."

"Do you?" he asked, his eyes now piercing in the light of the late afternoon sun. "Because I really need you to."

Before Mal could answer, the rumbling sounds of a car coming up the dirt path rent the air. It was coming fast toward them, into the parking lot, kicking up a shitload of dust. Her Hunter instincts kicking into high gear, Mal grabbed Xavier's hand, and took off for the shelter of the trees down near the swamp.

Silently, they watched the car slide into a parking space and stop with a sputter and a groan. When the door opened and a woman got out, Mal turned to Xavier and whispered, "She look familiar? From any of the shop pictures on the drive?"

He shook his head.

She pressed him. "You sure? There had to have been a ton of film."

He turned and gave her a lopsided grin. "I have a photographic memory, Beautiful."

Her heart freaking swooned, and she uttered dryly, "Of course you do."

He laughed softly. "It's a damn inconvenience. Every inch of your body…" He tapped his temple. "All up here and never going away."

"Good." It was her turn to grin now.

He motioned for her to follow. "Come."

"You have the cabin number, right?"

"I think so," he said, following the water, keeping to the shadows, the shade. "If I can remember it."

She gave him a playful push, laughing softly. At which he growled, and yanked her to his side. But as they drew closer to the cabins, they quieted, moving swiftly, listening, eyes wary as they passed the rustic dwellings, their screened porches overlooking the cypress swamp, now tinted peach in the light of the late-afternoon sun.

"Are we breaking and entering?" she asked, wiping sweat from her brow. "Or just lying in wait to grab the guy?"

He turned his gaze on her. "That's the Hunters way, isn't it, Amalie? No talk, all action."

"Not this Hunter," she said in a hushed voice as they approached the rear of the cabin. "I like talk. Lots of it. In my ear is good. Against my mouth even better."

With a soft snarl, he whirled around and caught her up in his arms. His ice blue eyes narrowed with heat. "Don't make me regret bringing you."

"Oh, you won't." With a crooked smile, she pulled away from him. "I have the nose after all."

"The nose, the eyes, the mouth, the ass…"

She glanced back and winked at him, then darted away, quick and quiet, to the side door of the cabin. She was there only a few seconds, when Xavier came up behind her, whispered in her ear, "Well?"

She shivered. In the ninety-plus degree weather, she actually shivered. "No one's in there."

"No body heat."

She glanced over her shoulder and grinned. "No body heat and no heartbeat. Should we wait inside?"

He shook his head. "Maybe in another cabin close by. Maybe in the trees."

She looked up at the massive cypress overhead. "If only I could access my puma," she whispered. "I hate that we can't shift outside the Wildlands. It's so inconvenient." Then her eyes slid down to meet his and she added, "And that pussy of mine really knows how to dig in her nails and climb."

Her suggestive tone and words had Xavier's nostrils flaring, and he took her hand and led her away from the cabin and back toward the swamp. "I think we'll stay out of the trees for today," he grumbled. "Come, Female."

CHAPTER EIGHT

"Liar!"

"Excuse me?" Xavier didn't spare her a glance, though he wanted to. Shit, he always wanted to. After all, she looked hot. Jeans, tank, smooth, tanned skin with a light sheen of sweat. His tongue twitched inside his mouth at the image, at the yearning to taste her salty skin. But he had to set his position, make sure he could see if and when someone returned to that cabin.

"You said no trees, and look at this," she said behind him.

Crouched inside the shelter of a massive fallen cypress, Xavier shrugged. "No climbing was needed." He narrowed his eyes at the screened porch a couple hundred yards away. "We're protected here. We can see everything, and no one can see us."

"We could be protected inside one of those cabins bracketing our camera owner."

Xavier glanced over his shoulder. Damn, she looked beautiful. Edible. "You looking for some comfort on this mission, Hunter?" he asked.

Her lips twitched. "No," she returned haughtily, the leaves of the cypress overhead traveling back and forth across her back. "I'm just saying there are options..."

"Like carpet and walls and indoor plumbing?"

She shook her head. "You're such a guy."

"Damn right," he said, then growled softly. "Wait, what does that mean?"

She laughed. "With what you have between your legs, you don't need indoor plumbing. Us females...well, let's just say it's an awkward act without it. Out of our fur, at any rate. "

He laughed with her. "I can ask if there are any vacancies here. Hell, maybe I'll just kick out some nice couple celebrating their mating night if it would please you."

She sobered suddenly, and her expression went soft, sensual. Even her tone was far more tantalizing than teasing. "You want to please me?"

Christ, she made him insane. His hands curled into fists, and a low, husky growl exited his throat. "Don't act so surprised, Hunter. I may be a closed book when it comes to sharing feelings and all that sappy bullshit, but don't pretend you don't know how affected I am by you. How my body twitches and hardens and sweats every fucking moment you're around. Pleasing you?" He laughed darkly. "It's on my mind constantly."

Her breathing quickened, making her cheeks flush and her spectacular chest rise and fall.

"Well, you're not the only one," she said, her eyes pinned to his.

"What do you mean?"

A slow, sexy grin played about her lips. "Pleasing me is on my mind constantly, too."

"You!" With a fierce growl, Xavier forgot everything—where he was, why he was there—and leapt on top of her, forcing her to her back on the soft moss. Snarling down at her, he rasped, "You...Dammit...You..."

She gazed up at him, breathing so hard, she could hardly get the word, "What?" out of her mouth.

"You make me crazy," he growled.

She raked her hands up his chest. "Good."

"You make me hungry," he continued, his eyes narrowed slits as he ground his hips, his hard cock, against her sex.

"Finally," she uttered, grinning, her hands moving down, over his stomach toward his hips.

He groaned, knowing where she was headed. "You make me... God, Amalie..."

"What, Xavier? Tell me. Please, tell me."

"You make me so fucking happy."

The words were out of his mouth before he could take them back. Not that he wanted to. They were true. He'd never felt anything close to this with anyone. He wanted her. Not just a night—or three—of hot, mindless fucking. No. He *wanted* her.

Amalie's hands froze near his hipbones and her eyes searched his. Within their incredible green depths, he saw her heart. Saw how she felt about him. How she'd always felt about him. And if he wasn't mistaken, he saw his own heart reflected there, too.

Suddenly, her face broke with a grin, and she whispered, "By the way, I don't think anyone would be having their mating night here."

"Why not?" he asked, his hands cupping her face. Her soft, beautiful face.

"It's just not very romantic. The swamp, the bugs."

He ran his thumb across her lower lip. "You sure you're a Hunter, Amalie?"

Her soft, sexy laughter went straight to his dick. "All I'm saying is that when you mate, or marry as the humans say, you want that first night to be special."

His expression grew serious and he leaned down and kissed her lower lip. "No bugs?" he whispered.

She nodded, lifting her chin instinctively. "Preferably."

He kissed her top lip, then swiped it gently with his tongue. "No swamp?"

"If one can help it," she said breathlessly, her arms wrapping around his waist.

Heat surged up from her skin into his and he stifled a groan. "What if one can't help it?"

Her eyes cut to his mouth and she licked her lips. "Xavier..."

"Because I don't think I can help it. I don't think I want to, Hunter."

She smiled softly, sweetly. "That's '*Beautiful*' to you."

441

"Yes, it is." He kissed her, a kiss that conveyed his hunger and his need, but there was so much more. More he had to say. The one vital thing that would change everything between them. He pulled back and forced her gaze to lock with his. "I want you, Amalie."

She arched her back and purred, "Then have me."

His cock felt so hard it was painful. "It's your first mating."

"I know," she thrust her hips up, ground her sex against him brazenly. "I want it to be with you. I've always wanted it to be with you."

Pain and pleasure battled within him. "I want that too. Fuck…"

"Then take it," she said harshly, desperately.

"Here? Now?"

"Do you care where we are?" she demanded. "Do you care who sees us right now?" She cursed. "Do you care if everything is put on hold for however long we need? However long it takes for this to happen between us?"

"Fuck no. Fuck. No." His mouth was so dry. He needed her, her heat, her saliva, her cream. He didn't give a shit about where they were, but he needed her to understand something. He needed her to know what he was asking of her. "Amalie, I won't take it unless I can keep it."

Her eyes widened, a flash of confusion moving through them. "What do you mean?"

"You know what I mean." He rose up, his eyes pinned to hers, but his fingers moving to the waistband of her jeans. "I want you. But not for a night or three." He flicked the button, eased down the zipper. "I want you always, forever, until the Wildlands are no longer filled with magic and we are dust that a new species calls their home."

For a moment, all Xavier heard was her rapid breathing and the sounds of the water and the wind through the cypress.

"I love you, Amalie," he said in a hoarse, desperate voice. "Fuck, Beautiful, I always have. I don't care about anything or anyone. Not anymore—not ever."

Tears sprang to her eyes, turning them a shocking leaf green in the light of fading sun.

"I love you, too," she uttered. "But you know that. You've always known."

He nodded. "Tell me," he nearly begged. "Tell me before I die of longing. Tell me before I strip you bare and taste you, fuck you, claim you. Tell me I'm yours and you're mine."

"Are you sure?" she said as he pulled down her underwear and jeans and tossed them aside. "Forever is—"

"What I want more than anything in the world, Beautiful," he said, easing her tank over her head and her bra from her shoulders. "There's nothing, no one, who can stop this, can stop me from claiming you." His eyes flipped up to lock on hers. "Except you."

Shock barreled through Xavier as Amalie grasped both sides of his T-shirt and ripped it up the center. The sounded echoed across the bayou, but he barely heard it. Her words next drowned out everything else.

"Mate me, Xavier," she said, her eyes flashing. "Mate me for life."

She had the black fabric off his body in seconds and was working his jeans down his hips before he had time to register her movement. Once he did though, he was like a male possessed, growling, taking over, his jeans off and discarded, and his head between her thighs.

The liquid heat that hit his tongue made come leak from his cock. She tasted like heaven, like honey, and he licked her over and over, nothing gentle, nothing sweet. Fuck no. Right now, he just wanted to eat her. And if the way her hips were jacking up, pumping hungrily against his mouth, was any indicator, she liked his slight roughness, his need to consume her.

"Oh god, Xavier," she said on a moan. "I can't...it's too much."

Damn right. It was all too much. But so what? They both needed this, needed each other. More was good. More made her buck and groan. More made her pussy so wet and warm and soft, he couldn't wait to get inside her.

Her fingers plunged into his hair, her nails digging into his scalp as he tongued her deep, then pulled out and suckled her clit.

"You're making me crazy," she whispered, then gasped as he pressed his tongue against her and jerked his head up and down.

Xavier felt her violent shudder beneath his mouth, coming hard and intense against his tongue. His entire body went up in flames as her juices rushed him. He lapped at her, drank her up, but left enough wet heat to coat her pussy walls and make his thrust easy and pleasurable.

With one last possessive suckle to her swollen clit, he rose over her, catching his weight on his elbows, holding his position so they were face to face. Breathing heavily, her eyes filled with heat and deep desire, Amalie wrapped her legs around his waist, arched her back and brazenly and seductively licked him from chin to nose.

"Mmm," she uttered, her eyes lifting to his. "I taste good on you."

Xavier, the male, died.

While the animal within him flared to the surface of his skin and took hold, took control. His cock poised at her entrance, the head hard and wet with pre-come, he growled. "Mine."

She nodded. "Yours."

And he pushed inside her.

———

He was deep.

Breathstealingly deep.

Every thick, hard inch, was deliciously impaled inside her, all the way to her womb, and nothing—*nothing*—had ever felt so amazing. There was no pain, just a wondrous full feeling. God, they were truly made for each other. She'd known the first time she'd seen him. Too young to understand the bond, the connection, it had surfaced as a lust and a hope for the future.

But now, now as he started moving inside of her, claiming her with his body as he looked down into her eyes, connected with her, she understood the true symmetry of love. Him and Her. Even in their puma forms, they would know this bond, feel this bond.

"I love this," he rasped, nipping at her lips as he thrust gently inside of her, getting her body ready for the intense, possessive thrusts to come.

After all, he was a Pantera male. They could fuck gently, of course. But it was only a matter of time before they went wild, attacked, demanded, their animal nature ruling their sex drive.

And being a Pantera female, Mal couldn't wait.

"I love being inside of you," he continued, dropping his head, taking one hard nipple into his mouth and suckling it deep. To her gasp, the rush of wet heat inside her pussy, he growled. "Kissing you, sucking your sweet, pink tits. Feeling you go tight and hot around my cock whenever I do."

His words, uttered against her breast, his breath teasing her wet nipple, made Mal feel like she was going to come again. She fought against it. She wanted to come with him this second time.

Then he look up and smiled. "And shit, Beautiful, I just love you."

Mal didn't know if it was the words, his voice, or how his ice blue eyes had melted into lazy, erotic pools of emotional blue, but she couldn't stop herself. Her Hunter strength kicked in, and she pressed her hands to his hips, eased his cock out of her, and flipped to her belly.

"Fuck me now," she demanded, coming up on her hands and knees. "Fuck me hard and deep until we both come. Outside, under the sky, near the bayou. This is how you should claim me, and how I should be taken. My pussy—both the one who purrs for you, and the one you're looking at right now—need it."

Xavier didn't say a word. Maybe he couldn't. Maybe his animal was right there, hissing and snapping and snarling near the surface of his skin, just as hers was. But it was no more than a second before she felt him behind her, his thick, stone-hard cock pressed at her entrance.

His thrust wasn't gentle this time.

Thank. Fucking. Christ.

He knew what she wanted, and he was giving it to her. Gripping her hips, he rode her hard, working her so deep she moaned and keened and circled her hips trying to feel him from every angle. Shock waves of pleasure moved through her. How could something so primal feel so good? So beyond amazing. She wanted to cry and scream and laugh and warn him to never stop. That as mates she would demand he fuck her every day and every night for the rest of her life. But she didn't have the voice. He'd stripped her bare in too many ways to count.

And then she felt it. The thing—the amazing, magical thing she'd only heard about from her Pantera female friends. The sign of a true mating. She felt his claws against the skin of her hip, and as he pounded into her, and she stretched around him, he marked her. She cried out, from pain, from pleasure, and from the absolute wonder of having a long-realized dream come true.

"I love you, Amalie," he said on a fierce growl.

He drove up into her, so deep she gasped, then reached around to palm her drenched pussy. With one pinch to her clit, Mal came, spasming around his cock as her body went wild and uncontrolled, and a rush of hot seed filled her sex.

CHAPTER NINE

Coming down from the fuck of the century wasn't easy or fast.

Xavier was shaking. Christ, shaking. And his dick was still hard. Nothing had or would ever compare to this. Mating Amalie. She was his everything now. His life, his breath, his vision, and his reason for waking up and…god help him, hitting the sheets every night. Looking at her, sitting before her, gloriously nude, her skin sweaty and pink, his mark on her hip, her sex still glistening with their shared climaxes, he wanted her again.

And again.

Shit, he didn't even want to take her back to the Wildlands, let other males see her. He knew that was an irrational thought, and he wasn't about to share it. But it was there. Oh yeah, it was there.

But he'd sensed something, his Pantera instincts overriding his post-orgasmic shakes. A male. Human. Near the bayou.

Xavier's narrowed gaze searched the green, the trees, the calm surface of the water.

"I scent him, too," Amalie said, the vigilant Hunter back in her eyes. She grabbed her clothes and yanked them on. "Maybe it's just another guest, but we need to be ready if it's not."

Xavier had his clothes on in under ten seconds, his eyes back on the cabin. "I don't see him. I don't see anyone."

"Bayou," Amalie whispered.

Xavier turned back toward the swamp. "What the hell?"

A heavy mist now coated the surface of the bayou. A low hanging cloud moving toward them. It swirled, and seemed to have an eye in the center like a tornado. Xavier slipped in front of Amalie, closer to the four foot tall and ten foot wide mass of white haze. He didn't know what was coming, but it wouldn't get near his mate.

As it touched down at the shore, and a male emerged from that 'eye' Amalie gasped under her breath, "Holy shit."

Still hidden from view within the massive tree, Xavier stared, riveted, ready to pounce. This was a human walking past them only ten or so feet away, but clearly he was so much more than that. And when the man drew closer to the cabin, and his hand reached for the screen door, Xavier knew in his gut, they not only had their camera owner, but they might very well have The Shaman, Chayton as well.

Clearly thinking the same thing, Amalie pushed past him and ran toward the cabin and the male. Cursing, Xavier burst out of the shelter of the tree and went after her. He reached her just as she cornered the male inside his screened-in porch.

"Who are you?" she demanded.

Xavier drew closer to his mate's side. "I believe this is the human we seek, Amalie." He eyed the confused and fearful older male. "Chayton, I presume?"

"Isi is in the Wildlands?" he repeated, shocked and amazed. "Oh, thank the gods."

Seated across from Chayton, who had only a short time ago emerged from the bayou like a spirit, Mal nodded. "You didn't know?"

He shook his head, his nearly black eyes softening. "I couldn't find her. I've been so worried—"

"Because she wasn't in her shop?" Mal finished. "Visible on the camera you hid?"

He looked at her for a moment, his eyes searching hers. Then he nodded, "That's right. I wanted to know she was safe, even if it wasn't safe for me to watch over her in person. She is my daughter. I love her."

"Then come back to the Wildlands and see her," Mal said quickly.

It was as if an icy wind blasted through the porch. Chayton shook his head. "Impossible."

"You don't understand how vital this is," Xavier began. He was seated beside Mal, and had his hand resting protectively on her lower back. "One of the Pantera's greatest enemies is growing in power."

A different kind of heat glinted in those dark eyes. "You speak of Shakpi."

Mal's heart stuttered. "You know?"

The male pushed his long, black braid over one tanned shoulder and nodded. "Of course I know. I have come to suspect that I am the one who accidentally opened the portal."

Mal turned to Xavier, who gave her a worried look before she turned back to Chayton. "How?"

"That doesn't matter."

"Of course it does," Mal insisted harshly. "Isi is being blamed for it. The elders claim that your vision proves—"

"That damned vision," Chayton said passionately. "It has ruined so much, so many. '*The blood of The Shaman's firstborn shall carry the taint of Shakpi, releasing her powers upon the lands of the Pantera.*'" He stood and walked over to the screen that faced the bayou. With the sun's retreat, the sky was giving itself over to twilight. "It doesn't mean Isi is destined to hurt the land. The Wildlands, after all, were created by the blood of both Shakpi and Opela. The rot of the land began long before Isi's birth." He glanced over his shoulder. "If you and your kind want to blame the spread of poison, then you should point the finger at the elders who were too eager to use my powers to walk among the spirits."

Mal understood his passion, his fear. But right now, they needed his help. His daughter needed his help. "You believe it was your connection to the spirits that caused the damage?"

He sighed. "I fear that the connection unknowingly opened the portal that Shakpi is using to touch this world."

Xavier cursed, stood. "Then you have to come back and close it."

A flare of anger vibrated through Chayton, and his lean face grew tense. "No. It's too dangerous. This swamp is protected with deep magic. If I leave, they'll find me."

"Who?" both Xavier and Mal said together.

"Shakpi's followers. They'll force me to open the portal to Shakpi's prison completely."

"We won't allow them to take you," Xavier said firmly. "Come back. Let this nightmare end for us all."

He shook his head. "I'm sorry."

His resignation sent Mal into desperate mode, and she tried another tactic. "Then at least come back and see your daughters."

His face went blank. "Daughters?"

She walked over to him, put her hand on his bare arm. "Ashe is there, too, Chayton."

"What?" The word came out so softly it was a mere exhale.

"She's mated to a Pantera."

Tears pricked his dark eyes, making them glitter like polished stones. "Ashe," he uttered. "I haven't seen her since..." He shook his head, too emotional to continue.

"She's pregnant."

His eyes widened. "No."

"Yes," Xavier confirmed, moving to stand beside Mal, his hand reaching for hers. "The first cub in so many years. Our miracle."

Mal squeezed her mate's large, warm hand, but to the Shaman male, she smiled and said, "They need you, Chayton. We all need you."

CHAPTER TEN

Night blanketed the Wildlands, and though the scent of the Dyesse Lily still clung to anything with leaves or moss, the brilliant moon overhead had returned to its natural state of white. It glowed down upon them, lighting their way as they raced, in their puma state, side by side over rocks and snaking around trees, toward town. Xavier carried Chayton on his back, while Amalie, after leaving the motorcycle in its garage near the border, had been vigilant about anything or anyone following them.

As they broke through the final barrier of brush and entered town, Xavier felt the male on his back shudder. He didn't blame Chayton for his fears and concerns. With what awaited Xavier when Aristide left the confines of quarantine and learned of his and Amalie's mating, he certainly understood them. But unfaced challenges had a way of growing out of control. It was always better to deal than run.

Beside him, Amalie slowed, growling as many Pantera, both in and out of shift, came out of their dwellings to watch the arrival of The Shaman. Clearly, the text he'd sent both Raphael and Parish had gone through. He wouldn't be surprised if the elders were at the foot of the path leading to the clinic, waiting, hungry for blood and information.

But the only Pantera out in front of the clinic were Raphael, Parish and Isi's mate, Talon. All three had tight, apprehensive expressions under the stark light of the moon, and when Xavier came to a halt in front of them, he gave a quick growl of warning. Chayton had come to help, to see his daughters. Scaring him or demanding from him before he'd even set his foot on Wildlands soil was not going to happen.

Catching his puma's eye, Raphael gave Xavier a clipped nod of understanding, then turned to face Chayton. "It's good to have you here."

"I wish to see my daughters," Chayton said, climbing off Xavier's back.

"Of course," Raphael said, though his tone had a trace of warning, of protective male. "Ashe is my mate."

For a moment, Chayton didn't speak. He glanced back at Xavier, and at Amalie, who remained in her puma form, too. He gave them a tight smile, then turned back to Raphael. "I must give you my congratulations."

It was what the Suit had obviously needed to hear. His entire body relaxed and a broad grin broke on his features. "And to you," he said, then gestured toward the clinic. "Come. Both your daughters are here together."

Both, Xavier mused, watching Chayton move up the steps behind the three Pantera males. *If Isi is with Ashe, then she's out of quarantine. Which would also mean that Aristide—*

A growl rent the night air. It was a growl Xavier knew well. He'd heard it beside him a thousand times. His gaze flicked up. Chayton and the three Pantera males were gone. But something else far more problematic sat outside the doors to the clinic; a massive light-brown puma, black eyes flashing fire. Amalie started forward, but Xavier hissed at her to stay back. She was Aristide's sister, true, but she was also Xavier's mate, and no matter what—or who—threatened their bond, Xavier would always protect what belonged to him.

In a flash of color, Xavier shifted to male form. True to his style, Aristide shifted mid-step as he moved toward his friend. They stood at about the same height, both broad shouldered, both heavily muscled, but where Xavier was dark with light eyes, Aristide was light with dark eyes.

Beside Xavier, Amalie also shifted. And she didn't wait for either one of them to speak. "Aristide, you have no right to be pissed," she began. "You know I've been in love with this male forever. No one will make me happier. No one will love me more or protect me more fiercely or—"

"It's all right, Beautiful." Xavier stepped in front of her, and faced Aristide. This was his fight, his best friend, his betrayal. "I love her, and I've mated her."

Aristide's black eyes locked with his, and his pale brows lifted. "You've mated her?"

Xavier nodded. "There won't be an apology or a question, but there will be a promise. I'll make her happy."

For several long seconds, the dark-eyed male just stared at him. Then he gave a little shrug, and a broad grin split his features. "I know you will." His grin widened further. "Brother." Laughing, he grabbed Xavier and embraced him. "Shit, I've waited a long time to call you that for real."

"You asshole," Xavier muttered, clapping him on the back. "How long have you known there was something here?"

"For-freaking-ever, bro."

Xavier laughed. "Then you'll be expecting your eviction notice. She's moving out. Or you are."

"Finally. I've been waiting forever." He pushed back, turned and gave his sister a smile. "Take the house, sis. Start a new family there."

"Unbelievable," Amalie said, giving her brother a fierce glare, even when he came in for a hug. "If I'd have know this, I would've seduced Xavier a long time ago."

Aristide stiffened, and Amalie pulled away, her turn to laugh. She gave him a little wave. "Night-night, *bro*."

As she walked away, she heard her brother growl at Xavier. "Wait? What did she just say? She seduced you?"

"Damn right. Best thing that ever happened to me," Xavier said with a grin in his voice. "Later, A."

Amalie was barely down the path when Xavier came up behind her and scooped her up in his arms. She let out a squeal of delight.

"Where are you taking me, mate of mine?" she asked, grinning up at him.

His smile was wide and hungry, and his eyes glowed blue fire in the moonlight. "Home, Beautiful."

"Mine or yours?"

He leaned in and kissed her, growled against her lips. "There is no mine or yours anymore. Only ours. So says the mark on your sexy hip."

Her skin tingled with his words, and her heart squeezed. She'd hoped and wished for this for so long, and now he was finally hers. The love of her life.

"You don't have to rush, Xavier," she giggled as he stalked through town toward their house. "We have so much longer than three days. We have forever. We have a lifetime."

But he didn't slow. In fact, he quickened his pace. "I need you now, Beautiful," he rasped. "I need to carry you home and get you in our bed. I need to strip you bare and lick every inch of your skin." He growled. "That quickie in the swamp only wet my appetite."

Her entire body flared with heat. "That was a quickie?" she nearly choked out.

He chuckled, low and sexy. "Oh, yeah."

She sighed and snuggled deeper into his chest as he rushed through the gate of their house, their home. "Oh, I have so much to learn, Xavier."

"And I can't wait to teach you, Beautiful." With a fierce snarl, he kicked down the door. "Don't worry, I'll fix that later."

"Much later," she teased.

"Tomorrow," he rasped, stalking down the hall.

She grinned when he entered their bedroom. "Next week."

He tossed her on the bed and growled. "Next year."

And then he was moving over her, kissing her, and neither one of them spoke for a very long time.

———

As a seer, a shaman, a human with extraordinary powers, Chayton knew instinctually what he was capable of and what he was not.

But that didn't matter.

Not today.

The Pantera had gathered in the square, the square where only a few nights ago, the birth of their kind had been celebrated. Ashe had told him all about it, regaled him with stories of dancing and feasting, then begged him to help her—help the Pantera—preserve their wonderful tradition. And perhaps their very existence. They all wanted him to stop what was happening on their land, and they believed Shakpi's power was to blame. He didn't know if this was true or not. But he did know that he played a part, and that if he didn't attempt to fix what might have been broken by his hand, his daughter would suffer the stigma forever.

He wouldn't let that happen.

His eyes lifted to look at her. Isi, and beside her, a very pregnant Ashe. So beautiful, their hands clasped as they watched him. They looked so hopeful. A shock of pain went through him, weakening him, his resolve. He had failed them in the past. He wouldn't fail them now.

He slammed his eyes shut, and called upon the spirits of his ancestors. Dark thoughts and needs and wants snaked through his blood. Yes, she was here, below his feet, wanting to rise, wanting to be released. His hands balled into fists, but he forced himself to relax. Air moved over his skin, and he allowed himself, his soul, to leave his body. Sound ceased to exist, even his heartbeat, and he fell. Down, down, down, below the surface of the Wildlands, down to where she was imprisoned. Instantly, he felt rage and heat and sadness burden his mind, but he once again forced himself to relax, to be like water.

The portal was not visible to the eye, only to the soul, but Chayton knew well where to look for it. Power surging into him, granted by those who shared his blood, by those long dead, he pressed against the gaping hole, the wound, in Shakpi's prison. As expected, it pushed back.

Remaining at peace, a wave on the water of his subconscious, Chayton pressed once again. But this time, something strange happened. It was as if his soul crackled, as if lightning exploded inside his mind, and he was thrust upward, out of the ground and into the sky.

He felt the magical connection to his body break. But it was too late to do anything to repair it. He could only watch from above as tiny particles of light rose from the earth.

The crowd of Pantera gasped, some drawing back, some inching forward. Then the particles of light let out a shattering scream, surrounded Chayton's body and entered it.

Staring down at the chaos below, Chayton could only grieve his failure. That is, until he saw the eyes of his physical body open and his mouth curve into a wicked smile.

"I am free," came an otherworldly voice.

Once again, the crowd gasped. But over the din, Chayton heard the word, the name, he feared above all others, uttered by a single Pantera voice.

"It's Shakpi."

BAYOU NOËL

Chapter One

Paris, 2005

Night had just fallen when Garrick Loriot strode into his opulent Parisian apartment with a scowl on his lean, starkly handsome face. After months of delicate negotiations, he'd at last reached a tentative deal to purchase an apartment building in Montmartre to use as a safe house for Pantera Diplomats, only to have the negotiations fall apart when it was declared a historical landmark.

Seriously. Was there anything in this city that wasn't a fucking historical landmark?

His pissy mood, however, swiftly disappeared when he flipped on the light and caught sight of the envelope that had been slipped beneath his door.

It was from her. He could just catch the scent of vanilla mixed with earthy cypress. His heart did that familiar leap as he bent to grab it off the priceless Parisian carpet.

He always looked forward to hearing from Molly. Especially this time of year. With his father deceased, these letters were his one and only connection to the Wildlands and the mother who had never fully recovered from a near-fatal accident.

Like both his parents, Garrick was a born Diplomat which meant he never knew where he would be from one week to another. He depended on those letters to keep him connected to his home.

461

Unlike those of the previous Nurturers who'd cared for his mother, Molly's letters weren't dry reports of medical facts. Hers felt like family, and were filled with wit and humor, and captured his mother's spirit, making him feel as if he were there.

And after his shitty day, he could use a pick-me-up.

Tearing open the envelope, he dropped into a chair near the window, his six-foot-plus frame dressed in one of the Armani suits Molly always called his "stick up his ass armor." And by the white glow of the Noël lights strewn on buildings, lampposts and even the Eiffel Tower in the distance, he read:

Dear Mr. Loriot:

I am writing to inform you of my resignation as caretaker to your mother, Virginia Loriot, effective December 24.

This was not an easy decision for me to make. These past five years have been very rewarding, but it's time for me to move on. I have accepted a position at Medical, and will be starting straight away.

Thank you for the opportunity to work with your mother. I wish her nothing but the best. You'll be pleased to know I've found a suitable replacement. Virginia has met and approved her.

Best regards,
Molly Cochell

What. The. Fuck.

It was as if all the air had been pulled from the room. And the lights, which had only a moment ago twinkled merrily behind him, dimmed. Garrick crushed the letter in his fist, wondering if it was some kind of sick joke.

No. It couldn't be. Molly didn't play cruel jokes. It wasn't in her nature. She was kind and sweet. *Too damned sweet.*

So what the hell was going on? She'd seemed happy and content the last time he was there. When was that now...? Nine, ten months ago? Had something happened while he was gone? Had someone made her unhappy? What was this new position she'd found? At Medical...

His jaw tightened.

At Medical, with all the other Nurturers. Females, yes. But many single males, as well. Christ, maybe she was looking for a mate…

The thought had him out of his chair and heading toward the phone to order a car before he even realized he'd made the decision to leave.

Screw the negotiations.

It could wait. Everything could wait.

He was going home for Noël.

CHAPTER TWO

Molly glanced around the room that had been her home for…
What was it now? Five years.

God almighty.

How had time passed without her ever noticing?

It seemed only yesterday that she'd arrived at the elegant, rigidly formal house near the center of the Wildlands. As a newly trained Healer she'd been eager to prove her worth by tending to the infamous, always acerbic Virginia Loriot. The female was considered one of the finest Pantera Diplomats ever born.

Of course, Virginia was the reason she'd come to this home. But Garrick was the reason she'd stayed.

With a low hiss she slammed the door on her traitorous thoughts.

She was done thinking about the male who'd stolen her heart. After five years, only an idiot would continue to hope that her feelings would be returned.

And while Molly was many things, she wasn't an idiot.

Time to pack it up and call it a day.

Closing the lid on the last suitcase, Molly shoved her fingers through her unruly mop of golden curls that contrasted with the dark, velvet beauty of her eyes. She'd often regretted her resemblance to a china doll.

Who wanted to be cute and cuddly? Even if she was a Nurturer. She wanted to be a tall, super-slinky brunette who screamed SEX APPEAL. Ha. She'd bet her favorite pair of Jimmy Choos that Garrick wouldn't have ignored her then. Hell, she would've had to lock the door to keep him out of her bed.

Dammit.

She was doing it again.

On the point of grabbing her bags, she hesitated as she heard the unmistakable sound of Virginia's cane hitting her door and shoving it open.

The older female might be frail, but she still commanded the entire house with the precision of a military general.

She even had the look of a general.

Entering the room, Virginia stood with a rigid posture, her body tall and thin and her face angular. As always, her dark hair was pulled into a tight bun at the nape of her neck.

"You sure you have to leave?" the older female demanded.

Molly swallowed a wistful sigh.

She didn't know when or how it'd happened, but at some point she'd started to think of this place as her home.

Perhaps not so surprising.

She'd lost her parents in an accident years ago, and while she'd been taken in by other Nurturers, she'd never truly had a place to call her own. It was understandable she would ache to build a sense of home and family.

A pity that the male she loved didn't feel the same way.

The painful reminder was all she needed to stiffen her spine.

"It's time."

Virginia arched a dark brow, a mysterious smile tugging at her lips. "You know Garrick won't be pleased about this."

"I can't worry about him anymore." Molly shrugged, though just the mention of his name sent curls of awareness through her. "I have to get on with my life." *Before it's too late*, she silently added.

"You know you always have a home here with me," the female affirmed.

Molly did know.

Virginia could be cool, even aloof, but over the years, Molly had slowly discovered the caring female beneath the proper façade.

"I appreciate that," she said, her gaze skimming over the room that looked starkly bare now that she'd packed away the small touches that had, only a few days ago, made it seem like home. "But I don't truly belong."

The older female looked as if she might argue, before she gave a small shake of her head. "Maybe this is for the best," she said beneath her breath. "Garrick needs a little wake-up call."

Molly frowned in confusion. "What do you mean?"

"Ms. Loriot," Sylvia called, poking her head in the doorway. The Nurturer who had been sent to take Molly's place was a young, fresh-faced, innocent, with dark hair and kind blue eyes. Molly didn't doubt for a second that she would be a more than adequate replacement for her. "Time for your medicine."

"You go with Sylvia," Molly urged. "I'm going to take my suitcases downstairs."

The female cast her a warning look. "Don't forget to say goodbye before you leave."

"Course not," Molly assured her.

She felt a pang of loss as Virginia left the room. She would miss the older female. Despite her sharp-edged tongue, Virginia had become a true friend. And the closest thing Molly had to family.

With one last look around the room, she grabbed her bags and easily carried them downstairs.

Virginia had offered the assistance of her household staff to haul Molly's belongings back to the dormitory used by unmated Nurturers, but she'd declined.

She needed to leave as she'd arrived.

Bags in hand…her heart filled with hope for the future.

Call it closure.

The thought had barely flared through her mind when the door flew open, hitting the wall with enough force to make the priceless paintings rattle on the wall.

Molly shivered, but it wasn't because of the blast of chilled, early evening air. No, that honor belonged to the tall, dark-haired male with rich caramel skin and eyes the color of melted honey.

466

Garrick.

Molly felt as if she'd been kicked in the gut.

God. Even after five years the sight of him still managed to steal her breath.

He was so freaking gorgeous.

The chiseled perfection of his features. The ebony gloss of his hair that had been neatly trimmed. The whipcord body that was encased in one of his outrageously expensive suits, this one a pearl gray with a dark burgundy tie.

He looked like he should be stepping off the cover of GQ. Until you glanced into those honey eyes.

Then it was easy to see the razor-sharp intelligence and lethal danger of his cat that lurked just below the civilized surface.

And tonight, his cat was more obvious than usual.

"What the hell are you thinking?" he snarled, his powerful presence cloaking her.

Molly had always found it ironic that this male was so distantly elegant, and yet carried the scent of the wild elements.

Tonight he smelled like an impending thunderstorm.

"Garrick," she breathed, the suitcases dropping from her suddenly numb fingers. "You're supposed to be in Paris."

He prowled forward, his expression clamped down tight. "Your letter brought my ass home." He halted mere inches from her, his anger whipping through the cavernous formal living room. "You aren't going anywhere, Molly. So you can bring those bags right upstairs. Better yet," he reached down and picked up one of her bags. "I'll do it for you."

Finding her backbone, and ignoring the flutters of excitement that raced through the pit of her stomach, Molly snatched it back.

Not this time.

She wasn't going to allow her aching awareness of this male to blind her to the fact that he saw her as nothing more than just another Healer.

She lifted her chin and feigned impassive, business-like composure. "If you read my letter, you know I'm no longer your mother's caregiver. If you want to bark orders at someone, find Sylvia."

"I don't know Sylvia," he snapped. "And I have no intention of knowing her." He grabbed her shoulders, his voice softening to a low rasp as his gaze swept over her face. "You belong here, Molly."

She let him touch her, a deep sadness settling in the center of her soul. "No, Garrick. I don't. And that's the whole point."

Without warning, Garrick's face paled to an ashen shade. "You met someone."

She pressed her lips together. *If he only knew. If he only understood and cared and wanted...* "I told you in the letter that I have a new position."

"One you clearly don't need, since you already have a position here," he returned hotly.

Frustrated at him, at herself, she pulled away. "I think I'm capable of deciding where I want to work."

She watched the glow of his cat reacting to her rejection, snarling, upper lip curling.

"And caring for my mother is no longer good enough for you?"

"Don't you dare imply I don't love your mother," she rasped, her chin tilted to a defiant angle.

She'd be damned if he demeaned the devotion she'd offered over the past five years. Virginia was not just a patient, not just a friend, and he knew it as well as she did.

Reaching up, Garrick tugged on his tie, his irritation clearly being replaced by genuine confusion.

"Why are you so mad?" He gave a baffled shake of his head. "Why are you acting like this? Or *reacting* like this? It's not you."

Her heart squeezed painfully. "You don't know me." She met his gaze squarely. "You never wanted to know me."

He stiffened at that, the predictable wariness settling on his fiercely beautiful face.

It was exactly what Molly expected. Had come to expect. They might share the most intimate details of their thoughts and desires through their letters, but whenever Garrick returned to the Wildlands, to this house, he reverted to treating her like a mere employee.

It was ridiculous.

And insulting.

To be sure, she knew more about this male than anyone else in the world did. Including his own mother. But he only revealed that true self when they were a thousand miles apart.

Enough was enough.

"Will you say goodbye to your mother for me?" she asked coolly.

His nostrils flared and those honey eyes turned molten gold. "What about me, Molly?" he demanded, the air prickling with the heat of his cat. "Were you going to say goodbye to me? Or was that what the fucking letter was about?"

She was done with this conversation, this back and forth. She had made her decision. Hell, should've made it a long time ago. She tightened her hold on her suitcases, and, slapping an expression of determination on her face, she swept past his rigid form.

"Goodbye, Garrick."

Chapter Three

Garrick felt feral as his puma slashed through moonlit grass and darted around fragrant cypress, hissing at anything that had the misfortune to cross his path. Flora, fauna, and if it had a heartbeat—*so long, sucker.* He couldn't believe Molly had just walked out.

On his mother.

On...him.

He snarled at a lone squirrel as he ran past, even bared his teeth and licked his chops, though he despised the taste of small game. The thing froze, then turned bushy tail and fled.

A new job.

Fuck. If she was going to leave him, didn't he have the right to know what kind of job it was? Why she wanted it? Who had offered it to her?

And if it had anything to do with a male?

The thought had his blood surging hot and fast through his veins. Growling, he picked up speed, zipping from tree to tree. Only when he heard the high-pitched and very pissed-off cry of a fellow puma did he stop short. Breathing heavy, his puma's sides heaving, he realized he'd startled off the prey of the massive male puma who'd obviously been on the hunt. And not just any male. He cursed inwardly and shifted into his human form. The other puma shifted as well.

"Garrick?"

Backlit by the moon, the tall, blond Suit stared at him, confused and more than a little irritated. "What the hell are you doing here? I thought you were finishing the contract for the safe house."

"It fell through." Garrick's gaze lifted and connected with that of Raphael, his superior and mentor. "I have another space in mind, but I had something to deal with here first."

The irritation in the male's gold eyes waned. "Your mother?"

"No," Garrick said quickly as a sudden breeze off the bayou moved over him, cooling his hot skin and his hotter blood. "She's well. It's her damn caretaker who's got my fur ruffled and my fangs out."

"Sweet Molly?" Raphael said, his eyes widening with disbelief. "She's too nice for such frustration. Although," he amended with a wicked grin, "with that perfect face and lush body, there is a line of Pantera males who wouldn't mind her ruffling their fur or coaxing their fangs out."

The instant explosion inside Garrick's brain was rabid and uncontrolled. He rushed at the male, and in seconds had his back against a tree trunk. "Is that right?" he snarled, his pulse slamming against the cord of muscle in his neck. "And who would be at the front of that line?"

Raphael didn't move. He didn't look angry or fearful. Instead, he said in a calm, curious voice, "That's a reaction which should be examined, brother. Don't you agree?"

Nostrils flaring, Garrick backed up. As the realization of what he'd just done, and to whom, snaked through his burning blood, he shook his head and growled. "I apologize. I must be jetlagged."

Unfolding from the trunk of the cypress, Raphael moved forward, amusement lighting his eyes. "So where is she?"

"Medical," Garrick uttered tersely. "She quit. After five years." He sniffed. "Claims to have a new position."

"Then she'd be in the dormitory with the other single Nurturers."

Garrick's gut clenched. He'd forgotten that part of Nurturer housing. "When you referred to the other males who might be interested in her, were you speaking in general or do you know—"

"I know nothing, brother," Raphael assured him. "But if you're this jacked up over the idea of such a thing…well, what does that tell you?"

"That she doesn't belong there," Garrick tossed out.

"Try again."

His eyes lifted sharply to connect with Raphael. "That this new job of hers is a bad idea. She was safe and comfortable where she was. She was happy…" He broke off. *Happy? Shit, clearly not.* Because if she had been, she'd have stayed. And wouldn't have looked at him like that in the hall before she'd walked out. Like he was her jailer. Like she wanted nothing to do with him anymore.

He swallowed thickly.

Like she wanted something else. Or someone else.

Without even a grunt of farewell to his mentor, Garrick shifted back into his puma form and took off into the trees. He would fix this. Offer her more money, more challenges to her Nurturer nature, whatever she required. Anything to get her back home where she belonged.

Then he could return to his work, to where he belonged, with peace of mind once again.

CHAPTER FOUR

Molly was given her old rooms at the back of the dormitory. She didn't have a lot of space. A small bedroom, a living room and bathroom. Still, they were hers. With no aggravating male thinking he could stroll in and out of her life whenever he felt the urge.

After unpacking her belongings, she'd headed to the communal storage shed to gather lights and holly, as well as the small box of decorations she'd left there after the death of her parents.

Once back in her rooms, she'd set about creating a Noël atmosphere, all the while forcing her heart and her mind to accept what was. Yes, she was back to where she'd started. Yes, her spirit was bruised. And yes, it felt as if she'd wasted the last five years of her life.

But she'd be damned if she was going to allow her heavy heart to ruin these last precious days of a holiday she adored more than any other.

Bayou Noël was going to belong to her now.

At last, satisfied that she'd replaced the institutional boredom of her space with a festive cheer, Molly moved to the window that overlooked the bayou, remembering the last Noël she'd shared with her parents. A smile touched her lips.

She'd tried to pretend she was too old to be excited by all the presents that had been neatly and beautifully wrapped and stacked both around the fireplace and inside their stockings. But she'd been secretly thrilled when her father had refused to listen to her protests, and had swung her into his arms so she could place the angel goddess on top of the mantel.

That's what she missed. What she wanted.

The laughter. The love. The sheer comfort of family.

A family of her own again.

She wiped away a tear. Dammit. Maybe she'd make a stocking for herself this year. And some hot chocolate with extra marshmallows.

This was her place. Her new start.

Repeating the words in an attempt to convince herself that she hadn't made a terrible mistake by walking out of that house earlier, Molly abruptly stiffened as she caught the familiar scent of an approaching cat.

Garrick.

Shit. Pulse pounding, she moved forward, wishing she'd locked her door. But she was too late, as the angry male simply barged into her rooms, his aggression filling the space with prickles of heat.

Glancing around, his brows slammed together as his gaze took in the pictures and personal items that had already been set around the room, as well as the Noël decorations.

His clever mind wouldn't miss the less than subtle displays of nesting.

And he wasn't pleased.

"What is this?" he growled.

"My home." She wrapped her arms around her waist, acutely aware that he'd left behind his jacket and tie. With his shirt unbuttoned to reveal a glimpse of the chiseled muscles of his chest, and his dark hair ruffled, he'd never looked more outrageously male. A shiver shook her body as the image of licking her way over that smooth, caramel skin seared through her mind.

No.

She was not supposed to be fantasizing about the annoying puma. She'd spent too many years in that daydream. She forced herself to meet his burning gaze. "And I don't recall inviting you."

His hands landed on his hips, his eyes reflecting the twinkling lights. "You had a home."

"No." She shook her head, refusing to be intimidated. "I was an employee who happened to live beneath your roof."

He looked shocked at her blunt words. "That's bullshit. You know my mother considered you family."

Molly rolled her eyes. Of course he would try to use his mother to convince her. God forbid he actually said that he might think of her as family.

"But I'm not," she insisted, turning to pace toward the mantel where she'd placed a photo of her mother and father. Her father had his arm around her mother's shoulders and they were gazing into each other's eyes with blatant affection. Loneliness sliced through her heart. "Not in any real way." With an effort she turned back to Garrick, willing him to understand. "Tonight, when you and your mother light your family candle on the Noël tree, I'll be alone." Her lips twisted into a sad smile. "Next year, I want to light a candle with someone."

He prowled forward, his presence seeming to shrink the already small room. "Don't do this, Molly. We've shared five years together."

"Through letters," she snapped, ignoring the magic of their almost daily correspondence. She might have discovered the real Garrick beneath the composed Diplomat, but it wasn't enough. She wanted a flesh and blood lover who would share her life. The good, the bad. The ups and downs. To hold her during the night and stand at her side during the day. "While you were thousands of miles away."

His eyes softened, and he reached out to lightly brush a finger over her cheek, his touch agonizingly gentle. "And yet I never felt closer to anyone in my life."

Oh, his words...his gaze...Pleasure seared through her, her cat surging toward the touch of the male she considered her mate.

It was the logical side of her brain, however, that was currently in charge. With a deliberate motion, she brushed his hand away.

"The distance was safe. But as soon as you came home, you treated me like a stranger. You put up barriers between us."

His expression became guarded. "That's not true."

"No?" Her voice revealed her pent-up pain. "How many times did I wait at the door for you to arrive, only to be treated with an aloof politeness when you finally made your rare appearance? Or how about when I invited you to take an afternoon to spend alone with me? Every time, you told me that you had too much work to get away." She gave a shake of her head, feeling raw as she exposed just how deeply she'd needed him. "It might have taken me awhile, but I finally got the message."

Ignoring her warning glare, he once again trailed his fingers over her cheek, tracing the line of her stubborn jaw.

"What message, Molly?"

Her cat clawed beneath her skin, desperate to reach the male she desired with every fiber of her being.

"I might be good enough to relieve your boredom when you're far from home, but obviously I'm not the type of female you want to have an intimate relationship with." She shrugged, pretending she wasn't melting beneath the feathery stroke of his fingers. "That's fine. I'll find someone who does."

Those honey eyes darkened to molten lava, and his expression went feral and hungry with the power of his beast.

"Any male touches you, Molly," he snarled. "And he dies."

And just to accentuate the point, he kicked the door closed with his boot.

CHAPTER FIVE

The fire, the heat, the madness that raged through Garrick was barely contained. Maybe it was because he'd thought about Molly for too many years to count. Or shit, maybe it was because he'd tried not to. Whatever the reason for the onslaught of desire, he couldn't stop himself now.

As he closed the distance between them and took her in his arms, he felt ready to consume her. And hell, anyone who might be foolish enough to walk into the room at that moment.

Her head back and her dark, velvety eyes pinned to his, Molly whispered in a pained voice, "Why are you doing this, Garrick? It's not fair."

"I don't care about fair," he nearly growled. "Do you?"

She didn't answer him. "You had your chance and you lost."

He bent his head and took her mouth—that perfectly pink mouth he'd dreamed about every damn night when his head hit the pillow—kissing her with all the hunger he'd been storing up and shoving away.

When he pulled back, her eyes were glassy and she was breathless. But she still managed to utter, "You lost me, Garrick."

"No," he said on a growl. "Never."

He kissed her again, hungry and impatient, and pulled her even closer until her breasts were pressed against his chest, and his thigh was wedged between her legs. And when he heard her moan, felt her tongue slip into his mouth, and her fingers slide into his hair, he felt his male's stoic mind and his puma's desperate heart collide.

This was right. *She* was right. She tasted so warm and so sweet, and he knew that he could do this—kiss her hungrily, suckle at her lower lip, feel her taut nipples brush his chest, revel in the sweet heat of her pussy against his denim-clad thigh—all day and all night if she'd let him.

Desperate to know the feeling of her skin under his palms, he gripped the edges of her shirt and dragged the fabric up, up, breaking their kiss just long enough to pull the thing over her head. Then he dropped it to the floor and took her mouth again. She groaned and raked her hands up his back.

He eased back an inch. "Do you know how many times I've thought about this, Molly?" he uttered against her wet lips.

"Oh, Garrick," she whispered, a cry in her voice.

"How many nights I've touched myself, wishing it was you. Your hand. Your mouth." He nipped her bottom lip. "Your wet pussy."

She arched her back, pressed her sex harder against his thigh. "Oh god, Garrick. Please."

"Have you touched yourself, Molly?" he whispered in the curve of her ear as he pressed her back, groaning when he felt how wet she was, even through the fabric of her jeans. "Have you wished it was me? My hand? My mouth?"

"Yes," she answered breathlessly. "In my bed. In the shower."

Garrick's puma growled and snarled beneath his skin. Just the thought, the image, of her lying back on her bed naked. Or under the hot spray of the shower with her hands between her thighs, her nipples beading, her hips swaying. It made him insane with lust. Fuck. She'd wanted him as he'd wanted her. He was such an idiot male. It was something he'd always known, always felt—but had pretended was nothing more than a casual connection.

And, like a true bastard, he had stayed far away to keep it so.

He drew back. No more. Not now. He wanted this—needed it. Needed her. Her touch, her taste on his tongue. With forced gentleness, he eased down the cups of her bra to reveal her heavy breasts. For a moment, he just stared at her, every inch of him going hard and anxious.

"Damn, Molly," he uttered hoarsely, his hands clenching with anticipation. "You are one beautiful female."

Her eyes flickered downward. "No…"

"Yes," he insisted, almost harshly. "Fuck yes." He reached out and cupped her right breast, then ran his thumb over one puckered nipple. "The most beautiful female I've ever seen."

Her breath caught.

"And I don't deserve you," he finished.

"Garrick," she began. But when he bent his head and lapped at her other taut peak, suckled it into his mouth and flicked it with his tongue, she said nothing more.

She was only gasps and moans, her hands fisting in his hair as her hips danced against his thigh.

Fuck, she was so responsive. So perfect. So right. So…

His.

His puma snarled, ripped at his chest with its claws. What was he doing? Thinking? Every taste, every goddamn touch, was like the hottest, most addictive drug.

As he suckled her dark pink bud into his mouth, flicked it gently with his tongue, he released her other breast and let his hand venture down, let it follow the warm trail to the wet treasure it sought. When his fingertips met denim and zipper, he made quick work of them. And, taking his mouth from hers for a moment, he dragged the offending fabric down over her hips, her legs and to her ankles, where she instantly stepped out of them. His cock pressing fitfully against his zipper, he drew back and stared at the vision before him.

The five-year fantasy come to life.

She was all soft curves, lightly tanned skin, and erotic wet heat, and Garrick didn't know what he wanted to kiss, taste or fuck first. She had such a glorious body. Granted, he'd thought about it, imagined it a hundred times with his fingers wrapped around his shaft. But his imaginings were nothing to the reality. Heavy breasts, berry-pink nipples, small waist, shaved mound. All that, and the face and heart of an angel, besides.

It was no wonder then that he dropped to his knees before her.

Her eyes widened. "Garrick...what are you doing?"

"Worshipping you, Mol." He dipped his head and lashed at the outside of her sex with his tongue.

She cried out. "Oh my god."

"So soft," he murmured, nuzzling her shaved pussy with his nose, then drawing his tongue through her hot, wet lips. Christ, she tasted so sweet. Honey and cream.

"Garrick," she cried again, her hands reaching for his shoulders to steady herself.

"I got you, sweet thing. I won't let you fall."

He grasped her hips, held her firmly, then dipped his tongue inside her again, groaning when a hot wash of moisture met him. He could feel her clit humming under the thin layer of skin just above him, and he wanted to feel it in his mouth. Wanted to suckle it hard at first, then soft, then light as a feather until she came apart in his hands.

But first, he wanted inside of her.

His hands tightening on her hips, he titled her toward him slightly, then slowly thrust his tongue up into her pussy.

She gasped, cried out. "Oh, god! Oh, Garrick!"

Her walls fluttered and creamed around his eager tongue, spurring him on. He thrust inside her, going as deep as his mouth would allow. His cock screamed to get out from behind his zipper and into her tight, hot body, but he ignored it. He wanted her climax this way. He wanted to feel her shudder against his mouth as he drank her down.

He fucked her as she pumped her hips against him, and it was only when she stopped, froze, her entire body going rigid, that he slowed. His gaze drifted upward, and he saw her stomach muscles clench, her ribs showing with every quick breath, her nipples so dark and hard he nearly came at the sight. But it was her face, her beautiful face, so flushed, so ready to fly, that made him pull out and lick her all the way to that pulsing clit.

"Oh, yes!" she cried out. "Yes! Garrick, don't stop!"

With feather-light flicks, he teased the bud until it swelled, until it went dark pink. She was so worked up, moaning, crying out, begging, her legs unsteady, that he had to hold her firmly. Then, like lightning flashing, fireworks booming, she fell apart, crying out, creaming against his chin, trembling in his hands.

And Garrick lost what was left of his mind.

That was the only explanation for what he did next.

Or tried to do.

It happened so quickly he almost didn't believe it. One moment he was the Suit enjoying the female who he'd dreamt and fantasized about for five long years, the next he was lost to his cat. The puma inside of him snarled fiercely and claws formed on his right hand. Before he could stop himself, his hand was poised just above her abdomen, those claws ready to strike.

Molly's head dropped. Her eyes were glassy and heavy-lidded as she stared at him. "Oh my god!" she rasped. "What are you doing?"

"I don't know," he lied.

Christ, he knew exactly what he was doing. Or wanted to do. He wanted to mark her.

Mark. Her.

Shaking the insanity out of his head, he backed away, stood up. This wasn't happening. He hadn't done that. He glanced down at his right hand. Fuck! The claws were still there. How was this happening? Why? He'd been with females before, and nothing like this had ever occurred.

Until Molly.

Oh, shit…of course Molly.

She was the goddam mating kind! And he was most definitely not. What an asshole he was. He didn't even know what mating looked like. He'd grown up with parents who were never together, who were completely, utterly and unapologetically devoted to their jobs. It was all he knew. And no matter how much he wanted Molly, she deserved a male who could be that for her. A mate. Give her a home, family, something real and lasting.

His puma snarled fiercely at the thought.

"Your puma wanted to claim me."

Her voice brought his head up, his eyes narrowed and his cock pulsing once again at his zipper. She was standing beside the bed, with a pink, wet pussy, and a bra that remained below her swollen, delectable breasts. God almighty, he'd never seen anything so fucking hot.

The claws on his right hand elongated.

He swallowed hard. "Yes. My puma wants you."

Her eyes glistened. "But you don't."

Was she kidding? Couldn't she see his cock tenting his zipper? Hadn't she felt his desire? His uncontained, desperate desire? "Molly—"

She shook her head, then turned to grab her shirt. "I think you should go, Garrick."

Fuck, he hated that she'd just covered herself. "Don't, Molly. Don't be angry with me. I want you. Dammit! I want you so fucking much, I ache with it. But…"

Her eyes, those incredible sable eyes, lifted and pinned him where he stood. "But what?"

There was nothing Garrick wanted more in that moment than to fly at her, get her back to the mattress, get her legs spread and bury himself inside her. But he didn't deserve her touch, her warmth, her cream—or, more importantly, her heart.

"I wasn't cut out for mating," he said, his voice a dark thread. "For being anyone's male. I don't have what a good female deserves. I can't be what you deserve, Molly."

She held the shirt to her chest, but lifted her chin. "Shouldn't I be the judge of that?"

He frowned. "I can't disappoint you."

"There's only one way to disappoint me, Garrick," she said. "And that's by not taking what you want. What's being offered to you. Goddess," she sighed. "What's right in front of you."

She didn't know what she was saying. She couldn't. She had no idea what had been instilled in him and what had happened. He would only hurt her more by staying, by taking what he so desperately wanted.

"I'm sorry," he uttered.

Turning away from the warmth and goodness, sweetness and hunger that was Molly Cochell, Garrick walked out the door.

CHAPTER SIX

Stubborn, pig-headed…jackass.

One cold shower and a half a bottle of Jim Beam later, Molly was pacing the floor of her living room. How dare the bastard come into her home and set her on fire with his kisses, his hands, his magic tongue, and his wicked words, and then walk away?

And how could she be so stupid as to allow him to hurt her?

Again.

He was the master hit and run artist.

Was it some sort of game to him? To keep the pathetic Healer so enthralled with him that she stayed to take care of his mother? It certainly made his life easier to know he could dash around the world while she stayed behind, keeping him constantly up-to-date.

Well, enough.

Really and truly enough.

Taking another swig of the hard liquor, she was staring aimlessly at the twinkling lights she'd strung around the window when there was a knock on her door.

Molly frowned, not so drunk that she didn't recognize the familiar scent.

Setting the bottle on a low table, she hurried across the room to pull open the door, her gaze running an expert examination of Virginia's angular face. Her color was high, but that could be from the crisp night air, and she didn't appear to be in any pain.

"Virginia?" Molly gave a shake of her head, trying to clear it. To say she wasn't used to drinking was a massive understatement. "What are you doing here?"

The female's expression was set in lines of stern determination. She could be as stubborn as her son—

No, no, no.

She'd stopped thinking about Garrick.

The bastard.

The hot and brutally sexy bastard.

"Something I should have done years ago," the female said in cryptic tones. "May I come in?"

"Course." Molly instantly moved back, urging the older female toward a chair near the fireplace. "Sit down." She waited until Virginia had perched on the edge of the leather wingchair before she grabbed a blanket and tucked it over her lap. The older female wasn't disabled but she was frail, and despite her protests she enjoyed being fussed over. "Do you want some hot chocolate?"

A small smile touched Virginia's lips. "You're such a good girl, Molly."

Pain stabbed through Molly's heart. "Good girl." She gave a humorless laugh. "Yeah, that's me."

Virginia frowned. "Is there something wrong with being good?"

"It boring, predictable. Insanely dull," Molly said, pacing toward the window. In her mind, she could visualize how Garrick had probably once thought of her. The tedious homebody who was in bed by eight and spent her days off baking cookies. While he was surrounded by sophisticated, beautiful females who could no doubt speak a gazillion languages, dance the tango, and make a male have multiple orgasms with just her kiss. "I don't want to be house slippers. I want to be four-inch stilettos."

"Because of Garrick," Virginia murmured.

Had he seen her that way tonight? Molly wondered. Naked, calling out to him, climaxing against his hungry mouth? She supposed he had, and yet he'd still walked away.

"It doesn't matter." Molly heaved a sigh, wrapping her arms around her waist. "Not anymore."

The older female cleared her throat. "Can I give you a little insight into the mind of my son?"

Molly hunched her shoulders. *Do I have a choice? Do I really want to know more about this male I can't seem to get out of head? Or my heart?*

"Garrick is brilliant, there's no doubt about that," Virginia said. "And he's one of the finest Diplomats the Pantera have ever known."

Molly turned back to meet the older female's steady gaze. "He had good genes."

Surprisingly, Virginia grimaced. "Not so good when it comes to the important things in life."

"What do you mean?"

Virginia touched the plain silver band on her finger. Pantera didn't exchange traditional wedding rings, but mated pairs often had matching bands made to symbolize their union.

"Before his death, Garrick's father and I were always a pretty non-traditional kind of couple. We both loved our jobs and traveling the world, which meant that we spent very little time together." She smiled as Molly tried to hide her confusion at any couple being happy to live apart. "Oh, occasionally we would meet somewhere for a weekend, but it was rare for us ever to be home at the same time. As a result, Garrick grew up being raised by various relatives and friends."

Molly wondered if Virginia was feeling guilty. "He turned into a fine male," she was swift to reassure her. "You must be very proud."

The older female nodded, her expression difficult to read. "Very proud, but I also understand that his lack of a stable home has made him doubt his ability to become the sort of male who would make a good father and husband."

Molly frowned. She'd never really considered how Garrick's past might have influenced his obvious fear of commitment. Was that what he'd been saying before he left her place? Why he'd thought she deserved someone else? Someone better than him?

She had to wonder if he also thought that she expected him to become a Mr. Homebody, when that would obviously drive him nuts.

"I'm not asking him to change," she said.

"Of course you are, my dear," Virginia reprimanded, her expression softening. "Garrick knows firsthand the trials of having a family who weren't there for him. And if you're being honest with yourself, you would admit that the thought of having a mate who was constantly gone would eventually destroy you. You have an emptiness inside you that needs to be filled with a male who can give you all of himself, not just a small part."

Molly blinked back the stupid tears that filled her eyes.

Virginia was right.

Even if she could somehow manage to convince Garrick they were destined to be together, he would either leave her for months at a time, or he would force himself to stay, and eventually grow to resent her.

A savage pain ripped through her heart, nearly sending her to her knees.

"So there's no hope," she rasped.

Virginia rose to her feet, moving to lay a hand on Molly's cheek. "There is if you're willing to compromise."

Molly frowned in confusion. "How?"

"Think outside the box," she urged. "Garrick can take a more permanent position somewhere that needs your skills. The Goddess knows that a trained Healer is always welcome among the Diplomatic faction outside the Wildlands." She shrugged, her expression thoughtful as she mulled over the possibilities. "Or he could stay in the Wildlands to train the new Suits half the year, and the other half you could travel with him. So long as you're together, everything will fall into place." With a smile, Virginia squared her shoulders and turned to make her way back to the door. "Now I must leave."

"Wait." Molly hurried behind her. "Where are you going?"

"To remind my foolish son it's almost time for the candle-lighting ceremony."

"But..."

Molly gave a slow shake of her head as Virginia briskly stepped out of the apartment and closed the door behind her.

It felt like she'd just been hit by a mini-tornado.

Or manipulated by a very fine negotiator, a voice whispered in the back of her mind.

Catching her lower lip between her teeth, she moved to the mantel and touched the small star ornament next to her parents' picture. It was the last gift she'd ever received from them. Her mother had told her that she'd chosen it so Molly could have something to make her Noël wishes come true.

Now Molly closed her eyes and made the Noël wish that came from the very depths of her soul.

CHAPTER SEVEN

"You're a fool, Loriot."

The statement brought Garrick's head around. He frowned. Raphael was headed his way, following the path of moonlight leading to the water's edge.

Garrick snorted and turned back to face the bayou, and all the barges moving lazily down it with the current. "Tell me something I don't know, brother."

"All right." Raphael came to stand beside him. "You're scared."

With a half-assed snarl, Garrick turned and gave his mentor a curious glare. "How the hell do you know about my fight with Molly?"

"I don't," Raphael said with a small grin. "But if you're out here, staring into space—"

"I'm not staring into space," Garrick corrected, gesturing toward the throng of barges in the water, and the yards of spruce trees bracketing the bayou on either side.

"Right," Raphael amended. "It's actually worse than that. Staring at all the Pantera heading down the bayou in their barges, huddling close together, the spirit of the season in their eyes and their smiles—waiting for the moment when they get to light the candles on their family tree. Yes. Staring at them instead of being with Molly, taking her in your arms, showing her just how goddamn much you want to claim her—"

"Enough, Raphael," Garrick nearly growled. He didn't want more images of his and Molly's highly erotic time together sifting through his mind.

But they came anyway.

Christ, he could still taste her.

"Is the truth too painful to hear?" Raphael asked.

"That's not my truth," he grumbled.

"Bullshit. I've known you a long time, brother. And ever since Molly came to work for you, you've made it a priority to both stay away from her, and to know everything she's doing or who she might be seeing when you're not around." His brow drifted up. "If that isn't wanting, needing, *loving*, I don't know what is."

Garrick's gut twisted. He hated his mentor's words, but despised the truth in them more. At first when he'd hired Molly, things had been so easy. He'd come home for a day or two, then leave again. No problem. But as they'd started to get to know each other better, and their letters had started taking on a flirtatious edge, things had changed. Whenever he was home, whenever he was around her, in the same room, he couldn't take his eyes off her.

He wanted to touch her.

Kiss her.

Claim her.

It was then that he'd decided it was better to stay away. He'd known what he didn't have to offer. And god, what she did.

"Do you want to be with her, Garrick?" Raphael asked, cutting through his thoughts.

"More than I've ever wanted anything," he said without hesitation.

The male cursed. "Then why stay away?"

Garrick turned to him, grimaced. "Like you said, brother, I'm a scared fool."

Raphael nodded his understanding. "Glad you can admit it. And shit, welcome to the club."

Garrick arched a brow. "What do you know about it?"

"I'm sure someday down the line I too will be faced with my fear. Giving myself to a female who holds my once-caged heart in her hands." Raphael inhaled deeply, thoughtfully. "But perhaps there's something worse for us to fear."

Garrick's brows knit together. "What's that?"

The male's gold eyes flashed. "Losing your mate. Watching every damn day as the female you adore above all things gives her love to another."

The words took only seconds to sink in, but when they did, they took root and spread like wildfire. Molly giving her love, her body, her wonderful soul to another…

Never.

Goddess, never.

Garrick shifted into his puma and took off. He was several yards away when Raphael called to him.

"Hey! Don't forget the lighting ceremony. Starts in an hour."

Oh, that's exactly where I'm going, Garrick thought. *To get my family, bring them back for the Loriot tree lighting. This year, and, Goddess willing, every year thereafter.*

Garrick gave his mentor one last growl before turning away and darting into the trees.

Chapter Eight

Molly waited until she was sure the families would all be in their barges, headed down the canal to find their trees.

It wasn't that the other Pantera wouldn't go out of their way to make her feel a part of the festivities. They were always eager to ensure that she was included. Sometimes to the point where she wanted to scream.

Still, watching the others light their candles, while she stood alone by her tree, was always a painful duty.

At last, confident that the majority of the Pantera were gone, Molly slowly left the dormitory and headed toward the canal. In one hand she held her candle, and in the other was the small picture of her parents. They might not physically be with her, but she knew they would be with her in spirit.

Lost in memories of happier times, she was suddenly caught off guard when a shadow detached itself from a nearby cypress tree and prowled to stand directly in her path.

"I was beginning to think I was going to have to come in there and drag you out," a low male voice teased.

Molly gave a small gasp, her heart slamming against her ribs as she ran an avid gaze over Garrick's painfully familiar face.

She'd intended to spend the few minutes it would take to reach the canal shoring up her defenses before having to endure an awkward confrontation. Now she felt too raw…too exposed.

"Garrick," she breathed, her tongue peeking out to dampen her dry lips. His eyes darkened to the color of melted honey as he allowed his gaze to linger on her mouth. "Where's your mother?"

"She went to the tree with her new Healer," he said, his voice distracted as he lifted a hand to gently push a stray curl off her flushed cheek.

Her heart squeezed with a wistful regret that she wouldn't be with the older female.

Cutting all contact might be for the best, but it didn't make it any easier on this special night.

"You should be with them."

"No." He stepped close enough to wrap her in the heat of his body, and for the first time she noticed that he wasn't wearing his usual suit. Instead he was dressed in a casual pair of jeans and a cashmere sweater that emphasized his dark beauty. God. He was...divine. "*We* should be with them."

We? She frowned.

"I told you, I'm not returning as your mother's Healer."

He cupped her chin in his palm, staring at her with an intensity that made her shiver.

"How about you return as her daughter?"

Molly's mouth fell open, her heart forgetting to beat. "Garrick—"

"Wait." He pressed a finger to her lips. "Just let me speak."

Bossy Diplomat. She sent him a dry glance. "You do a lot of that."

"Point taken," he wryly conceded, his thumb absently brushing her bottom lip. "I'm going to show you that I can do something very, very good that doesn't take any words at all. But first..." He grimaced even as Molly trembled in anticipation. She might be pissed at this male, but that didn't keep her body from craving him again and again, and with a vigor that was downright indecent. "I have a confession."

"I'm listening," she said.

He studied her upturned face for a long, tender moment, almost as if he were memorizing how the moonlight played over her features.

"I've devoted my life to my career, always convinced that I could never be a good mate or father if I was thousands of miles away." Regret was threaded through his voice. "But the thought of actually losing you has made me look at myself and admit that I've been a coward."

Molly felt her cat crouch inside her, warily curious to discover where this was going. "Coward?"

His hand slid to circle her neck, holding her gaze as his thumb pressed against her thundering pulse.

"I loved my parents, and more than that, I respected them, but I never truly felt like I had a home," he confessed, unknowingly echoing the words his mother had shared earlier. "When I was small I used to think if I could just be good enough, or smart enough, or talented enough, my parents would want to be with me. Then, one day, I just stopped hoping." He leaned down, pressing his lips against hers in a kiss that made her knees weak. "Until you."

Her hands grabbed his upper arms, her heart melting at the thought of the lonely little boy who was afraid to wish for a true home. "Oh."

"It terrified the hell out of me to suddenly long for something I'd spent so many years denying I could have," he continued, his hand compulsively stroking up and down her neck, as if he was hungry for the feel of her warm skin. "So I kept you at a distance, even when every single part of me was aching to draw you closer."

A fragile, terrifying hope began to spread through Molly's heart. "What do you want from me, Garrick?" she breathed.

His eyes glowed with the power of his cat, his enticing musk teasing at her senses.

"Everything," he growled, sweeping his lips over her forehead. "Your heart." He used his tongue to trace the shell of her ear. "Your soul." He nipped her lower lip. "Your body." He skimmed his lips down the curve of her neck. "Your future." He lifted his head to study her with a wistful expression. "Be my mate, Molly."

She tentatively reached up to touch the face that had haunted her dreams for years.

"You're sure?"

"I've never been more sure of anything in my life," he rasped.

"But your career—"

"Is just that," he interrupted, wrapping his arms around her waist so he could haul her tight against his body. "A job. You are my life."

She hesitated. She'd been disappointed so many times. Then, seeing the stark need that glowed in his honey eyes, she allowed a slow smile to curve her lips.

It might have taken her walking out to bring him to his senses, or maybe a wish upon a Noël star, but she wasn't about to allow happiness to slip through her fingers.

Wrapping her arms around his neck, she went onto her tiptoes to press a kiss to his mouth.

"And you're mine." Another kiss. This one deeper…lingering. "All mine."

He growled low in his throat. "As much as I'd like to stay and complete our mating, we don't want to miss lighting our candles." He gently took the candle and picture from her hands, threading their fingers as he pulled her toward the bank of the bayou. "Together."

"Together," she echoed, pure joy filling her heart as they stepped onto the barge that Garrick had thoughtfully decorated with sprigs of holly. Minutes later they began floating down the canal lined by trees already glowing with candlelight. "*Joyeux* Noël, Garrick," she murmured softly.

He sent her a smile filled with the promise of a thousand tomorrows. "*Joyeux* Noël, my sweet Molly."

About the Author

New York Times and *USA Today* Bestselling Author, Laura Wright is passionate about romantic fiction. Though she has spent most of her life immersed in acting, singing and competitive ballroom dancing, when she found the world of writing and books and endless cups of coffee she knew she was home. Laura is the author of the bestselling *Cavanaugh Brothers* series, *Mark of the Vampire* series and the *USA Today* bestselling series, *Bayou Heat,* which she co-authors with Alexandra Ivy.

Laura lives in Los Angeles with her husband, two young children and three loveable dogs.

Alexandra Ivy is a *New York Times* and *USA Today* bestselling author of the *Guardians of Eternity* series, as well as the *Sentinels* and *ARES Security* series. She also writes the *USA Today* bestselling series, *Bayou Heat,* with Laura Wright. After majoring in theatre she decided she prefers to bring her characters to life on paper rather than stage.

She lives in Missouri with her family. Visit her website at alexandraivy.com.

Made in United States
North Haven, CT
15 February 2023

32642331R00280